I0823382

CARNIVAL FANTÁSTICO

Also by Angela Montoya

Sinner's Isle

A Cruel Thirst

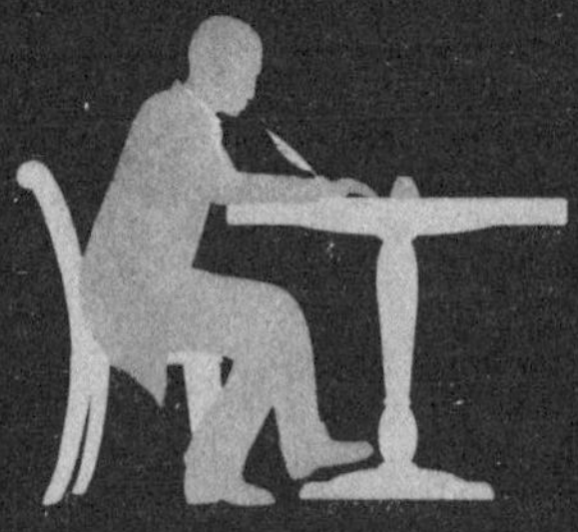

Carnival Fantástico

Angela Montoya

joy revolution

Joy Revolution
An imprint of Random House Children's Books
A division of Penguin Random House LLC
1745 Broadway, New York, NY 10019
penguinrandomhouse.com
getunderlined.com

Jacket design and art by Trisha Previte
Acrobat by LaInspiratriz/shutterstock.com and mask by VectorArtist7/shutterstock.com

Library of Congress Cataloging-in-Publication Data is available upon request.
ISBN 979-8-217-02446-9 (hardcover) — ISBN 979-8-217-02448-3 (ebook)

The text of this book is set in 11-point Warnock Pro.
Interior tent icon, bird art, textured parchment paper art, and circus poster art background used under license from stock.adobe.com.
Interior design by Cathy Bobak

Manufactured in the United States of America
1st Printing

The authorized representative in the EU for product safety and compliance is Penguin Random House Ireland, Morrison Chambers, 32 Nassau Street, Dublin D02 YH68, Ireland, https://eu-contact.penguin.ie.

Random House Children's Books supports the First Amendment
and celebrates the right to read.

For anyone who has ever been told you are too much
or not enough, listen to me well:
You are fantastical in every damn way.

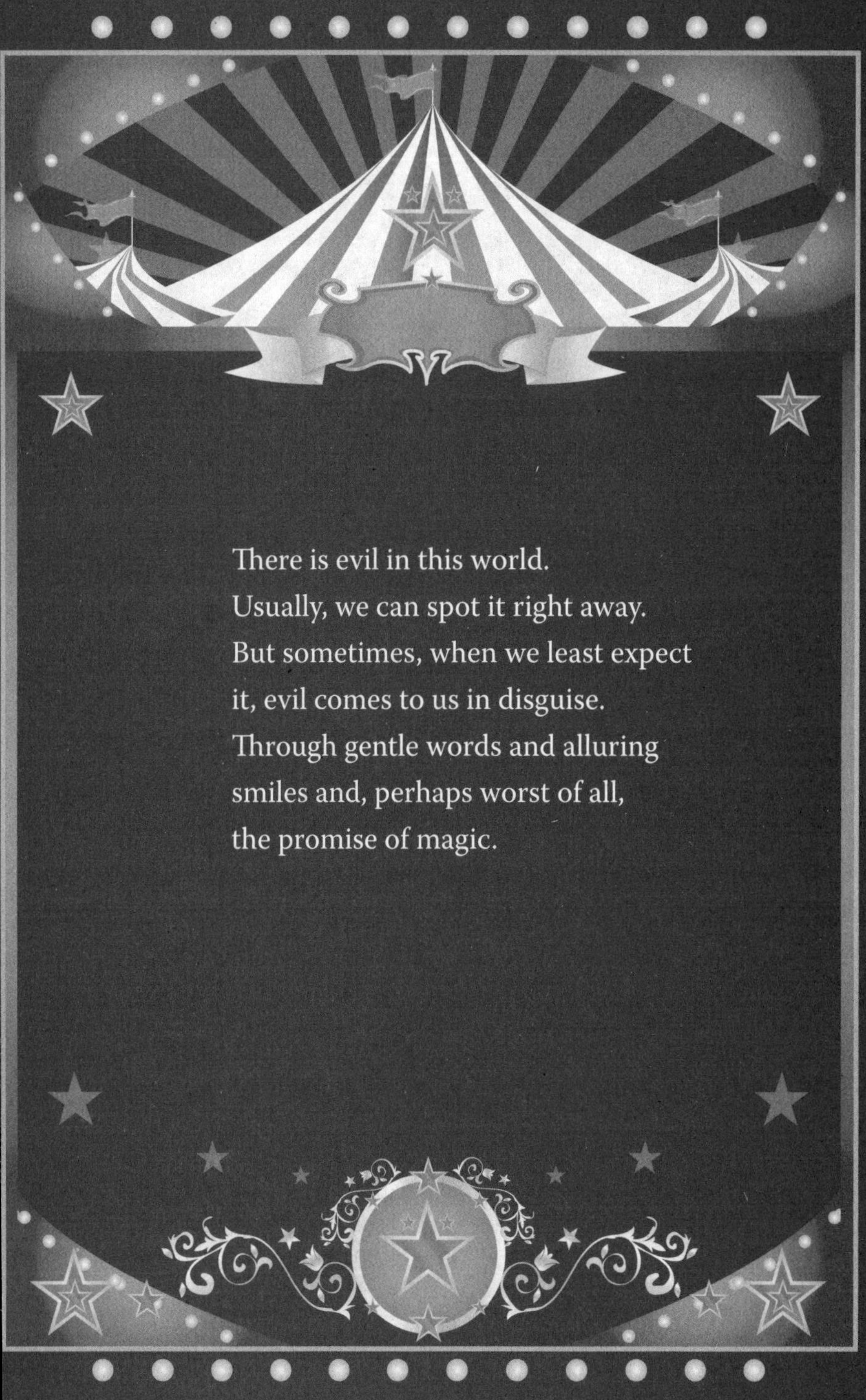

There is evil in this world.
Usually, we can spot it right away.
But sometimes, when we least expect
it, evil comes to us in disguise.
Through gentle words and alluring
smiles and, perhaps worst of all,
the promise of magic.

CHAPTER 1
Esmeralda

A sugary-sweet breeze whirled in the air. The miniature billboard hanging above Esmeralda's head swung on its hinges. The glittering words painted on the sign sparkled as they caught the light from glowing lanterns that never dimmed. It said:

To enter Carnival Fantástico, a person must do three things.

1. *Pay the ticket fee.*
   Begging for a discount will not be tolerated. This is a carnival filled with mesmerizing magic, well worth the monies to get in.

2. *Wear the most outrageous costume the mind can fathom.*
   But beware of dressing in something that sparkles. Estefan the ostrich has an affinity for all things shimmering.

3. *Be young in heart, body, and mind.*

The carnival is a riotous and reckless place, lasting from sunset to sunrise before disappearing into the morning horizon. There will be dazzling dangers, death-defying distractions, and electrifying explosions at every turn. Our attractions have minds of their own and a penchant for mischief.

No admittance will be offered to bores, fusspots, or sticks-in-the-mud.

Esmeralda Montero was certainly no stick-in-the-mud. In fact, anyone who spent a sliver of a second with her would probably liken the soon-to-be-nineteen-year-old fortune teller to a dandelion puff. Which was quite the opposite of any sorts of sticks in any sort of mud.

As for being a bore, Esmeralda had never let a dull remark slip from her tongue. Never forgotten to flirt and wink with charm. *Some* people might call her fussy, but she could easily make them forget with a twirl of her hair around her finger or a well-timed jest to lighten the mood.

A bell clanged from the small tower to her right, followed by the familiar roar of excited guests.

Hidden in the shadows, she turned away from the billboard displaying the carnival's rules and watched as revelers jumped up and down, shrieking and clapping with glee. The man in charge of the strong-arm game, a worker named Ramón, pretended to be shocked that someone could possibly win. His jaw dropped, his hand flattened over his heart, and he shook his head in disbelief—as if a hundred other guests hadn't already swung the mallet hard enough to make the disc shoot up and ping the metal chime.

"We have a winner!" Ramón shouted. He pointed to the victor as the crowd around them swelled. "You must be blessed by magic, señor, for it is rare for one to be mighty enough to make the bell sing!"

The winner in question, a short young man in a Chihuahua costume, beamed sheepishly and toyed with his little brown tail. In a country where the spectacular was outlawed and conformity was required, being told they were special always made the guests of the carnival merrier, which made their pocketbooks open wider in return.

"Care to make things interesting?" Ramón asked with a wiggle of his painted-on brows, causing them to look like two caterpillars dancing.

The twentysomething man dressed as a dog tilted his head, eyes shining and curious. "What do you mean?" he asked Ramón.

Esmeralda chuckled. "Here comes the hook," she whispered to herself.

"It is rare for someone to have the strength to make the bell sing once," Ramón said, loud enough for all to hear. "Rarer still for them to do it twice. How about this?" He leaned close to the man as if to tell him a secret. "For the low price of thirty silver bits—cheaper than the first time you paid for the game, mind you—you may try again. If you make the bell sing a second time, I'll let the lovely doll by your side choose any prize she desires."

A woman sporting whiskers and a long fur coat took the man by the wrist. She batted her long white lashes. "Please try again, cariño. *Please.* I want a teddy bear desperately."

The prizes within Carnival Fantástico *were* rather awe-inspiring: stuffed animals that could grow to the size of a house when soaked in tea, snow globes that called forth real snow when rubbed just right, tiny toy soldiers that served their owner's every command. Esmeralda's favorite prize was the wooden pistols, which blasted glitter bombs that stuck to the skin and couldn't be washed off for weeks.

She pulled her focus away from the crowd. The man wouldn't win. The mysterious magic fueling Carnival Fantástico never hastily gave up its possessions.

Esmeralda scanned the bustling throng of excited patrons, searching for someone in need of her services. Her heart gave a little squeeze. The carnival had stopped only a town away from Río Norte. The city where she'd grown up, the city that had sharpened that very heart into the prickly thing it was now.

Her only comfort was knowing she wouldn't be recognized behind her costume. Hopefully, she wouldn't recognize anyone in return. She couldn't handle seeing certain people from her past. *Especially* if they were enjoying themselves. Her nose scrunched up beneath her porcelain dove mask at the mere thought.

But she knew she'd never see *him* here.

People learned Carnival Fantástico was coming to their town just hours before the train arrived. Bell-shaped flowers showed up first, fluttering onto the doorsteps of mansions and penthouses. Then the carnival's flyers would appear and plaster themselves onto lantern posts and building walls and town square monuments. Only those who were starved for enchantments and excitement shoved the monotony they faced to the side and purchased tickets so they could be lost for the night.

He had never had a strong taste for fun nor freedom. *He* would never be caught dead in a place known for wayward enchantments.

Two young women giggled as they scampered by. They danced and skipped to the music thumping throughout the carnival. The melody was joyfully haunting and played over and over all night, only stopping when the sun rose and the last guest exited beneath the twinkling marquee. There was no band, no maestro to keep the bouncing tune in tempo. The music was simply there, sewn into the fabric of the circus tents and within the floorboards of the wagons.

Ángel Veracruz's Carnival Fantástico wasn't the typical traveling circus. It was alive.

Once the stars shone bright in the night sky, the carnival stirred. The young and young at heart poured in at every stop within the sprawling country of Costa Mayor to witness its sparkling magic, spending whatever money they earned or begged for or took just for a few hours of pleasure and a chance to forget about their humdrum lives.

Meanwhile, life before joining the carnival had been far from dull for Esmeralda. So much so that she often fantasized about what sort of girl she would have been if she had grown up with doting parents, or simply parents that didn't betray her the first chance they could. She might have been a teacher. Or a seamstress. Or a dancer. Instead, she became a liar.

At least she was a good one.

The two young women she had spotted stopped before a floss joint. The sapphire-colored booth sold cotton candy that tasted different with every bite. After paying a few silver bits, the taller of the two girls, who was dressed as an angelfish, tore off a piece of the sugary floss and stuffed it into her mouth. Her face contorted with disgust. "Pickled eggs," she complained.

The girl with her, sporting a swordfish costume, laughed. "Let me try!" She snagged a portion. Tasted it. She gasped. "Cream pie!" She giggled as she placed the remainder of the floss on top the angelfish's awaiting tongue.

"Easy marks," Esmeralda said to herself.

They were clearly in love, judging by the way they gazed into each other's eyes, but they wore no courting pins on their costumes. No rings on their fingers. Perhaps their relationship was in a limbo and needed a little coaxing.

"Perfect," Esmeralda whispered.

She slipped from her hiding spot. Stuffing her mass of black curls into the hood of her cloak, she stepped into the chaos of the carnival. There wasn't a square inch of empty space; the ticket agent never turned anyone away. Grinning brightly, Esmeralda dipped and slinked through the throng with ease, all the while keeping her eyes locked on the two young women devouring their treat.

When Esmeralda neared them, she pulled out two cards.

They were crafted from the prettiest purple cardstock, but it was the kaleidoscopic ink that made them truly exceptional.

Because just like the carnival, the ink was alive.

Bell-shaped flowers had been drawn onto the back of every card in the deck along with her stage name—La Paloma Blanca: Fortune Teller Extraordinaire. The flowers fluttered and swayed. Fat-bottomed bumblebees whizzed on and off the card. Sometimes, Esmeralda swore she smelled something like jasmine emanating from the blooms themselves.

She flicked a card over. The illustrations on the front shifted from stars and the planets to laughing faces to birds in flight. They would continue to transform until a person pressed their fingertips to the iridescent ink. Once touched, the ink formed into a depiction of the person's deepest hopes and dreams.

Using the enchanted cards made being a fortune teller rather easy. All Esmeralda had to do was try her best to interpret what the pictures meant while putting on a great show for her customers.

When she had customers.

People weren't often eager to hear their future when they had an entire carnival filled with magic to experience in the present. So, Esmeralda had to take matters into her own hands. She had to go out and find people who looked like they might be stuck in their past or need a push into something new.

Like two young women who required a gentle nudge toward love.

She flicked the cards in the air and watched with greedy

anticipation as they fluttered toward the girls. The lustrous ink shimmered like fish scales underwater. When the cards stuck into the remaining cotton candy and the pair gasped, Esmeralda smirked.

The girl dressed as an angelfish plucked one out and read aloud the inscription. "La Paloma Blanca: Fortune Teller Extraordinaire." She shrugged. "I've never heard of her."

Esmeralda's smirk fell flat.

The girl flipped the card over. "It's a drawing of two fishes swimming in the sea. And look! Their wake makes a heart. That's . . . rather romantic." She blushed. "What do you say? Want to have our fortunes told?"

The other girl nodded emphatically. "Yes, let's!"

Esmeralda gave a tiny victory dance.

Someone bumped hard into her shoulder. She whirled around and sneered, but the woman dressed as a chicken paid her no mind. She was too busy raising her feathered arm and downing a full bottle of glowing liquid. The woman's eyes bulged as the cerulean tonic slipped down her throat. She wheezed.

Esmeralda snickered. *Serves her right for not watching where she was walking.*

The magic elixirs were meant to be sipped slowly over days, not taken all at once. Whatever the woman drank would be in her system for at least a month. The tonics sold in the shops did whatever they wanted and often acted like naughty children, forever switching labels from hair growth to nose growth tinctures. From love potions to potions that induced gas. Magic was as devious as it was wonderful.

The woman gasped and coughed. The man wearing a rooster costume beside her patted her back, causing the fleshy red comb on his head to wobble.

"I told you to taste it first," he shouted over the music and mayhem.

The woman opened her mouth to speak, but the screech of a hen came out instead. She clutched her neck. Her eyes bulged. She tried to say something else, but all she could do was cluck.

Esmeralda pulled the last card from the pocket in her cloak and slipped it into the man's hand. He blinked in confusion.

"La Paloma Blanca can help you with your troubles," she said in her most mysterious and alluring tone. She spun away. Laughter bubbled out of her at the thought of telling fortunes to an oversized fowl.

Cutting right, she entered Clown Alley—the backstage area where the Big Top performers readied themselves for the show. Gone were the sugary-sweet scents of the carnival, quickly replaced by skunky smoke and puffs of the powder used by the aerialists.

A hand shot out and grasped her arm. Esmeralda froze.

"How many times do I have to tell you that this area is meant for performers and crew only?" a gravelly voice said.

Esmeralda wasn't in any of the Big Top acts *yet,* but this path led directly to her fortune teller's wagon.

She smiled and batted her lashes at the large rata. She had taken to calling the guards of the carnival ratas because they were like rats—always around to nibble away at anything fun.

"I'm just passing through," she said sweetly.

The rata's thick brows furrowed, making him look like a bulldog. "You're always just passing through."

"Perhaps so I can see you. I do so love our spirited exchanges."

He wasn't impressed. "Go the long way like the rest of you third-ringers."

She ignored the slight. To have a wagon or booth situated on the outer edge of the carnival meant you lacked luster. But she wouldn't be a third-ringer for long. And this *rata* would be the first person she'd stick her nose up at once she made a name for herself.

"Esmeralda!" a familiar voice called.

Camila jogged toward her with an extra bounce in her step, weaving through rowdy clowns and stretching ax throwers. Her sequined bodysuit was a vibrant shade of lime green and fit her muscular frame perfectly. The costume was nothing like the all-white atrocity Esmeralda was made to wear.

Esmeralda jerked her arm free of the rata's grasp and raced into Clown Alley. He yelled after her but made no move to give chase. There was no point. He had to know by now that she'd keep taking this route anyway.

"Why do you look like you're in such a good mood?" she called out.

"Wouldn't you like to know," Camila shouted back.

Esmeralda laughed. "Yes, actually, I would!"

Camila stopped before her, towering over her like always. Her skin was the same golden brown as Esmeralda's, but that was where their similarities ended. Esmeralda's black hair could never be tamed by a comb. Camila's was straight and silky and forever parted into two plaits. Esmeralda was small enough to go unnoticed. *Everyone* noticed Camila.

"Did the new boy finally sweep you off your feet and give you the smooch you've been dreaming about?" Esmeralda teased.

"Har. Har. *No.* But close. He smiled at me today."

"*Wow.* That's progress." Esmeralda nodded approvingly but in a sarcastic sort of way. She had been trying to get Camila to make a move since the young man joined the carnival five days ago.

"Slow and steady . . . or whatever they say," Camila said.

"Personally, I prefer fast and sporadic."

Camila scoffed. "Are we talking about potential love interests here? Because I haven't seen you so much as speak to a boy in that way since I met you."

A splinter of sorrow pricked Esmeralda's heart at the thought of being romantic with anyone ever again. She ignored the sadness. "Shouldn't you be getting ready for the show?"

Camila rolled her eyes. "Unfortunately, yes. Instead, I'm hiding from my ridiculous sister. She won't shut up about trying out a new act." She snapped her fingers. "I nearly forgot. Gabriel is searching for you. He had that wicked glint in his eyes, so you know he's up to no good again."

Esmeralda huffed. "He probably doesn't even know what the word *good* means. I better get a wiggle on it." She started to walk deeper into Clown Alley. Leaving Gabriel alone for long was never a smart idea. He was too clever, always building new contraptions. But just as many times as he created something wonderous, he also failed and saw disastrous results. "I need to find him before he accidentally sets my underthings on fire . . . for the third time."

"I'll walk with you," Camila said. "I'd prefer to avoid Pilar at all costs. She wants to attempt to stand on my shoulders while juggling dumbbells."

"Your sister couldn't catch a cold if she tried. How does she expect to juggle?"

"Tell me about it. But she says we must have something new to perform for the Running."

Esmeralda halted. "The Running?" She whirled toward her friend. "Does this mean . . ."

"We got our invitation thirty minutes ago," Camila said. She blew out a shaky breath. "I'm not sure if I should be excited or terrified. I've heard the stories. I know how often people get hurt during the challenges just to impress the ringmaster. But Pilar has her mind set on it."

Esmeralda's jaw dropped. And so did her stomach.

If the Sánchez Sisters were in the running to be the next lead act in the Big Top, Esmeralda didn't stand a chance. Pilar and Camila's strongwoman act was mind-blowing. And Pilar was a hound for attention. So was Esmeralda, but at least she had a good reason. She didn't just want to be the carnival's next main act; she was desperate for it.

She had joined Carnival Fantástico ten months ago, which meant her time with the carnival and the safety it offered her were nearly up.

The rules to join the traveling circus were simple:

1. Earn your keep.
2. Always smile.
3. Never mix or mingle with officers of the law.
4. Do not let the ringmaster catch you stealing from guests.
5. You must stay for the entirety of one year.
6. Leave promptly, with no fuss, once your year is up.
7. Most importantly: The show, no matter what circumstance may arise, must always go on.

Esmeralda's year with Carnival Fantástico was nearly complete, so she had to find a way to stay on. Her savings, amassed from her fortune teller earnings and the valuables she'd slyly nicked from patrons, would be enough to venture to the southern port of Costa Mayor and book passage on a ship that would smuggle her out of the country. But then what? She'd be alone and flat broke in some foreign land she'd never heard of.

She couldn't let that happen.

She needed more money. More time. Because if she truly wanted to escape her miserable life in Costa Mayor and start somewhere new, she required a small fortune. Being the next lead act would solve everything. She could stay in the carnival for as long as she wished. And when she was sick of being dazzling and beloved by all, she could take her riches and run away for good.

But she hadn't received any sort of invitation for the

Running. Her heart sank. Did that mean she hadn't been chosen to compete? The ringmaster must've thought she wasn't special enough. And why would he? She didn't have any sort of extravagant talents. She couldn't hold a candle to the other acts. Hell, if she didn't lie through her teeth half the time, no one would ever want her around.

Stop that, she hissed to herself. *You don't know you haven't been chosen yet.*

Perhaps her invitation was waiting for her at this very moment. Perhaps it was at her wagon, ready for her to squeal with delight.

She started to walk once more. This time, her steps moved at double speed. Camila's long legs easily matched her pace.

"What do you think about us being in the Running?" Camila asked.

"I'm thrilled for you two," Esmeralda said. That wasn't a complete lie. She wanted the best for her friends. Though, she wanted the best for herself a *tiny* bit more. The Sánchezes had joined the carnival at the same time as Esmeralda, but they didn't need to escape the country like she did. They didn't have a one-way ticket to the front lines of war, where all criminals ended up, looming over their heads.

"I didn't want to join the Running," Camila admitted. "But you know Pilar, she loves attention. And all the money we'll make for being the lead act will help our family back home."

Esmeralda painted a smile on her face and nodded numbly.

Damn Pilar and her brilliant showwomanship.

They moved through the performers gossiping and dressing before the Big Top show began. They passed beneath a string of bulbous lanterns. The sparkly lights flickered as Sophia the Juggler's pickpocket of a monkey swung from left to right. Esmeralda led Camila away from the pesky primate. She'd avoided the little beast since he'd stolen one of her broaches. Granted, she'd nicked the broach first, but that wasn't the point. She stuck out her tongue at him. The monkey offered a vulgar gesture in return. Esmeralda gasped.

"My sister is so concerned about catching the ringmaster's eye," Camila said. "She never shuts up about how dreamy she thinks he is." She jerked her chin toward a poster glued to the back wall of a tent. Drawn in that same enchanted ink used on Esmeralda's cards was a painting of the famed ringmaster and owner of Carnival Fantástico, Ángel Veracruz.

In the poster, he was bowing, his top hat resting on his trim torso. The ink shifted like sand caught in a gust of wind. Now, the ringmaster stood to his full height, a knowing grin on his handsome face. He was young and charismatic. Half of the carnival's customers came just to catch a glimpse of him. Perhaps even more of him if the opportunity arose. Ángel Veracruz was a notorious philanderer.

Then he was gone, and the ink changed once more, revealing glittering letters.

Do you long for fame and glory?
Then you're in luck!
I am searching for my next main act.
Performers: Add your name to the Running if you dare.
Try your hand, prove your worth, and see if good fortune is in the air.

The posters had been the talk of the carnival since they started sprouting up two weeks ago. Melanie the Marionette had been the star of the show up until then. Her act was like nothing anyone had ever seen. She'd built a massive mechanical dummy, but instead of her holding up the dummy, its strings were attached to Melanie. *She* became the marionette, dancing and twirling and soaring in the air. Until, one day, she disappeared. Some people speculated she'd run off with a wealthy patron. Others said something suspicious was afoot. The ringmaster insisted she was simply ready to retire and live her life in peace.

Whatever the case might be, the carnival needed a shiny new performer to lure in the crowds. Audiences were eager for something different. For a fresh face to wow them into oblivion.

Esmeralda was eager to *be* that face.

Sure, she didn't perform any daring tricks that would awe crowds. She was only a fake fortune teller, and a pitiful one at that. But she had charisma. She could *wow*.

Not like Nicola the Escape Artist, or David the Knife Thrower, or the bear trainer, or the trapeze artists, or the Sánchezes' strongwoman act, or any of the other acts currently performing in the Big Top for that matter.

That was a minor detail, though.

She'd figure out how to be even better as soon as she was chosen.

If she was chosen.

No.

She wouldn't let an *if* ruin her night.

When she was chosen. Because she *had* to be chosen.

She and Camila dipped to the side to dodge a bull elephant's trunk as he reached for his favorite snack—the fresh fruit bouquets the concessions slinger painstakingly prepared every day. The elephant swiped three bunches and stuffed them into his mouth, paper packaging and all. Esmeralda grabbed one for herself and took a bite out of a candy-coated strawberry.

Camila clicked her tongue.

"What?" Esmeralda said with her mouth full. "Krystal should know better than to leave her cart where the menagerie lines up before the show."

"Good point." Camila tugged a skewer filled with sour-coated grapes from the bouquet. "I wonder who else will be in the Running," she mused as they wove around the black-and-white-striped canvas that made up the Big Top.

Anyone could add their name into the Running, but only the very best, the brightest, the shiniest of stars—in the ringmaster's eyes—got invitations to join. Those who were special enough to participate then had to pass three separate challenges that started and ended according to the ringmaster's whims. Until only one remained. That person would be the new face of Carnival Fantástico. The gilded feather on Ángel Veracruz's top hat.

"So far, I know of five other acts that got invitations. And ten others who received rejection letters," Camila said.

Esmeralda winced at the thought. She'd die of shame if she got one of those letters. Or simply crawl into a dark cavern and never leave.

Camila went on, "The ringmaster always picks eight to start with."

Two acts left, then. Esmeralda still had a shot. She could still be chosen. Perhaps he was saving the best for last.

The best what? she asked herself. *You don't even have an act.*

But she was savvy. She trusted she'd come up with something when the time came. She'd written *La Paloma Blanca: Fortune Teller Extraordinaire and Renaissance Woman* when she had signed herself up for the Running. She might have fibbed and said she could perform as an aerialist, singer, fortune teller, cobra tamer, and all-around star. Upon reflection, the cobra-tamer part might have been too much.

Camila eyed Esmeralda with a raised brow.

Esmeralda did the same. "Why are you looking at me like that?"

"You seem awfully distracted this evening. Normally, you're going on and on about everything and everyone."

"I have no clue what you're talking about." She shoved two berries from the stolen fruit bouquet into her mouth, chomping noisily.

She hadn't told Camila or Gabriel that she had added her name into the Running, for fear of not being chosen. She had just over two months left with the carnival; she couldn't live out the rest of that time with them knowing she wasn't good enough to be picked. Knowing she wasn't special enough.

She was forever being pushed aside for something or someone better. Her parents did it when she was ten. The boy she once loved did it even after he told her he'd love her forever.

Even Gabriel, who had also joined the carnival with her on the same day and was also on the run from the law, didn't entertain the idea of fleeing with her when their term ended because he had someone he loved more waiting for him on the outside. She needed to prove to herself that she was worth something to somebody. That she could be loved and wanted. And chosen.

They exited Clown Alley and continued through the carnival until they made it to the third ring, where the least popular attractions were situated. They slowed as they neared a shabby wagon. Esmeralda had painted fortune telling cards on the front to give the impression that a great seer resided within.

That was a scam, of course. She could see into the future as much as the next person. Still, she made do.

Esmeralda peeked around the corner, where a short queue of customers had formed. She deflated. There weren't nearly as many as she'd hoped. The cotton candy girls were there, at least.

"You're going to watch the show tonight, right?" Camila asked.

"And miss another opportunity to witness you and Pilar argue in front of the entire audience again? Not a chance."

"That only happened once."

"And it was hilarious."

"Glad you find disagreements with my sister entertaining." Camila held out her hand. "You're the bee's knees."

"And you're the cat's meow." Esmeralda licked her thumb—gross, but she'd done worse—and sizzled it into Camila's palm.

She couldn't exactly remember why or how they had started that tradition, just like she couldn't remember why or how Camila had decided Esmeralda was worthy of her friendship. But Esmeralda supposed that was how friendships worked. They weren't forced; they simply were. Not that she was an expert on the matter. Esmeralda had had three close friends total throughout her nearly nineteen years, one of whom was now dead to her.

She started for the metal steps leading to the back entrance of her wagon but stopped abruptly. She blinked hard. Rubbed her eyes. Then blinked hard again.

Her eyes were not deceiving her. A black envelope was waiting on the top step. Beside it sat a box wrapped in shiny cellophane.

Her pulse began to race.

She whirled around, searching for Camila, but her friend was already lost amongst the throng of revelers in ridiculous costumes. "Drats." She faced what lay on the step, gluing her eyes to the envelope as if it were a mirage that might melt away. Fortunately, it remained.

With a nervous squeal, she snatched up the envelope. A hand mirror framed in the familiar bell-shaped flowers had been stamped onto the parchment—the official symbol of Carnival Fantástico. She let out another squeal before grabbing the box and racing into her wagon, shutting the door behind her.

She took a deep breath.

"If it's not an invitation, you will be okay."

That was a lie.

"If this is a rejection, you will be fine."

She wouldn't.

She needed this. She needed to be chosen. To be picked. To be believed in. To be seen as worthy.

No, those things weren't practical. What she really needed was the opportunity to earn her weight in gold coins.

Ravenously, she tore open the envelope. She tugged out an obsidian-colored card.

And her heart plummeted to her toes.

CHAPTER 2
Ignacio

Ignacio used to believe that everything in life could be categorized into one of two options: right or wrong. He had lived, quite rigidly, within the boundaries of what he'd been told was right by his father, a man Ignacio had idolized.

He was a perfect son. A perfect student. A perfect . . . *everything*. He listened to his father. He obeyed his teachers and leaders. He said yes to whatever they asked of him.

Until he didn't.

The heat of the day still lingered on the stucco, warming Ignacio's back through his coat and shirt. His fingers slid over the rough walls as he inched toward the back entrance to the staff's kitchen. It was well past midnight. Everyone who worked in the great and powerful Comandante Olivera's home would have fallen asleep long ago.

Ignacio turned the knob gingerly. His brows pinched together. Someone had engaged the bolt. *Odd.* No one ever locked this door or *any* door within the gated manor. Who would have the nerve to break into the home of the Blackbirds' leader?

There had been only one person who had dared to try. And she was long gone, having scurried off to some country across the sea, never to return. He clenched his fists and willed his thoughts to flee far away from the girl who had run away with his heart—and his savings.

He knelt beside the planter box that flanked the door and lifted the small statue of a dove. The clay figure had been here since he was fourteen and so had the master key it concealed.

Ignacio shook his head in disappointment. The comandante was cautious enough to keep the doors locked, but he didn't think highly enough of Ignacio's competence to remove the key to said door.

With a sigh, Ignacio brushed the dirt off the rusted metal and slipped it into the keyhole. He eased into the familiar space.

It smelled of soap and vinegar, just like he remembered. Shiny pots still lined the walls, kept perfectly clean and hung impeccably straight like the comandante ordered. The wooden countertops were clear of clutter, and the checkered floors gleamed in the moonlight let in by the spotless windows. There wasn't a single speck of dust within the entire space. Not even the dust's ghost would dare remain.

Comandante Olivera often proclaimed that his home, staff, soldiers, and family were extensions of him. Therefore, they must be perfect. *Always* perfect. As he saw himself to be.

Ignacio scowled at his boots. He should wipe the dirty soles on the rugs out of spite. But that would only get the serving staff in trouble. His qualms didn't lie with them, only with the comandante.

Tiptoeing through the shadowy hallway, he focused on the

staircase at the opposite end. He wouldn't dare risk his gaze slipping to the room three doors down on his left. Even after a year, the thought of the final moments he spent inside that cramped space made his guts gurgle with resentment.

He bounded up the steps leading to the comandante's office. He'd been up and down them so many times, he knew the rug would conceal any sounds he made. There were no longer portraits on the walls. Any sign of the family the comandante once boasted about had been wiped away as if they never existed. As if Ignacio's mother had never mattered. As if Ignacio himself didn't matter.

That shouldn't come as a surprise. Even before his mother had died at the hands of Dos Palos spies, Ignacio's father had kept him at arm's length. It seemed his father wanted an obedient soldier, not a son. Ignacio had given him what he wanted until he couldn't any longer.

And his disobedience fractured what little relationship they had into a thousand shards that could not be pieced back together again.

The door to Father's office was ajar. Ignacio peered back over his shoulder, searching for a single looming shadow in the darkness. But Father wasn't home. Ignacio had memorized his weekly routine.

The comandante would have supper at El Portal del Rey first. It was a known haunt for members of the Blackbirds. Then he'd make an impressively fast stop at Muñeca's, a secret establishment where Blackbirds could also be found, but under silk sheets instead of sitting at linen-draped tables. Such businesses had been banished by the king of Costa Mayor several years ago, but, unsurprisingly enough, his soldiers were beyond the laws of the land they served. Father's final stop of the night would be a swanky speakeasy on the other side of town, where other arrogant worms assembled in tucked-away rooms and bragged about their great wealth while drinking booze that cost more than what most people earned in a month.

Father wouldn't be back before daybreak.

And yet, Ignacio couldn't force himself to move past the threshold and into his father's office. His fingers twitched at his sides. Memories poured over him. The smell of leather varnish. The mausoleum-like quiet. The sting of Father's wrath when Ignacio was five years old and burst into the office without being summoned. How many punishments did he suffer for not knocking properly, for not showing enough regard, for not being exemplary in every way? Enough to still feel the repercussions deep in his marrow even now when he was a few days shy of turning nineteen.

Ignacio shook his head. That was the dreadful thing about memories. One could try to flee from them, but they always caught up. And often at the most inconvenient moments.

Nevertheless, he had a job to do. A task far more important than his own discomforts.

The day after Ignacio turned eighteen, Father had enlisted him in the training core to become one of his elite soldiers—the Blackbirds. Ignacio grew up believing he would follow in his parents' footsteps. Mother had been King Amadeo's comandante before she was killed protecting him. Father was given the title of comandante soon after. Both his mother and father had served in the military with honors. When he was a boy, Ignacio had believed he would do so as well, but as he matured, his dreams had begun to change. Still, he went to training camp, and he endured it for six long months, even while suffering a broken heart.

The day before he was going to receive his official Blackbird marking, he and the cadets had been called to action. They stormed into a tiny village across enemy lines and destroyed everything, believing their adversaries to be lying in wait. But there were no opposing forces. The army of formidable soldiers constantly trying to demolish the barriers between his country of Costa Mayor and the neighboring kingdom of Dos Palos, the villains he'd been taught to despise and fear, were nowhere to be found.

As Ignacio marched into the village, he quickly realized the people he had been ordered to take down were only farmers and their families. The rulers of Dos Palos and their soldiers had retreated north, leaving their subjects who couldn't escape at risk. And they were so obviously lacking in provisions because King Amadeo's army had cut all supply chains going in or out of the village and between Costa Mayor and Dos Palos.

These citizens were the monsters he was supposed to kill? These thin and weary people who hardly had clothes on their backs?

When the first shots rang out, screams tore through the sky. And Ignacio did nothing but stand there like a shell-shocked fool as the Blackbirds obliterated whatever lay in their path.

General Keara, the leader of the platoon and his father's

right hand, commanded the cadets to stand guard while she and the other officers charged ahead. Ignacio followed them. He didn't know why. Probably to ease his guilt. To try to convince himself that he was wrong, that what they were doing was imperative to the safety of Costa Mayor.

That didn't happen.

Whooping and laughter led him to the truth. The general and the senior Blackbirds were digging through a steaming stream in the middle of a meadow. Water sloshed around them as they filled thick satchels to the brim with whatever was inside the hot springs.

"We've hit a payload!" one of the Blackbirds yelled.

"I was starting to believe we'd drained these lands dry," another added.

"Just keep digging," General Keara ordered. She stood, stretching her long back. "I'll send word to the comandante. Congratulating him on his magnificent find."

Ignacio had tried to get a look at what they were stashing away, but he couldn't without being spotted. He felt sick. The Blackbirds under Keara's command were not hunting for enemies of Costa Mayor. They were searching for whatever lay within that meadow. The enemy he had been taught to hate all his life was not trying to infiltrate Costa Mayor. Costa Mayor was trying to infiltrate them because they wanted something Dos Palos had.

In a haze, he ran until he reached the next village, thinking he could at least warn the citizens of the soldiers nearby. But it had already been decimated by the Blackbirds. The corpses picked clean by vultures.

That was the day Ignacio defected. The day he turned his back on everything he thought he knew.

He'd once thought his father was the epitome of what it meant to be righteous and noble. But there was nothing righteous or noble about what Ignacio had witnessed in the war. Under Father's command, innocent people had died. And Ignacio had done nothing to stop it. He was going to do whatever it took to make up for that now.

Emboldened by these memories, he took a deep breath and stepped into his father's office. The place was still cold and bare, much like his father's soul.

Ignacio reached under the desk and pressed a nearly imperceptible button. For most of his life, he'd never known the hidden switch existed. He might never have known if his first and only love hadn't told him of it right before she squished his heart under her shoe.

The well-greased mechanisms engaged, and the door to his father's real office opened as quiet as the swish of a horse's tail. His pulse quickened as he entered.

At the center of the circular war room stood a massive table with a detailed map unfurled over the glossy wood. Figures in the silver-and-black regalia of Costa Mayor stood in a dense line far past the borders of Costa Mayor and into the northern territories of Dos Palos. Father had marked *X*'s over landmarks. The markings might seem random. But Father's actions were never random.

These *X*'s must have been other places where they had found whatever material General Keara and the Blackbirds had stuffed into their satchels in that village. Ignacio's eyes roamed over the map. The *X*'s were almost all the way to the farthest tip of Dos Palos. Nearly the entire country had been overtaken.

This was possibly incriminating, but people in Costa Mayor had been taught to hate and fear people from Dos Palos for a dozen years. Without proof that the war wasn't Dos Palos's doing, Ignacio's countrymen could only be glad to see the Blackbirds fighting so *valiantly*.

He needed hard evidence that the war had never been about protecting Costa Mayor from invaders. That it was, in truth, the Blackbirds who had been chipping away at Dos Palos's borders. That thousands of lives had been lost on both sides because King Amadeo wanted to obtain whatever resources were in their springs. Ignacio had to find something he could take without his father's notice. Correspondence with his generals or the king, notes about what lay beneath the *X*'s on the map . . . *something* to give to the Defiant, which operated the one printing press in all of Costa Mayor that was ready to expose what was truly going on.

He thumbed through ledgers and notes. There was nothing there. It was as if his father didn't even trust the walls of his own home with his sins.

Horse hooves clopped on the cobbled road outside. Ignacio paused. From within the hidden office, it was hard to decipher if the sound was close or a street over.

Did I get the days wrong? Perhaps Father changed his plans?

No. Ignacio was merely being hyper-vigilant. Father wouldn't be back yet. And he preferred to use his motorcar. Their carriage hadn't been hitched in years.

Either way, Ignacio didn't want to be inside his childhood

home any longer than necessary. He strode over to the lone bookshelf. A broken hand mirror lay face up on the dark wood. That wasn't like Father, to keep around things of no value. Ignacio's gaze landed on a tattered spine tucked amongst the tomes.

"My stars," he whispered.

Slowly, so as not to rip the fraying edges, he pulled out a small book. The cover had been torn off, but Ignacio still remembered it clear as day. It had been a vibrant drawing of two young men smiling before an inky-black locomotive. Ignacio hadn't seen this book since before his mother died. She had read the peculiar fable to him on nights his father was away because Father loathed fantastical tales about the gods of old. He claimed it was blasphemous to our true god, the crown.

Ignacio had thought this book had been lost to him for good. Not a single shop in Costa Mayor sold such stories any longer. If a work wasn't in praise of King Amadeo, it was forbidden. As were most vices, like alcohol consumption, gambling, and other illicit affairs, unless you were part of the court or the Blackbirds.

Dogs barked outside.

Ignacio quickly placed the book back. There was no time to reminisce.

He started for the desk but stopped when the rubbish bin caught his attention. The metal basket was filled with crumpled parchment. Ignacio quickly snatched a wad of paper from the top of the pile and flattened it.

His eyebrows flew up in confusion.

It was a flyer for a traveling circus. *Carnival Fantástico.*

He'd heard the name many times over the years. Boys from

school dared each other to climb the fences that lined the perimeters whenever it suddenly showed up outside of town, but the guards were good at finding anyone who hadn't paid the entry fee. Authentic magic was rumored to exist within the carnival. His bunkmate at cadet training swore he saw a man fly there once.

Ignacio didn't believe in magic, but there must have been something strange at play because the carnival was the one place the king and his men never touched.

Scratching his head, he flipped the paper over.

Héctor,

Please come and see me.

"Héctor?" Ignacio whispered. No one ever called his father by his first name. Even when his mother was alive, she used honorifics.

Ignacio grabbed a few more crumpled flyers and smoothed them out.

Héctor,

We need to speak.

Héctor,

We have business to attend to. Don't be such a wet blanket. Come to Carnival Fantástico. It is magnificent indeed.

Héctor,

The carnival will be stopping near your home on the 16th of March. Will I see you then?

The sixteenth? Ignacio checked the clicking timepiece on the desk. That was tonight.

Héctor,

Don't make me angry. I know your secrets. And I know who you wish to keep your sad secrets from.

Ignacio straightened his spine.

Secrets? What sort of secrets would someone in the carnival know about Father?

He grabbed the last balled-up flyer and opened it. His stomach plummeted to his boots.

A drawing of a hand mirror framed with flowers winked up at him. The words "We See You" were woven around it. But it wasn't the sketch or the peculiar phrase that quickened his pulse. It was the familiar silvery-black ink with shifting hues of purple, blue, and gold.

"This cannot be," he said. "It can't be the same ink."

Still holding the flyer, Ignacio stuffed the rest of the papers back in the bin and bolted out of the office. He cut right, heading straight for his old bedroom. He burst through the door, not caring who heard. Ignacio wrenched open his armoire and dug through old clothes and dusty toys until his fingers grazed over a wooden box. He yanked it out and flung open the lid.

Panting as if he'd run across the world, Ignacio gazed down at the items still perfectly placed inside. Odd trinkets he'd been given or secretly collected. Painted soda-pop caps. A photograph taken of his mother, the sepia tones doing little to capture the spark in her hazel eyes, the soft warmth of her dark brown skin. Gingerly, he scooped up an old mint tin. His thumb grazed over the initials he'd painstakingly scratched into the front only a few years ago.

His insides no longer fluttered like startled birds when he thought of the tiny notes he and Dovie had passed through the vents. Now, his insides soured with regret. Ignacio stuffed the container into his coat pocket. He wasn't sure why. Perhaps he enjoyed torturing himself.

His eyes fixed on something at the bottom of the box. He hesitated for a moment, then grabbed the folded letter that had nearly destroyed him. He placed the box onto his old bed before unfolding the paper. His vision blurred. But he didn't need to see to know what it said; he had memorized every word of the letter. They were practically tattooed on his soul.

But the ink? Could they really be written in the same ink? He raised the letter and the carnival flyer so that they were side by side. He blinked hard, then chewed on his bottom lip as he scrutinized them. The strange ink *was* identical.

His heart slammed so hard against his chest that he thought his ribs might crack. There was no such ink in all of Costa Mayor. He would know. In his desperation to find the author of the letter, he had gone to every stationery shop he could find, and no one had seen anything like it. He had never thought to go to Carnival Fantástico and ask there. Why would he? Magic wasn't real.

A door shut at the front of the house. Ignacio's head snapped toward the hallway. Father's telltale footsteps thundered like a war drum. He was moving fast.

Shit.

Ignacio stuffed the letter and flyer into his pocket and looked for a place to hide. Though he took after his mother in coloring and demeanor, he was as tall as his father and nearly as broad. And he had left his father's secret office door ajar. The second his father saw that, he would know someone had been inside.

There was only one option.

Ignacio ran for the window. Grimacing, he eased it up, hoping that the hinges had been recently oiled.

The window opened without a sound. He draped one of his legs over, followed by the other. He swore. The tree that had stood outside his window for his entire life had been chopped down. A piece of him broke at the mere thought. But Father was still coming; he had to go. Ignacio was only on the second story, but there were nothing but rosebushes to break his fall.

The floorboard on the landing step gave a recognizable creak. Father was not twenty paces away. There was no choice but to jump. His father's boot squeaked against the polished tile. He was ten paces from the door.

Ignacio pushed himself off the ledge.

He clamped his mouth shut to hold in a hiss as angry thorns tore at his clothing and dug into his skin.

From above, the comandante's voice roared.

Guards raced out of their small post near the front gate and barreled into the manor. Ignacio bolted from the bushes the second the area was clear and ran as hard and as fast as he could.

And he would not stop.

Not until he reached Carnival Fantástico and found out who wrote these notes to his father. And how in the hell they had access to the same ink that had once been used in the letter that shattered his heart.

CHAPTER 3
Esmeralda

Esmeralda couldn't believe her eyes as she gazed at the notecard in her hand. It was blank. There wasn't a single word marked onto the paper. Not *Congratulations! You're in the Running* or *Better luck next time*. Was she that insignificant that the ringmaster would have forgotten to write something so simple?

Tears welled in her eyes. She sniffed.

"It's his loss," she said. Even though she knew that was the opposite of the truth. She needed the ringmaster far more than he'd ever need her.

She was about to tear the card and envelope to shreds when something sparkled on the paper. Tiny firecrackers began to fizzle over the black cardstock. Her jaw dropped when words started to form.

She sucked in a jittery breath as the entire message came into view.

Dearest Esmeralda Montero, also known as La Paloma Blanca: Fortune Teller Extraordinaire—or should I say Renaissance Woman?

Congratulations! You are in the running to be the lead act in the most fantastical circus the world has ever seen. Now it is up to you to prove what you have to offer my enchanting, astounding, gloriously magnificent Carnival Fantástico. Be ready, darling dove, your first of three tests will come a-fluttering tomorrow.

With love and devotion,

Ángel Veracruz, your enchanting, astounding, gloriously magnificent ringmaster

She read it again, for good measure. Thrice. A fourth time.

"I got in," she breathed.

Esmeralda squealed. She waved her hands in the air and stomped her heeled slippers on the floorboards as if she were a child being gifted a pony.

"I got in!"

She thought she might cry.

"What are you so excited about?" a sinister voice hissed into her ear.

With a gasp, she dropped the card and gift box and spun. She swung out her arm in pure reflex, and her fist connected to something hard and scratchy.

But no one was there.

Someone groaned.

Un fantasma? A ghost?

Esmeralda scrambled back until her knees bumped into her cot. She grabbed the first sharp object she could find, a hideous clown sculpture, and held it before her.

"Who's there?" she yelled.

The space directly before her blurred like heat waves.

She gripped the statue tighter and held it like a club.

"Show yourself!"

The heat waves shuddered. Something popped. Then sparkling fog filled her wagon. Within the haze stood the figure of a short young man.

Esmeralda gaped. "Gabriel?"

Her friend and coconspirator rubbed his temple. "King's toes, Esmeralda, you clocked me real good this time. I think I might faint."

The tension in Esmeralda's shoulders dissipated, and she lowered the clown weighing heavy in her hands. "Serves you right. You should know by now not to sneak up on me like that."

Gabriel grinned as he flapped the fog away from his face. "I'll gladly risk getting clobbered if it means scaring the daylights out of you." He chuckled and put his arms up in surrender as she lifted the statue once more. "I'm teasing. I think I learned my lesson this time. But I wanted to try out this new tonic. Turns a person invisible for a whole twenty minutes. We can use this while you're giving fortunes."

"What are the repercussions, though?" Esmeralda inquired. Magic always asked for something in return.

Gabriel scratched at his fluffy curls. "I can't remember." He shrugged. "Must not have been terribly bad, then."

She placed the clown on a small shelf and pulled off her cloak. The wings of her sequined costume sprouted out like paper fans. She was supposed to appear as the beautiful white dove she was named after, but the wings were too small and made her look more like a cherub than a delicate bird. It was a silly getup. Not nearly as fancy as those worn by performers in the Big Top, but that might soon change. Glee filled her chest. If she completed all three challenges and was chosen to be the new main act, she'd have enough money to purchase all the costumes she desired.

"What's that?" Gabriel asked. He jerked his chin toward the gift box on her cot. It had been left beside the letter from the ringmaster.

"Nothing." Esmeralda batted her lashes. She feigned nonchalance. "Just an invitation . . . to the Running."

"You're razzing me," Gabriel said.

She thrust the letter toward him. Gabriel took it, his thin brows raised. He mouthed the words as he read. He hadn't gone to school a day in his life but had taught himself how to read while selling week-old newspapers to bored men as they waited for their significant others at luxury retail shops. Esmeralda had never been to school either, but her parents had taught her how to read, write, and pick locks. At least they'd gifted her that.

As he read, she smirked and turned toward the periwinkle cabinet she'd painted with Camila a few months back. They'd found it abandoned near the train tracks in a gleaming city called Montecino. Esmeralda hated leaving unwanted things behind and simply had to have it. So, they lugged it into her tiny fortune teller's wagon and spruced it right up to store even more discarded knickknacks.

She opened one of the doors and peeked at herself in a small mirror to ensure her porcelain dove mask wasn't crooked.

Gabriel huffed from behind her. "How did you con your way into the Running?"

She might have been offended by that statement if she hadn't wondered the same thing.

"Perhaps the ringmaster has taken notice of my magnificent fortune telling skills."

Gabriel guffawed in reply.

She changed from her plain slippers into heeled boots that tied up to her shins. Now that she was in the Running, she thought it wise to put her best foot forward. Or in this case, her only pair of unscuffed shoes.

"I heard Melanie the Marionette practically whirled herself into oblivion to earn the top spot," Gabriel said. "How do you plan on wooing our ringmaster for all three rounds?"

"I suppose the same way I have wooed you into helping me tell fates."

"By lying through your teeth?"

"I was going to say by being the charismatic wonder that I am."

Gabriel chuckled. "I love how delusional you are."

Esmeralda laughed off the sting Gabriel's jest inflicted. She knew he was only teasing, but the sorry truth of it was, she survived on delusions. Esmeralda was a nobody with no one to look after her. At every turn in her life, it seemed she was doomed to be left behind, to be deemed unworthy. But the invitation from Ángel Veracruz was a new start. Becoming the lead act in the most famous carnival in the world would change everything. She would finally be a somebody. And she would have something that would never turn its back on her. Money.

Someone banged on the wagon's front door. "Is anyone in there?!"

Gabriel checked the timepiece hanging from his pocket. "You're fifteen minutes late," he mouthed.

Esmeralda winced. She cleared her throat, letting her words smooth out into a sultry tone. "The great Paloma Blanca is nearly ready, señor. The spirits are waking as we speak." She waved Gabriel on while quickly reapplying her plum-colored lip paint.

He placed the invitation on her bed beside the gift box and grabbed cards from her cabinet. He set them on a table covered with a deep purple fabric.

"Find any good candidates to scheme while you were out amongst the throng?" Gabriel asked before shoving a bowl of dry ice under the tablecloth.

"I did." She grabbed the large palm leaf she used for decor and fluttered it in the air, dispersing the manufactured mist. "I gave my cards to a pair of young women who need my help to advance their relationship. And to a clucking hen."

"I wonder if hens know how to tip properly," he replied.

Giggling, Esmeralda handed Gabriel the leaf. He gave her a crystal ball in return. She took a seat behind the table and fluffed out the feathers that made up her skirt. "How about you?" she asked. "Any leads from the guests in line?"

"Plenty." Gabriel pulled a curtain closed around her cot and personal items. She never told him how grateful she was that he thought to do such a thing. That he thought enough of her to realize she was desperate for some sort of privacy. But it also offered him a perfect place to hide while she told fortunes. So perhaps it wasn't really for her at all.

"The handsome young man in front of the line is a known

bootlegger. He sells hooch to anyone with coin. Even seventeen-year-olds like me." Gabriel winked as he opened his jacket, revealing a shiny flask. "Clearly, he doesn't care for the laws of the land and prefers money over most things. Oh, and the woman wearing butterfly wings has three children and a husband she despises."

"Does she despise just the husband or the children as well?"

Gabriel pursed his lips in thought. "Let's go with both. She does have rather large bags under her eyes."

Esmeralda nodded as she shuffled her cards, taking mental notes as Gabriel prattled on about the necessity of a good nightly face serum. With each reorder of the stack, the ink shifted and glinted. It was ready to work its mischievous magic.

"There's a pair of siblings who want to know if their goldfish is at peace," he said as he placed the needle on a record that played ghostly melodies mixed with ethereal chimes.

Esmeralda stopped her shuffling and eyed him.

He shrugged. "Must have been one hell of a fish."

She set the cards down and pressed on a hidden button on the base of the crystal ball. Glowing light emanated from a concealed bulb. For a moment, she saw her own reflection. Was this truly what she wanted out of life? To swindle people? To be a fraud?

She smirked and blew a kiss to herself.

Why not? This was the one thing she was good at, after all. And it was better to be the swindler than to be swindled. She'd learned that the hard way.

"Ready?" Gabriel asked.

She nodded.

He tucked himself behind the curtain where various pullies had been rigged. Gears began to grind and the main door to her wagon slowly opened, revealing a small but hopefully generous queue.

Gabriel's voice, disguised through a loud-hailer, roared to life. "Come one, come all! Please, don't despair. Come have your fate told by La Paloma Blanca, Fortune Teller Extraordinaire."

"It's about time," someone grumbled.

Esmeralda's eyes narrowed for a fraction of a second before she put on her most dazzling smile. *When you become the lead act, you'll never have to kiss any customers' heinies for measly tips again,* she told herself. She'd once overheard Melanie the Marionette bragging that her monthly salary was twenty thousand silvers. That was twice as much as Esmeralda had saved after ten months in the carnival. No wonder Melanie left without a word. With that sort of loot, Esmeralda would probably disappear too.

"First in line may come through," Gabriel's voice boomed. "Just add a silver coin into the coin box before you do."

A few voices objected. One person, a woman dressed as asparagus, left the queue altogether. Esmeralda took a calming breath. She needed every silver coin if she wanted to add to her savings *and* pay Gabriel for all his help. He always tried to refuse, since he made a good salary building haunts for the Fun House, but she never wanted to be in debt to anyone for anything.

The wagon swayed as her first customer clambered up. The

clink of a lone piece of silver thunking into the empty coin box nearly gutted her. The man wore a black mask in the shape of a wolf. His bowler hat was tugged low down his forehead, almost to his snout.

Trying to be mysterious, I see.

The door swung shut with a thud. The man reached for something, most likely a weapon tucked inside his coat. *Ah yes, he must be the bootlegger Gabriel spoke of.* Esmeralda wasn't afraid of some rudimentary thug. She'd been brought up by a far scarier man.

She lowered her voice to something husky and equally mysterious. "No need to fear, señor. It is only you and me in this wagon." She raised her arm and fluttered her fingers. "And the spirits of course."

The chandelier suddenly shook. A fun innovation Gabriel had come up with after she'd gone a week without a single customer. Though, the first time he'd tried it, the entire thing crashed onto the table, spooking her customer so much that Esmeralda had to pay the customer for his troubles instead. Now, it seemed to be a fan favorite.

The bootlegger wasn't impressed, however. He sat down unceremoniously. "Let's get on with it, then."

Why even come to a fortune teller's booth if you're going to be a bore? Being a bore goes against carnival rules anyway.

"What is it you wish to know?" she asked, smiling. "Would you like to hear from a loved one? Is there a secret you want brought to light? Perhaps you wish to understand the comings and goings of the officers in the county? My guides have told me the prohibition laws are quite strict around these parts."

His eyes pierced into her from behind his mask. "What did you say?" he growled.

She waved her hands over the crystal ball. "I only repeat what the spirits show me within this enchanted stone."

He leaned forward, peering at the ball. "I don't see nothing."

Obviously, she wanted to say. But she held her annoyance back. "That is because you aren't looking with your mind's eye."

She circled one hand over the crystal while the other pressed the hidden button once more. Swirling shadows danced within the sphere. To any onlooker, they might appear as whirling phantoms trapped inside.

Gabriel came up with this particular idea after he and Esmeralda had snuck into a real fortune teller's shop while Carnival Fantástico was stopped in one of the larger cities in the south several months back. Watching someone actually speak to souls from the Land of the Dead was rather interesting, especially when the king's church proclaimed that all souls were reincarnated after death, and that the new lives they were given would be based on how well they served him in this one.

Esmeralda had never believed such a ridiculous notion and therefore happily lived her life spitting on King Amadeo's portraits wherever she went. She never spat on the queen's portraits, though. There was a steeliness in Queen Hermosa's eyes that Esmeralda admired. Plus, she'd heard the queen went around telling the court about her husband's thumb-sucking habits. Apparently, their arranged marriage wasn't to her liking, and she tormented him whenever the opportunity presented itself, which was something Esmeralda couldn't help but respect.

The bootlegger's lips parted ever so slightly, and he leaned closer to the crystal ball.

Got him.

The chandelier rattled harder.

"The spirits are ready to communicate," she said, fluttering her lashes. "Now, what would you like to know specifically?"

The bootlegger popped his knuckles. "Will this next shipment set me over the top?"

The crystal throbbed with orange light. "My guides wish for me to consult with the cards."

When she was younger, she had seen a woman use cards in secret to help people find guidance. The woman had pulled several for Esmeralda the second she spotted her. None of them had been encouraging. But at least she'd learned some tricks.

She grabbed her deck and began to shuffle. She shut her eyes and spoke in a language she'd made up to sound more enigmatic. The table shook.

"What's happening?" the man said.

"The spirits have much to say," she whispered.

A burst of cold fluttered her hair. The man gasped.

"They are ready to answer your question," she said. "Hold out your hand."

The man did as he was asked. She placed the card onto his skin. The enchanted ink needed contact with her customers to work. Esmeralda hummed and the table rattled louder. The air whipped harder, sending some of her deck flying. Her eyes flicked to the curtain and narrowed. Gabriel was using the wind machine too generously.

She pulled her attention back to the man in the wolf mask, who was practically salivating with excitement. A smirk pulled at her lips. *I've got you right where I want you.* She flipped the card over. The kaleidoscopic ink began to shift into the shape of a sleek-looking motorcar. The front hood popped open, and cash tumbled out like a waterfall.

"The spirits have spoken," she said. "You will enjoy your spoils and be greater than the ones who came before you." She added for good measure, because she knew these sorts of men liked to hear these sorts of things, "You are untouchable."

Elation sparked in his pupils. She didn't need to see the face behind the wolf's mask to know he was thoroughly pleased.

She glanced at the tip jar on the table. Now would be as good a time as ever to remind him it was there, waiting to be fed a few more silver coins, but it was the man who spoke first.

"You know, I had my bet cast on the strongwoman act." He suddenly stood. He dug his hand into his coat pocket before dropping a golden coin into the tip jar. Esmeralda held in her gasp. That single coin was worth seventy silver ones. She'd been so focused on it that she had missed what he'd just said.

"I'm sorry, can you repeat that?" she asked sweetly.

"I said, I plan on switching my betting card and placing you right at the top. Who can compete with someone who speaks to spirits?" He turned and stomped toward the door, which was already opening. Over his shoulder, he growled, "Don't disappoint me, birdie."

Gabriel's head popped out from around the curtain. "What is he talking about?" he mouthed.

She shook her head.

"What sort of bet has been cast?" Esmeralda called after the man.

But he was already gone, and the two young women she'd seen earlier in the evening were entering, giggling and holding each other's arms.

Esmeralda grumbled at their happiness. Perhaps she'd read their fortunes and tell them their love was doomed. That love was a lie. But she was too practical for that. A happy customer always paid best.

When the final guest had been conned, Esmeralda grabbed her cloak and whirled it over her shoulders.

"Where are you going?" Gabriel asked as he greased the door pulley.

"To the Big Top," she said. "If I'm to be the next lead act in Carnival Fantástico, I've got to study my competition." Under her breath, she added, "So I can outsmart them."

1st of April, 1913. D+P: Age 10

To Esmeralda,

If you'd like to make a proper paper dove you must first:

1) Cut a piece of parchment into a perfect square.

2) Fold the parchment in half from point to point. The paper should appear as an isosceles triangle, to be precise.

(If you have any questions, I do not mind helping.)

To the boy I don't care to know,
1) I did not ask for your assistance.
2) Don't pass me notes. It's odd.
(I refuse to get in trouble because of you . . . again.)

You won't get in trouble. I promise. And we can give each other nicknames. That way, no one will know it is to you whom I'm passing notes. Though, we won't get caught.

I'll call you Dovie.

If you're wondering, <u>Why Dovie?</u>

1) I can now only think of you whenever I fold paper doves.

2) There is a large tree outside my window with a nest in it. A tiny white dove with a scowl just like yours glares at me whenever I come near. I swear I heard it growl once.

Don't be silly. Doves cannot scowl.
But I like this dove all the same.

CHAPTER 4
Ignacio

"The cheapest seat in the house is five hundred and twenty silvers," a woman with magenta hair and a gravelly voice called down from the elevated ticket booth.

Ignacio gawked. "Five hundred and twenty bits?! For one ticket?!" He pointed beyond the entrance, toward the wagons, games, and roller coasters teeming with people. "Can't I just enter to enjoy the sights?"

The woman shook her head while blowing a giant bubble of iridescent gum. With a single long fingernail, she pointed up toward the sign hanging above her head.

The Fun House, Giggle House, Tailor Virtuoso, Weather-Altering Tent, Siren Exhibit, Games, Treats, Foods of All Shapes and Sizes, Roller Coasters, Tonics, Ales, and All Other Unnamed Amusements are for guests with tickets to the Big Top show.

No exceptions.

Not even for handsome young men with light brown eyes and close-cut shaves.

Ignacio blinked at the last line. That was far too specific to not be speaking about him. Not that he was vain and went around thinking himself handsome. But he had caught the attention of a person or two in his day, and he *did* have light brown eyes and a close-cut shave.

Her bubble popped and glitter fluttered onto Ignacio's shoulders and boots. Scowling, he tried to brush his clothing clean. His brows pinched together even closer than they already were when the damn glitter wouldn't come off.

"What will it be, babe?" she inquired. "The show's starting soon."

"Hurry up, man!" A gentleman with cat whiskers drawn on his face called from the queue. "I caught a buggy from three towns over as soon as I heard the carnival arrived. Who knows when it's coming back. I'm not missing my only chance at a bit of happiness because of you."

Ignacio turned his head, eyeing the line of twenty or so people behind him. A few had on extravagant costumes with pearls and gems sewn into the seams. The hardships of war clearly hadn't touched their homes. But the man with cat whiskers had holes in his slacks and dirt in his nails. He also favored one leg, which made Ignacio wonder if the man had suffered at the front lines of the battlefield and lived to tell the tale as well.

Memories flooded Ignacio's senses. The screams of the dying and pops of gunfire filled his ears. The smell of blood and dirt and sweat stung his nostrils. The acidic taste of bile as he realized what he'd done.

"Señor," the ticket agent said sweetly, pulling him out of his miserable remembrances. "Are you going to pay or not?"

Ignacio chewed on his lip. Something was off. Five hundred and twenty silvers was the exact amount he had in his coin purse. Quite literally. Not a coin or bill more. The Defiant—the small organization who dared to resist the king, the comandante, their confining laws, and the war they'd forced upon their people—had given him the sum for travel, shelter, and bribes, along with a falsified officer's badge, while he hunted for clues to bring his father down.

How could the price of admission be that precise total?

"Hurry up before we miss the show!" a woman in line snapped.

Scowling, Ignacio retrieved his money and slapped it onto the tall counter above his head.

"Hold out your palm," the ticket agent commanded. "And try to smile, for king's sake. You're entering an enchanted wonderland full of magical mysteries. What's to be so blue about?"

Ignacio's scowl only deepened. "I'm not the smiling type."

"Then you have come to the right place because Carnival Fantástico always turns bitter frowns upside down."

She spit her gum into her hand. Ignacio knew he made a face, but he didn't care. That was absolutely foul. Quick as a viper, she bent over the booth and smashed the gum into Ignacio's awaiting palm.

His jaw dropped. "What are you doing?!"

The young woman pulled her arm back. The bubble gum was gone. In its place lay a gleaming ticket with bell-shaped flowers drawn around the words.

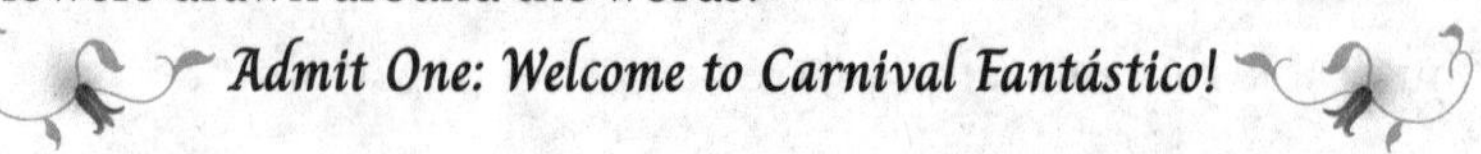

“Have fun.” She winked, chewing on something new, before yelling, “Next!”

Wiping his hand of germs, he stepped into the chaos. Music blared around him, thumping so loudly, he felt it in his solar plexus.

The air smelled of sugar and cinnamon. Bells clattered. People twirled and laughed with unbridled joy. In the distance, a wooden roller coaster shot people into the sky like a catapult. There were no ropes or cords attached to the carts the guests were in, and he wondered where they’d end up as their screams and laughter faded into the night.

How in the world was his father linked to this sort of place? Ignacio didn’t think Father even *could* consort with anyone from the carnival. Because King Amadeo cut trade and supply chains between Costa Mayor and Dos Palos, the railroad tycoons were losing a hefty profit. To reward their loyalty, the king turned a blind eye to all their other dealings. Thus, Carnival Fantástico was free to move along the tracks of Costa Mayor and continue to propagate magic and mayhem.

So, what would Father have to do with anyone here?

Ignacio glared at the costumed people flittering around.

Who could the author of those notes possibly be? How did they know my father well enough to call him by his first name? How did they get that ink? Could it be her?

Fingers wrapped around Ignacio’s bicep and yanked him to the side.

“Hey!” he yelled. “Let me go!”

“Not until I’ve done my job,” a slight man sporting a goat mask said.

He thrust Ignacio into a dull-yellow tent. Masks of all shapes and sizes hung from the canvas walls, along with fluffy tails, feathered jumpsuits, and two bottom halves of what appeared to be a donkey's ass.

"Didn't Rosita tell you the rules?" the man asked.

Ignacio shrugged him off. "The ticket agent? She only told me I had to pay to get in."

"There's that, yes, of course. But you cannot go any further without donning a disguise. It's the rules! Lucky for you, you've come to the right place."

"I had little choice in the matter."

The man waved him off. He cleared his throat and raised his arms. "Welcome to the prodigious tailor virtuoso!" He cupped his mouth as if telling a secret and whispered, "That's me." He raised his arms once more. "Everyone must wear a disguise while on these unsanctimonious grounds. That is the second and most important rule, in my not-so-humble opinion."

"Why?"

The tailor blinked. "Why not?"

Ignacio's already frayed nerves were starting to split. "I have no more money to give."

"What of that ring on your pinky?" the tailor asked.

Ignacio's fingers instinctively traveled to the ring in question. Protecting it from the man's greed-filled eyes. "Absolutely not. It was my mother's."

She had been the king's comandante nearly twelve years ago. She was killed on her journey back from Dos Palos, where she had gone to discuss new trade agreements on behalf of the king. Within hours of her murder, Dos Palos closed the borders between itself and Costa Mayor, then claimed they would no longer trade goods with Costa Mayor unless they could inspect every shipment entering or exiting its lands. King Amadeo took her death and the new barriers as a sign of deepest disrespect. And thus, the war began.

The tailor tapped on the temple of his porcelain goat mask. "What about the tin box in your coat pocket?"

Ignacio balked. "How did you—"

"Or what about that badge hanging around your neck?" the man queried. "Though, I don't suppose it's worth much. Might want to hide that, matter of fact. You officers are unwelcome here." He put a hand to his heart. "Not by me, certainly, I welcome all. Especially if they pay well."

Ignacio stuffed the aforementioned badge inscribed with the king's crest beneath his shirt.

"What about the shiv at your hip, then? That seems like a nice compromise."

A deep unease clenched Ignacio's gut. How did this man know what he had hidden in his clothing? This place was off. Wrong. He felt dirty for even being there. The faster he found whoever wrote to his father and used that mysterious ink, the faster he could leave. The war was continuing; more lives would be lost if he didn't give the Defiant some sort of damning evidence against his father and the king to print up and share with the world. And if he also found out where the ink came from, maybe, just maybe, he could find his way back to her. Though, he had no clue why he would even want to see the girl who had decided he wasn't good enough to love.

He unsheathed the dagger. The tailor virtuoso plucked it from his grasp and flung it into a wooden box as if it were scraps.

Ignacio scowled. That dagger wasn't cheap. The blade was specially made for the Blackbirds and was nearly indestructible.

"Now to spiff you up." The tailor spun and scampered to the wall of masks.

"Perhaps you can help me with something?" Ignacio asked.

"It will cost you," the tailor said over his shoulder.

"That was an expensive piece of weaponry. Surely, it's worth more than a silly costume."

The tailor held up a finger. "You get one question."

Ignacio clenched his jaw. He turned his face away, trying to calm his temper. A poster lay face up beneath the counter. A young man with a curling mustache winked up at him from the parchment. Ignacio balked. He rubbed his eyes. The young man was gone. In his place glistened sentences written in the exact ink he was searching for. He raced to the poster and snatched it up.

"Who wrote this? Where can I find whoever used this ink?"

"That's two questions," the tailor said.

Ignacio grasped the tailor and whirled him around by the collar of his goat-hair cape. "Tell me . . . *now*."

The tailor giggled boyishly as if this were all some sort of game. Ignacio's grip tightened.

"All right," the tailor said. "Kindly unhand me first."

Ignacio released him.

The tailor hopped onto a small crate and cleared his throat. In a theatrical fashion, he announced, "You will find your answers with our beloved ringmaster. But he is neither here nor there. He is everywhere and all at once. He *is* the carnival. Ángel Veracruz, inventor of the most fantastical carnival there ever was, is a wonder. A friend to the gods. A magical provocateur!"

Outside the tent, a woman dressed as a chicken clucked and pecked at the empty peanut shells on the dirt. A man in a rooster costume tried to stop her to no avail.

Ignacio shook his head. *I've got to hurry this along.*

He refocused on the tailor, who was still going on about the glorious Ángel Veracruz.

"Where might I find this *magical provocateur*?" Ignacio asked.

"Let me think." The tailor rubbed his chin. "Where does one find a ringmaster, I wonder?" he said, sarcasm dripping from his tone. "Where might a *ring*master be found? Somewhere with a center ring perhaps."

"The Big Top."

"He's handsome *and* intelligent, folks!" the tailor yelled out. He held his hand to his ear. "Sounds like the show is getting ready to start as we speak. Perhaps if you stay and watch the performance, making sure to ooh and aah at all the right parts, our Señor Veracruz will feel generous enough to meet with you after."

"Perhaps?"

The tailor nodded. "He's a very busy, very important man."

Ignacio cursed. This wouldn't do. He needed answers now. During his last correspondence with the Defiant, they'd told him the debtors' prisons had been emptied out and the prisoners carted to the front lines to take over for the fallen officers. They weren't soldiers. They had no place in battle.

"Better scram before you miss the show." The tailor shoved something into Ignacio's chest.

A mask made to look like a weasel.

"Is there deeper meaning to you giving me this animal in particular?"

He looked up then, but the tailor was already walking away, getting ready to wrangle some other sucker inside his buttercup-colored tent.

CHAPTER 5
Esmeralda

Esmeralda tugged the hood of her cloak tight over her face as she walked toward the black-and-white-striped tent that stood erect at the center of the carnival. She still wore her dove mask and didn't want anyone to stop her and ask for a free fortune telling. Or worse, have no one recognize her at all as she greedily watched the other performers in the Big Top.

But watch she would. Because if she was going to become the next main act, she needed to understand what captivated the audience the most.

Would it be the way Pilar and Camila worked in tandem as they lifted a ton's worth of marble pillars over their heads? Perhaps it was how Anella the Contortionist bent her body at the oddest of angles? Or how Paco appeared so calm and collected while he strutted over scorching coals? Hopefully, a death-defying act wasn't a requirement for the Running because Esmeralda couldn't do any of those things.

She had her own sort of magic to offer, of course. She was

brilliant with her cards and could woo a crowd with her dazzling smile, but how could she make that translate to the center ring? How could she add the entrancing spark of danger that lifted audiences into a standing ovation? Having people scream her name would be thrilling indeed.

The Big Top grew closer. She winced. The entrance felt like a gaping mouth filled with sharp teeth. Except instead of teeth, it was a passageway filled with thousands of dark mirrors that forced you to look at your own reflection. Which she hated. All the strange mirrors, the way her face and body contorted as she walked through, made her cheeks flush from dread. So much so that sometimes she even felt feverish after exiting on the other side. Bogged down as if she'd been drained of all her energy. Esmeralda shivered at the thought. But besides going to Clown Alley and entering via the performers' accessway, the mirrored tunnel was the only path into the massive tent.

Cheerful horns began to blare. The first act was about to start. She quickened her pace.

"Oof!"

The sound burst from her lips as she ran beak-first into something hard and unyielding. Her eyes watered, and she lost her footing from the sudden force.

Hands wrapped around her biceps, steadying her.

"Apologies," a deep but youthful voice said. "Are you okay?"

"Hardly," she huffed.

The tall young man wore a stiff coat with a hood over his head. He sported one of the weasel masks from the tailor's shop—which signified they had someone untrustworthy in their midst. He could be an officer. A tax collector. A scorned lover. Someone who the tailor deemed deceitful. One of the ratas would find him soon enough and kick him on his rear out of the gates.

She lowered her head even though she had on her mask.

If it was an officer, she was done for. *No,* she reminded herself. *You are part of the carnival. You are untouchable by the comandante's cronies.* But still, best not to push her luck. "If you'll excuse me . . ." She tried to back out of the weasel's hold, but his fingers tightened ever so slightly around her arms.

She went rigid but recovered her charm quickly. "You can unhand me now, doll. You have saved me from tumbling onto the ground." She freed herself and offered a tiny bow. "My hero."

Quickly, she swept around him.

He stepped forward. "Wait . . ."

An explosion rattled inside the Big Top, followed by the screams of the audience. The young man ducked to the ground. His hands went over the hood covering his head as if trying to shield himself from some invisible bomb that was sure to drop. He must've been a soldier. One who'd seen the terrors of Comandante Olivera's bloody war. She wasn't sure if she should snicker at him for being one of the comandante's puppets or feel sorry for him. Either way, he was safe now. Wars weren't being waged within this circus tent. Ilda the Rocket Woman was just being blown through the air by a cannon.

Esmeralda used the distraction to slip away from him. She burrowed herself into the crowd that had yet to enter the Big Top. She glanced over her shoulder as the customers surged forward, anxious to get to their seats. The weasel slowly rose. He didn't even flinch when a juggler on a unicycle nearly crashed into him. His gaze was scouring over every reveler.

She gulped and pushed deeper through the throng to shield herself.

If he figures out who you are, he will arrest you.

"No," she whispered to herself. Officers held no power within Carnival Fantástico because of the king's not-so-secret deal with the rail masters.

You're fine.

You're safe.

And yet, she was terrified. She would not go back to a cell. She would never feel manacles around her wrists again.

She decided not to trap herself within the Big Top tent. Just before she made it to the tunnel of mirrors, Esmeralda cut right. Shielded by costumed guests, she bolted away as fast as she could.

There was no chance she was going to let herself get caught by some weasel in a weasel mask.

CHAPTER 6
Ignacio

Ignacio thought he might be sick.

His fingers instinctually went to his mother's ring. He spun it in circles around his pinky finger as his mind raced.

That voice. He knew that voice.

A single word came to mind: *Impossible.*

CHAPTER 7
Esmeralda

The screams and cheers of the Big Top crashed over Esmeralda like a tidal wave as she quickly walked through Clown Alley. The backstage area was empty of the performers, of the animals from the menagerie, of the tiny buggies used to cart in dozens of clowns, of the pesky monkey that was forever eyeing her trinkets. Not even the ringmaster's ratas were around.

Everyone must have been inside the tent still after they performed the march of showstoppers. It was similar to the opening parade, in which the carnival performers sauntered through whatever town they arrived in to lure guests to the show. Though the march of showstoppers was much more magnificent. The energy of the crowd in one tight space heightened every sense. The costumes were bigger. The tricks were more daring. Even the popcorn smelled better.

Jealousy nipped at her. She should be in there winking and waving to awed patrons. Instead, she was scrambling through the dim shadows to get away from a weasel who probably wasn't even looking for her.

She risked a glance over her shoulder. Her heart jolted. A figure in black stood only yards away, half hidden by a pile of empty barrels.

She clamped her hand over her mouth to seal in the scream rising in her throat.

A warm breeze swept through the alley. The figure began to flutter in the air like a ghoul. Esmeralda slowed her pace and circled around. Panting, she squinted into the twinkling dark.

It was just one of the ringmaster's coats hanging out to dry.

A laugh escaped her. "Esmeralda, you chump. There isn't a soul out here."

Camila had once commented how strange it was that Esmeralda spoke to herself so often. Sometimes, Esmeralda had full-on conversations and arguments with herself. Which, to her, was completely normal. She didn't have a sister to speak with while growing up like Camila did. She certainly didn't have loving family members who asked her about her day.

She was an only child from a broken family of thieves. No one had paid her any mind unless they needed her to fit into a tight space, so she made do with her own company. And she thought herself to be perfectly entertaining most of the time. But if she were honest, she didn't want to always be alone. It would be nice to find someone who wanted her. Who loved her enough to see past all the jagged edges.

Sure, she was a thief. Esmeralda knew she could be rude and arrogant. Sometimes selfish and maybe even a little rotten. But there had to be *something* worth loving inside her.

The poster hanging on the wall shifted from the handsome face of the ringmaster to a congratulatory banner.

¡FELICIDADES, TO THE EIGHT PERFORMERS
CHOSEN BY SEÑOR VERACRUZ!
BEST OF LUCK.
DON'T FORGET TO SMILE.
BECAUSE ONE OF YOU WILL BE OUR BRAND-NEW MUSE!

Pride swelled in her chest. The ringmaster thought her worthy. And *when* she was selected to be his lead act, she would show everyone who had ever left her behind that they should be sorry. Someday soon she would be inside that big tent being cheered on by troves of loving fans instead of standing outside running from imaginary foes.

Until then, she needed to come up with a plan on how to wow the world. Just as she turned on her heels and took a step, something hard clamped around her shoulder, holding her in place.

"Stop," said the deep voice she had heard minutes before. But it was hard to be certain when her pulse thundered so hard against her skull.

She forced herself to stay calm and fluttered her fingers to the left. "Baños are on the other side of this alley, señor."

"I'm not here for the bathroom," he said. "I'm here for you."

That was all she needed to hear. Esmeralda stomped on the man's boot. His hold on her loosened, and she darted forward. She grabbed the first thing she could reach, a large egg made from fool's gold sitting on a vanity.

"Wait!" he yelled.

She did not, in fact, wait.

Whirling around, she flung the egg with the whole of her

might. The egg didn't hit the man in the skull as she hoped but instead pounded deep into his throat. Both his hands wrapped around his neck. He wheezed, gasping for air.

Esmeralda was not surprised to see that it was the weasel she had bumped into. Nor was she surprised to see the shining officer's badge that had untucked itself from the collar of his shirt. But how quickly he recovered *did* surprise her entirely.

He launched himself at her. She tried to dodge out of the way, but her boot snagged on one of the tension wires holding the rear of the menagerie tent in place.

Her face skidded across the dirt. Something snapped.

Thankfully, it wasn't her nose, but her dove mask had shattered into tiny pieces, falling like raindrops onto the ground.

For stars' sake! That mask wasn't cheap.

Cursing under her breath, she tried to rise, but a giant boot stomped onto her cloak.

She swept out her leg and kicked the young man's feet right out from underneath him. She'd learned that trick once from the boy she had loved. The man landed on his back with a comical huff, but his long-limbed body sprawled out across her cape.

She grabbed the fabric with both hands and yanked. He didn't budge.

"Get off, you mule!" This was the only cloak she had. She couldn't just slip out of it and leave it here.

"Wait," he rasped, still trying to catch his breath.

"So you can arrest me? Ha!"

I won't go back to a cell. I won't ever be so cold my bones feel brittle. Especially not so close to where I once lived.

She yanked again, and the seam tore. A frustrated shriek came from her.

"Get off!" she repeated. "Are you that terrible of an officer that you have to pick on a girl?"

"I see no girl here," he countered. "Only a lying, scheming coward."

That was strangely personal.

"Enough!" he roared.

He jumped to his feet just as she tugged. With the fabric free, she jerked back, landing hard on her rear. The officer stood to his full height.

"You can't arrest me here," she panted. "You can't take me with you."

"I only want to talk, dammit!" He shoved back the hood of his coat, gripped his weasel mask, and tore it from his face.

Esmeralda's jaw dropped. She blinked hard, not believing her eyes were seeing what they were seeing. This couldn't be. He shouldn't be here. It made no sense.

"You," she whispered.

His right eye twitched. "*You,*" he snarled.

The badge swung between them like the pendulum of the grandfather clock his father kept inside his manor.

She barked a bitter laugh.

"Of course you took after him. Looks like dear old daddy bumped you right up to officer, then. You should be so proud."

She glared at the boy she once cherished most in the entire world. The boy who was not a boy anymore. He was a man. He'd grown up in the year since they'd seen each other. Muscles had filled in around his once gangly limbs. His jawbone seemed more defined, even though that shouldn't be possible. A few scars marred his brown skin. Skin she had once kissed and pressed against under the stars.

"What are you doing here?" he asked.

Now she could hear the familiar richness of his voice. She hadn't known it was him at first because the tone had deepened since their parting. He'd truly grown up without her. Just like he wanted. And yet, he had the gall to ask her questions.

Fiery rage burned through her body. He was working for his father. He was here to arrest her for running away from the comandante before her indenture was up. Or throw her back into a cell and leave her to rot like his father had done before. Or worse, ship her off to war.

Like hell he was.

She reached for the golden egg in the dirt. The second her fingers clasped around the heavy mass, she chucked it as hard as she could.

The egg bopped him right in his thick skull.

He stumbled back but regained his footing. He glared down at her, gaze unfocused. "You little—" His eyes flashed with fury before they rolled back. The boy she once loved collapsed in a limp heap next to her feet.

And, of course, he'd fallen right onto her cloak.

She breathed hard through her nostrils. "Ignacio Olivera, you are the very worst."

17th of May, 1914. D+P: Age 11

Dovie. What do you want to be when you grow up?

Rich. Filthy, stinking, rotting rich. I want to lie on a lounger all day and have people feed me cherries.

I think you mean grapes.

Nope. Grapes are boring. Rich people eat cherries.

I hate cherries.

I've never had them, but they look divine.

Remember the dove I told you about a year or so ago? The one that scowled at me, and I said it looked just like you? Anyway, guess what? She's back. And she isn't alone. I believe she has a husband.

Can doves marry?

I just returned from the library. Turns out the answer is yes. Well, sort of. Mourning doves often mate for life.

So do pigeons.
But still, that's rather sweet.
Do you think you'll ever marry someday?

Of course. You?

I'm not so sure anyone would want to be stuck with me for that long.

I would.

I've just realized what your nickname should be! Pigeon.

But pigeons are like rats with wings.

I know.

CHAPTER 8
Ignacio

Ignacio's body jostled violently, wrenching him from his dreams of being clobbered by a little bird.

Strange, he thought. He didn't recall falling asleep.

He opened his eyes but quickly slammed them shut when white light flooded his vision and an all-consuming pain lanced through his skull. He groaned and rubbed his hands over his face.

What happened?

The muscles in his stomach tensed. He had seen Esmeralda Montero. Really and truly. The girl he thought was lost to him forever was there, dressed as some bird inside Carnival Fantástico. And she had clocked him. *Him*, of all people!

What right did *she* have to be so mad at *him*? If anyone had a right to be so angry that they'd throw a golden egg, it should be him! *She* had gone back on all the promises they made to each other when they were younger. *She* was the one who didn't show up under the dove tree that night. They were going to run away together. But what did she do instead? The little chicken.

She left him a coldhearted letter. The one currently tucked away inside his coat.

Whatever bench he was resting on shuddered viciously.

"Watch the potholes, Mini," a gruff voice called. "We've got a long way yet to go until we get to the clinker."

The clinker?

The sound of clopping hooves and smell of dried grass jerked his mind to full alertness.

He shot up. Ignoring his pounding headache, he opened his eyes. His jaw dropped. Somehow, he'd been put inside a barred cart. And there was nothing but yellowed wheat fields for miles on end.

"What is the meaning of this?" he hollered.

The man driving the wagon peered over his shoulder. He had a wispy beard, a knife-sharp nose, and devilry in his eyes.

"The sleeping beauty has awoken, I see." He chuckled to himself.

Ignacio wrapped his fingers around the rusted bars and shook them. "I demand you let me out of here at once."

"Or what?" The man flicked the reins and the sturdy horse pulling the cart trotted faster.

"I'm an officer of the law!" Ignacio lied. In fact, he was wanted by all officers of the law on account of his desertion from the Blackbirds and his suspected ties to the Defiant. But that was none of this man's business.

The jailer chuckled. "You'd be surprised how often I hear that one."

Ignacio's hand went to his collar to find proof. But his falsified badge was gone. *No.* His fingers dug into his coat. The letter and flyer remained. He tunneled into his pants pocket. Found nothing but lint. His entire body went ice cold with dread. The tin box he'd taken from his room with dozens of rolled-up notes written between her and him was gone.

"Esmeralda," Ignacio growled. The brat. The thief. The coward. "How did I get in here?" he asked. "Why am I under arrest?"

"That pretty girl with the wild hair caught you stealing. Said you were after her golden eggs."

"After her . . ." Ignacio could breathe fire, he was so furious. "I wasn't stealing anything. You have an innocent man."

He shouldn't be surprised by this. Esmeralda had always been the first to throw a low blow in a fight.

The jailer huffed. "If I had a silver coin for every time I heard that, my girl Mini here would have horseshoes made of Blackbird obsidian. But I will soon enough. Once I deposit you to the military barracks."

"The what?"

"Didn't think I'd recognize you, eh? I've been around long enough to remember when your mother was still in charge. I know who you are, son, *and* who's looking for you right now."

Bloody hell.

"I demand you release me!"

"Not a chance. Your daddy will put up a fair amount of dough for your return. What he plans on doing with you, one can only imagine. I doubt even the son of the great comandante can be pardoned for abandoning his duty as a soldier."

If this man knew half of the things Ignacio knew about "the

great comandante," he wouldn't be so worried over Ignacio's desertion. Or perhaps the jailer wouldn't care at all. There were so many people in this world who would happily turn the other way, so long as their lives were left unaffected, or they could benefit.

Ignacio eyed the bars. They were old but well made. He obviously couldn't break himself out by prying them loose. He turned to the small door at the rear. The lock sealing him inside was the size of his head. But the hinges . . . now those looked as if they hadn't seen maintenance in ages. The welds were even cracked in some spots. If he was going to chance an escape, he'd have to do it fast. He wasn't sure how long he'd been knocked out. Who knew how far he was from the carnival now or how close they were to the barracks.

Ignacio had to get away. He had to figure out who knew his father's secrets. He needed to bring the comandante and King Amadeo to justice for what they'd done.

Was it Esmeralda who wrote to his father? She had used this ink before.

No. She would never. She hated Father. But who knew if that was still true? There was no telling what Esmeralda was capable of anymore.

But, dammit, she looked good. Distractingly so. When she had worked as his father's runner, she'd been the prettiest girl Ignacio had ever seen. Now she was beyond beautiful. Her cheeks had filled in a bit. Other places too. She had never donned makeup when they were growing up, but the deep purple lipstick she wore when he caught her behind the Big Top brought out the plumpness of her mouth. A mouth he'd once tasted.

He shook his head to break his thoughts apart.

She had you arrested. She knocked you out with a blasted egg.

It was his turn to return the favor. Not the knocking out part, of course. But he could be cold. He could be callous.

Perhaps it was petty to want to hurt her. Perhaps it was wrong. But Esmeralda Montero had cut him to his very core, and he'd been living in a state of brokenness ever since. Getting back at her might be the thing to finally mend the damage caused to his heart.

But first, he had to escape this jailer.

Carnival Fantástico did not stay in one location for long, and the train pulling the attractions from city to city moved at an incredible speed. Knowing how skittish she was, he doubted Esmeralda would even be there by the time he caught up to the traveling circus again.

The jailer began to hum the same irritating tune that played on a loop at Carnival Fantástico. Silently, Ignacio slithered to the other end of the barred cart. He lay on his back and placed his boots on the iron slates of the small door. He heaved.

Saints, the door is heavy.

The lock made a great clatter. The jailer peered over his shoulder.

"Stop that right now!" he yelled.

"I'd rather not." Ignacio gritted his teeth and grunted as he shoved his legs upward yet again.

"Stop that!" the jailer pulled back on the reins.

Tiny dots danced in Ignacio's vision, but he didn't rest. Not until the hinges gave out and the door broke, held up by only the giant lock. He scrambled to his hands and knees and squeezed through the opening, tumbling onto the dirt.

"I said stop!" the jailer screamed.

But Ignacio was already running away, bolting as hard and as fast as he could in the direction they had just come from. Praying to the gods once written about in fairy tales that he wasn't too late.

CHAPTER 9
Esmeralda

Esmeralda grunted as she tried to lift one of Camila's dumbbells. Camila grinned and took it, jesting about Esmeralda's weak arms before chucking the heavy metal into an already heavy trunk.

Sometimes they stayed in a town for multiple days. Sometimes only one night. When the ringmaster decided he'd had his fill or the laughter in the Big Top dulled, the carnival was immediately packed up into wagons, which would be wheeled onto the train or stuffed into boxcars and secured for departure once the carnival closed. In the ten months since she, Gabriel, and the Sánchezes joined the carnival, they had almost always convened at the sisters' wagon to help the girls pack . . . and to gossip.

"What happened after you knocked him out?" Gabriel asked as he exited the wagon Camila and Pilar shared, brushing the sweat from his brow.

"I checked his pockets of course," Esmeralda said. "He didn't have much to offer. A flyer for the carnival. A tin box and an officer's badge, which I snagged." His mother's ring was on his pinky finger. She wasn't so heartless that she would steal that. Although, the thought had crossed her mind. He *had* given it to her once upon a time.

She grabbed another dumbbell. "I found one of the ringmaster's ratas and had them contact a jailer. I told them I found Ignacio trying to steal some golden eggs."

Both Camila and Gabriel snorted.

"Remind me not to cross you," Camila teased.

"He'll be fine," Esmeralda said, rolling her eyes. "His father is the second most powerful man in Costa Mayor."

Gabriel gaped. "He's the son of Comandante Olivera? The commander of the entire army? How did a thief like you meet the child of the most prestigious man in Costa Mayor?" He added a "No offense" to soften the slight.

"Offense taken," she replied. "I'll have you know it was the comandante's son who pursued me. Anyway." She flicked her hair over her shoulder to prove she didn't care that Gabriel assumed Ignacio was too good for her. Ignacio clearly thought so too. He did betray her a year ago. And what was his excuse for breaking her heart? *I can't turn my back on my father.* "I lived in the comandante's manor from the age of ten, all the way until I ran away before my eighteenth birthday."

"Lived there? Why?" Gabriel asked.

"Yeah, why?" Camila chimed in. "And why did you never tell us this? It's like you talk and talk but don't actually say anything about yourself."

"That's because I'd rather speak about anything in the world other than my past."

Camila and Gabriel stopped working altogether.

"I think we're beyond that," Gabriel said. "You've already spilled most of the beans anyway. You can't leave us hanging now."

Camila chimed in. "You can tell us stuff, you know. It's kind of what friends are for."

Esmeralda couldn't help but feel a timid sort of warmth gathering inside her chest, but she ignored it. Her parents had given her up the second she wasn't of use to them. Ignacio left her once she told him she wouldn't wait for him to return from the Blackbirds. Comandante Olivera had her thrown into a cell when she no longer served as his trustworthy spy. The moment she wasn't what someone needed or wanted or expected, the moment she didn't offer anything of value, people were done with her.

She made Gabriel and Camila laugh. She trotted around with an arrogant grin and lackadaisical manner that put them at ease. What would happen when they saw the serious, sad side of her that didn't offer them joy? They'd probably stay away, and she couldn't risk that.

"We better hurry up and finish before the train leaves us. You know how much I hate running after things." She moved to pick up one of Camila's trunks. It didn't budge. Camila had placed one of her sandaled feet right on top of it.

"Talk," she commanded.

Esmeralda placed her hands on her hips. "Is the truth about

my wretched history more important than getting ready to depart?"

"Yes," Camila and Gabriel said in unison.

"You're both insufferable."

"We learned it from you," Gabriel said. "Now spit it out before I expire from the morning heat."

Esmeralda breathed hard through her nostrils before saying, "When I was ten, I was caught stealing from Comandante Olivera's home. Instead of sending me to the dungeons, he turned me into his spy. Ignacio and I became friends as I worked off my indenture."

"And then you became more," Camila added with a wiggle of her brows.

"Unfortunately," Esmeralda grumbled.

Gabriel narrowed his gaze. "When you and I met inside the jailer's wagon . . ."

"That was two months *after* I ran away from Comandante Olivera. Like I said, I scuttled off before my indenture was up, but his officers found me easily enough. The comandante then left me to rot in a dark cell as punishment until he decided all us criminals would serve him better in the war. And that's where I met you, another pitiful prisoner heading for certain death."

"And aren't you lucky for it," Gabriel said. "If I remember correctly, it was I who got us free from our manacles before we reached the trenches."

"I think that hooch you procured from the bootlegger has done something to your brain. *I* freed us from the jailer's cart. *You* got us out of the manacles long after we escaped."

“You *both* played pivotal roles in your freedom,” Camila said. “Now back to you and Ignacio falling in love.”

Esmeralda groaned. “Do we really need to talk about it?”

“Yes,” her two friends said again.

This brought on a wave of giggles.

Pilar’s head popped out of the wagon. “What’s so funny?”

Pilar Sánchez looked nearly identical to her sister Camila, though she was eleven months older. She was tall and lanky but with muscles that showed themselves whenever she had need for them. And Pilar, like her sister, wore her black hair in two plaits that she pinned up like a crown. There was no denying her queenly beauty.

The sisters grew up on a massive farm in El Sueco. Their unnatural strength was built through years of exertion like the rest of their family. But because half of their uncles, aunts, and cousins had been called to war, the Sánchezes had fallen on hard times. The girls came to the carnival to earn enough coin to send home to their grandparents and keep their home afloat. But once Pilar got a taste of fame, her priorities shifted. She wanted to be a star not a ranch hand.

She hopped onto the grass and lifted one of the marble columns she and Camila used to show off their strength during their act. The post was weighty. Esmeralda could only lift it inches from the ground with both arms. But Pilar rested it on one shoulder and walked up the step to her wagon with ease. She placed the column down next to the others that had already been stored.

“We were just talking about Esmeralda and her beau,” Gabriel said.

Pilar's pretty face knotted in surprise. "You have a beau?"

"He is not my anything." Not anymore.

Once, Ignacio Olivera had been her everything. He was the one person in the entire world she loved with every fiber of her being. Her veins and bones and organs buzzed whenever she so much as thought of him.

In fact, they were doing it now. She grew feverish when she thought of those long lashes curled over his light brown eyes. Of the last night they'd spent together. The warmth of his bare skin against hers.

Stop it, she hissed in her mind.

But her body didn't listen. Seeing Ignacio for the first time since he left her for the Blackbirds had brought back a thousand sharp memories *and* the feelings that came with them.

She remembered the way he smelled. The way her head fit perfectly against his chest. The shy smile he'd give whenever they saw each other after being apart for long. Almost every good memory she had of her life before the carnival involved Ignacio in some way.

They were so young when they found each other, just ten years old. The first time she'd seen him in the daylight was when she caught him watching her from his bedroom window.

She had been in the courtyard of the comandante's estate, waiting for Comandante Olivera and his general to finish whispering to one another so they could tell her what to do. She didn't mind being the comandante's errand runner so much. Having a warm bed to sleep in and food in her belly was rather nice. Plus, someone kept leaving her little treats on her pillow and extra socks in her dresser.

Growing bored while waiting on the comandante, she tried to crease the parchment in her hand into the shape of a bird. She had seen a few paper doves left about the estate and wanted to try, but she couldn't get it right. Frustrated, she let her eyes roam over the grounds and spotted him, the gangly boy who had been responsible for her having to work for the comandante in the first place. He'd been the one to find her when she and her family snuck into the comandante's home to steal his prized collection of rare figurines. Ignacio had been the one to rat her out.

She stuck out her tongue at him. His eyes widened, and he disappeared behind his curtains. But when she got to her room in the servants' quarters that night, she spotted a small bird made from folded paper hanging through the overhead vent.

Esmeralda had been ecstatic to see the fluttering dove, but that emotion was quickly devoured by suspicion. She stood on a chair and plucked it from the fishing wire it was attached to. Two words had been scribbled onto the wing.

Open. Please.

Hastily, she pulled the bird apart and was stunned to see that he'd written instructions on how to properly fold a paper dove. She'd laughed at his audacity and had replied with some rude comment. But that had been the beginning of their friendship. They passed tiny notes using fishing wire through the vent that led from his palatial room on the second floor, through the stairwell, and into her windowless chamber on the bottom level.

Ignacio Olivera was the great war commander's only son.

She was the great war commander's tiny spy. They both had their roles to play in the commander's life. But their worlds were never meant to collide. She was too far below Ignacio's station.

The letters had been rudimentary at first, just the naïve thoughts of two children who had no other friends. And then, as they grew older, the letters grew deeper.

Ignacio would ask questions like:

What do you think of when you look at me?

If you weren't you, who would you wish to be?

Have you ever loved someone before?

When he turned fifteen, Ignacio asked:

Will you meet me under the stars?

And that was where their tragic love story began, because she had said yes.

The train whistle blew three sharp shrieks, cutting through the memory. They would be departing within ten minutes.

"Less chisme. More packing," Pilar, ever the older sister, ordered.

Esmeralda grabbed whatever items she could lift and brought them into the sisters' wagon. She placed the bejeweled shoes she held next to Camila's cot. An open gift box caught Esmeralda's attention. Cellophane wrapping lay crumpled beside it.

"Is this the gift the ringmaster gave you?" she asked over her shoulder.

She had yet to tell the sisters that she was in the Running as well. There hadn't been a proper time between knocking out her first love and framing him for burglary. Esmeralda had been so distracted that she hadn't even glanced inside the box she had been given.

The compact wagon rocked slightly when Camila placed another column down. She dusted off her hands and stepped beside Esmeralda. She peered at the four cloth cuffs resting on a nest of glistening confetti.

"Yup," Camila said. "The greatest ringmaster of the most magnificent carnival there ever was has *generously* gifted us with cuffs to wipe our sweat on." She plucked one up. The stitching glimmered in the early morning light like the ink used on Esmeralda's cards. "But they are rather spectacular."

"Let me show them!" Pilar said.

Camila flung one of the cloth cuffs to her sister. Pilar missed the catch but quickly plucked the cuff off the wagon floor. She brushed off the dust and slid it onto her wrist before holding it up. Wiggling her fingers, she grinned.

"Is it doing something?" Gabriel, always the innovator, had to know.

"The second I slip these on, my arms feel light as air," Pilar said.

"That's saying something. You've got bigger muscles than me," Gabriel added.

"Not hard to do, but I'll take the compliment," Pilar teased. "Watch this." She walked over to one of the columns. She bent low and scooped her arm around it.

Esmeralda gaped as Pilar stood, holding the heavy column as if it were made of feathers.

"Amazing," Gabriel whispered. "What does it feel like?"

"Like it weighs next to nothing."

"The ringmaster gave you enchanted cuffs?" Esmeralda asked in awe. No one had a clue where the magic came from or how it worked. As far as she knew, magic didn't even exist outside Carnival Fantástico. Esmeralda didn't care about its origins. It was there and it could benefit her. That was all she needed to know.

"What did you get inside your gift box?" Gabriel asked her.

"*Your* gift box?" Pilar asked with an incredulous tone. As if Esmeralda couldn't possibly have been chosen for something as momentous as the Running. Granted, Esmeralda was still in shock, but that didn't mean Pilar should be in shock as well.

She batted her lashes. "Silly me. I nearly forgot to mention it. I've been selected for the Running too."

A moment of stunned silence permeated the wagon. Then Camila screamed. She jumped up and down and wrapped an arm around Esmeralda's neck, tugging her in for a too-tight hug. Esmeralda stiffened. She was never the affectionate type.

"What will your act be?" Pilar asked. "Surely reading cards won't do for a crowd of thousands."

"Shut your yapper, Pilar," Camila said through her teeth. "I'm sure Esmeralda has a plan."

"Of course I do! Lots of them, actually."

She had one: Do whatever it took to become the ringmaster's new lead act.

To keep things fresh and exciting, the ringmaster only let his performers and staff work within the carnival for a single year. That was how long it took to tour all of Costa Mayor. But his lead acts got to stay on and gain wealth and fame until they wished to leave. Melanie the Marionette, though, had been the main attraction for less than twelve months before she suddenly quit. Meanwhile, other lead acts in the past remained with the carnival for years.

The whistle screamed five times. The train carrying all of Carnival Fantástico would be departing in minutes.

"I better get to my wagon," Esmeralda said. "It's been a long night, and I'm beat."

The girls and Gabriel waved her off. They teased her about dreaming of her first love. But Esmeralda's mind was far from Ignacio Olivera. All she cared about right now was finding out what lay inside her cellophane-wrapped box.

CHAPTER 10
Ignacio

He thrashed through the wheat field. That brat, that villain, the person he once thought held his future in her hands, the girl who had framed him and sent him to jail, was getting away.

He stumbled to a stop. The sun had crested over the eastern side of the valley, casting the sky in a dusky pink. There should have been wagons and booths in this very spot, but the carnival was gone. There were no towering tents. No whirling roller coasters. The marquee he'd walked through upon entry was nowhere to be seen. The only hint that there had ever been a carnival at all was glistening glitter near the train tracks.

In the distance, he heard a blustery howl of a whistle. His head snapped to the left. Just beyond the small hill he saw puffs of pearlescent smoke from a train's engine stack. People often mused that magic pushed the locomotive to impossible speeds. If he had any hope of catching up, he needed to sprint. *Now.*

Ignacio took off at a crackling pace. His muscles moved on instinct. Father had kept him on a strict exercise regimen since he could walk, but the six months spent training with the Blackbirds had made him even faster. He tucked his head low and sliced his hands through the air, pushing his body past the edge.

When he made it up the hill, he saw the massive train.

The locomotive gleamed like obsidian. The boxcars it pulled were painted in purple hues or the same black-and-white stripes as the Big Top. After those came caged carts filled with slumbering beasts. Behind them were wagons chained on top of trailers of various sizes and makes, trailed by even more boxcars.

Thankfully, the train wasn't moving at its full momentum yet.

Ignacio pushed his legs harder than ever before. He needed to cover the space between himself and Esmeralda.

Gritting his teeth, he doubled down.

He couldn't let this opportunity slip away. Not when it was so close.

Someone whistled. People popped their heads out of wagon windows and from the tops of boxcars. Ignacio saw the surprise etched on their faces. The incredulity. They didn't think he could catch up. But once he set his mind to something, there was no stopping him.

He raced through the weeds and hurdled boulders. He was getting closer.

"Almost there!" a person yelled from within the train.

"He'll never make it!" someone else shouted.

A young man with curly hair cupped his hands over his mouth and hollered, "Best hurry! The valley drops off into a gorge!"

Ignacio chanced a glance at the tracks leading north. His

stomach dipped. He'd forgotten about the massive canyon that flanked the valley. His family home in Río Norte wasn't so far from this very basin, and yet, he'd never come this way. Father didn't allow Ignacio frivolous explorations when he was young.

The only escapades he'd partaken in were sneaking out of his room at night with Esmeralda and lying upon his roof to gaze at the stars. Just once were they able to steal off and leave the manor grounds. They spent a single night laughing and running about the boardwalk like two regular teenagers in love. That had been enough for him. Being able to look straight into Esmeralda's deep brown eyes had felt like the most adventurous thing in the world.

The toe of his boot smashed into a stone he didn't see. Pain lanced through his foot.

"Dammit," he growled.

This was what happened whenever Esmeralda slipped into his mind. Stubbed toes and stinging memories of broken promises.

"Hurry up, man!" that same curly-headed boy yelled.

Ignacio thrust himself onward. The train was moving faster now, but he was trailing right behind it. He hopped onto the tracks. He was almost there. Yards away. Now only feet.

The door to the caboose banged open. A tall man with a distinctly coiled mustache stepped out onto the small platform. Ignacio recognized him at once from the posters he'd seen. He was Carnival Fantástico's ringmaster.

"Need help, kid?" the ringmaster yelled over the train wheels grinding against the tracks.

"Is that an honest question?!" Ignacio panted. His lungs were starting to constrict.

The ringmaster laughed heartily. He grasped the copper railing and leaned forward, his body hovering over the ground. He extended an arm. "If you can reach me, I'll let you board."

Let me board? Not even King Amadeo himself could stop him from boarding right now.

A blaring whistle sounded from the front of the train.

"Hurry up, kid!" the ringmaster yelled. "We're headed for a bridge, and I don't think even you can run on those tracks."

Ignacio clenched his jaw and forced himself to give it everything he had. He sprinted with all his might. The whistle blew three more times. The landscape was beginning to change, the weeds on either side of the tracks giving way to unstable rocks.

"Now or never!" the ringmaster hollered, smiling as if this were all a game.

Grunting, Ignacio leapt. He stretched his arm as far as he could. Strong, callused fingers clasped around his wrist. Ignacio's toes scraped against gravel and crossties before the ringmaster yanked him up the rest of the way. With a clank, Ignacio landed on the small metal balcony welded onto the back of the caboose. He panted, sucking in greedy breaths.

His eyes bulged as the earth on either side of the train suddenly disappeared. The bridge they were crossing was hardly more than a few pillars and planks soaring over the deep canyon.

"That was some stunt you pulled off, and not a moment too soon." The ringmaster helped him rise to his feet. He patted his back. "What's your name, kid?"

The ringmaster had called Ignacio *kid* three times now, yet he couldn't have been many years older than Ignacio's nearly nineteen. He appeared to be in his early twenties at most. *Strange.* The tailor virtuoso had made it sound as if this man had created the carnival, but Carnival Fantástico had been mesmerizing audiences for some forty years.

"I'm Ignacio."

"Ignacio." The ringmaster said his name slowly as if he were chewing on each syllable to see how it tasted. "And do you have a surname, *Ignacio*?" He did it again.

"Just Ignacio." He wouldn't give out his last name for many reasons. The carnival and officers of the law weren't meant to mingle. If the ringmaster had even a sliver of a clue that Ignacio was the son of Comandante Olivera, there was no telling what he'd do. If Esmeralda hadn't written to Father, then someone else had. He might still need the ringmaster's assistance, seeing as that same ink was used all over his carnival.

The ringmaster held out his hand. "The name's Ángel. Ángel Veracruz, proprietor of the most fantastical carnival there ever was." Reluctantly, Ignacio shook his hand. Ángel grinned. "Now, tell me why you were so desperate to trespass onto my train. If you offer me a good enough reason for your intrusion, *Ignacio*, I'll let you stay."

Ignacio blinked at the challenge tucked within the ringmaster's tone. "And if I don't?"

Ángel whistled and made a falling motion with his hand.

"You'll throw me off this train?" His eyes snapped to the canyon they were currently hovering over.

"You said it, not me." Ángel winked. He crossed his arms and leaned against the wall of the caboose, which boasted a mural made in his likeness. "Choose your words wisely."

Ignacio thought about pulling out the flyer with the ink on the back, but he didn't want to show all his cards yet. Though, he certainly didn't want to take a nosedive over the gorge either.

"I am searching for someone," he admitted.

"Oh?" Ángel toyed with his curled mustache. It was the same russet brown as his slicked-back hair. "And who is this someone?"

"I'd rather not say."

Ángel's brow rose. "Afraid they will give you a bad reference?"

Esmeralda certainly seemed to hate him. She had framed him and sent him away in a jail cart. Even though it was *she* who should be put away. Not for being a thief or a liar. Both of which she was. She should be sent to the clink for being a terrible human being. For stomping all over an innocent boy's heart. Ignacio had heard people say the pain of losing their first love faded over time. If anything, the ache had worsened.

He took a deep breath to calm the bitter anger fighting for purchase in his thoughts. "The person I'm searching for . . . we . . . we were friends. I . . . I saw her and . . . um . . ."

Ángel's eyes softened. "You are trying to reconnect? Perhaps rekindle your love?"

Ignacio shook his head. "There is no love between us."

"Sure, kid. Anyone would be willing to risk their life and run *that* hard for someone they were once *only* friends with." Ángel pushed himself from the caboose wall and edged closer to Ignacio, clearly intrigued. "What happened between you and your love? This answer will tell me if you stay or go."

Ignacio tried his best to ignore the way his insides clenched as he told the sorry truth. "I don't know."

They'd been thick as thieves growing up. Their first meeting wasn't a great circumstance by any means. She and her family had snuck into his home at night. Someone tripped the alarm. Esmeralda's family bolted away, but she had fallen behind. She hid under a table as Father's guards scoured their home for intruders. Ignacio had been the one to find her.

At first, he was shocked that someone so young was burgling his home. His shock tripled when she bopped him in the nose and tried to flee. She ran straight into Father's chest. Like a trapped animal, she began to fight. But she was a tiny thing. All hair and eyes. There was no chance of squirming away from a man like Ignacio's father.

Father scooped her up and then stomped out of the house. Ignacio followed, cupping his bloody nose. Meddlesome neighbors had already formed outside and had to part for the jailer cart pulling up to the gate. Father had flung her into the wagon. Alone. This little girl was all alone, but she did not cry. Ignacio was in awe. Surely, even he, the stoic son of the comandante, would shed a fretful tear.

"Who does this child belong to?!" Father roared to the onlookers. "Come forward right now and you can take her place!"

Ignacio watched as her eyes quickly found a man standing in the back of the crowd. He had her same full lips. Same sharp nose. His gaze fell to the ground as the silence grew.

Ignacio's fingers balled into fists. This coward was going to remain quiet. He was going to let her take the fall.

"Fine," Father snarled. He turned to the driver. "Take her to the king's dungeons."

"Wait!"

Everything went silent.

All eyes flicked to Ignacio.

He gulped. Had he just said that?

Yes. He had.

He started to point toward the man in the crowd, but the man was already gone.

In the span of a heartbeat, Ignacio had decided his new fate. *He* would protect this girl for the rest of his days. *He* would stand by her side when no one else would. And he would start at that very moment.

He stuck his chin up and marched toward his father, pretending to be the soldier he was being raised to be. "You said you needed a new errand page. What of her? Let her pay off her debts to you here."

Father's eyes narrowed. He looked behind Ignacio, speaking to the head of his house staff. "What do you think, Señora Sevilla?"

The white-haired woman scrutinized Esmeralda. "We could use some youth to help with the running of things."

"Fine," Father had said.

From that day forward, Esmeralda had stayed in the servant's quarters and paid off her debts. From that day forward, Ignacio had watched her from afar. Always making certain she was okay. Always making sure she had the things he thought a kid would need.

His mother would leave him chocolates on his pillow whenever she was called to the palace for more than a few days. And she would bring him back little treasures like silly colored socks. Ignacio did the same for Esmeralda.

But after months of silently observing, he saw her struggling to fold a slip of parchment into the shape of a bird. He couldn't sit back and let her continue to fail. So, he folded up a scrap of paper into a dove and sent it down the vent shaft between their rooms, hoping to soften the scowl that was always on her face.

He didn't know it was love until years later. They were fifteen, and he couldn't think of anything but her. So, he asked her to meet him on the rooftop one summer night.

And after he turned eighteen, and his father told him it was time to start his training, his first thought was of her. Of the fact that he would be leaving her behind for who knew how long. Like her family had done years before.

He had told her he had to leave. She begged him to run away with her instead. He told her that he couldn't just turn his back on his father. She'd given him until midnight to change his mind. But when he went to meet her, she was already gone.

The girl he longed for most in the universe didn't even say goodbye. All she left behind was his mother's ring that he'd given to her the night before, a broken statue they'd earned at their one trip to the boardwalk, and an angry letter written in iridescent ink.

His gaze flicked to the ringmaster on the caboose of a magical train. He was still waiting for an answer. Ignacio thought of the words she'd written him that day.

"She stopped loving me because I wasn't enough," he admitted.

"And you would like to find out why?"

More than anything. "I suppose I would."

Veracruz grinned excitedly. "Pray tell, who is the little birdie who hurt you so?"

"Her name is Esmeralda."

The ringmaster's mustache twitched. Humor danced in his eyes.

"*Ignacio*, you said your name was?"

Ignacio nodded.

After a moment, the ringmaster spoke. "I normally make anyone who joins up with my most precious carnival sign a strict contract, but I will make an exception this one time. You may enter this train but on two conditions." He held up a finger. "One, so long as you are here, you will work. No dillydalliers allowed in my zoo. Everyone earns their keep."

"Of course." Ignacio had no intention of staying long. He'd get the answers he needed from Esmeralda, find out who was blackmailing his father and why, then send everything he learned to the Defiant and be on his way.

The ringmaster lifted another finger. "My second condition is this." He fluttered his hand in the air. From seemingly out of nowhere, an intricate pocket mirror appeared in his grasp. It was a strange thing, made of dark glass, with bell-shaped flowers etched into the sides like a frame. Just like the symbol that had been stamped onto the back of one of the discarded flyers. A chill ran through Ignacio even though his body was still warm from his sprint.

"You must gaze into the mirror of truth. Then I shall let you enter my train."

Ignacio snorted. Of all the ridiculous things . . . But when he saw that the ringmaster's expression held no humor within it, he straightened his shoulders and cleared his throat. "Um . . . erm . . . sure. I guess."

"Spectaculous!" Veracruz fluttered his fingers. The mirror disappeared, then quickly reappeared in his other hand. "You'll learn these fun tricks too if you stay in my world. It's all very entertaining."

"I'm sure."

"Ready?" Veracruz asked.

The man acted as if looking into one's reflection was a difficult task.

Ignacio took hold of the mirror.

"Do be careful with it," the ringmaster said. "It's a family heirloom, and the material used to make it is hard to come by nowadays."

Gingerly, Ignacio held it up.

The ringmaster angled his body so he could see the reflection staring back at Ignacio.

But the reflection wasn't of Ignacio exactly. It was an older version of himself. He stood in the living room of his childhood home as a grown man. An older version of Esmeralda was there too. She was laughing as she played tug-of-war with a scruffy dog. His father entered the room, a warm smile on his face as he carried a bowl of mints.

Ignacio's heart thawed at the sight. At the vision of the two most important people he'd had in his life actually looking happy to *be* in his life.

A faint whisper came from within the mirror. It wasn't the ringmaster's voice. Nor his.

"Yes," it sighed, low and thrumming through Ignacio's core. "Yes."

Ignacio frowned. He felt suddenly numb from his head to his toes.

The ringmaster plucked the mirror from his grasp. "That will most certainly do."

"What was that?" Ignacio asked. He flexed his hand, noting the strange numbness was gone.

"What was what?" the ringmaster asked.

The mirror had disappeared. Vanished into thin air.

"I saw a most bizarre scene. And I heard—"

"It was magic. Enchantments to frazzle the mind. Just a crumb of fun, kid. This is a carnival, no?" He winked at Ignacio. "Now . . ." The ringmaster held up a fist. "Are you ready?"

"For?"

"For the time of your life, of course!" Veracruz knocked on the metal door. A window Ignacio was certain hadn't been there moments ago slid open, revealing the ticket agent he'd seen last night.

"What's the password?" she asked, chewing on her gum.

Ángel faced Ignacio. "Tell her," he urged.

"Tell her what?"

"That you're ready to have the time of your life, kid."

Ignacio scratched his head. "I . . . um . . . I'm ready to have the time of my life."

The ticket agent slid the window shut. Then the door leading into the caboose opened. A cacophony of sounds and smells washed over Ignacio like a sudden storm. He stumbled back.

"Unbelievable," he breathed.

He couldn't quite understand what he was seeing.

From the outside, the caboose looked like any old boxcar. But within rocked a speakeasy filled with flappers and sheiks, dancing and drinking and swinging from crystal chandeliers. A woman strolled by, carrying a miniature giraffe with pink spots. Ignacio thought it was a stuffed animal until the little creature stuck out its long tongue. Two men whirled about, bopping to the bouncing jazz in heeled boots as tall as Ignacio.

He rubbed his eyes. How could all this fit inside such a small space?

Perhaps it was the adrenaline finally leaving his body or the shock of the entire day and previous night, or being clobbered by a golden egg, twice, but Ignacio suddenly felt quite ill.

"We've got a newbie!" a man with a tattooed face hollered.

People cheered. Arms wrapped around Ignacio's shoulders and yanked him in. Drinks were pressed into his hand. Calls rang out, urging him to *chug, chug, chug.*

"What is it?" he asked a young man beside him.

"It's giggle water," the boy yelled. "Give it a try."

Before Ignacio's brain could argue, he guzzled the liquid down. He was very parched.

He gasped and coughed. Someone patted his back.

"That isn't water," he rasped, which caused an uproar of laughter.

The young man pointed at the cup Ignacio held limply. "Good stuff, right? I bought it from a bootlegger at our last stop. The guy said moonshine will put hair on your chest."

"Alcohol is illegal in Costa Mayor," Ignacio reminded him.

"But we are on the tracks. We are untouchable here." The boy filled Ignacio's cup with something from a silver flask. "Drink up, buddy boy. You're officially part of the most fantastical menagerie of misfits the world has ever seen!"

CHAPTER 11

Esmeralda

As the train crossed the tracks on the rickety bridge that towered over the canyon, Esmeralda grabbed the cellophane-wrapped gift from Ángel Veracruz. Her greedy hands tore at the packaging and pried open the box. She sucked in a breath. Lying inside were the most beautiful silk gloves she'd ever laid eyes on. They were pearly white with intricate needlework of doves flying in a starry sky.

"Wow," she whispered, before hastily shoving them on.

The stitching glimmered as she raised her arms. She squealed at their beauty. She'd stolen lovely things for herself before, but nothing so striking had ever been gifted to her. Ignacio's mother's ring didn't count.

But what could the gloves do? Camila and Pilar's cloth cuffs gave them extra strength. With that sort of help, their strong-woman act would be hard to beat. The sisters were impressive enough without any sort of enchantments. Esmeralda needed her gift to be damn near miraculous if she wanted to compete.

She tried to lift her cot to see if they made her exceptionally strong as well, but the bed was as heavy as before. She chewed on her lip, contemplating why the ringmaster would gift her gloves.

Inspiration struck. "If the Sánchezes received something that helps them with their act, I must have too!"

She rushed to her cabinet and pulled out her deck. A thrilling buzz shot from the tips of her fingers down the length of the gloves to where they stopped below her elbows. The cardstock used for her deck began to glow a beautiful kaleidoscope of brilliant purples, blues, blacks, and golds.

She turned the cards over, her eyes alight at the shimmering magic, but there was nothing different about them.

She shuffled the deck. Nothing extraordinary happened. She twirled the cards with her fingers. They looked pretty, casting rainbows against her wagon walls, but that wasn't anything to brag about. She flicked a card with her wrist, aiming for her bed.

But the card did not spin away.

Instead, it twirled in the air, the cardstock folding into itself. Her mouth fell open as the card formed into the shape of a bird. A bird that was now flying in circles around her head.

"King's toes," she whispered. She blinked hard, watching the bird flap its tiny wings. "This is sensational." A laugh escaped her. "This is amazing!"

Her smile faded ever so slightly when she realized the bird was a dove.

She'd only called herself La Paloma Blanca—the white dove—

because it was the first thing that popped into her mind when she joined the carnival. The ringmaster had said a stage name would make her seem more mysterious. So she gave herself one. But she'd regretted naming herself that instantly. Because every time she saw a damn dove, she thought of *him*.

Esmeralda shook her head to rattle all thoughts of Ignacio from her mind. He was gone. If only she could have left her memories of him in that jailer's cart too.

She threw another card to see if the transformation was a fluke. It wasn't. A second paper dove fluttered about her wagon. Giggling, she flung the entire deck into the air. A bevy of doves flapped their paper wings.

Her laughter grew.

She raised her arms and twirled in a circle, her skirts whirling around her legs. The doves followed her movement. She lowered her arms. The doves flew low to the floor.

"This is wonderful! Incredible! The bee's knees!"

She danced, and they danced too.

When her hands fell to her sides, the doves tumbled to the floorboards, landing flat and uncreased as if they had never shifted shape.

"Absolutely astounding," she said. Her front teeth scraped over her bottom lip as she peered down at the mess of cards on the floor. She rested her hands on her hips. "Now I need to figure out how flying doves will make me so unforgettable that Ángel will have no choice but to pick me."

The next morning, the train slowed to a stop in the undeveloped lands just beyond the next city they were set to perform in. As far as cities went, it was nothing remarkable compared to some of the wealthier metropolises crowding Costa Mayor's three coastlines. But as the locomotive passed by the outer edges of the city, she could tell that it was large, with extravagant cathedrals built in the name of King Amadeo and buildings gleaming with new money, so it made sense why Ángel would choose such a place.

Like a swarm of ants finding a picnic platter, the scores of performers and carnival hands funneled out of their boxcars and wagons and got to work. Tents needed to be raised. Games and roller coasters put in place before the day's end.

The enchantments that fueled the traveling revelry were never as illustrious when the sun was up. Magic was lazy during the daylight hours. Carnival Fantástico had to be built like any other humdrum circus.

Elephants used their trunks to pull the bale ring—a massive steel hoop that helped raise the center poles of the Big Top. People worked in tandem, singing about pretty ladies and money as they clanked their heavy mallets onto stakes. The ringmaster's newest recruits scampered back and forth, running errands for the stars of the Big Top show. Ángel was forever adding new crew to the carnival, needing to fill in the spots of those whose twelve months had come to an end.

When Esmeralda was the lead act, she would have all sorts of new recruits to boss around. She pictured the scene now. Someone would cool her down with a feathered fan while she lounged on a chaise in her expensive costume. She'd be eating cherries, just as she told Ignacio she would when they were younger. People with money were always lazing about eating grapes in the pictures she'd seen. But cherries? Now those were a luxury indeed. She'd only had cherries on a few occasions in her life. Each time it had been with *him*.

She stomped her foot. "Stop letting your thoughts drift to that rodent of a boy," she told herself. "You need to stay focused."

Wit and panache wouldn't earn her the lead spot alone. Her personality would only take her so far. She needed a glamorous new costume to fit the bill. It might bite into her savings, but this was an investment for her future.

Esmeralda slinked out her wagon door and headed straight to the tailor virtuoso. She burst through his tent with the full breadth of her excitement on display.

The tailor yelped, and the bolt of fabric in his arms thumped to the ground.

She winced. "Sorry, Jorge. Didn't mean to frighten you."

He fanned himself with his fingers. "I thought you were one of my creditors finally come to do me in!"

She giggled and bent down to retrieve the fabric. It was a stunning shade of pearly white. Her thumb brushed over the cloth.

"This is perfect," she whispered.

"It is!" He took it from her, scratching at his strawberry blond hair. "But for what, I haven't decided."

"Good thing I am here, then, because I just decided for you. I need a new dove costume." Something that was as beautiful as her gloves. She couldn't wear her old getup now. She'd look ridiculous.

"This material isn't cheap, you know?" he said.

"I can't expect all reward with no risk."

"Might you have other reasons for wanting to dress beyond your means?" He wiggled his brows.

"Like what?" she asked.

He chuckled to himself and made a zipping motion on his lips.

She ignored him. She never trusted someone who spoke in riddles and exclamations. "I'll need a new mask too." To herself, she grumbled, "Some weasel made me break mine."

When her purchase was completed, she skipped toward the very rear of the carnival where her wagon was normally placed by a team of horses. Esmeralda halted. She blinked at the empty space.

The rata who was forever pestering her about walking through Clown Alley stomped by. She grabbed his arm. "Can you tell me where my wagon has gone?"

"Moved you to the first ring," he said. He looked her up and down with a scowl. "I can hardly see why."

The first ring? That was where the most prized booths and acts were stationed. It wasn't as good as having an act in the Big Top, but this was certainly something.

"May I go now?" he asked, his eyes darting to her hand.

"Certainly." She started to release him, but then she remembered all the times he'd accosted her, the times he called her a third-ringer and tried to make her feel inferior. She clenched her nails into his skin. "Remind me again, where has my wagon been moved to?"

His eyes flared with irritation. "The first ring."

"Oh my." Her free hand went to her heart. "It looks like you'll be seeing even more of me now. I do believe first-ringers have access to Clown Alley. Isn't that right?"

"It is," he growled.

"Pardon? I didn't hear that?"

"You are correct."

"How fabulous." She released him and fluttered her fingers. "Off you go. I do thank you for the information."

Cursing, the rata marched away.

She did a silly dance. *The first ring.*

Obviously, this upgrade was because she was in the Running to be the lead act. She could only imagine how many more patrons she would have tonight. With the tips she'd earn, she could buy herself all sorts of costumes. Hell, she could get those lacy boots Jorge had on display. He'd said they were for Anella the Contortionist, but they would look much better on Esmeralda.

With a squeal, she ran toward the center of the carnival.

Just like the posters plastered near the ticket booth illustrated, Carnival Fantástico was built like a bullseye. At the center stood the most cherished spot, the Big Top. The first ring that circled around the Big Top boasted all the most entertaining things: booths that sold enchanted tonics, games that left guests giggling and gasping, the Fun House, the carousel, popular acts. And now, La Paloma Blanca: Fortune Teller Extraordinaire.

She clapped her hands.

Ring two was where the food booths and speakeasies that sold mezcal could be found. The menagerie was there too, as well as the siren enclosure and a roller coaster that had spinning cars that sometimes left the tracks.

Up until now, Esmeralda had been all the way out on the third and final ring of the bullseye. There, kiddy games and unenchanted prizes could be found, and a grouchy clown named Ronaldo who lurked around the corners, waiting to squirt unsuspecting guests with his flower broach. The third ring was for duds. Esmeralda hated it because she wanted to shine.

And now she would.

She hummed and sang to herself as she neared her wagon, which looked dreadfully shabby amongst the other gilded ones. That was fine. What did she care if the shingles were missing in some spots? Nothing would bring her mood down ever again. The ringmaster had given her the very best gift she could ever ask for: He gave her a chance.

The door to her wagon was ajar. Not terribly abnormal because Gabriel and Camila were forever in and out. Sometimes to add more contraptions. Sometimes to steal the confections she had stolen from guests first.

But she remembered Camila and Pilar would be practicing their new act. And Gabriel would be helping the crew ready the animals for the opening parade.

Esmeralda rolled up her sleeves. If someone was riffling

through her things, she'd be sure to give them the wallop they deserved. She marched past the other performers preparing their booths and mini stages. Her heeled slippers clanked on the metal steps. She didn't need to be stealthy. Let whoever was inside her private quarters squirm with fear.

She banged the door open the rest of the way but quickly froze in place. Her stomach plummeted to her toes as if she were on the slapdash roller coaster that spun and flipped people upside down.

The ringmaster stood in the center of her wagon amongst the scattered cards she had yet to put away. In his hand was the officer's badge she'd stolen from Ignacio. His other hand was hidden behind his back.

"So, the rumors are true," the ringmaster said. He faced her. Seeing him in the daylight was always a shock to the system. He was dangerously handsome, and his blue eyes shone like sapphires when the sun was out. "An officer came into my carnival. Was he looking for you?"

"I don't know what he wanted," she said quickly, which was true. She hadn't exactly given Ignacio time to explain. "He's gone now. I got rid of him."

"No people of the law are allowed in my sacred carnival. I have taken great pains to set those protections in place so my magnificent patrons feel free from the worries of the world. Costa Mayor is at war. People come here to escape that. To forget. I cannot allow my performers to fraternize with members of the law. You know that."

"I do, señor! Very much so. I had him removed at once."

"Yet you held on to his badge. For what purpose?"

Why *did* she keep it? Just like she kept the tin box she'd taken from him. Her heart thumped heavy and hard in her chest. She knew the reason. She couldn't part with something that belonged to him. Even if it hurt her to her very core, she was desperate for a tiny piece of Ignacio. Although it lacked all his comforting warmth.

"I also found this," the ringmaster said.

He brought his other hand from behind his back, and she thought she might faint or cry or simply cease to exist. He held the box where she stored all the jewelry, watches, broaches, and trinkets that she'd stolen from the customers over the last ten months.

"I . . . I . . ." Her mind scrambled for something to say. "There—there are no rules about stealing," she stammered.

"No." He sighed, disappointed. "But there *are* rules about being caught. *And* about fraternizing with officers."

"I didn't . . ."

"My lead acts are nearest and dearest to my heart. They are an extension of me. Therefore, I can only choose someone who I trust implicitly. Someone who holds no lies."

"I'd never lie to you. I promise." She would promise the world if it meant she would remain in the ringmaster's good graces. Her wagon had been moved to a revered spot. He'd given her enchanted gloves. He might let her be the main act and stay on for as long as she wanted. He had chosen her. He believed she was special enough to be in the Running. And he currently held half of the funds she had saved that could pay for her passage out of Costa Mayor in his grasp.

She couldn't lose that. If she wasn't chosen to be the main

act and had to leave in two months, she would be a sitting duck for the Blackbirds. Without those stolen trinkets, she'd make it as far as the southern port, but that was it. She'd be caught, again, and find herself in a cell or shipped off to war, again. And this time, Gabriel wouldn't be there to help her escape.

She pushed deeper into her wagon and held up her hands. Pleading. "Please, Señor Veracruz, tell me what I can do to make this right."

The ringmaster's eyes widened. "Dearest Esmeralda, I'm not angry with you." He smiled compassionately. "But I do wish you would have felt comfortable enough to have come to me when this officer pestered you. I could have taken care of him myself."

Relief filled her.

"And, please, none of that 'Señor Veracruz' stuff. That makes me feel old. And I'm not that. Call me Ángel."

Her cheeks warmed.

"I wasn't even coming in here to talk to you about this." He slipped the badge into his jacket pocket. He could chuck it into the sea for all she cared now, but what about the box of treasures in his other hand? Her fingers itched to snatch them from him. But she didn't dare move. "I came to give you this." With a flourish, he pulled out a small black envelope.

Esmeralda sucked in a breath. "Is that . . ."

"Indeed. This is your first challenge."

She wanted to be excited, but how could she be? He still held the box with all her stolen goods. She'd be doomed without it.

"To win my esteem, one must show that they can mirror Veracruz's three *V*'s," he said. "Versatility. Vivacity. And Vibrancy." His gaze met hers and she forced herself to smile. "I've seen all three of these attributes in you, Esmeralda." He held out the envelope to her. "Now you need to prove it to the world."

She took the card as if it were an ancient tome filled with the universe's mysteries.

"See you soon, kid." He started for the door but stopped when she shouted, "Wait!"

Slowly, he faced her.

"Um . . ." She gulped. "About the box." She licked her lips. "I . . ."

"There's no need to apologize," he said. "We all make mistakes. But the best of us don't make them twice."

With that, he was gone.

Esmeralda slumped. He'd taken her only hope of fleeing Costa Mayor. If she didn't earn the top spot now, she'd be done for. Tears pricked her eyes, but she willed them away. She couldn't let herself start to cry or she might never stop.

"It's okay," she said to herself. "You'll be fine. You'll figure something out."

But there was nothing to do now but win the Running.

With shaking fingers, she tore open the envelope.

The time has come!

Time to show me attribute number one.

You have five hours to prove your VERSATILITY.

Demonstrate your adaptiveness, resourcefulness, and not-so-humble utility.

**You may use whatever it takes to pass the challenge.*

She had five hours to prove she was versatile. To show she could be resourceful. How in the world would she do that?

She chewed on her cheek and sank onto her bed.

Something clattered onto the floorboard.

Esmeralda leaned down and scooped up the tin box she'd taken from Ignacio's pocket. For the first time since their scuffle, she truly looked at the box. The label was no longer there, but she could tell by its size and curvature, it had once been used to hold lemon mints. Ignacio's favorite.

She ran her thumb over the smooth metal and turned the box around. Her brows rose. She hadn't noticed there were letters scratched into the back. *D+P.*

"Dovie and Pigeon," she whispered.

The bells clanged loudly from the direction of the meal tent. Her stomach growled on instinct.

Rising to her feet, Esmeralda tucked the box under her pillow and straightened her shoulders. She'd force herself to eat. She'd put on her bravest face. Then she'd get to work trying to figure out how in the hell she could prove her worth to the man who now held her life in his hands.

5th of January, 1915. D+P: Age 11

Dovie. What were your parents like before . . . well . . . you know . . . before you came here?

They were only ever kind if they needed something of me. One time, they wanted to steal jewels from a nobleman's caravan. I was so scared because I would have had to hold on to the axle under the carriage for an entire mile before I could slip inside. But my parents promised me they'd take me to the boardwalk if I was a good girl, so I did it.

I think they forgot that promise, though.

How old were you?

Six.

I'm sorry.

I've never been to the boardwalk either. Maybe we could go together someday.

I'd like that.

I know what my father would say about your past. "Hardship was created to build character."

I can hear his voice now in my head. I shiver at the mere thought.

What was your mother like?

She was magic. She used to sit with me and tell me all sorts of stories until I fell asleep.

What were they about?

All kinds of things. Adventure. Love. Gods. Monsters. You name it. I was little but I could take it.

Can you tell me one of her stories?

I'll just mess it up. I can hardly remember them anymore.

Try anyway. Even if you get it wrong, I'm sure
she'd be happy knowing you're still thinking of her.
I know I'd want my loved ones to think of me
when I'm gone.
And who knows, maybe there was some sort of
lesson she wished you to learn—and share.

CHAPTER 12

Ignacio

A rumbling purr emanated from underneath Ignacio's ear, luring him awake. But awake was not what he wanted to be. He was so cozy. So relaxed. He shifted his body, nuzzling deeper into his unbelievably soft mattress. With a sigh, he drifted back to sleep.

Until something hot and rough, like wet sandpaper, slid over his cheek.

He frowned but wouldn't let whatever it was interrupt his rest. When the strange sensation happened again and again and again, Ignacio had no choice but to pry his booze-heavy eyelids apart.

The world spun. He thought he might vomit. This had been exactly how he felt after he and the Blackbirds in training attacked that village. Like the edges of his vision were squeezing in. Like he would be sick all over himself.

With a shaky breath, he forced his eyes to focus on the pink dot directly above him until the dizziness waned. But the pink dot wasn't a dot at all. It was a moist triangular nose with long whiskers sprouting out on either side.

He didn't understand what he was seeing. Never in all his days had he witnessed such a large cat. The massive feline bent down, and its wide tongue lapped over his forehead. Unnerved, Ignacio went still. His eyes traveled left, then right. Sleeping soundly around him lay three pearl-white tiger cubs. Ignacio's gaze flicked to the beast hovering above him.

"Holy shit," he mouthed, his pulse thundering.

He'd somehow locked himself in a cage with a tigress and her offspring.

The only comfort was the fact that he wasn't already dead. But how did this happen? *When* did this happen? Last thing he remembered was entering that impossibly large speakeasy somehow stuffed into the caboose. And then being handed a drink. Well, *several.*

Ignacio shifted ever so slightly but accidentally pinched one of the cubs' tails. It whimpered. The tigress's ears flicked back.

"Easy girl," he said in a singsong way.

The tigress hissed. That horrifying sound was all Ignacio's body needed to set itself into motion. He shoved himself over the cubs and lunged for the cage bars. His fingers wrapped around the metal. He shook with all his might.

This wasn't the same sort of rusted cage like the jailor's cart. There was no getting out of this. It would only be a matter of seconds before the beast sank her claws into his back. He could picture it now. Steel-sharp daggers digging into his flesh, tearing him into shreds. And before he had a chance to take down his father, before he had a chance to right his failures from battle, before he got to see Esmeralda again.

He shook the bars harder. "Help!"

Howls of laughter echoed from the shadows beyond. Young people with rolled-up sleeves, aprons, and dirt on their faces clapped each other's backs and pointed at Ignacio as if him being eaten by a ferocious animal were hilarious.

"Let me out!" he roared.

A boy who appeared to be a year or two younger than Ignacio jogged forward. He sported a fedora that was tilted low over one eye. "Look behind you, cabrón!" he hollered.

Ignacio forced himself to peer over his shoulder. The mother tiger had one leg up in the air as she primped herself.

This brought out wails of laughter from the people outside the cage.

"Here," the boy in the cap said, lifting a latch. The cage door swung open with a squeak. Some of the onlookers grumbled and called the young man a wet blanket for ending their fun. As the rest of the pranksters dispersed, Ignacio scrambled out. He recognized the boy. He'd been the one to offer Ignacio a drink when he first entered the caboose. *Several* drinks.

The boy—Gabriel, he had introduced himself as—checked the timepiece hanging from his pocket and started to walk away.

"Aren't you going to lock up the cage?" Ignacio called after him.

"Nah. The animals are free to do whatever they like within the menagerie confines." He gestured around them. Ignacio hadn't even realized they were inside a colossal tent. Animals he'd only seen in the storybooks his mother read to him when he was little milled about, munching on bones or grain while being groomed by their human keepers. Long oval mirrors hung on either side of the entrance. They reflected the sunlight from outside, making the tent appear as bright as a spring day.

Gabriel motioned toward the tigress. "Isadora here prefers to sleep in the cage with her cubs so they stay out of trouble. She's a sweetheart, though. She's only bitten off a man's leg once that I know of."

"What?"

"Might have been an arm." Gabriel shrugged. "We usually throw the newbies in with the ostrich, but the manager of the menagerie put him in his enclosure and brought it outside because he causes a ruckus whenever the menagerie mirrors first go up. He goes nuts for anything that sparkles."

"You're telling me you and your cohorts put me in a cage with a beast that has dismembered someone? I could have been next. Or killed. Do you find murder amusing?"

"Only sometimes." Gabriel chuckled. "I'm just kidding. The prized animals at Carnival Fantástico are treated so well and fed so often, they hardly ever attack. And if they do, the ringmaster says they must have had good reason."

Ignacio couldn't tell if Gabriel was joking again or not.

A bell clanged from somewhere outside the menagerie.

"Come on," Gabriel said. "I'll show you where to get some grub."

He took off at a surprising pace for someone who'd also drank far too much the night before. Ignacio lengthened his stride to catch up. It wasn't hard. He towered over Gabriel and his legs easily matched his speed.

"Who's in charge of the menagerie?" he asked.

"That would be Jade." Gabriel jerked his chin toward a young woman who was busy scrubbing down the back of a tutu-clad alligator. "Are you looking for a gig?"

Ignacio shook his head. He couldn't help but notice that every worker and performer he had seen within the carnival seemed conspicuously young. The ringmaster and supposed owner of the carnival himself couldn't have been older than twenty-five.

"How long has Ángel Veracruz been the ringmaster?" he asked.

"Couldn't say. I've been here less than a year, and no one except the main act stays on beyond their twelve months. But I think he got the position from his father years back." He elbowed Ignacio. "Nepotism, am I right?"

Ignacio huffed a weak laugh. If nepotism had its way, he would be next in line for his father's title too. If his father had his way, Ignacio would be leading a battalion deeper into Dos Palos to murder more innocent people. But for what exactly? He still didn't know what General Keara had been stuffing into those satchels.

He'd tried to track her comings and goings across the northern border of Costa Mayor for the last month in hopes she might lead him to wherever she brought those bags, but she was a slippery eel. He'd lost the general in a major city and only spotted her again through the window of a train heading west.

That was when he decided he had to go to his father's home and see if he might have better luck gathering information there.

They neared the exit. The mirrors hanging on either side had the same inky coloring as the one he'd looked into before entering the caboose.

"They're enchanted," Gabriel said. "They keep the animals in."

A strange feeling of wrongness spread through Ignacio's core as he passed between the mirrors. As if his body was trying to tell him something. What that something was, he had no clue. He stopped. After the cowardice he'd shown in Dos Palos, he had promised himself he'd never turn his back when he sensed trouble. He'd failed those people, and it haunted his every waking moment.

"What are the mirrors made of?" he asked.

"For as dark as the surface is, my best guess is that it's some sort of obsidian, but what do I know, I'm no glazier. Never mind that," Gabriel said. "The parade is going to start in half an hour, and we haven't had lunch. I've been hungry enough times in my life to know never to take meals for granted." He shoved Ignacio on.

Commotion washed over him the second he stepped out of the menagerie. Brilliant sunlight beamed in his eyes. He squinted and blocked the strongest rays with his arm. To his surprise, an entire tent city bustled before him. Almost every game and ride was up and in place. People shouted orders at one another as they decorated their booths. Others sweated and sang a merry tune as they built up the sideshow stage.

"How long have we been stopped?" he asked, impressed.

Finding Esmeralda amongst this chaos would not be as easy as he thought. In the daylight, he could see that the carnival grounds stretched on for acres.

"We pulled up to Aldama in the morning. It's lunchtime now. So . . . a few hours, give or take."

Ignacio had boarded the train at roughly eight o'clock in the morning yesterday, which meant he'd been out cold for nearly twenty-four hours. That wasn't true. The memories were less fuzzy now. He spent quite a bit of time inside the caboose, raising his cup and shouting, "Death to love!" a few too many times. Still, building an immense carnival with so many intricate parts in a few hours was no small feat.

"I can't believe all of this was constructed in that time."

"Carnival Fantástico is a magical place," Gabriel said.

They passed by a cart that popped outrageously large kernels of corn. The scent of salt and butter permeated the air.

"Where does the magic come from?" Ignacio asked.

Gabriel eyed him with suspicion. "Why the inquisition? First the mirrors, now this. Are you a Blackbird or something?"

Ignacio huffed. "Far from it."

A pair of young ladies who might have been twins passed by. Ignacio locked eyes with the taller of the two. She gasped then shielded her mouth, whispering into the other girl's ear. The girl inhaled sharply.

"Gabriel!" the taller one shouted. "Who is that?" She pointed at Ignacio as if he were a rotten egg.

Ignacio's fingers wrapped around the ring on his pinky. He twisted it in circles whenever his stomach made that weird sort of nervous lurch.

Gabriel jerked his thumb toward him. "This is . . . erm . . . actually . . . I don't think I caught your name. We were just calling you *cabrón* all night."

The girl's gaze flicked to Ignacio's hand. Her focus zeroed in on the ring. A startled laugh escaped her. She whispered into her companion's ear again before grabbing her by the arm and jerking her away.

Gabriel rubbed the back of his neck in confusion. "Do you know the Sánchez sisters?"

"I doubt it very much."

The girls were both beautiful and had faces one wouldn't easily forget, but Ignacio had never had eyes for anyone but Esmeralda. Even after she turned her back on him. Perhaps that was his problem. Perhaps he should have tried harder to move on. But Esmeralda wasn't the kind of person one simply got over. Her smile was engrained into his heart. Her laughter fused into his marrow.

He wished it weren't so, but she was as much a part of him as his own soul.

The smell of fried eggs and perfectly burnt chorizo wafted into Ignacio's nostrils. His stomach growled viciously.

Gabriel chuckled. "Cook's food does that to me too."

He led Ignacio into an open-sided tent littered with picnic tables that were filled with carnival performers and staff. People laughed and gossiped while sipping their café or scraping their utensils over empty plates. Ignacio's heart thumped a bit harder as his eyes scoured the bustling throng.

Was she here?

He grinned as he imagined what her pretty face would look like when she saw him. Her nose would scrunch up like it always did when she was mad. Her upper lip would quirk to one side.

"Here," Gabriel said, offering Ignacio a tray. "Best hurry and eat before the fire breathers get in line. Those guys must consume three times as much as us on account of all the smoke in their guts."

Ignacio hardly heard a word Gabriel was saying because the world around him had frozen in place.

There she was.

The girl with wild curls and a mouth that could kiss you into oblivion or curse you into the dirt.

She was sitting alone at the opposite end of the tent. She tapped her empty fork against her chin. Her eyes looked glossy with worry, and she was mumbling to herself like she so often did.

Her talking to herself was how Ignacio knew they could communicate through the vents connecting their rooms when they were children. At first, he thought he was being haunted. But it was only Esmeralda arguing with her own conscience.

The Sánchez sisters ran to Esmeralda's side. Their arms flailed about as if telling her a horrifying tale.

Ignacio's muscles tensed.

The fork in Esmeralda's grasp clattered onto her plate. She gaped. Even from across the busy tent he could see her lips form the question "Where is he?"

She jumped to her feet. Her furious eyes scanned the open space.

Ignacio's fingers tightened around his tray. His heart hammered in his chest.

He knew then and there—he was a dead man.

CHAPTER 13

Esmeralda

Esmeralda shoved her mass of curls back from her eyes and glared around the picnic tables. "Are you sure it was him?" she asked the Sánchezes.

Camila nodded. "You said he was tall and had brown skin and a shorn head. And he had a ring with three black gems on his pinky finger."

"Did you also say he was a real-life heartthrob? Because he is that," Pilar added.

Esmeralda growled.

Camila smacked her sister on the arm. "You aren't helping." She gave a cheeky smile. "But you're not wrong. He's easy on the eyes." The sisters giggled.

Bitter jealousy nipped at the edges of Esmeralda's heart. *Stop that,* she hissed to herself. *You have nothing to be jealous about because you do not care about Ignacio Olivera.* But she had to admit, Ignacio was devastatingly beautiful. If a person was into perfectly honeyed eyes, and perfectly soft lips, and perfectly perfect everything. *Ugh.* She could scream. She hated him so very much. She hated him for making her love him, for making her trust him enough to give herself to him completely, and for then leaving her in the dust.

Finally, she spotted him at the opposite end of the tent.

Her nose scrunched tight as if she were smelling a wet dog. Her fingers clenched around the fork she had dropped onto her tray. She should stake him through the heart. *No. He doesn't have one.*

He was the worst sort of boy. One who lured a girl in with his tenderness only to then watch her crack when he was finished with her. Esmeralda wouldn't give him the satisfaction of thinking he hurt her. She would be indifferent. She would pretend he was nothing and no one to her.

Leaving the fork where it lay, she pushed back her shoulders and brushed away the wrinkles on her loose skirts. With the wretchedness of losing half her savings, she hadn't even thought to ready herself for the parade.

She wore no face paint and hadn't properly brushed her hair, which was unfortunate. Dolling herself up had always felt like putting on armor. But she'd pretend she felt powerful all the same. Plus, her blouse was draped low over one shoulder. Ignacio had been a sucker for the curves her body held. Since he'd abandoned her, her figure had become a thing of wonder. She wasn't above using it to snap the boy's resolve.

"If you'll excuse me, ladies," she said to the Sánchezes. "I'm going to go kill this man . . ." The sisters gasped. "With kindness," Esmeralda added.

She sauntered forward, trying her best to hold on to her nonchalance as the sisters' giggles traveled after her. Her gaze met Ignacio's. Crackling energy buzzed between them. He gulped, looking absolutely horrified.

As he should.

Someone spoke to him from a nearby table. He tore his eyes away from Esmeralda and turned to the right. Butterflies fluttered in her stomach. His profile was worthy of a museum.

Stop that.

The rodeo girls tittered and winked at him. They asked him his name. He offered them a tight smile. Told them he was called Ignacio in a silky tone.

He was flirting. Right in front of her. Typical cake-eater. Well, she could return the favor. Let him see how it felt.

"Gabriel," she said breathily the second she was close enough. She draped her arms around her friend's shoulders and squeezed perhaps too aggressively. She kissed him on both cheeks. When she stepped back, she batted her lashes slowly and seductively. "There you are."

Gabriel had the nerve to seem thoroughly repulsed. She kept her doe-eyed smile.

"I missed you this morning in my room," she said, tapping the bill of his cap.

"Were we supposed to meet there?" Gabriel asked. "I thought you didn't need me until after the parade."

She bit down on her lip as coquettishly as she could. "You know I always need you."

"If you say so." Gabriel took off his hat and scratched at his greased-back curls. "Esmeralda, this is . . ." He huffed. "I'm sorry, I still don't know your name."

Ignacio started to speak, but she cut him off. "This is Ignacio," she said.

Gabriel's brows shot up. "*The* Ignacio?"

A sly grin tugged at Ignacio's lips. "You've been talking about me," he said in such a smug manner that the tips of her ears went hot.

Dammit, Gabriel.

"Not flatteringly," she quipped. She held her composure and toyed with her hair. "Besides, I could hardly pass up the opportunity to tell my dear friend—I'm sorry, I meant lover—Gabriel about the time I pummeled a boy with a golden egg."

Ignacio's eyes flared. "You could have killed me."

She snorted. "You have a thick skull."

"You had me thrown in a jail cart."

"I knew daddy would bail you out."

"I could have been hanged!"

His voice had risen three octaves. The noise and gossip swirling around them suddenly stopped. Esmeralda couldn't have this drama in her life. Not when she'd already been a disappointment to the ringmaster before she even competed in her first task for the Running.

She ripped the tray from Ignacio's grasp and passed it to Gabriel. "Excuse us for a moment, love. I need to have a word with this pest in private."

"Sure thing, *sugar plum*," Gabriel said.

Now he gets what I was trying to do.

Clearly, she wasn't with Gabriel in any fashion. He'd recently parted with the love of his life, Javier, when Javier's time with the carnival was up. But they had plans to be together soon. Plus, she hadn't felt that pull of attraction toward another soul since Ignacio the weasel crushed her heart.

She squeezed the weasel in question's wrist and jerked him forward. She led them away from the meal tent, down the back alley, and behind the ginormous metal cage that kept Estefan the ostrich from escaping and wreaking havoc. The bird had quite an affinity for sequins. And in a carnival full of costumed performers, letting him roam free simply wouldn't do.

She released Ignacio with a shove.

"What are you doing here?" she snapped. She peered behind the cage. People lingered about. Someone might tell the ringmaster that the officer she'd gotten rid of was back. She lowered her tone. "Are you going to arrest me?"

"Arrest . . ." He shook his head and chuckled. "I nearly forgot you stole my badge." His body tensed and the humor evaporated from his face. "The tin box—"

"Is in my possession."

"You haven't . . . Have you . . ." He gulped. "Did you open it?"

An incredulous laugh escaped her. "Do you think I have time to sit around and peek into your little mint box? I am in the Running to be the lead act of Carnival Fantástico. I have more important things to do with my life."

"Like flirting with that boy," he suggested.

She flung her hair back, revealing her neck and collarbone,

her shoulder exposed. His eyes slipped over her skin and a gleeful, angry thrill ran through her. Ignacio had grown older and more muscular, but at least not everything had changed. He was still attracted to her.

"Flirting with *lots* of them, actually. But that is none of your concern. What you should be worried about is the fact that the ringmaster does not take kindly to officers in his carnival. I've already gotten myself into a pinch because of you. So, whatever you're up to, leave me out of it. And if you think for a second you can come here and arrest me for skipping town before my indenture to your father was up, you've got another thing coming. There isn't a single chance in the king's green—"

"I haven't come here to arrest you, Dovie."

A shock of pure heat bloomed over her cheeks at hearing that nickname.

"Don't call me that," she hissed.

He had the nerve to appear hurt.

"If you aren't here to arrest me, then why are you following me like some lost pup?"

His jaw flexed. He crossed his arms. Arms that had become much more defined in their year apart.

Stop that, she reprimanded herself. *You do not need to concern yourself with his arms.*

"Have you ever thought that my being here has nothing to do with you?" he asked.

She scoffed haughtily. But her arrogance stalled. What if he wasn't here for her? What if he couldn't care less about her being here? That somehow felt worse.

"Then why *are* you here? Surely you aren't at the carnival for a job. Looks like you're following in your daddy's footsteps by becoming a law keeper." They'd had an argument about his future nearly twelve months ago to the day. She'd never forget it because it was the day after his birthday, which was on the twenty-first of March. And she *only* knew that because her birthday was three days after his. Certainly not because she cared to remember anything about *him*.

"How little you know," he said. "And you will continue to not know because you've lost those privileges."

Her body blazed with fury. "*I* have lost those privileges? Ha! *You* have lost those privileges with me!"

"That's not how this works, Dovie. You—"

She shoved her finger into his sturdy chest. "Do not call me that."

"Esmeralda," the ringmaster's voice rang out.

She spun around, attempting to shield Ignacio's hulking body from Ángel Veracruz, but there was no use. Ignacio loomed over her like a clown on stilts.

This was it. The ringmaster was going to think she'd gone behind his back again. There was no doubt he would kick her out of the Running now.

"Señor Veracruz," she said, smiling shakily. "I didn't see you there."

His curled mustache crept upward. "You were rather busy. And it's Ángel, remember?" He grinned and met Ignacio's eyes. "I see you have found your long-lost *friend*."

Esmeralda's jaw dropped. "Pardon?"

The ringmaster chuckled. "The kid nearly lost his life trying to board my train. He said he was searching for someone." He leaned forward and dramatically whispered in Esmeralda's ear. The hairs on the back of her neck stood on end. "A special sort of someone, if you understand my meaning."

Ignacio had been lying. He *was* looking for her.

And he thought her special.

Ángel winked as he stood to his full height, which was identical to Ignacio's.

"You knew he was here?" she asked Ángel. He hadn't said a thing to her when she saw him in her wagon. When he punished her for stealing and took the badge. "But . . . he . . . he's the officer . . ."

The ringmaster waved his hand. "What's in the past is in the past. Let's move on to more important things, shall we? What are you two discussing? Anything fun or scandalous?"

The ringmaster must know Ignacio was the officer she had dispatched from the carnival. He knew everything. Everyone who wished to work within carnival grounds had to gaze into the ringmaster's enchanted mirror. It was how Ángel understood their intentions. Perhaps Ignacio wasn't here to arrest her or anyone else, then? Either way, she didn't want the ringmaster to think for a single second that she wasn't serious about becoming the lead act.

Because she *had* to be the lead act.

"Ignacio and I were discussing the first challenge," she said.

The ringmaster's brows rose with surprise. "Were you now? And have you two come up with something?" he asked, curiosity playing on his face.

She had his attention. She needed to keep it. "We have indeed. It'll blow your socks off. But you'll just have to wait and see what it is," she said flirtatiously, and she could have sworn she heard Ignacio growl behind her.

Ángel guffawed. It was a boisterous sound that reminded her of how Ignacio laughed the night they snuck out of his father's estate and went to the boardwalk. They had played ring toss a thousand times and eaten ice cream too quickly to beat the summer heat. They held hands on the Ferris wheel and danced to the pretty harmonies of a barbershop quartet. Truly, it was the most fun she'd ever seen him have. It was far more magical than any enchantment within the carnival.

Her heart pinched. That boy was gone. She had known that would happen once he joined the Blackbirds. Once he joined his father's war.

"I, for one, look forward to seeing whatever the great Paloma Blanca has in store." The ringmaster pulled out the timepiece from his pocket. "You have four hours left in this challenge. Two of your competitors have already passed. You'd better get on with it."

With that, the ringmaster swept away like a phantom.

Slowly, she turned to face the boy who had apparently chased after a moving train to see her.

She put her hands on her hips. "Not here for me, huh?"

He mimicked her, placing his large hands onto his toned waist. "*Paloma Blanca, huh?* Did you, perhaps, name yourself after the nickname I gave you when we were kids?"

"Ha!" she barked, rather childishly. "You wish."

Rosita the ticket agent passed by the other side of the

birdcage. She sported a twinkling tiara and sequined jumpsuit. The ostrich in the enclosure chomped his flat beak. His bulky body flopped down from the swing he'd been perched on and landed with a hard thunk. Estefan was a strange and ugly bird. She'd never even heard of an ostrich enjoying a swing. Or sequins for that matter. He'd once chased a customer dressed as a silver fox through the menagerie for hours until he could be caught.

An idea sparked.

She turned to Ignacio. "Why are you here? And be honest."

"You once told me my father had a secret office." He shifted his weight as if he were uncomfortable. She hoped he was. "I finally went inside it. I found flyers for Carnival Fantástico discarded in the rubbish bin."

He stared at her as if she should know about this, but why on the king's green earth would she know such a thing?

"Someone from within the carnival invited him here. They acted as if they knew him enough to call him by his first name. I'm looking for that author."

"But Ángel said you were searching for me." Realization doused her like icy water. "You can't possibly think I wrote to your father."

"You know him better than anyone."

She held up her hand. "I'll stop you right there. You and your father are the last people I'd wish to see or speak to again."

He studied her for a long moment before looking away. "*If* it wasn't you, then someone else is in communication with my father."

If? There was no *if* about it. Of course he'd never believe her, though. He never did when it came to anything about that man.

But Ignacio was wrong. And no one within the carnival would reach out to Comandante Olivera. Most of the performers and circus hands were either wanted by the law, on the run from drafting agents, or trying to earn enough to pay off their loved ones' debts so they'd be released from prison before they were sent to the front lines of war. Ángel was the only person who could offer them protection, and he was the only person willing to help them earn enough coin to get away.

But if Ignacio really thought someone was speaking to the comandante, then she would work with that. Because if she was going to pull off the glorious idea that just popped into her brain, she'd need someone like Ignacio to assist. Someone who had brute strength on their side.

"I can help you find this person." When she saw his lips part with surprise, she added, "*After* you help me."

Ignacio scowled. "Why don't you ask the ringmaster? Or your many lovers?"

"Because it is him"—she jerked her chin toward the direction Ángel had escaped to—"I'm trying to impress. Being a fortune teller is fine enough, but I need more."

"You like it here, don't you?" he asked quietly. "You want this life?"

"I want what it can offer me. And if I don't become the main act, I will only have two more months before my term is up."

"And then where will you go? What will you do?"

The softness of his tone nearly pummeled her. It offered her a glimpse into their past. Into how he used to speak to her. He was once so gentle. Ignacio had treated Esmeralda like she was some sort of broken bird. She had needed that tenderness then.

She needed someone to care for her, someone who offered her a safe space to lay out all the sharp shards of her heart so she could piece them back together again.

But Ignacio choosing his father over her had changed her. Those months spent in the cold cell his father had thrown her into had changed her too. She'd hardened herself. And she wouldn't break so easily this time.

A few carnival hands walked by, pulling carts filled with outlandish novelty items.

Yes, she thought, *that's exactly what I need*.

Her arm shot out, and she snatched a handful of bright blue whistles that sang like an operatic singer when blown.

"What was that?" Ignacio asked.

"What?" She held the whistles behind her back.

"Do not play coy. I saw you steal something from that basket. You've taken to thieving right out in the open, I see."

"I don't know what you're talking about."

Ignacio put his palm out. "Hand it over, Dovie. I'll return whatever you took to its rightful place at once."

"You're absurd."

He reached behind her, and she dodged him.

"Give it here."

He lunged forward, gripped her shirt, and hauled her to him until her chest pressed against his. Esmeralda froze as the heat of his body melded with hers. His warm breath tickled her skin, reminding her of their first kiss. It had been sweet and filled with longing. And they had been standing exactly as they were right now.

The notch in his throat bobbed. Was he remembering too?

Who cares, she told herself. *You have only four hours to impress Ángel.*

"Do we have a deal?" she managed. "I'll help you after you help me."

"Helping a thief isn't a good idea."

She half smiled. "You won't know for certain until you try."

His light brown eyes bore into hers. "Hand me what you stole, and we have a deal."

"I was hoping you were going to say that," she said.

Ignacio's brows quirked in confusion as she placed the blue whistles into his awaiting palm. The metal gleamed in the afternoon sun. And Estefan the ostrich went wild for them.

"Better chuck those," she said.

"Huh?"

Esmeralda reared back and unleashed the ostrich from his cage.

CHAPTER 14

Ignacio

"What are you doing?!" His voice had risen to a prepubescent pitch.

The ostrich, a massive, beastly thing with tufts of frizzy hair on its head, lunged out of the open cage door, snapping its beak at the shiny whistles in Ignacio's hand. He leapt back right before the bird, more like a dinosaur, ripped off his limb.

"Throw the whistles, you fool! Or Estefan will get you!" Esmeralda shouted.

"Estefan?"

"The ostrich!"

Something like a growl emanated from the bird's outrageously long neck.

With a horrified gasp, Ignacio flung the whistles into the main alleyway to his right. Esmeralda grabbed him by the collar and yanked him to her as Estefan bolted forward. Ignacio crashed into her and tripped over her skirts. They tumbled onto the dirt. He caught himself as best he could so he wouldn't squish her with his full weight.

He hovered over her. That mass of black curls he'd always thought were so pretty fanned out on the grass. Her blouse hung down one shoulder. Ignacio tried his very best not to look at her soft bronze skin. Or the constellation of beauty marks he once traced with his lips down to her stomach. He tried not to breathe in her familiar scent. Oranges. Mangoes. Vanilla. And jasmine. Always jasmine.

She winced. "I bumped my head on a rock. Way to clobber me, you goof."

He frowned. "It's what you deserve for trying to feed me to a monster bird."

A group of trapeze artists sporting shimmering costumes that clung to their lithe bodies walked by, speaking about what sort of new stunts they might try during the parade to impress Ángel for their first challenge.

One of them gasped. "Estefan got out!"

The infamous ostrich opened his wings and did a strange sort of dance. They tried to calm him down, but instead, the beast barreled after them.

"Run!" the eldest girl in the bunch yelled.

The trapeze artists whirled around and bolted away, their shiny leotards refracting rainbows of light in their wake. Estefan chomped his beak as he took chase after them.

"Hurry!" Esmeralda ordered, shoving at Ignacio's chest. "Help me."

She scooted from underneath him and crawled on her knees toward the bottom of the enclosure. With steady fingers, she began releasing the fasteners holding the wheels in place.

"What are you doing?" Ignacio whisper-yelled.

Voices rang out. People were cursing and yelling Estefan's name.

"I'm stealing this cage." Esmeralda jumped to her feet. "Help me push it to the parade floats. They're getting ready at the front gate." The voices grew quieter. Estefan must have gotten away. Yelps of surprise rang out from the direction of the meal tent.

Esmeralda tried to push, but the grass made the massive cage hard to move.

"Help me," she grunted, her lovely cheeks spotting with red.

"Why should I?"

"We made a deal. I told you I'd assist you, didn't I? But you must come through for me first," she said through clenched jaws.

Cowboys ran past swinging lassos over their heads. They'd catch the wayward ostrich and bring him directly back. This was Ignacio's chance to get the answers he needed from his first love.

Something loud crashed nearby. That ostrich was a terror.

Ignacio wrapped his fingers around the bars of the cage and shoved. They cut left, passing by a tent that rumbled and flashed bright light from inside. The marquee above the entrance warned of shifting weather patterns and sudden storms.

They moved through the inner ring and then toward the entrance to the carnival. He watched her from the corner of his eyes as they gained speed. Watched her nose scrunch up as she focused. There were so many questions he wanted to ask her. Mostly he wanted to know if she was happy. Happy without him. But he decided to start with something simple. Esmeralda clammed up when things got too hard. The girl had always been quick to cut a person off if they pushed to know her too fast. She deflected emotions like it was a sport.

"How long have you been part of the carnival?" he asked.

"I joined just over two months after you left."

You mean after you *left,* he wanted to volley back. But he held his tongue.

"What were you doing during the months before you joined?"

Her knuckles turned white as she squeezed the metal rungs. "Are you trying to make me angry?"

"No. Why?"

They shoved the cage through an empty alley at a steady speed.

"Ask your daddy what I was doing."

"What did he do?" he questioned. But he could tell by the bitter snap in her tone she was ready to end this conversation. He led them into a safer one. "How did you come to be a fortune teller? I don't remember you speaking to spirits before. Only to yourself."

A hint of a smile fluttered over her pretty face. She steered them to the right. Then to the left.

"It was Gabriel's idea," she said. "We arrived at Carnival Fantástico together. The ringmaster was excited to have someone like Gabriel added to the team. He's so smart. He can fix just about anything." Ignacio ignored the stab of jealousy piercing his heart. "Me, on the other hand, I didn't exactly have a skill to offer, unless sneaking around to find out intel or running top-secret missives counted. Luckily for me, I've always been good with cards, and I'm decent at reading people. Gabriel mentioned that to the ringmaster, and Ángel said his previous fortune teller had recently met the end of her term, so it worked out."

Ignacio had seen her playing cards with tourists perusing

the markets a time or two growing up. Locals didn't dare try their hand with her. She was a masterful cheat.

"And Gabriel? Is he your—"

"Stop," Esmeralda ordered. They dug their heels into the ground and halted the cage. And not a moment too soon. A shrieking clown with sparkles in his wig ran past, followed by a frenzied Estefan, and lastly, a pack of lasso-toting carnival hands.

Esmeralda had the decency to appear mortified. But then, she giggled. She whooped and laughed so hard that tears fell down her cheeks. He liked her like this. Liked her free from all the angry burdens of life. And her laugh was always so infectious. His own lips pulled into a grin, and he couldn't help but chuckle.

She'd been the only person to ever truly make him laugh after his mother died. Before Dovie barreled into his life, he'd been a quiet and sad boy with no one to talk to. Sure, he'd had his nanny, but she didn't really care. Not like Esmeralda. Whenever they were able to talk face to face, she'd look up at him with those big brown eyes as he spoke about the most ridiculous things, and she'd listen. She'd laugh and then tease him and then make him smile through his sorrows. And he'd loved her desperately for being a true friend.

Merry bells began to clang near the carnival gates. She cursed.

"The parade is about to start. We must go faster!"

Together, they shoved and grunted and cursed as they pushed the heavy birdcage through the gates. The parade floats were like nothing Ignacio had ever seen. They were massive and each made up with their own unique theme.

The tiger's enclosure, which wasn't an enclosure at all—it was more like a stage—was painted to look like a vibrant forest. Ignacio spotted the tiny mirrors situated within the falsified trees. Gabriel had mentioned that the mirrors inside the menagerie tent kept the animals in place. They must be working there as well. Isadora the tigress didn't seem too pleased. She paced back and forth, without her cubs, huffing a dangerous sort of growl.

They passed a float shaped like a volcano. A banner bearing the name *Paco the Fire Breather* hung from the side. Foam fizzled from the vent before an angry burst of flame exploded from the top. A young man, wearing nothing but a cloth to cover his bits, greased himself down with something that smelled of old musty books.

"Why did you think it was me?" Esmeralda asked.

An enormous bull elephant stood behind the volcano float. A dozen smaller elephants flicked their ears and sniffed at the ground with their trunks. Dogs dressed up like tiny elephants ran around their long legs.

"What was you?" he asked, thoroughly distracted.

"Why did you assume it was me who wrote to your father? Honestly, I should bop you in your nether region for even suggesting such a thing."

The last time they had seen each other, she had made it very clear what she thought of Ignacio's father. She'd used words like *bastard* and *villain* and *good-for-nothing monster*.

"Because of the ink that was used. I've seen it once before," he said. He waited for her reaction, to see if she'd flinch, realizing she'd been caught, but no such reaction came. Still, he didn't completely believe she wasn't in communication with his father.

They shuffled by a float that literally floated in the sky. It was in the shape of a kite with ribbons twirling down like tails. Below it stretched the aerialists Ignacio had seen just after the ostrich was let loose. Half of their costumes were torn to shreds. One man had a black eye. Another was missing a chunk of hair.

Ignacio tilted his body away before they recognized him as one of the contributors to their clothing loss. Though, hauling Estefan's cage might raise some suspicions.

Two heads popped up from within a float that was built to look like a warrior's colosseum. Ignacio recognized them both. Gabriel and the taller of the Sánchez sisters.

"What in the world are you up to, Esmeralda?" shouted the young woman.

"I'm proving how versatile I am!" Esmeralda shouted back. "I'm joining the parade!"

"You're what?" Ignacio asked, incredulous.

"I always get stuck in a float with all the lackluster acts. No one pays any attention to us. So, I'm making my own float."

"Dressed like that?" Gabriel yelled down.

Esmeralda winced. "I didn't have time to run back to my wagon . . . or to think things through."

The two heads disappeared. Just as quickly, Gabriel and the young woman scurried out of the side of the colosseum. They ran to meet Ignacio and Esmeralda. Gabriel was now dressed in all black and the young woman wore white robes. Instead of pushing the cage, as Ignacio imagined they would, they got to work rouging Esmeralda's cheeks and pinning up half of her wild hair.

"The horse opera float has a few extra costumes you can use," Gabriel offered. "They keep them around in case one of them falls into dung." He said that part to Ignacio as if that fact might interest him. It didn't. Not in the slightest. In truth, he didn't want to hear a word from this guy's mouth. Esmeralda had moved on to someone else. The mere thought made Ignacio feel hollow inside.

"We can use the feathers in the birdcage to jazz you both up to resemble doves," the young woman added.

You both? They were speaking about putting on costumes and masks in a plural sense. As if Ignacio was part of this charade. *No way. Nope.* That wasn't going to happen. "The deal was to help you get this cage to the parade, and that was it. I'm not joining you in any fashion."

"Fine," Esmeralda snapped. "Whatever. I don't care." She turned her attention to the girl and smiled. "That's a brilliant idea, Camila."

"Do we want to know how you got Estefan's enclosure?" Camila asked.

"I'm sure you'd prefer not to be implicated in such an outrageous scandal."

The three of them laughed as if unleashing a hell bird upon an unsuspecting crew were hysterical. It was diabolical. Unhinged. Only a little impressive.

"What's the plan?" Gabriel asked.

"To cause a scene, of course."

Gabriel chuckled.

Esmeralda's face lit up. And Ignacio thought his heart might collapse in on itself. She liked Gabriel. He made her smile in this silly, comfortable sort of way.

Jealousy scorched Ignacio's cheeks.

But as they pushed the cage to the very rear of the parade, he watched her laugh and tell the story of their harrowing adventure with Estefan. All the jealousy and hurt and anger he felt melted away. He found himself smiling too. He found himself laughing. Until Gabriel's eyes met his.

Ignacio's grin turned into a sneer.

Gabriel grimaced. "I'll go get that costume," he said to Esmeralda. He spun on his heels and ran toward the horse opera.

Using rope and chain, they hooked the cage up to a float that was as large and intricately fashioned as the carnival's carousel.

Somehow, in the span of moments after Gabriel returned, Esmeralda had been transformed. Her hair was pinned up, loose curls falling around her face. She had on lip paint and rouge. And she wore a corseted leotard that showed off her thighs and arms.

A lump formed in Ignacio's throat. He had seen the full beauty of her figure once before. On the night of his eighteenth birthday.

Camila started sticking the soft white feathers from Estefan's underbelly that littered the bottom of the cage onto Esmeralda's costume. She had also somehow procured a tiny white mask and handed it to Esmeralda.

The cage lurched forward. The procession was beginning.

"We better scram," Camila said. "But first, take these. They'll go perfectly with your look." Camila yanked off the clip-on earrings she wore before snapping the pearly clusters onto Esmeralda's earlobes. "You're the bee's knees." She held out her hand to Esmeralda, who beamed. Esmeralda licked her thumb and pressed it into Camila's palm.

"And you're the cat's meow," Esmeralda said breathily.

"Best of luck!" Gabriel yelled over the clatter of rumbling floats.

Esmeralda thanked her companions. She kissed their cheeks.

She disregarded Ignacio altogether and climbed into the cage. She started to close the door. But she hadn't kept her part of the bargain. She'd offered to help him. Yet he was no closer to knowing who might have written to his father. They'd barely scratched the surface.

His hand shot out, and he took hold of the door before she could shut it.

Her nose scrunched. "What are you doing?"

"I'm coming with you."

CHAPTER 15
Esmeralda

"*No,* you're not," Esmeralda said.

Ignacio wasn't going to destroy the first challenge she had received from Ángel.

She clenched the cage door harder and tried to jerk it from his grasp. He didn't budge.

"We made a deal," he said. "Or are you going to go back on your word like always?"

She barked a bitter laugh. "That's rich coming from you."

The parade was picking up speed. The carnival was only half a mile or so outside the city limits. Soon, they'd be rolling into the main square amongst the excited crowds that had gathered to see the extravagant floats . . . and an ostrich cage bouncing on its axles in the very back.

Ignacio started to jog. "Let me in."

"No. You'll ruin the look I'm going for."

"And what's that? Are you trying to play the part of desperate dingleberry?"

She sneered. "Beat it, Ignacio."

"Not until you help me like you said you would. You have to hold up your end of the bargain."

She glared at him. But Esmeralda already knew she'd lost. Ignacio was as stubborn as a mule when he had his mind set on something. It had once been one of her favorite things about him. Like when she'd counted her favorite scarf lost after a strong gust snatched it from her throat. Ignacio wouldn't give up until he found it, tangled in the limb of a tall tree. He brought it back to her, a little worse for wear, but she didn't care. In fact, she cherished the scarf even more knowing he'd climbed all the way up to retrieve it for her.

To show her gratitude, she made sure to mend any rips in his sleeves before his father could see. She'd also written him a note and slipped it under his door. Normally, he was the first to write. So, she thought he might find it special that she had taken the lead.

A bit of her softened at the thought of a younger version of him. She eyed the man who was a stranger to her, but also not, and her heart squeezed.

"You may join me, but on one condition," she said.

"No," he panted. "No conditions."

"I can't have some random person inside a cage with me when I'm dressed like this." She gestured toward herself. She knew she looked amazing, thanks to her friends. And she could tell Ignacio thought so too by the way his eyes went to anything but her. "I'll let you in, but you must be in a costume."

"I don't see too many clothing options nearby."

She smirked. "I'll make do."

4th of December, 1916. D+P: Age 13

Dearest Pigeon,

I've learned my lesson. The next time a windstorm sweeps through Río Norte, I shall tie my scarf in knots around my throat. I patched up all the tears in it with the pretty scraps of cloth that I've been saving. I'm like a squirrel, always storing little treasures away for the winter. Even discarded things can come in handy.

Anyway, thanks for retrieving my scarf. I think I might just love it even more than I already did.

Because of the lovely patches.

Not because you rescued it for me.

But thanks, I guess.

Dovie

CHAPTER 16
Ignacio

"I refuse," he said.

Esmeralda smiled. A genuine, bright-as-the-sun smile. One that would melt the rubber soles of anyone's shoes right to the concrete.

"Come on, Ignacio. It's the only option we have," she replied.

"Taking my shirt off cannot be the only solution to this problem."

She rolled her eyes. "Don't be such a bore."

That hurt. She must really think him the dullest man to ever live, especially now that she'd surrounded herself by stars. How could he compete?

Esmeralda squeezed her face against the cage bars and peered toward the front of the procession. "We're nearing the city now." She whirled around. "I've got to get you to at least look like you belong in this cage with me."

He felt another sting; this time it hit him right in the chest. She was right, he didn't belong. Not here. And not with her.

They weren't meant for each other like he once thought. Their lives were so vastly different. He had a war to end. All she cared about was having her name on billboards.

"I'll do this," he said. "Then you will answer my questions."

"Every single one of them."

Grumbling, he tore off his jacket and then yanked his button-up shirt over his head. He folded them both and placed them in a neat pile to the side.

"Still like to keep things tidy, I see," she said.

"Some habits die hard." Like the way she made him laugh even if he didn't want to, or the way she made his stomach dip to his knees.

He had to get his mind together. Esmeralda Montero did not want him. She never did. She was a liar. But she hadn't lied about one thing. His father *was* a bastard, which stood as a reminder that Ignacio's mission was more important than old feelings.

Frowning, he stood to his full height.

Esmeralda's gaze fell to his bare torso and her lips parted ever so slightly.

"Like what you see?" he teased.

She scoffed. "I was only trying to figure out why one of your pecs seems so much larger than the other."

His eyes fell to his chest.

"Now," she said as she began scooping up the remainder of Estefan's fallen feathers. "Let's figure out how we can stick these onto you."

CHAPTER 17
Esmeralda

She had the appearance of a beautiful dove. Ignacio, on the other hand, looked more like a pigeon that had been run over by a buggy. Estefan's stinky feathers stuck out at random angles from his sweat-slicked shoulders. He wore a black strip of cloth across his eyes. A rudimentary mask, but it was the best she could do given the circumstances.

But now Ignacio was pouting.

"Stop acting like a baby," she said.

"You tore my only jacket," he huffed.

"I needed something to make a mask. Someone might recognize you."

He offered no retort. His muscular arms were crossed, and he was scowling at the quickly changing landscape. A hundred or so rickety shacks stood around the outer edge of the city. Children ran about the parade begging for food and water. They wore tattered clothing. Some had on no shoes. These sorts of settlements had been growing larger as the war continued.

With so many adults lost in battle, who would be there to take care of the little ones left behind? Certainly not the king or his cronies. Queen Hermosa was rumored to be the only person pressuring the king to offer them shelter. But the big-city elite fought her at every turn. They preferred the nobodies be left somewhere out of their line of sight. Esmeralda tugged off the clip-on earrings Camila had given her and tossed them to a tiny boy who stood alone, sniffling. The costume jewelery probably wasn't worth much, but it was all she had to offer. She couldn't pretend she didn't see these poor souls as the procession went on. Because she knew how it felt to be left behind. Because she understood what it felt like to be counted as a nobody.

She caught Ignacio staring at the little boy as if he might be sick.

"Don't like what you see?" she asked. "Don't like what your father and his king have done to Costa Mayor?"

Ignacio met her with a hard glare. "I don't."

The small wheels that carried the birdcage hit a divot. Esmeralda lost her balance. Ignacio's hand shot out. He clutched her arm, holding her protectively in place. Her sightline was in perfect alignment with his torso. Her cheeks went flush. His pecs were so symmetrical, they were truly a work of wonder.

"Eyes up here, Dovie," he said.

Angry heat flared within her. "Don't be so arrogant."

"Hmph. Now . . ." He lifted her up and plopped her onto Estefan's swing.

Lifted her up like she was nothing!

"What are you doing?" she asked, taking hold of the swing ropes to balance herself.

Ignacio rested both hands on either side of her hips. "I'm making sure you can't get away or distract me. It's time for you to keep your end of the deal. Time to answer some more of my questions."

A seedling of worry sprouted inside her. Why did he have that menacing look upon his face? And why did his lifting her up like that have to be so cursedly hot?

"Why did you join Carnival Fantástico?" he asked.

"My personal life is off-limits."

"I have feathers stuck to my skin. I helped you steal this cage. I think you owe me this in the very least."

She scowled down at him. She had joined to get away from the officers hunting for her. To escape the comandante's wrath. To forget Ignacio.

Her attention roamed upward to the city they were bumping toward. It was so unlike what they just rode through. The buildings were ornate and made from polished stone. The streets were bursting with people in fine clothes that had been dyed in bright hues. It was against the law to wear anything too outlandish, but that was how one knew a person came from wealth. Only the rich could afford to pay the fines accrued by standing out.

The onlookers were jubilant as they waved their pretty flags made in the carnival's colors. A giant billboard with glowing bulbs showcased some of the carnival's attractions. At the very center, painted in scrawling letters, it said:

WHO WILL BE CARNIVAL FANTÁSTICO'S NEW STAR?

She returned her gaze to Ignacio. "I joined the carnival because I didn't want to be a nobody anymore."

Ignacio's jaw flexed as if her answer had irked him.

The bell wagon leading the parade began the carnival's signature ragtime tune. A few more yards and the procession would be fully engulfed between the towering buildings of the city. Not a single officer was in sight, even though the carnival was known for its speakeasies and for harboring fugitives. But Ángel's alliance with the railroads and the towns they supplied was so strong that not even the king dared to soil their parade.

They were crossing the rim of the city limits. She had to come up with something to make herself stand out. She must get past this first challenge.

"Can you breathe fire by any chance?" she asked.

"Stay focused. I still have questions for you."

She rolled her eyes.

"If you didn't write to my father, then I need to find out who did. My only clue is that they used a very peculiar blend of ink. It has a dark undertone but glistens like a kaleidoscope in the light. It can move and shift. Like the posters hanging in the carnival. I know you know the ink I'm speaking of."

"Of course I do. The deck I use to tell fortunes is drawn up with this very ink. It's enchanted. One touch, and it can reveal your hidden desires." She wiggled her brows. "Care for a reading?"

"Who did you get the ink from?" he asked. "I . . ." He frowned. "I searched high and low for that ink this past year and found it nowhere but within the carnival."

The past year? I thought he only recently started searching for whoever was writing to the comandante.

"How did you get it?" he asked.

"The cards show up in my curio cabinet before the carnival starts each night."

"So, it would be the ringmaster, then?" he asked.

"I don't know. Perhaps. No one discusses where the magic comes from or how it works."

"But you've used that ink before. You have personally written letters with it." He said it like an accusation more than a statement.

"*No*. I haven't." She spoke slowly so each word would find its way to his brain.

He shook his head bitterly. "Are you so callous that you would forget?"

She barked a harsh laugh. "That's funny coming from you."

The cheers of the expectant crowd drew her attention. People were shouting out the names of the other acts before her. They called out for Camila and Pilar. They screamed when Paco the Fire Breather blew out a heart-shaped flame from his lips. Anella the Contortionist—her float was situated right in front of Esmeralda's stolen birdcage—was standing on top the rotating carousel and twisting her body into shapes that shouldn't be legal. Clearly, these acts were putting on their best shows. They were in the Running as well and understood the stakes.

But none understood them better than Esmeralda.

She had to get the audience to love her. To force all the attention onto her so Ángel would see how she shined.

Ignacio was trying to say something to her, but she paid him little mind. She couldn't let Anella the pretzel one-up her. But no one was calling Esmeralda's stage name. No one knew who she was.

That simply wouldn't do.

She clambered onto her feet, the swing only slightly wobbling because Ignacio was holding it steady.

"What are you doing?" he asked, his tone exasperated per usual.

"Let go of the swing," she ordered. "I need to put on a spectacle."

But he didn't budge. "We aren't finished speaking."

"Yes, well, as you can see, I have other matters to attend to at present. Now, move it," she snapped.

"One more question and then maybe I'll let you go."

She started to complain, but she knew he wouldn't back down. "Fine."

"Why did you name yourself Paloma Blanca?"

Warmth spread across the apples of her cheeks.

He knew why. *Of course* he knew. But he wanted her to say it.

She hated him so much at that very moment. And she was mad at herself too. That after all the hurt he'd caused her, she still wanted a piece of him with her. A reminder of the love she once had.

"Doves symbolize hope, and all that nonsense people want from their readings." She wiggled the swing. "Let go."

"Tell me the truth."

"That is the truth. Beat it before I knock you out again."

"Dovie . . ."

Esmeralda groaned. "All right. Yes! I called myself Paloma because of you."

"Why?" The word came out in a whisper.

"I . . . I don't know," she lied.

"Did you miss me?"

A sunburst flared inside her chest. She always missed him.

"No," she said.

"Then why?"

"It was the first thing that popped into my mind. Now, let go of the swing before I make you."

He smirked. "What's the magic word?"

"Don't be childish," she snapped.

His fingers dug into the wooden seat.

He was such a pest.

She took a deep breath and said through her false smile, "Please."

Chuckling, Ignacio stepped back.

Esmeralda pushed her feet out and in, slowly building momentum until the swing was in full motion. Anella was busy stuffing herself into a small glass box. All eyes were glued on her. Esmeralda had to do something quickly.

"I am La Paloma Blanca! Fortune Teller Extraordinaire!" she yelled over the cheering crowd. She raised and lowered her pitch to match the melody of the circus song. "I can tell you your fate or see how you and your lover will fare! Ask me anything. Ask me if you so dare!"

She didn't have her cards to help her cheat her way through

fortunes, but she'd make do. Still, no one paid her much mind. She cleared her throat and repeated the chant louder.

"I am La Paloma Blanca!
Fortune Teller Extraordinaire!
I can tell you your fate or see how you and your lover will fare!
Ask me anything.
Ask me if you so dare!"

Some people's attention had begun to turn to her. She wouldn't let this opportunity pass.

"You there!" she called down to the first person she saw that was an easy enough mark. He had a forlorn expression and was alone. "The spirits tell me you were stood up. Could this be so?"

The young man's chin wobbled. He clutched a bouquet of baby's breath against his chest and nodded.

"Do not be disheartened. True love awaits you. You've only got to be your sincerest self." Unless he was the child of thieves. Unless he was a nobody. Then love was rather cruel.

The man gulped. But then a smile lit up his face.

"That was too easy," Ignacio grumbled.

"Hush," she snapped.

"You!" She pointed toward a woman with splotches of paint in her golden hair. "The spirits tell me you are an artist. I can see your passion so clearly. Keep going, doll. Your big break will come!"

"Ridiculous," Ignacio huffed. But the woman appeared happy as could be.

"Pick me!" someone called.

"No, pick me!" another yelled.

"Me!"

A swarm of people chased after the birdcage as it bounced down the cobbled city road. Most of the women wore ritzy garments with elegant cloche hats. The gentlemen sported smart suits perfectly tailored to their forms. The way they jogged beside her float, one would think they'd make capable soldiers. But no, that role was only for those who couldn't afford to pay for a way out. She stomped down her bitterness. Now wasn't the time.

She still had to pass the challenge. She had to prove how versatile she was.

"I will open my fortune teller's wagon tonight as soon as the sun sets. Come and see me, dear friends."

As the bells clanged, she started to belt out a different song, keeping in tune with the carnival's melody.

"I'm Paloma Blanca, Fortune Teller Extraordinaire.
I can tell you if you'll find riches.
Or lose all your hair!"

The crowd laughed.

"I'm Paloma Blanca, Fortune Teller Extraordinaire.
I can tell if you'll get that promotion.
Or need to search for a job somewhere."

No one really laughed at that one.

She cleared her throat and tried again.

"I'm Paloma Blanca, Fortune Teller Extraordinaire.
The spirits speak to me often.
Even when I'm just in my underwear."

This had the audience howling. It wasn't even that funny, but she went with it.

"Tell the ringmaster how wonderful I am, so he never forgets!"

The audience cheered and clapped for her as she swung. They made Esmeralda feel as if she were a queen waving down at her subjects from a high tower.

"There's no need to tell the ringmaster!" a voice boomed over the onlookers.

Esmeralda gasped. Ángel was there, standing amongst the throng. How had she not seen him? He so easily stood out with his striped pants, his gleaming jacket made in the shade of amethyst, and velvety top hat.

He raised his arms wide. "For your ringmaster is right here!"

The audience hurrahed and whooped and begged for autographs.

Ángel winked in her direction before disappearing in a puff of glittering smoke.

Esmeralda could do nothing but smile. Surely, she had impressed him this day.

A shriek rang out. Someone screamed for help. The parade came to a jarring halt. Esmeralda lost her grip on the ropes and flung forward.

Ignacio caught her around the waist before she face-planted

into the metal bars. The momentum of her weight slamming into his arm squeezed the air out of her lungs.

"Are you okay?" he asked, his breath tickling the back of her neck. The sensation brought on a storm of chills. She couldn't handle him being so close.

"Let me go," she hissed. *"King's toes."* She scrambled away from him. "Did you have to catch me so aggressively hard like that?"

"You're welcome," he deadpanned.

She adjusted her costume. "I would have caught myself."

"Sure."

"She's suffocating!" a woman shrieked. "Somebody, please help!"

Ignacio's head whipped in the direction of the scream. Three carnival hands were clambering onto Anella's float. Her hands were banging against the glass box she'd stuffed her body into.

Esmeralda gulped. "She's trapped inside."

Ignacio shoved her aside and slammed open the cage door, running off to assist.

Bitter jealousy stung inside her chest. Of course he'd try to help Anella. But why did it always feel like Esmeralda was the first one to be pushed away whenever Ignacio Olivera had something more noble to do?

CHAPTER 18

Ignacio

As he raced through the panicking crowd, their screams morphed and reshaped into the cries of the terrified farmers he'd failed to protect in Dos Palos. His ears began to ring. His insides burned with remorse. He'd failed them. He'd let them die. He'd done nothing but stand there like a terrified child.

That would never happen again.

He wouldn't fail the contortionist. He couldn't. He had to stop the suffering before it was too late. Had to stop the screams.

He wedged his body between two finely dressed onlookers pointing up at the glass box that was situated on top of the carousel. An elderly man covered a small child's eyes.

"Let me through!" he barked to a gaggle of ladies who were too busy giggling to notice they were blocking the staircase that led to the float.

He scrambled onto the main platform, which was a smaller replica of the carnival's carousel. He'd seen the original while shoving the ostrich cage through the grounds with Esmeralda.

This version even had the ornate carvings of the menagerie animals and the mirrored ceiling. But the contortionist and the box she was trapped inside were positioned on the rooftop.

Ignacio clambered up the ladder and made it to the ridge in seconds. Three carnival hands were trying their best to open the bolt sealing her inside with a master key, but the lock wouldn't disengage.

Anella banged ferociously on the glass. The panic in her eyes, the fear, set Ignacio into frantic action. He ran back to the edge of the rooftop, reached down, and snapped the top ladder rung clean off.

"Watch out!" he ordered.

The carnival hands jumped aside.

Ignacio bashed the lock once. Twice. Three times.

It should have broken already. But it held strong as if the bolt had been welded shut.

He reared back and smashed the metal pole onto it again and again and again.

Snap.

The bolt fell away with a heavy thud. He shoved the glass lid open and pulled Anella out.

She gasped and sucked in greedy breaths of air.

"Thank you," she panted. Tears streamed down her freckled face.

"It was nothing," he said. "I'm glad you're—"

She flung her arms around his neck. "You saved my life."

The audience who had gathered around the float cheered uncontrollably.

"You're my hero," she whispered.

"Please, it was—"

She popped onto her tiptoes and kissed him hard on the lips. Whistles rang out. The spectators applauded.

Ignacio's cheeks warmed. Not because of Anella's kiss but because Anella wasn't the one he longed to be kissed by.

He eased back and offered a tight smile so as not to be rude. "You should see a physician to make sure you're all right."

She shook her head. "I can't stop my act, or I'll be out of the Running."

But her body began to tremble against his. He knew this feeling. He'd experienced the tremors that ravaged the muscles after terror subsided.

"You should sit," he said. "Take a moment to breathe."

"The show must go on no matter what. Those are the rules." She released him and stepped back, but her knees gave out. He caught her before she fell. More gasps echoed throughout the onlookers below. Their exuberant grins had started to fade. The whistles and cheers were quieting.

"No," Anella whispered. "They aren't smiling."

A woman in the crowd yawned dramatically into her silk gloves. A few others joined her.

Anella gaped at them. "How can they be so cold?"

The parade started to move suddenly. The bells at the front of the procession clanged louder than ever, and the performers on the floats ahead of them carried on. Anella clung tight to his forearms as the crowd's attention shifted away from her.

"No," she cried.

Her chin wobbled and then she buried her face, sobbing into his bare chest.

Ignacio chanced a glance back at Esmeralda. She paid him no mind. He didn't know why that hurt but it did. Esmeralda was swinging on the ostrich's perch. Singing and calling out made-up fortunes like nothing had happened. Showing off that charismatic smile she seemed to reserve for everyone but him.

Bitterness churned in his gut, and he glared at the floor. The broken lock snagged his attention. He gently pried himself from Anella's hold and knelt beside it. Something glistened where the arm of the lock entered the mechanism. It had that same kaleidoscopic shimmer that was within the ink.

He swiped his finger over the substance and rubbed it between his pointer and thumb. His fingers instantly stuck together. Wincing, he pried them apart. Someone had glued Anella's lock shut. The pads of his fingers started to burn. He quickly wiped off the excess on his pants, but sparkling fragments remained, reminding him of the ink. Had the glue been enchanted too? It'd explain why he had a hard time busting the lock. But why? Did someone want the contortionist dead?

"Who fastened the bolt?" he asked.

Anella wiped at her tears. "There should never have even *been* a bolt. This was my first time using the box in the act. I wanted to impress Ángel during the challenge. I told Gabriel to simply shut the lid once I shoved myself inside."

Gabriel? Did he do this?

Esmeralda had said her cards had the enchanted ink on them. She and Gabriel were clearly close. He could have been the one to place the cards inside her wagon. He might very well have access to whatever magic this was.

A gasp came from Anella. Her finger shook as she pointed

to the glass box. Ignacio blinked with confusion as his eyes caught on what lay inside.

A black envelope stamped with bell-shaped flowers surrounding a hand mirror.

"How did that get in there?" he wondered out loud.

He plucked it up and handed it to her, but she shook her head. "I can't look. Please, open it."

He broke the seal and pulled out the obsidian-colored card.

Dearest darling Anella,

It brings me sorrow to inform you that you are henceforth disqualified from the Running. You broke rule number 7: The show must always go on. I'm sorry, but you stopped my parade, and thus, the show cannot go on for you. I can only let the right sort of showstopper continue at my most fantastical carnival. You have twenty minutes to pack your bags once we return to camp. Please see the treasurer for your severance pay.

With love and a shattered heart,
Ángel Veracruz

"This can't be happening," Anella sobbed. "I'm supposed to be a star! I can't go back home to my wet blanket of a husband."

She cried harder, draping her arms around Ignacio's shoulders once more. He sighed and patted her back, trying not to flinch as her hot tears slid down his skin.

CHAPTER 19

Esmeralda

Where was a golden egg when she needed one?

She could have chucked it right at Ignacio's thick skull. She wouldn't blame Anella for wishing to kiss Ignacio. He *had* saved her, and he *was* exceptionally handsome. For a weasel. He had no ties to Esmeralda. And, truthfully, she had no ties to him.

She had turned around right after Anella's lips smashed into his. If she spent one more second watching that horrendous scene unfold, her lunch might have found its way onto the cage floor. And that wouldn't do. Not when people were finally taking notice of her.

Ignacio could kiss the damn queen for all she cared. What mattered to her was becoming the lead act. Impressing Ángel was imperative. Not just because he held her livelihood in his hands. But because he saw something in her. She wasn't just a nobody to be left in the dust to him.

The door to the birdcage swung open, and Ignacio bounded in. She ignored the flutter her heart made.

He came back.

“What are you doing in here?” she deadpanned.

He wiped bubblegum-pink lipstick from his mouth. “You and I made a deal. You said you were going to help me.”

She scoffed, almost made a remark about him getting help from Anella instead, but then she remembered she wasn’t supposed to care.

Kicking out her legs with more force than necessary, she swung harder.

She called out to the crowd as they turned down another street, “Follow me! Get in line! Carnival Fantástico is a wild time!”

Ignacio’s hand smacked the wooden plank, holding her in place.

Her eyes widened, but she forced an exuberant grin. “What are you doing?” she asked through her smile.

“We need to talk, Dovie.”

“It’s Paloma Blanca, payaso,” she said in a singsong way. She raised her voice so the revelers nearby could hear. “Paloma Blanca, Fortune Teller Extraordinaire! Some even call me a Renaissance woman, for my gifts know no bounds!”

She placed her toe on his chest and nudged him back, but he didn’t let go. “Scram, you stubborn ox.” She shoved him harder.

His fingers wrapped around her ankle to stop her. The warmth of his touch did something terrible. All her defenses cracked. The anger. The hurt. They tried to break through. They tried to reach out to the boy she once loved. To be soothed by him. But they were her wounds to carry.

“I wish I never laid eyes on you,” she snapped.

"Yeah, well, the feeling is mutual." He let go of her ankle and held on to her swing on either side of her hips. "But we made a deal."

She leaned forward so their noses almost touched. "Consider it broken. If you need help, go back to Anella's float."

Dammit. She hadn't meant to say that.

"Is that what you want?" His eyes bore into her. "To leave you to impress that rat of a ringmaster?"

"Don't you dare call him that," she snapped.

"He doesn't care about you. He just cut Anella from the Running for stopping the show. For something she couldn't control. She nearly died!"

"Quiet down," she hissed. The spectators still following the parade were casting her curious glances. They had departed from the city limits and were now rattling up a dirt road toward the carnival grounds. With the buildings no longer holding the sound in on both sides, the noise of the bells and hooves clomping dispersed, and anyone nearby would easily hear them.

"You don't care, do you?" he said. "You don't care about the danger you might be in."

"I'm not arguing with you."

"Why not?" he asked. "Talk to me. I haven't seen you in a year. We used to care for each other."

Someone eavesdropping in the crowd gasped. People were starting to chatter. Her first instinct was to glare at them all. To yell that they should mind their own business. But now knowing Anella had been cut for forgetting the cardinal rule cemented the fact that Esmeralda couldn't rest on her heinie now. People were taking notice of her, *true* notice of her, for the first time. She needed to show she could adjust to the crowd at the drop of a hat. This was her shot. And Ángel could still be watching.

They were nearing the carnival entrance, where the onlookers would stop following and gather to wait in line. She had to give the audience something that would make them desperate for more.

She flipped her hair over her shoulder dramatically. "I only have room in my life for the spirits that guide me. I have given myself, my heart, and my life to the cause of telling the dear guests at Carnival Fantástico what fortunes fate has in store for them."

She didn't need to see Ignacio to know what sort of face he was making. His fingers digging into the plank of her swing was enough. He was furious.

"That is the answer you have for me? That's all you can say?" His tone was unexpectedly void of anger. Void of any emotion at all. "After all we—"

"There is no *we*," she spat. She quickly regained her composure. "Paloma Blanca belongs to the carnival alone." She raised an arm and blew kisses to the crowd. "Come and see me, friends, for I have many more futures to share!"

The parade rambled through the gates of the carnival, and the crowd that had assembled behind it was ushered toward the ticket line.

Her smile faded at once, and she slumped. Entertaining droves with her charisma alone was rather draining.

She peered down at Ignacio and found his eyes cold and closed off to her. A bit of her spirit broke when seeing him this way. She had fallen in love with him because of the words he wrote on those paper doves. He was so open and honest and free with his heart. He'd tell her whatever was on his mind.

I love you.

I feel like I cannot breathe without you.

I will always protect you.

Because of his openness, she had felt confident enough to answer every question he fluttered her way. One exchange floated to the surface.

Dovie. What scares you most in this world?

To be left alone with no one to love me. You?

To be a disappointment.
Dovie. Where do you dream of living someday?

I think I'd like to live in a meadow filled with flowers. Somewhere where I can twirl and sing and laugh and be as loud as I want.
What about you?

I've always loved looking up at the galaxies.
So, I suppose someplace that offers a clear view of the sky.

You're in luck. I heard meadows are perfect for stargazing.

Hot sorrow clogged in her throat. Where had that kind boy gone? When did he decide his father and the Blackbirds were more valuable than her? The day he learned of his enlistment into training camp, she'd told Ignacio everything his father had done. She'd been the comandante's little spy for years by then; she knew the horrors he'd inflicted upon the people in this kingdom. She knew about the business owners he blackmailed. The family members he ransomed to keep court officials in line. She'd told Ignacio that. But he didn't care. He joined the Blackbirds anyway.

"You and I have both made our choices. What is in the past is in the past," she said.

He glared at anything but her. "Fine. If that's how you want it, I won't bring us up again."

The word *us* sliced against her heart.

He lowered his voice. "But I must tell you about Anella's lock. Someone tampered with it. It has the same makeup as what is inside the enchanted ink. I need to find whoever has access—"

"That's really all you care about? Getting answers for your daddy. Hiding his secrets."

"I'm trying to do what's right."

"Your version of right is much different than mine. It always was. It always will be."

He scoffed. "How little you know."

The parade floats entered Clown Alley, where they would be hosed down and readied for the march of showstoppers when the Big Top show began. The moment the floats came to a full stop, Ignacio left the cage.

Esmeralda gulped. She had half a mind to chase after him. To kiss away the marks Anella had made and squeeze him until he loved her back. Instead, she slowly eased off the swing and straightened her shoulders.

When she stepped toward the cage door, she blinked rapidly in surprise.

Lying on the grass was a black envelope stamped with bell-shaped flowers surrounding a hand mirror.

She snatched it up. Tore the seal open and pulled out the card. The words on it were written in iridescent ink.

Congratulations to our reigning birdcage thief!
Your fast thinking has shown versatility beyond belief.
Your resourcefulness has gotten you through.
Now get ready, Paloma Blanca, for challenge number two!
(But first, kindly return Estefan's enclosure to the menagerie before Jade loses her temper.)

26th of August, 1917. D+P: Age 14

Dovie. Today I got into my first fight.

With whom? And, more importantly, did you win?

With some officer's son at school. He called me a dud because he said I have no friends. But I do have friends. Loads of them.

And yes. I knocked him right on his sorry ass.

Such language! I'm so very proud.
Who are these friends you have, by the way? I have never seen them. Are they imaginary? Are they in the room with you right now?
You can tell me, I won't judge . . . too harshly.

There's Doña Bria, Señor Duenas, and Victoria.

The governess. The gardener. And the maid.
They hardly count.

There's you.

Honestly, sometimes I think there's no one in this world who gets me more than you. I swear I miss you even though we haven't been in the same room together since we were ten. Is that weird?

I don't know. But I quite like weird.

CHAPTER 20

Ignacio

Ignacio needed to get away from Esmeralda—no—from Paloma Blanca, Fortune Teller Extraordinaire or Renaissance Woman, or whatever the hell she wanted to call herself. She was so arrogant. So self-centered. So frustratingly stubborn. And she'd gone back on their deal. He should have known she'd break her promise.

He slowed as he entered the alleyway between booths and games. Posters of the ringmaster hung on every pole. The enchanted ink shifted with the breeze. The first night he arrived at the carnival, Ignacio had passed by a lemon-drop scented booth that sold shimmering tonics and bubbling concoctions. He had stopped before it, thinking perhaps the ink might be there amongst the other merchandise. He'd even asked the worker with jewels for teeth if she offered magical ink. The woman shook her head. She said that would belong to someone far more enchanting than she.

There was only one person Ignacio could think of. Not Gabriel. Ángel Veracruz.

With the performers and carnival so busy readying for the evening, now would be the perfect time to find the ringmaster's quarters.

Ignacio spun on his heels and jolted.

The ringmaster himself stood before him. He wore his signature sequined jacket, top hat, and mischievous grin. "Hello, *Ignacio*."

There he went again. Saying Ignacio's name as if each syllable held a joke only the ringmaster was privy to.

Ignacio straightened his spine. "Didn't see you there."

"Hard to miss me, isn't it?" Veracruz chuckled. He raised his hand. "I believe you left these behind."

Ignacio gawked. "My shirt and coat." With all the commotion of the parade, he'd forgotten he was walking around half naked and covered in Estefan's foul feathers.

He took the clothing and quickly dressed with a word of thanks.

"You showed great fortitude today, kid." The ringmaster took off his hat and placed it over his heart. "Allow me to express my gratitude for saving Anella. What a tragedy that might have been. I count my performers as family. I couldn't imagine losing someone so dear to me."

"Yet, you so quickly kicked her out of the carnival." Ignacio couldn't hide his bitterness.

"A game with no consequences is rather boring, wouldn't you say?"

Judging from the way Esmeralda acted, and all the tears Anella shed, the Running wasn't just some game to them. It was a lifeline.

"Walk with me?" the ringmaster asked. Though his tone implied it wasn't a question but a command.

Ignacio nodded.

A group of performers dressed in figure-hugging costumes with plumes of purple feathers bobbing on their heads giggled and waved to the ringmaster and Ignacio as they passed by. Veracruz winked at them. He bent down and pecked one of the women on the cheek while slipping her a discreet note.

Ignacio frowned. He never treated any of *his* family members in such a flirtatious manner. Not that he had many. His father never spoke of his childhood. The only hint about his past was the web of scars lacing the comandante's right arm. Mother said he had been wounded when he was a young man, but he never explained why or how because he was ashamed. His mother had siblings, but they lived in the southern regions of the country and rarely wrote. But if Ignacio did have close relations, he was positive he wouldn't offer them any winks.

The two young men wove through the bustling carnival. The sun was starting to descend. Soon, thousands of guests would be walking beneath the marquee to experience a night full of enchantments beyond compare. But where did those enchantments come from? What was fueling this strange place?

"How goes your reunion with Esmeralda?"

"Chillingly," Ignacio said sourly.

The ringmaster laughed. "I figured as much. Esmeralda has spunk, yes? She reminds me so much of another brilliant showstopper I know." He beamed. "It's me, of course. I'm the brilliant showstopper." He snickered at his own jest.

Ignacio didn't find the ringmaster funny, but he smiled

courteously. An old habit he'd never been able to stop. Father always said a well-mannered child was the jewel on a parent's crown. Ignacio never had a choice about being rude or not. His father didn't give him one.

"Tell me, what do you think of my fantastical festival?" Veracruz asked.

One of the gondola lifts that took guests from the entrance of the carnival to the opposite end of the third, outermost ring started to sway overhead. With a squeak, it began to spin. The carnival hands screamed and shouted with exhilarated glee as they tested the ride themselves. Ignacio saw no ropes or wire carrying it. The only sign the gondola was held by anything at all were tiny specks of light glinting off a cable so thin he could only compare it to fishing wire.

"Carnival Fantástico is like nothing I've ever seen before," he said honestly.

The ringmaster nodded proudly. "Nor will you ever."

Ignacio watched Ángel Veracruz from the corner of his eye. For someone who couldn't be past the age of twenty-five, the ringmaster had more crow's feet than Ignacio had realized. Perhaps it was because the man was always smiling like he had won some great prize.

"Where does the magic come from?" Ignacio asked.

The ringmaster cupped a hand behind his ear. "Do you hear the music?"

Only the sounds of the carnival surrounded them. The clopping of horse hooves. Performers chattering. The people in the gondola screaming. There was no music.

As if it were waiting for its cue, the music began to play.

"The tune is called 'The Tale of the Valerio Brothers.' Ever heard of it?" Veracruz asked.

That surname sounded familiar, but Ignacio couldn't place where he'd heard it before.

"I'm not sure," he said.

"The story isn't widely known. Especially not since King Amadeo began banishing stories about gods and magic years back." He clicked his tongue. "Such a shame."

They stopped before the Fun House. The entrance to the striped tent had been constructed to look like a menacing face. The eyebrows of the face cut in angry lines. Its eyes moved in hypnotizing circles. Beneath its ruddy clown nose waited a gaping mouth that billowed with glowing red smoke. Nothing about the tent looked fun to Ignacio. Though, he supposed, people who had never witnessed true horrors might find being frightened to near death exhilarating.

"Let's see what you interpret from 'The Tale of the Valerio Brothers.'" The ringmaster cleared his throat and sang the song perfectly in tune to the bouncing melody just like Esmeralda had done with her ridiculous rhymes during the parade.

"There once were two brothers called Valerio.
They worked for a circus and its impresario.
One day, the brothers came upon something
inconceivable.
A window to the gods. A portal once believed
unreachable.

The god of smoke and mirrors spoke to them from the
Land of the Dead.
'I'll give you whatever you wish so long as you do as I
ask,' the god said.
That day, a delightful deal was made.
The brothers received enchantments and gifts for a tiny
trade.
The Valerios shared their magic for the world to see.
So, we celebrate their great find. For a small fee."

Performers and carnival hands had stopped to listen. They clapped and whistled once he finished. The ringmaster made a great show of bowing for his doting fans.

"What do you think, kid?" he queried.

"You're saying Carnival Fantástico's magic comes from a god?"

Veracruz shrugged coyly. "Stranger things have been true, no?"

Have they? Ignacio didn't think there was anything stranger than a god blessing a carnival. Especially since gods didn't exist. His mother had been devout in her prayers. Before she died, she had told him about the hundreds of gods who dwelled beyond the realm of the living. She'd told him that most were good, shining blessings upon those who worshiped them. Some were benign, not caring what humanity did or did not do. But a handful were made from pure wickedness and waited for any opportunity to wreak havoc. Ignacio had seen enough evil in humanity to understand mere mortals didn't need the help of devious gods to destroy the world.

"Maybe the song means everything is smoke and mirrors," Ignacio said. He gestured toward the Fun House, a tent quite literally filled with smoke and mirrors.

The ringmaster laughed. "Can it not be both?"

Ignacio crossed his arms. "You answered my questions with more questions."

"Did I?" Veracruz chuckled. "When one grows up in a carnival, they find themselves forever speaking in riddles. But I wouldn't have it any other way."

He sat on a bench that had been sculpted to look like a cloud. In fact, from the way it swayed and misted around the ringmaster's striped britches, Ignacio wondered if it was one.

"Look around you, kid. This carnival is as magical as the mind wishes it to be. Our country is in the middle of a terrible war. I am here to give our people an escape. There is no harm in that. In fact, bringing joy to people is honorable, I think. There are some who long to steal what I have created. They'd like to harness all these enchantments and use them in malice. I cannot and will not let that happen." His expression turned serious. A heavy sort of anger blazed behind his eyes. "I know who your father is, kid."

Cold ice slithered down Ignacio's spine. "You do?"

The ringmaster flicked his wrist, and two crinkled pieces of paper appeared from thin air. One was the flyer Ignacio had taken from his father's secret office. The other was the breakup letter Esmeralda had left him a year ago. They had both been tucked inside his coat pocket. The one the ringmaster had just returned to him.

"You went through my clothing."

"Nah." The fury burning in Veracruz's eyes dissolved. With a wink, he gestured toward the tear in the seam. Esmeralda had ripped his jacket up to make him a mask for the parade. "These letters fluttered out when I picked up your things. But I've known you were Olivera's son since I first saw you on the caboose."

"How?"

The ringmaster raised his other hand with a flourish and his intricate hand mirror poofed into existence. "The mirror never lies. It told me who you were. But judging from the letter our dear Esmeralda wrote to you, perhaps I *should* be wary. She seemed to believe you were very much your father's son."

She was wrong. Ignacio glared at the letter. Each word written scorched inside his chest. His heart still stung knowing that she'd run away with only those hateful words as her goodbye.

"I understand what is going on here," Veracruz said. "And I believe you have come to make amends with your one true love while also sabotaging your dear old daddy."

He really did know. Not about the Esmeralda part. There were no amends to be made. But the part about his father was certainly true.

"I have a question for you, though," the ringmaster said. "Well, I have one *why* and then a *what*. *Why* are you at odds with your father? And *what* made you think coming here would help you in your mission?"

Ignacio held his tongue. He did not trust Veracruz. Not in the slightest.

"Shall I take a guess, then?" the ringmaster queried. "You finally understand that your father is leading us deeper into war. His Blackbirds aren't trying to defend our country against a formidable foe, they are trying to steal Dos Palos's resources. Seeing how you helped Anella, I'd say you're the type that cannot sit back and do nothing as innocent lives are taken. *Or* perhaps you did sit back and do nothing, and now that deep well of guilt inside your belly is starting to drown you."

Ignacio's pulse thumped hard in his temples. His palms began to sweat. Veracruz somehow knew everything. He even knew what a failure Ignacio was. That he'd stood by and done nothing to save those farmers.

"Now to my next question: What made you think coming here would help you in your noble cause?"

Ignacio surrendered. The ringmaster knew everything about him anyway. "I found notes addressed to my father. The sender wanted him to come to Carnival Fantástico. They claimed they knew his secrets. I figured this person might have some sort of intel I could use."

The ringmaster fiddled with his curled mustache. "So, someone in my carnival has been communicating with your father."

"It wasn't you?" Ignacio asked.

"I want to keep Comandante Olivera *out* of my carnival. I certainly wouldn't invite him in."

Veracruz stood suddenly. Ignacio readied himself for whatever punishment might come his way. He had lied to the ringmaster that day on the caboose. He'd told him he was there for Esmeralda, but that wasn't the only reason.

Fortunately, no punishment came.

Veracruz simply took off his top hat and scratched at his head.

"You aren't mad that I lied to you?" If Ignacio had gone behind his father's back like he had done with the ringmaster and Father found out, the man might have backhanded Ignacio right then and there. Instead of a wallop, the ringmaster simply shrugged and put his hat back on.

"Look, you seem like a smart kid. And I believe you are right. Your father is up to something. Perhaps whoever is communicating with him recognizes that. But I want to understand why they would want him to come here."

"That's what I'd like to figure out too."

"It's settled, then." Veracruz patted Ignacio on the shoulder and started to walk away. "When you find the answers we both seek, please be sure to let me know."

"That's it?" Ignacio called after him.

The ringmaster twirled around and offered a bow. "That's it."

The music grew louder. The sun had finally disappeared, and the carnival was ready to rise from its slumber.

"I best get ready for the show." Veracruz flicked his fingers, and the letter Esmeralda wrote to Ignacio years ago fluttered toward him. Ignacio caught it. He eyed the forever gleaming words scrawled on the page in her messy handwriting. Ignacio called after him. "What about this ink?"

"The ink?" the ringmaster questioned.

"Yes. The ink used to invite my father here. It's the same ink Esmeralda wrote this letter with. The same used to create the posters and her fortune teller cards." And the glue that nearly killed Anella had that same shimmering gleam. "Where is the ink?"

Veracruz was already halfway down the alley, walking straight for the Big Top. "We'll have time to talk again once my guests depart. In the meantime, enjoy yourself." He waved. "Thanks for speaking so freely with me, *Ignacio*. I have a good feeling about you."

Ignacio's eyes narrowed as the ringmaster strolled away. Something was off about that man. He was too calm, too easy-going. Anella had nearly died. Ignacio had just told him someone in his carnival was communicating with the commander of the king's army, despite his rules. Yet, the man only worried about his show.

Either way, Ignacio had work of his own to do. He ran to the bunk boxcar meant for carnival hands that he'd been assigned to. There, he transcribed his chat with the ringmaster so he wouldn't forget. He also wrote down what he remembered from "The Tale of the Valerio Brothers" because there was something eerily familiar to him about the story. When he was satisfied, he slipped the papers and the letter from Esmeralda under his stiff mattress, then smoothed the worn sheets and tucked them tight at each corner. He had never left a bed untidy since he was four years of age.

By the time he was finished, he was half starved, and the carnival gates had been opened for guests. He left his shared boxcar in search of something to eat. He rounded the first bend near the ticket booth before coming to an abrupt stop. His heart thundered faster than the bouncing beat romping around the fair. There, in her Blackbird black-and-silver uniform, stood General Keara, his father's right hand. The tailor virtuoso bowed as he escorted her into his costume tent. General Keara glanced over her shoulder.

Ignacio dove into the only hiding space he could find, a wooden coffin made for sawing performers in half. His jaw dropped when he lowered his eyes. His body was invisible from his torso to his toes. He really hated the magic inside this place.

When he peeked out toward the tailor's tent, Keara was gone. A few moments later, the tall and muscular form of the general sauntered out. Her uniform was hidden beneath a burnt-orange cape. She now sported a fox mask, clawed gloves, and a swishing tail.

She promenaded like the fox she dressed as. She was heading directly toward a purple wagon labeled ***La Paloma Blanca: Fortune Teller Extraordinaire.***

CHAPTER 21
Esmeralda

"I can't believe how many people are in line to see you," Gabriel said as he pressed an eye to the tiny cutout in the wagon wall.

"*I* can," Esmeralda said. "I was superb out there."

Gabriel cleared his throat.

"With your and Camila's help, of course. Thanks for making me beautiful. Well, even more beautiful than I already am."

"Always so humble." Gabriel sealed the hole shut with a cork and turned around. "The tension between you and that godlike, dream of a man didn't hurt. The crowd loved you two together."

Esmeralda harrumphed. "The only person who is godlike in this carnival is the tailor."

She gazed at herself in the looking glass. Jorge had done a fantastic job with her new costume. This time, her dove wings looked more angelic than cherubic. And the cut of her garment was to die for. Every curve of her body was on full, glorious display.

She turned to the side. "Does this make my rump look big?"

Gabriel paused his tinkering with the door lever. He eyed her. "Extremely."

"Fantastic." She wiggled the rump in question.

Her friend rolled his eyes. "You are so . . ."

"Delightful? Exuberant? Wonderfully clever?"

"Sure. Let's go with that. *Dammit.*" One of the screws in the pulley system fell out and clinked onto the floor. Gabriel bent to retrieve it.

Esmeralda returned to appreciating her reflection. She pulled back her lips and examined her smile. She gasped.

"Why didn't you tell me there was pepper in my teeth?" She started digging between her molars with her sharp nails. "Seriously, I haven't checked my face since supper. You let me walk around like this for a whole hour. What sort of friend are you?"

When Gabriel didn't reply, she checked for him through the mirror. He was sitting on the floor. Ignacio's mint box rested on his lap. She'd nearly forgotten she'd taken it from him and kept it under her cot. The lid was open, and what appeared to be dozens of tightly rolled-up papers had been strategically arranged inside.

Of course they were. Anything Ignacio touched had to be organized to annoying perfection.

Gabriel had already taken one out and unfurled it.

Esmeralda's entire body went numb when she recognized the carefully squared parchment.

"Fourteenth of February, 1919. D plus P: age fifteen," he read.

Her heart thumped heavy against her ribs. *What was this?*

Gabriel continued, "Dovie. What is your happiest memory of us? Pigeon. My happiest memory of us is the first time you convinced me to climb out onto the roof. I can't recall smelling fresher air or seeing more stars. We talked all night. I was so tired the next day, I fell asleep while scrubbing the dishes."

Gabriel's eyes met hers in the mirror. "Is this . . ."

Esmeralda couldn't reply. She couldn't even force her lips to move. Her hand went to her chest. Something like panic writhed behind her ribs. He'd kept some of their notes. Many of them, it seemed. And from the sound of it, he'd dated them too. Of course he did. He loved to keep thorough records of just about everything.

She started to pant. She couldn't get enough air inside her lungs.

Ignacio held on to their letters.

But why keep these when they had parted the way they did?

Her mouth went dry.

Why bring them here when he knew she was a snoop? Was he playing some sort of malicious game?

"What's eating you, Esmeralda?" Gabriel asked.

She couldn't catch her breath. "This dress is too tight."

Gabriel rushed to her side. He grabbed her hands. "Look at me." She did. "Now slowly inhale. Count to five." She tried her best. "Release that breath for another count of five." They did this several times until her pulse slowed, but nothing helped the burning inside her heart.

"Why would he have these?" she whispered.

"Is it not obvious? The boy cares for you."

"But . . . that can't be true." He'd been cold and indifferent since they'd reconnected. He let Anella kiss him, for stars' sake.

"Sure seems true to me. What happened between you two?" Gabriel asked gently.

Her brows furrowed. "He let me go."

"Have you asked him why?"

Of course she hadn't. Even the thought of asking him made her stomach clench. She wouldn't open herself up to getting hurt again. Not now, not ever.

She shrugged Gabriel off and returned to the mirror. "I've been too busy being fabulous to care why he left. It's his loss, anyhow."

"Don't do that," he said.

She fluffed her hair. "Do what?"

"Don't push aside your pain with that nonchalant arrogance."

She gaped and spun to face him. "I did no such thing. I *was* busy being fabulous."

Gabriel sighed. "You're insufferable."

"And you're a pest."

"Or am I just honest and that rattles you?"

"Dammit, Gabriel." She grabbed a nearby slipper and chucked it at him.

He dodged it with a laugh.

Someone pounded on the back door. "Dovie, let me in!"

Gabriel's brows rose. "The spirits must have been listening."

She rolled her eyes.

Ignacio pounded harder. "I need to talk to you!"

"Take this." Gabriel opened Esmeralda's palm and dropped the tin box into it. He wrapped her fingers around the cool metal before moving toward the door.

"Don't open it!" Esmeralda whisper-shouted.

"You said you didn't have time to speak to him. Well, now is a perfect time."

"I have guests to attend to."

"Let them wait. It'll make you seem important. I'll go out there and stir them up by muttering rumors about you. Only the very worst sort, of course."

The knocking grew more insistent. "Esmeralda. Please, let me in."

Gabriel cleared his throat. "We are through!" he yelled. "You have broken my heart too many times!"

"What are you doing?" she hissed.

"I'm breaking up with you!" Gabriel winked before he opened the door and exclaimed with dramatic flair, "You were never truly mine and now I see why."

Esmeralda's jaw dropped. *Oh, Gabriel is a dead man the next time we're alone.*

She watched him sweep out. But her attention quickly shifted to Ignacio as he rushed in, sweat dripping down his forehead. He slammed the door shut and slid the lock in place, then whirled around to face her.

Esmeralda stuffed the tin box behind her back.

"She's here," he blurted out.

"Who?"

"General Keara. I saw her at the tailor's. She's coming this way."

The box in her grasp clanked to the floor. General Keara terrified Esmeralda. Esmeralda was the comandante's errand runner and spy. General Keara was his hound. And she was always happy to sink her teeth into her prey. Ignacio's gaze flicked near her feet where his tin box lay. He blinked, then shook his head as if to say that didn't matter right now.

"We need to hide," he said.

"*We?* Why *we*? That's your father's second-in-command. She'll never get you in trouble because *daddy* wouldn't allow it."

Esmeralda, on the other hand, could be sent back to the cold cell she'd only barely escaped from. Her heart sputtered. *Stay calm,* she told herself. *So long as you're inside the carnival, General Keara has no claim over you.* But if she didn't get the lead role, once her year was up with Carnival Fantástico, that would be a whole different situation. Esmeralda had broken the law by running away before her indenture was completed, and then again when she and Gabriel broke free from the transport cart that was shipping them off to war. From all she knew about the comandante, he wouldn't forget or forgive those acts of defiance.

"I haven't spoken to my father since defecting," Ignacio spat out.

Esmeralda froze. "You deserted the Blackbirds? But . . . you're an officer. I stole your badge."

"The badge isn't real."

Her jaw dropped.

He ran a hand over his cropped hair, something he'd always done when trying to formulate the right words. His arm fell to his side as if in defeat.

"You were right," he said. "About everything. My father is a warlord. He and his Blackbirds are not battling Dos Palos because Dos Palos is trying to harm us. They are infiltrating Dos Palos because there is something within the lands he wants."

Voices sounded from outside the front of the wagon. Gabriel was arguing with someone who was demanding to be let inside. General Keara. Esmeralda recognized that voice so clearly.

Ignacio rushed forward and grasped her by the arm. "We've got to go."

Burning heat seared into every part of her skin he touched. It seeped into her muscles, her tendons, her marrow. And she craved it. She was desperate for more. For his warmth to cover her and shield her from the world as it once had.

The notch in his throat bobbed.

Did he feel that still-burning flame too? Did he look at her and long for what had once been?

She met his gaze. Praying. Hoping. Searching for a hint that he felt something. Anything.

"She can't know I am here," he said. "Someone inside the carnival has information I can use against my father."

Just as suddenly as the heat came, it disappeared. Ignacio didn't care about protecting Esmeralda anymore. He didn't feel the embers of love still smoldering. He was only worried about himself.

His hands on her felt suddenly suffocating. She tore herself free.

The voices outside grew louder. Gabriel and General Keara were at the wagon's front door.

Esmeralda closed her eyes and exhaled. "Leave."

"What?"

"You heard me. Scram. Go before she finds you. Clearly, she knows who I am already, or she wouldn't be trying to get inside. It's too late for me to hide, but she might not know you are here.

Find your information and wipe your conscience clean of your father . . . and of me." Her words hurt to even say.

"The latter is not what I want," he whispered angrily.

His confession nearly leveled her.

"I won't leave you," he said.

Her brows pinched together. "You said that once before."

The entry handle wobbled. Despite Gabriel's protestations, the door squeaked ajar.

Esmeralda met Ignacio's eyes. "Hide."

CHAPTER 22
Ignacio

She had shoved Ignacio into the one place his large body would fit within her tiny wagon: a cramped armoire bulging with costumes, garments, and all her intimate things. They smelled of her. Of oranges, and jasmine, and soft velvety creams. Even as he crouched inside, his body hunched and twisted at odd angles, it was clear to see that Esmeralda's organizational skills had not improved since they parted. And her wagon was cluttered with trinkets.

Her room in his father's manor had been kept sparse, but she'd had an entire drawer stuffed to the brim with knickknacks. Dovie had always collected things she liked, especially items she thought no one cared about. Scraps of pretty paper floating in the breeze. Broken dolls left abandoned in a park. Bottle caps thrown on the street. She'd bring them back and tell him that one day she'd pretty them up and display them on a shelf because everything deserved a chance to be cherished.

Voices mumbled through the walls of the armoire. He pressed one eye to the tiny crack between the doors. His fingers dug into the wood to hold him steady. That's when he saw General Keara. She still wore the fox mask, which covered the top half of her face, but there was no denying who she was.

Gabriel wove his body around the general, trying to stop her. "I must insist you wait in line, señora."

"My business with the fortune teller will be hasty," she said.

"It's all right, Gabriel," Esmeralda, who had quickly disguised herself with her dove mask and now sat behind a small table, said in a sultry tone. She began shuffling her cards. "I can make time for eager guests."

A sly smile crept over the general's lips. She sauntered toward the empty chair opposite Esmeralda and seated herself.

"Gabriel, be a saint, and ensure the customers in my queue know I will be with them shortly."

He hesitated but slowly slipped out the door, clicking it shut behind him.

As Esmeralda shuffled her deck, she asked, "What would you like the spirits to show you? Your future? Your past? Your deepest desires?"

"I did not come to have my cards read," Keara said. "I'm sure you already knew that, being the great fortune teller you are. In fact, I'm convinced you already know the answer to the question I have."

"Oh?" Esmeralda's posture gave no hint that the general's words made her uneasy. But that was exactly how Ignacio knew her nerves must be in a tizzy.

Esmeralda was loud in every way. When she spoke, certainly. But in her gestures, in her movements, in her face. Her thoughts danced over her features. When she was angry, it was written in the line between her eyebrows. When she was cross, it was evident in the crinkling of her nose. When she was happy, one could see nearly all her teeth. But when she was worried, or hurt, or scared, her face turned to stone. It went lifeless as if the magic inside her hid behind her heart.

The general rested an elbow on the table. The wood creaked as she leaned close to Esmeralda. Ignacio knew Esmeralda must hate it. She'd never been the kind to enjoy having people in her personal space.

"Where is the comandante's son?" Keara asked.

"Who?" Esmeralda placed a card down. Then another. Acting as if she were about to read the general's future.

"Do not play daft," Keara said.

"I don't know what you mean." Esmeralda placed another card down.

Keara slammed her hand on top of Esmeralda's. "Enough!"

Fuck this. Ignacio started to open the armoire, but Esmeralda met his eyes through the thin crack in the doors. She shook her head nearly imperceptibly.

"I know it is you behind that mask, Esmeralda Montero," Keara said.

Esmeralda tried to pry her hand away, but Keara clenched tighter, holding her in place.

"You can't do anything to me so long as I'm within carnival grounds." Esmeralda's words came out fast and breathless.

"Believe it or not, your capture is the least of my concerns. In fact, I did not come to the carnival to find you at all. Though,

I should have known to look here the moment he defected. The boy never could rid himself of his love for you."

Esmeralda's lip quirked up in disgust. Ignacio's heart plummeted. His love repulsed her. Of course it did. What would a shooting star want with a black hole? She was so dynamic. So full of life. He was a bore who took everything far too seriously.

"We know Ignacio was on carnival grounds. If he isn't here now, I'm certain he will find his way back. So, I came here to make you an offer." Keara released her hold on Esmeralda's wrist. She leaned back and crossed her arms, looking smug. "Bring Ignacio to me, and you will be pardoned for your past crimes."

Esmeralda blinked rapidly. "What?"

"You can leave this place as a free woman. Hell, with my recommendation, I'm certain the comandante would offer you a stipend for your assistance. We'll even help you go anywhere you'd like."

Sweat trickled down Ignacio's back. All Esmeralda had to do to fix her life was tip her head toward this armoire. If she did, he wouldn't blame her. He'd failed so many people in his life. He was never what anyone wanted him to be—not his father nor his schoolmates or fellow soldiers. Clearly, he had failed her too or she wouldn't have run away without him.

But he wouldn't go down without a fight. He'd have to barrel his way through Keara. Which was no easy task. The woman wasn't his father's right hand for no reason. She was a vicious combatant. Ignacio had seen her take on three men twice as large as himself. Their bones were snapped in terrible places before she was even out of breath.

He was mentally preparing himself for war.

But Esmeralda simply added more cards to the growing pile on the table.

"I haven't seen Ignacio Olivera in a year," she said.

"According to the jailer we spoke to days ago, a girl matching your description was the one to turn him in. Now, I won't make this offer again," the general said.

This was it. She was going to tell Keara where he was. Why wouldn't she? The general was offering her an out.

"Ignacio is not here, and even if he were, there would be nothing you could do about it. We are safe on carnival grounds."

An arrogant smirk flitted over Keara's features. "We might have to test that theory. Especially once Comandante Olivera is made aware that instead of serving your kingdom as a soldier, you're trying to be a big shot at a circus."

Esmeralda went statue-still. She didn't even blink.

"You do not frighten me, General," she said, far more quietly than Ignacio would have expected. Her confidence was wilting.

"Then you are as arrogant as I remember. The comandante *will* hear of this. Enjoy your last few days of freedom, girl."

Esmeralda pulled another card from the deck. Smiling, she spun it to face the general.

"Do you know what this illustration means?" She answered her own question. "This is the queen of thieves. The card speaks of power. Of trust in oneself. It tells me to rely on my gut. And right now, my intuition says I have dozens of customers in the queue, and you're wasting their time."

"That is your answer for me, then?" Keara probed. "You will not take the deal?"

"Well, how could I in good conscience when I don't know Ignacio's whereabouts?" Esmeralda batted her lashes innocently.

Keara jumped to her feet. "You are a fool."

"And you are desperate. Not a good look, babe."

Viper-fast, the general grabbed Esmeralda by the arm. The claws sewn into her gloves dug into Esmeralda's skin. Her cards fluttered to the floorboards. Ignacio was ready to shove the armoire doors open, but Esmeralda growled, "Don't."

He clenched his jaw so tight his teeth ached.

Keara must have thought Esmeralda was speaking to her because she spat, "Don't what?"

Esmeralda raised her chin. "Don't let the door hit you on the heinie when you leave."

"You'll regret this day," Keara snarled. "And I'll be there, front and center, to watch you fall."

CHAPTER 23
Esmeralda

The second that leech of a woman left her wagon, Esmeralda stomped to the armoire and tore the doors open. Ignacio tumbled out, landing on his hands and knees with a heavy thud.

"Ouch," he hissed. But then, he had the audacity to reach for the mint box that had slid near the foot of her cot.

"Oh no you don't." She bopped him on the back of the hand and snatched the tin up. "You're not getting this back until you tell me everything. What is going on? Why is General Keara willing to bribe *me* to find *you*?"

Slowly, Ignacio rose to his feet. He stretched his back and popped his neck. "I can't believe you can store so many things in one tiny armoire. And you still prefer the scent of jasmine, I see."

Lush jasmine vines had grown up one side of Ignacio's childhood home. Whenever they lay on the rooftop, she would breathe in greedily while the flowers were in bloom. One day, she had found a vial of perfume under her pillow that smelled exactly like them. The note on the paper dove lying beside it said: *Scents carry memories. Now you can think of our roof time chats as often as you'd like.*

"Don't change the subject, Ignacio," she snapped. "Why did you desert the Blackbirds?" She pointed at him. "You owe me the truth for covering for you."

Ignacio lifted his hands in surrender as if her finger were a weapon.

"Okay." He took a calming breath. "After you . . . after . . . When I left for the Blackbirds, I poured myself into my training. I moved up in the cadet rankings rather quickly. Quick enough that by the end of the first term, my troop was called into action to assist in a small battle across enemy lines. Keara ordered us to infiltrate a pueblo. She said known leaders of the Dos Palos infantry were hiding there. We did as we were told. We destroyed the town."

He gulped. His thumb ran over his mother's ring. It once fit so perfectly on Esmeralda's own finger.

"There were no infantry leaders in that pueblo. The only weapons the people living there carried were the ones they used for hunting. And I just . . . I stood there in shock as families screamed and begged for help. I did nothing." His eyes grew distant as if seeing it all replay in his mind. "The others celebrated our overtaking, but I threw up. I was keeled over in the back of some building when I spotted Keara and her closest soldiers sneaking up the hillside behind the town. I followed them. It went against our orders, which were to stand guard, but I didn't care. I had to know why we had just massacred these people."

Esmeralda felt like she might be sick herself listening to this story.

"Keara and her soldiers trampled through a field of purple flowers. Then they started laughing and cheering and patting each other on the back. I couldn't get a clear view, but I could hear them splashing through water. I saw them fill satchel after satchel with whatever was inside the stream. That's when I realized, the war was not about border control and safety. It was about finding whatever was in that water. It was about stealing from the land and people of Dos Palos. They killed for whatever they stuffed into those bags. *I* let people get killed for it."

"That wasn't your fault."

He blinked at her as if that thought had never occurred to him. He was forever wondering and worrying over how he could've done better. How he could be perfect. His bastard father was to blame.

Knowing how thick Ignacio's skull was, she said again, "It wasn't your fault."

"But I didn't do anything to stop it. And when I tried to figure out what was in those satchels, it was too late. Keara had already fled with them in her armored car."

He scowled at the floor. His jaw muscle flexed and unflexed. Pain, true pain, flittered over his handsome face.

The urge to wrap her arms around him and use her warmth to soothe him was so overwhelming it hurt. But she didn't dare move. The fear of him rejecting her touch was stronger than the ache inside her chest.

"Whenever I shut my eyes, I see the fallen families. Their anguished faces. The babes in their arms going still. I hear their cries for mercy. They haunt my dreams. And I deserve it. I can't take back what happened that day, but I aim to stop more days like that from happening. I deserted the Blackbirds and my father. I joined the Defiant."

She'd heard of the underground collective that printed unfavorable stories about the king and his men from Gabriel's beau, Javier. He planned on joining up with them once his term with Carnival Fantástico was over. It was one of the reasons Gabriel adored him so much. Javi wanted to help people. He wanted to end the war as well. Rumors swirled that the queen herself was funding the resistance on account of her disdain for the man she was forced to marry and the laws he had enforced.

"Two nights ago, I snuck into my father's home. I was trying to find hard evidence of his transgressions. Something the Defiant could use to expose what is happening in Dos Palos. We believe that if we can get the truth out to soldiers, to citizens, to lawmakers who really care, we can make a difference. If we can show that my father and King Amadeo fabricated this entire war for their own personal gain, people will revolt. We can force them to end their reigns of greed and terror."

She sighed. "The truth doesn't matter, Ignacio. People are going to believe what they want to believe. More like, they'll believe what the king and his cronies want them to believe. Cathedrals are sprouting up in King Amadeo's honor everywhere. And with the upper class growing wealthier because of the spoils of war, nothing will change. Us regular people will never have enough power to change the tides."

"We have to try anyway. When I was in my father's office, I found crumpled flyers for the carnival. It wasn't the flyers that caught my attention. There were notes written to my father on the back. Notes asking him to visit. Telling him that he and the author of the notes needed to have a chat. Whoever wrote those notes knows his secrets. I came to the carnival to investigate. And also, to find out who had access to that special ink."

"Well, you already know it wasn't me. The cards I use for fortune telling show up inside my cabinet every day."

"From whom?" he asked.

Her irritation spiked. "I don't know!"

"You don't find that odd? Someone enters your wagon without your consent?" Now his voice was rising to match hers.

"It's nothing new to me, Ignacio. I lived in your father's home from the age of ten to nearly eighteen. People were always in and out of my room. *You* came in yourself, leaving little things when I wasn't around."

He winced. "I am sorry for it."

That stung.

He must have caught on because he shook his head. "I'm sorry that I never thought about what an invasion of privacy that was. I should have asked first."

"No," she said simply. "I never minded with you. *You* were my home, not some stuffy room under the stairwell."

His lips parted, and he blinked at her.

The air grew thick between them as if she'd stepped into the butterfly exhibit. Only, the little creatures flapping around Ignacio and Esmeralda now were all their past pains. And they weren't nearly as pretty.

How had things gone so wrong? They had been so close. So honest and real with one another. She'd trusted him with her heart and her body. Perhaps that had been too much for him. Perhaps *she* had been too much for him. He might have grown tired of all her sharp shards. She asked too much of him. She should never have begged him to run away with her when she learned his father had enlisted him in the Blackbirds. She had known he idolized the comandante back then.

She cleared her throat. "What is your plan now?"

He seemed to regain his wits. "I must find whoever wrote to my father."

"Who are your suspects so far?"

"You." He grinned when she scowled. "I've taken you off my list."

"Well, thank the stars for that."

He chuckled. "Truth is, it could be anyone here. The ringmaster, the tailor, Gabriel."

She shook her head. "It couldn't possibly be Gabriel. I won't even let you think that for a moment. And the ringmaster hates the comandante as much as we do. Why do you suspect the tailor?"

"He welcomed Keara just now. She had on her uniform and yet he let her in. He dressed her as a fox."

Jorge *had* been acting a bit jumpy when she saw him earlier. "We should start there, then," she suggested.

"We?" he asked.

She licked her dry lips as his brows pinched together.

Gabriel poked his head in the doorway. He looked harried. Stressed. "I cannot hold your customers off any longer. People are starting to leave."

"Of course," she said.

What was she thinking in saying *we*? She couldn't go on wild goose hunts with Ignacio. She had to stay in the ringmaster's good graces. And Ignacio so obviously didn't want her help anyway. The look on his face when she'd said *we* had screamed of revulsion.

"Come in, Gabriel. Let's prepare for my guests," she said.

Ignacio opened his mouth as if to protest. Her heart squeezed with hope.

But he said nothing.

She inwardly deflated.

You're such a fool, she snapped at herself.

With a nod, Ignacio turned around and left.

Too easily.

Just like before.

15th of October, 1917. D+P: Age 14

Dovie. What is something that keeps you up at night?

Remembering that I was left behind.

If it's any consolation, that will never happen with me.

Oh, I know. Because I'd chase after you and tackle you to the ground.

That's adorable that you think you could actually catch me. You realize I'm fastest in my class, right?

What I lack in speed I make up for in spirit.

So you'll just spirit your way into tackling me?

Precisely. So don't get any ideas.

Never.

I knew you were smart from the moment I met you.

Was that before or after you punched me in the nose?

I thought we agreed to pretend that never happened.

CHAPTER 24
Ignacio

Ignacio left Esmeralda's wagon with a dull ache in his chest. He'd often felt that way whenever she was away from him for too long when they were younger. As if his heart forgot to beat without hers there to nudge its proper cadence.

Now that she was back in his orbit, his traitorous heart had begun its subtle protest once more. For a second, he had felt hopeful. When she said she'd help him, he thought, *This could be my chance to win her back*. He was a fool for thinking like that. She did not want him back in her life. Perhaps his mind was simply lost in the idea of her.

Seeing her in that costume cut so perfectly against her hips hadn't helped either.

He scrubbed his hands down his face.

No wonder his father often warned of the dangers of love. One person should not have so much power over another's thoughts.

The smell of buttery popcorn, fried churros, and fresh grass filled his lungs. The screams from patrons on whirling rides, the constant pinging of games, and the bouncing melody of "The Tale of the Valerio Brothers" swirled around him. It grounded Ignacio, reminding him he was still within the carnival. He and Esmeralda were safe for now, but that wouldn't last. If Keara couldn't get ahold of him, Father would come for him and for Esmeralda too, which frightened Ignacio more than anything.

He dipped into the throng of carnivalgoers heading toward the Big Top. Cutting right, he wound back toward the tailor's soft-yellow tent. Just as Ignacio neared, the tailor slipped through the door flap and flipped a glowing sign saying **DO COME IN** to **SORRY, GO AWAY**.

The tailor cast glances from left to right, and then slid his signature goat mask on. He took an envelope from his pocket before sauntering off.

Ignacio knew that crest stamped into the wax seal well. It belonged to his father.

He rushed forward. He had to see what was in that letter. But the crowd had grown so thick that it was impossible to move anywhere but forward, toward the opening of the Big Top.

"Pardon me," he said, trying to squeeze his way through the dense multitude. "Please, let me pass."

"Watch it," someone snapped when he stepped on their shoe.

Standing on tiptoes, Ignacio scoured the throng for the tailor. He couldn't see him anywhere.

A lone figure caught Ignacio's attention. She was standing still, watching the throng like a hawk in the sky. Keara.

Cursing, Ignacio ducked low, hiding behind a woman wearing

a costume that resembled a giant swan. He plucked a few feathers from the costume's rear and shielded his face as the crowd passed the general. He tried to nudge through two men, one outfitted as a leather-skinned rhinoceros and the other a glimmering unicorn, but they hardly acknowledged he existed. There was no weaseling out of the flow of pedestrians.

"I bet ten gold coins on the pretty dame from the parade," the rhinoceros said.

"Which one? There was a plethora," the unicorn replied.

They both chuckled.

"My bet is on the Sánchez Sisters," the woman dressed as a swan proclaimed. Her elaborate mask had diamonds dangling down her cheeks. "Camila and Pilar always amaze during their performances."

What exactly were these wealthy patrons betting on?

A person outfitted as an octopus with sweeping tentacles whispered to the tight-knit group, "I bet a thousand silvers that we see tragedy before the night's end."

"Señor Blanco," the swan scoffed. "What a horrible thing to say."

The man innocently shrugged his many appendages. "Oh, Doña Mariposa, you know how these challenges go. Half the fun is watching these poor little ragamuffins work themselves to death to impress the ringmaster." He gestured toward the unicorn. "Francisco here bet seven gold coins that the new main act would *retire* within a month."

Why did he emphasize retire *like that?* Ignacio wondered. As if the word had a different meaning altogether.

"Just a month, though?" the swan queried. "That seems so short."

The unicorn waved her off with a hoof. "During each Running, our performers grow bolder . . . or should I say more desperate. With the threat of war looming over their heads, they need the carnival and all its spoils more than ever. They're willing to take greater risks to earn our Ángel's praise. Whoever is chosen to be the next main act must be truly tantalizing if they want to keep us coming back for more. Hell, they'll probably saw off their own limbs to keep from having to retire."

"What about Melanie the Marionette?" the octopus asked. "Sure, her act was risky and all, flying in the air like that, but it wasn't jaw-dropping by any means."

"And where is she now? Hmm? She was put out to pasture in the blink of an eye. She went from a star to a nobody," the unicorn said. "Which is fine by me because now I get to cast my bet on someone new."

Ignacio's fingers snapped the feathers he was clutching. These bastards were gambling on the performers' demise.

These awful, no-good fiends were so pompous. So arrogant. So unfeeling. And judging from their use of honorifics and extravagant, complexly stitched attires, they were filthy rich. Most likely part of the king's own court come to escape the false piety they exuded across the kingdom and show their true selves behind their masks.

Ignacio ducked his head a bit lower. He doubted it, but one might recognize him as the comandante's son, like the jailer who had tried to take him to the military barracks.

Gasps of awe bubbled around him as they moved from the open air of the carnival into a strange sort of corridor. The entrance to the Big Top was large and arching. The voices and footfalls bounced around like an echo chamber. When Ignacio let his gaze roam upward like the rest of the crowd, he gawked.

A thousand pairs of eyes were blinking down at him. He squinted. They weren't eyes at all, but hundreds and hundreds of smooth black stones reflecting the spectators' faces back at them. There was something peculiar about their reflections, though. Something that made everyone appear a bit different than what they really were.

Ignacio caught his own reflection. He seemed . . . *better*. For lack of a proper word. He appeared as a man who moved around with confidence. Like a man who never made mistakes. Or failed anyone. He wished he could be this version of himself. If he were perfect, perhaps his father might have loved him more. Perhaps Esmeralda would never have left him. Perhaps those farmers would still be breathing. What Esmeralda had said to him inside her wagon came to mind. Their deaths weren't his fault. He couldn't have saved them. Had he openly allied himself with Dos Palos, he'd surely be dead too. Maybe he could accept Esmeralda's words one day. *After* his father and the king were dealt with.

The jazz music, which was always playing in the background, roared to an unignorable volume. People gasped and cheered. As the patrons funneled into the main hub of the tent, he could see why. The Big Top was alive.

Clowns on stilts walked by throwing handfuls of confetti

in the air. Massive elephants and pearl-white ponies pulled the floats from the parade. They marched around the tent in a wide circle, the performers waving and blowing kisses to the audience. There was a large center ring, flanked by two slightly smaller rings on either side. Inside each ring, people in jewel-toned dresses twirled in rhythmic unison. A medley of colors swept over the space from the glowing bulbs dangling overhead. Massive mirrors made from the same black stone that had winked down at him within the entrance tunnel hung from the tent walls and rafters. Inside the mirrors stood the ringmaster himself, with his curled mustache and top hat, waving and singing "The Tale of the Valerio Brothers."

With the guests headed to their seats, Ignacio could finally move more freely. He started toward the exit door flaps, which were on the other side of a row of bleachers, but he paused when the lights dimmed and the music lowered to a beating thrum.

A single spotlight sent a direct beam to the center ring. There was a quick explosion of sparkling dust and then the ringmaster appeared. Standing proudly on a rounded platform, his arms were spread wide. His teeth glinted as he turned in a slow circle. His purple coat winked with sequins.

Ignacio instinctively looked around for Estefan the ostrich, but he was noticeably not part of the show.

The audience stood and cheered, electrified.

"Fans, friends, and fiends!" the ringmaster roared. "Welcome to the most fantastical, most sensational"—people in the stands shouted the words along with him, including the woman in the swan costume and her companions, now sitting in a coveted box, who were yelling the loudest—"most deliciously delinquent, most wonderous, most death-defying, most enchanting show!"

People stomped their feet, creating a drumroll with their boots and heels.

The ringmaster's gaze drifted upward as he soaked up their praise. He took off his top hat and shouted, "Welcome to Carnival Fantástico!"

The audience whistled and clapped and hollered. Exhilaration was so thick in the air, Ignacio almost got caught up in it himself. But he pushed his legs to move. He needed to find the tailor and see what was in that letter.

Something in one of the mirrors hanging near the exit caught his attention and he halted. A face that was neither human nor beast stared at him hungrily. Its eyes glowed. Ignacio blinked, horrified. But in the next second, the face was gone.

Unease filled his belly. He stepped close to the oval mirror, but the only thing he saw was his own haunted reflection.

"As you may know, I am on the hunt for a new main act since our beloved showstopper Melanie the Marionette hung up her strings. During the welcome parade, you saw many of the amazing performers who are in the Running." The ringmaster put his hand to his ear. "Scream out your favorite act so far."

Thousands of voices barked out their darlings.

"Nicola the Escape Artist!"

"The Flying Córdovas!"

"Paco the Fire Breather!"

"The Sánchez Sisters!"

"Benicio the Bear Trainer!"

"David the Knife Thrower!"

"La Paloma Blanca and her handsome noviecito!"

Ignacio's head snapped toward the audience.

There had been a time when he had wanted nothing more than to be called Esmeralda's beau. Now? He couldn't deny how his body ached whenever he laid eyes on her. If only her heart wasn't as cold as the frozen abyss.

The crowd continued to chant their favorite performer's name.

The ringmaster laughed heartily. When the audience quieted, he said, "I hear you loud and clear, my lovelies. Lucky for you, a few of these acts are ready to put on a show for you tonight." He swept his arm to the smaller ring on the right. "Up first, I give you Paco the Fire Breather!"

A spotlight fell onto a tall young man wearing a red singlet. He waved with one hand. The other hand grasped a torch of blue flames.

Something popped near the center ring. Glistening smoke engulfed the ringmaster before he disappeared. The spotlight that had illuminated Veracruz swiveled upward to find him standing on a catwalk hanging below the rafters. A woman sitting in the stands nearest to Ignacio swooned.

"Next, we have Benicio the Bear Trainer!" he bellowed.

Another spotlight shone on the center ring. A giant man sporting a bear pelt roared before running to a bicycle. He leapt on and began pedaling. To Ignacio's surprise, real bears surged out of the backstage curtains riding on unicycles.

"And last but certainly not least, we have the Sánchez Sisters!"

A fourth spotlight hit the smaller ring nearest to where Ignacio stood. Camila and her sister wore matching leotards. They waved and blew kisses and dazzled the crowd. They dug their hands into a bowl of powder and clapped, sending sparkling puffs of dust into the air. The dust morphed into wispy butterflies and fluttered away, causing the audience to cheer even louder.

The cloth cuffs on the Sánchezes' wrists caught Ignacio's attention. They shimmered like the ink he hunted for, like the glue that had locked Anella inside the glass box. His eyes went to the other performers. Benicio's fake claws looked to be tinted with the iridescent paint. Paco had a string of gleaming beads glinting around his throat.

The phantom band ambled to life and played "The Tale of the Valerio Brothers." And with that, the show kicked off.

Ignacio remained transfixed but also on edge. Esmeralda swore the ringmaster would never write to his father. The ringmaster himself said so too. But when Ignacio questioned him about the ink, he had shrugged him off. How could this man not know where it came from when most of his performers sported something with those very glinting tones of blacks, purples, blues, and golds?

Camila readjusted her cloth cuffs as she squatted low. Her sister Pilar climbed onto her shoulders. She beckoned the audience to applaud. Camila extended her arm upward. Slowly, Pilar stepped onto Camila's palm. Camila didn't even flinch at the weight she carried. An amazing feat in and of itself.

In a measured and smooth motion, Camila bent down and

picked up a thick slab of marble. Small cutouts had been etched into the stone for her fingers like a bowling ball. She lifted the rectangular block, which had to have been at least one hundred pounds, with ease.

Camila flung it up. Pilar caught it and placed it on top her head. The crowd watching the act gasped, Ignacio included. How were these two so strong? Camila continued to bend and flick, bend and flick. Sometimes, Pilar missed the catch, and the heavy marble thumped onto the ground. The audience sighed with disappointment but leaned in a little closer with anticipation each time. The sisters continued until Pilar could no longer reach high enough to place the marble on top of the stack on her head. But Camila bent again. She threw the slab into the air. With a clink, the marble landed on the top piece of its own accord.

The audience stood and roared with excitement. As the cheers boomed around the giant tent, the bulbs swinging from the ceiling glowed a bit brighter. Ignacio squinted up, wondering why. It could be part of the act. But he saw no carnival hands up in the rafters.

He jolted.

That face appeared again. This time within the mirrors hanging high above their heads. But those glowing eyes were not focused on him. They were directed at the Sánchez sisters.

Time seemed to slow.

Camila let out a sound that was part grunt, part scream. The cuff on her wrist shimmered ever so slightly as her arm swayed.

"Drop the bricks!" she shrieked to her sister, who still stood on her palm.

But it was too late.

Camila's wrist snapped back with a sickening crack. A sharp cry tore through the tent. The marble slabs, and Pilar herself, came tumbling down.

CHAPTER 25
Esmeralda

Esmeralda sat on the steps of her wagon listening to the sounds of the Big Top as she counted her tips. She'd never earned so much before. She'd stolen that much, sure. But not earned it. Though, she wasn't certain if scamming people by telling them false fortunes truly counted.

None of that mattered now. If she didn't get that top spot, she'd never earn enough dough to purchase passage out of the country in her two months left with the carnival anyway. Ángel had taken her safety net when he found her box of snagged goods. And General Keara was without a doubt going to tell the comandante she was here, especially since Esmeralda hadn't been particularly helpful.

What else was she supposed to do? Rat Ignacio out to the general?

Never.

Even thieves had a code.

Her palms started to sweat. If the ringmaster found her

unworthy, he might very well hand them both over to Comandante Olivera himself. She wouldn't let that happen.

"I can't believe he left the Blackbirds," she murmured. "He turned his back on the man he practically worshiped." To be fair, she had worshiped the comandante just as much when she was younger. Perhaps more.

From the age of ten until she was sixteen, Esmeralda had watched Comandante Olivera with admiration in her eyes. He was so large and commanding. He intimidated everyone. His presence was enamoring. No one dared say no to the man. They would do whatever it took to please him. He was respected. Feared. Honored. Esmeralda had wanted to be like him because she thought that no one would ever brush her off or push her away again if she was that powerful.

Until one day she overheard him berating Ignacio for some insignificant mistake. Her hackles rose. No one should ever speak to anyone in such a manner, certainly not their child. Her resentment for the comandante grew. And when she decoded one of his missives to the front lines, she realized how terrible the man truly was. He'd ordered his Blackbirds to destroy everything in their wake. He told them to leave no home, school, or shop in one piece until they found their target. She had assumed the target meant enemy leaders, but now she wondered if it was whatever General Keara put in those satchels.

She had tried to tell Ignacio his father was a warmonger the morning she learned he was enlisted into the Blackbirds. But he refused to listen. He refused to see his father in a dark light.

At least *now* he knew the truth, and he was trying to do something about it.

That didn't mean she could ever forgive him for leaving her behind, though.

"Damn you, Pigeon," she whispered.

She shoved off the steps of her wagon and started to walk, stuffing her tips into her coin purse before concealing it amongst her curls.

Esmeralda nodded at a worker filling up balloons for a game. Preparing for the influx of new customers to come as soon as the main show ended. Nearly everyone was inside the Big Top. Their applause and *oohs* and *aahs* tumbled out of the tent and echoed in the air like a haunting fog. The sounds taunted Esmeralda. They whispered, *You aren't good enough to be in here with us.* It was clear she hadn't proved herself to the ringmaster enough or else he would have invited her to perform.

A scream tore through the sky. Esmeralda's head snapped toward the Big Top. She waited for the applause. For laughter.

But more horrified screams rang out.

Knowing the Sánchez sisters would be performing, she ran toward the tent.

She kept her eyes forward as she bolted through the arch of a thousand mirrors. She hated the things. Hated how it felt like a million eyes were crawling on her skin like spiders. She skidded to a halt as she met a wall of animals, performers, and carnival hands whispering and sobbing into each other's arms before the side ring.

"What happened, Jade?" she asked the manager of the menagerie.

Jade's green eyes met Esmeralda's. She shook her head. "I . . . I'm sorry, Paloma."

"For what?"

"There . . . there was an accident. Camila, she . . ."

Esmeralda shoved her way through the onlookers. She pushed them hard, with little care for manners. She needed to see Camila. *Now.*

She stumbled through a tight opening and gasped. Her hands clamped over her mouth to seal in her shocked cry. Camila writhed in pain on the sawdust-covered floor. The bottom halves of her legs were buried under a pile of the marble slabs she and Pilar used during their act.

But where was Pilar?

Ignacio, Gabriel, and two other carnival hands were frantically digging through the rubble. A sequined slipper lay upside down near Ignacio's knee.

"No," Esmeralda whispered.

She dashed forward and fell beside a thrashing Camila. She reached for Camila's hand but noticed it was bent at an awfully wrong angle.

"Where's my sister?!" Camila sobbed. "Where's Pilar?!"

Esmeralda's eyes met Ignacio's. He looked horrified.

His gaze flicked to Ángel, who was busy telling his ratas to usher in the next attraction. Ignacio glared at the ringmaster's back. All the while, he heaved slab after slab to free Pilar from the wreckage.

CHAPTER 26
Ignacio

Ignacio carried Pilar's fragile frame into the healer's boxcar. Every instinct inside him urged him to run as fast and hard as he could to get her help, but he didn't want to do any more damage to the young woman's body.

There was no telling how Pilar was faring. Her bones were twisted at crude angles and deep purple bruises bloomed from her chest and abdomen. His mind replayed the massacre in Dos Palos. All those bodies open and bleeding on the grass.

Bile rose up his throat. Sweat pricked on his forehead. But he kept his focus steady. He wouldn't let Pilar die.

Esmeralda and Gabriel followed close behind with a wailing Camila in their arms. Her cries were spine-chilling. And so was the face he'd seen in the mirror. The creature had smiled right before Camila's strength gave out.

Ignacio must have been seeing things. Monsters didn't exist. That was the stuff of fables. But he *was* in a carnival known to make the impossible possible.

The healer rushed forward as they entered.

"Lay her here," the woman said, gesturing toward an empty cot. "Gently." Ignacio did as she commanded. Esmeralda and Gabriel laid Camila in the bed parallel to her sister. The healer pulled back her long braids and tied them with a bit of ribbon as she assessed them.

"What happened?" she asked.

"Camila was holding up Pilar, but then her wrist snapped," Ignacio said.

It didn't just snap. A moment before it happened, the cuffs she wore started to glisten. Then whatever shimmered within them sputtered out like a dying sparkler. That was when Camila first screamed.

The ringmaster burst into the boxcar. "How are they?"

In this lighting, Ángel appeared different. The shadows cast by the amber candles deepened the crow's feet Ignacio had seen before. A few gray hairs had found their way into his curled mustache. He looked much older, as if the very weight of this incident had aged him twenty years.

The healer turned toward the ringmaster. "I can ease the pain and set the bones, but Pilar needs to be taken to a hospital. Immediately."

"Surely there's one in town. We can take her," Esmeralda suggested.

"No," Ángel replied sharply.

Ignacio clenched his fists when he saw Esmeralda flinch.

"What I mean is . . . this town does not have advanced facilities," he said.

"Nuevo Campos is our next stop, yes?" the healer asked.

"It is," the ringmaster replied.

"My sister is a physician there. We can take her—"

"The Sánchez sisters will remain in my carnival. Under my care."

The healer balked. "But señor . . ."

"We'll send a telegraph ahead asking for your sister to join us when we arrive. I'll ensure she has the necessary tools."

What a strange thing to do. Pilar needed a surgeon in a sterile environment if she was to survive. And time was not on their side.

The ringmaster's gaze traveled to a looking glass on a nearby shelf.

Was he searching for something . . . or someone?

Ignacio's pulse raced harder than before. First Anella the Contortionist nearly met her end by suffocation. And now the Sánchezes had been pummeled. He thought of what those people said in line. Of the bets they were casting.

He couldn't help but step closer to Esmeralda. If something or someone so much as thought they could harm her, they would have to go through him first.

"We should leave this very minute," the healer said. "We can pack up everything and be out of here within the hour."

The ringmaster watched Pilar. His gaze roamed over her battered body so unhurriedly, Ignacio nearly throttled him. They needed to move. To get her to a physician before it was too late. Yet Veracruz stood there like he was waiting for Pilar's breathing to slow.

Esmeralda must have noticed too because she rushed forward and took the ringmaster's arm. "Ángel, please," she said.

Heat seared through Ignacio at the intimacy of the touch.

The ringmaster gazed down at her almost lovingly. Ignacio clenched his fists so hard his knuckles popped. Veracruz's eyes flicked to him before returning to Esmeralda. He half smirked.

"You are right, darling." He patted her arm. "As soon as the Big Top performances are over, we will pack up and go."

"You must be joking," Ignacio said.

"I never joke about such matters. You should all know by now that the show must always go on." Once again, his gaze flicked to the mirror. "Come, let us leave the sisters here with the healer. The final act is readying to begin."

Ignacio planted his feet. He wouldn't leave the girls. He didn't know exactly why, but he couldn't trust they'd be okay.

"If you don't mind, I'd like to stay with them," Gabriel said to the healer.

He must be sensing the same thing Ignacio was. Sensing the wrongness permeating the air.

They looked to Veracruz for approval.

The ringmaster's jaw muscles flexed before he flashed his signature grin. "But of course. You're a good friend." He faced Ignacio. "Why don't you find some extra hands and begin discreetly packing up the third ring attractions? No one will worry much over those." He motioned for Esmeralda. "Follow me, love. I want you to take notes on how to thrill the crowd."

He placed his hand on the small of Esmeralda's back and urged her toward the exit. Ignacio saw her shoulders stiffen. He started forward but stopped himself. If she said nothing to the ringmaster, who was he to intervene? She'd probably scoff at him anyway.

Veracruz looked over his shoulder and found Ignacio's gaze. He winked before he and Esmeralda disappeared into the shadows. Through his nostrils, Ignacio breathed out the boiling rage filling his lungs.

It had taken much longer for them to tear down the carnival and pack everything onto the train than Ignacio liked. The moment the train started moving, he dashed out of his shared bunk. Something was terribly wrong with this carnival. He had to figure out what. And he was going to start by seeing what exactly was in those mirrors. He kept thinking about "The Tale of the Valerio Brothers." When the ringmaster recited the ballad, he spoke of a god of smoke and mirrors. Perhaps he wasn't speaking in riddles as Ignacio first thought but, unbelievably, in truths.

Ignacio had heard a tale similar to the Valerio brothers' before, but he couldn't remember how or when. And it was driving him mad.

With a grunt, he shoved open the rear boxcar door. Wind whipped across his skin. His eyes watered from the cold as train tracks whizzed beneath his feet. He slid the door shut and hopped onto the next wagon. He would do this until he made it to the boxcars that held the Big Top materials.

He passed through the menagerie car and opened the next door.

Ignacio halted.

Esmeralda lay in a tight ball on a small balcony welded onto the boxcar being tugged behind the one he was on. The healer's sign bumped against the metal door above her as the tracks sped by below.

With his footfall shielded by the rattling groans of the train, he jumped across the gap between cars and landed beside her. He shivered. It was a wonder she could sleep with the windchill so biting.

He couldn't leave her here. It wasn't safe, for one, but also, she'd freeze.

Kneeling, he scooped her up. He paused when her mass of curls fell away from her face. The skin around her eyes was swollen. She had been crying.

There had only been two times he'd seen her shed tears. The day he told her he had been enlisted into the Blackbirds was the most recent. The first time had been one summer night when they were fifteen. They lay under the stars on his roof. He told her about his mother and how the loss of her left a hollow cave in his chest.

Until he met Dovie.

That night, she had wiped the tears from his cheeks while her own eyes filled with them. Then she had scooted closer to him, offering him her warmth.

"I often talk to myself," she had said. "Keeps all the sad thoughts away."

He had smiled. "I've heard you."

"Maybe . . ." She chewed on her lip. "Maybe we can be each other's noise. It won't replace the people we've lost, of course, but maybe we can be there for each other to silence all those sad thoughts that like to slip in when things go quiet."

She had done that for him. Dovie had silenced the sad noise. But then she left and his sorrows began to scream once more. Esmeralda had hurt him deeply when she ran away. Still, he wouldn't leave her here in the cold.

Slowly, her eyes blinked open as he stood cradling her in his arms. She gazed up at him in a sleepy sort of way that burned his insides. She'd looked at him like this the night of his eighteenth birthday. When he climbed onto the rooftop to meet her, he'd been shocked to see that she was already there. She'd laid out blankets and fluffed them into a sort of nest. She patted the blankets, beckoning him to her.

"I've been pondering," she had said.

"Terrifying."

"I know." She bumped him with her shoulder. "Since my birthday comes three days after yours, I've been thinking about a gift that will suit us both."

He raised a brow. "Is that right?"

She nodded, then shifted onto her knees and faced him. "I want you."

He blinked in confusion. "You already have me."

She giggled and rolled her eyes.

Then, she did something that sent every nerve in his body shooting to the sky. She climbed into his lap. Her legs straddled him. Her warmth melted against him.

"I'll be your present and you will be mine," she said.

He had sucked in a breath, unable to control the irregular beating of his heart.

Her long lashes dipped and she met his gaze. "What do you say, Pigeon?"

Ignacio had tucked a lock of hair behind her ear. "I . . . I'd say there is nothing I've ever wanted more in my life."

They had given each other that gift. They had become one. And after, she'd looked up at him with sleepy stars in her eyes, and he never thought he could love anyone more than he loved her at that moment.

"Are you going to tell me why you're holding me like some sleeping princess?" Esmeralda asked, slicing through his memory.

"Oh . . . I . . . I was going to bring you someplace safer to rest."

Her lips flattened. "You sure you weren't thinking about chucking me off the train?"

"I would never."

She snorted. "I know. You're far too good."

Not good enough for you to love, he wanted to retort. Instead, he asked, "Any news on Camila or Pilar?"

She shook her head. "Pilar hasn't opened her eyes. Camila is up, though. She hit her head really hard, her wrist is broken, and her legs are pretty banged up. Otherwise, she's okay, physically. Mentally, not so much."

The train raced past a blinking lantern. The soft glow illuminated Esmeralda's beautiful face. This close he could see every soft curve and line.

"You can put me down now," she said quietly.

“Of course.” He set her gently onto the metal deck, already missing her jasmine scent.

Esmeralda wrapped her arms around her body, and she shuddered.

“Here.” He shrugged off his coat and placed it over her shoulders.

She sniffed. Did she remember his scent too? Did it make her insides burn like hers did to him?

“Camila didn’t want to be in the running for the lead act,” she said. “But she did it because Pilar loved the spotlight. She did it to make her sister happy.”

Perhaps this was selfish given the circumstances, but he thought back to the day he told Dovie he had been enlisted. Despite his desperate need to please his father back then, Ignacio had been willing to run away for her.

“Sometimes people are willing to risk whatever it takes to make their loved ones happy,” he said.

She scowled. “How foolish of them. Love only leads to heartbreak. Look at Camila. At every person you’ve ever known. Every time you open yourself up and trust someone, you’re setting your neck on a guillotine, waiting for the blade to drop.”

“You can’t really believe that.”

“Look at us,” she said. “We were . . . we . . .” She turned her face away.

“We were special,” he admitted. And saying so nearly broke him all over again. He hated using the word *were*. Hated that he couldn’t say *are*. We *are* special.

Over the past year, he’d thought of the things he would say to her. All the accusations and questions he would fling her way. But, at that moment, he couldn't say a thing because he felt too raw inside. Seeing her, being so near to her, recalling the unfathomable depth of their love, it all made her betrayal that much worse. And yet, he couldn't say any of the things he had wanted to say to her when she was right here because he was terrified of losing her again.

"And now we can hardly stand to look at each other," she said.

He smiled through his pain. "I wouldn't go that far. I've caught you eyeballing me quite a few times since I showed up."

"Don't be ridiculous. If I *was*, it was most likely because I was trying to burn holes through you with my intense scrutiny."

He chuckled. "Keep lying to yourself."

"You really think you're handsome, don't you?"

He didn't care if he was or wasn't, so long as she took notice. He shrugged. "Your eyes don't lie, Dovie."

She scoffed. "If anyone has been doing any sort of ogling, it's you, Pigeon."

Hearing her call him Pigeon had once peeved him. His nickname for her had been cute. Hers for him had been purposely snarky. But hearing it now was like cool aloe on sun-scorched skin.

He smiled. "The people lining the parade yesterday were *definitely* looking at me."

"They were paid actors."

"They must have been well compensated because I heard the townsfolk had to mop up all the drool afterward. Took them hours."

"You are conceited in every way," she said.

"Only in the ways that anger you, which is just about every one."

She huffed and crossed her arms, closing herself off. Panic set in. He had just had a glimpse of the old Esmeralda. He couldn't lose her yet.

"Before you dishonored me by calling me a pigeon, you mentioned it was I who ogled you. That might perhaps be true."

Her brow rose. Esmeralda had always loved a compliment, and he'd always been happy to oblige, especially knowing that she never received them as a child. Also because he truly meant them.

He edged closer to her. "I must admit that you are even prettier than the last time we saw one another. I would never have thought that possible."

She raised her chin. "Go on."

"When I saw you today in your wagon wearing that costume, I worried my jawbone would drop onto the floorboards."

A giggle escaped her. "Is that so?"

"Oh yes. Even when I dreamed of you after we parted last year, I never imagined a prettier picture."

She turned to him fully, suddenly serious. His stomach dropped. He'd gone too far.

"You dreamed of me?" she asked. Her eyes were so large and open. So full of . . . hope, perhaps?

He couldn't help it; he stepped closer to her. "Dovie, I . . ." Could he tell her the truth? That there hadn't been a night that went by where she hadn't come to him in his dreams.

Her brows pinched, and she turned her head. "Do you hear that?"

The sun had begun to rise, casting the sky in the same cotton-candy pinks he'd seen guests nibbling on so joyfully during the carnival. Rooftops of buildings from their next stop were beginning to pop up over the horizon. The train blared its horn three times. Loud cheers rang out in return.

Esmeralda scrambled close to the side of the balcony and peered around the boxcar in front of them. She rubbed her eyes as if seeing a mirage. Aching at the thought of her so near to the edge, he moved to join her. His hands ready to catch her if she fell. He gaped. Hundreds of people were lining the tracks. They held up signs.

Some offered well wishes for the Sánchez sisters. Some begged for the ringmaster to marry them. A few stated they were rooting for Paco the Fire Breather. But others—now Ignacio rubbed his own eyes. There were dozens of sketches of him and Esmeralda. No, of the masked man and Paloma Blanca staring lovingly at each other from within the ostrich cage.

"King's toes," she whispered. Her face glowed with a greedy sort of amazement. "They adore me." She pointed at a sign saying she must become the lead act. "They are rooting for me."

"Technically, us. I'm on those signs too."

"Well . . . sure . . . but you can tell they are here for me. I mean . . . Look there. I have a much larger portion on that sketch." She held her hands against her chest. "They love me."

"No, Dovie. These people are betting on you. I overheard some guests talking about it before the show."

"Of course they are. I'm worth the gamble. At least to *some* people."

What did that mean? He shook his head before spiraling. "They are betting on people getting hurt. They're hoping it happens."

"Good thing that won't happen to me, then. Because I plan on winning."

He took her arm so she faced him. "You aren't still going to go on with the contest after what happened to Camila and Pilar, are you?"

"Why not? They aren't going to keep me fed or safe. And, thanks to you, I don't have enough to pay for passage out of this country once my time is up in the carnival. I *have* to be the main act if I intend to survive. Because now, thanks to you, *again*, your father knows exactly where I am. The girls and I are close, but I can't let their tragedy stop me from living."

Ignacio stepped back, stunned. "How could you be so cold? They're your friends."

"And you were the boy who swore he loved me. You promised you'd always be there. Until you weren't. If I'm callous, it's because every time I offered my heart, the person who promised to keep it safe dropped it to the dirt. When you left—"

"I never left you!" he snapped. "How could you say such a preposterous thing? It was you! You left first!" He knew he should lower his voice, people were watching from the tracks, but he couldn't help it. She was lying right to his face even when he had been there.

"*I* left first?!" She laughed haughtily then returned to watching the excited gathering. "You might need to get your memory checked because you are—" Her skin suddenly paled, and her jaw went slack.

A man stood snarling amongst the onlookers holding signs. He wore a bowler hat tugged low to his nose. His jacket hung haggardly over a black-and-white-striped prison uniform.

"The bootlegger," she whispered.

She winced and gathered her curls, using them to shield her

face. But it must have done the opposite of what she was trying to do, because the man yelled, "It's you! I'd recognize that smug smirk anywhere."

Though her hair was over her eyes, the bottom half of her face was exposed. Just like when she wore her dove mask.

The man raised his finger and pointed at her, his cheeks reddening.

"You scammed me!" he shouted. "You told me I'd find fortune! But now I'm on the lam because of you!" He shoved his way through the crowd and started chasing after the train.

Esmeralda's entire body went rigid with fear. Ignacio couldn't stand the sight. He shoved his sleeves up, readying for a fight, but then he remembered what had happened to Anella when she'd lost the crowd's approval during the parade.

The people holding up their signs and rooting for La Paloma Blanca might start to think she was a fraud. He had to turn this around. Perhaps laughter would work. "Let me tell you a new fortune, buddy! One step closer and prison will be the least of your worries!" he shouted, flexing his biceps.

The man let out a string of curses.

Ignacio clucked his tongue. "Do you pray to the gods with that foul mouth? Perhaps that is why you've had such pitiful luck!"

People began to chuckle. Which made Ignacio feel strangely elated.

He went on, "Or maybe it's because you're a terrible crook!"

The crowd whooped with laughter.

Finally, Esmeralda regained her composure. Her shoulder brushed against Ignacio's arm as she moved beside him. "I'm seeing your new future now! The spirits tell me you will catch the fiery fever if you don't get lost!"

Ignacio gaped as dramatically as he could. "He's turning red already!" he hollered.

The bootlegger halted. His hands went to his crimson cheeks. Cackling, someone swatted his back and told him to beat it before he got the rest of them sick, or worse, gave them bad luck. More onlookers began to berate him until the man had no choice but to flee.

Esmeralda met Ignacio's eyes, and they both fell into a fit of laughter. Her hand rested on his bicep. His insides went warm. Then turned molten as her giggles calmed and her gaze roamed over his face.

"You were brilliant," she said softly.

The world beyond them blurred. He no longer heard the crowds cheering their names or the train wheels bumping on the tracks. There was only Dovie. There was only ever Dovie. He took a step closer to her. She didn't move. He stepped closer again. Her lips parted.

A whistle blared, snapping him from his trance. It must have done the same to her because she inhaled sharply.

"We've reached our next stop."

She swept back and offered a shy smile before jumping to the boxcar theirs was attached to.

"Where are you going?" he yelled.

"To get ready for the next challenge."

He shook his head. "You can't seriously still want to do this."

She pulled the boxcar door open. "The show must go on."

Still wearing his only coat, Esmeralda scurried away.

CHAPTER 27

Esmeralda

"Hey, kid."

Esmeralda's head snapped up. She was sitting near the siren enclosure, dangling her feet over the impossibly blue waters while writing out ideas on how to stand out during the next challenge. The page was empty, though. Her mind was too busy spinning in circles about everything that had happened last night with the Sánchezes and this morning with Ignacio.

She clamped the notebook shut and scooted around to face the ringmaster.

"How is Pilar?" she asked. She hadn't had the guts to visit the sisters since the train stopped in Nuevo Campos. How could she when they'd both nearly died and all she cared about was if she could use the aerialist's hoop for her act?

The ringmaster took off his top hat and scratched his thick brown hair. Bits of gray had begun to pepper his temples. She'd never noticed that before. And he was rather young to be so gray. She supposed stress could do such a thing.

"Camila is up and moving about, but I don't know about Pilar," he said. "The healer and physician are meeting right now."

He plopped down beside her, nodding at the performers dressed as sirens who were swimming about in the pool to work in their new fins. They had once been opera singers, but when they couldn't get their big break anywhere else, they joined the carnival.

The ringmaster's face turned forlorn. "I don't know if they told you yet, but, unfortunately, I had to disqualify the girls. They're no longer fit for the challenge."

Esmeralda stiffened. She didn't think the sisters could continue on in the Running, obviously, but she also didn't think he'd disqualify them before Pilar even woke.

"Such a pity," he said. "They had great potential." His focus went to the journal in Esmeralda's lap. "What are you working on?" he asked.

"Oh . . . um . . ." Esmeralda shrugged. How was she supposed to answer such a thing when he'd just told her that?

He nudged her shoulder with his. "Come now. I'm not the kind to judge."

"I was coming up with ideas for the next challenge."

"Is that so? You are thinking of such things even after what happened to the Sánchezes?"

Her eyes widened. "Is that horrible of me?"

"No. That is *circus* of you." He winked. "Only those with true sparkle in their veins understand that the show must carry on." His eyes crinkled at the corners. And for the first time she noticed that he'd powdered his face. "You are more like me than I ever realized."

"Really?" She scooted closer. "How so?"

"You are a performer through and through. You want to feel the spotlight on your skin. To be loved and adored by all. And you have spunk, kid. Did you see how many people held signs up for you when we entered the city? Did you hear them chanting your name?"

A twinge of annoyance spiked through her. "They were also chanting for Ignacio."

"News travels fast. That's exactly why you must capitalize on it. If you want to be the main attraction, you gotta do whatever it takes. Use this energy. Use him."

"Use Ignacio?"

"Sure. Pull him into your act. Tease the audience with a love story, even if it's a false one."

"I don't think he would be okay with that."

"Make him okay with it. And fast."

She blinked in confusion.

Ángel grinned brilliantly. The morning sun turned his eyes the same sapphire blue as the siren tank. He twirled his fingers, and a black envelope popped into existence.

He offered her the card. "Get ready, Esmeralda Montero. Challenge number two has just begun."

She took the card with both hands. "Thank you. I won't let you down."

"I know you won't. Especially if you heed my advice. Use the boy. Give the people what they want." With a grunt, the ringmaster stood. "See you soon."

She watched him go, his movements stiff as if he too hadn't slept well. She sighed and beamed, clutching the envelope. He still believed in her.

Her smile quickly faded when the ringmaster crossed paths with Gabriel, who held Camila up with her arm around his shoulder. Esmeralda tried to hide her excitement and the envelope, but it was too late. They had seen it.

Gabriel shook his head before escorting Camila away.

Away.

That's where people were always moving when it came to Esmeralda.

Away.

Maybe it was her own fault. She was selfish and greedy. But how else was she supposed to be? No one in this world would ever care for her like she did. People left her when they learned who she truly was anyway.

But the crowd, the audience, the coin they flicked in her direction, that would be there until she decided she'd had her fill. Ángel Veracruz was the only person who understood that fact. And he would be the only one to save her from Comandante Olivera.

She tore the envelope open and read the card.

Welcome. Welcome. To challenge number two!
Show me your vivacity and you will be through.

Do you sparkle? Do you shine?

Can you make the crowd feel divine?

Prove your effervescence tonight in the center ring.

And perhaps your name will be the final one I sing.

**There are currently six acts in the Running. Only three will continue.*

21st of March, 1918. D+P: Ages 15 and 14

Dovie. It is my birthday.

Yes. I'm aware. The cook had me run to the market for extra flour to make pie. It's weird. Who wants pie on their birthday?

Thanks for ruining the surprise. Just razzing you. The pie was my idea. Cake is disgusting. But pie, especially cherry pie, now that is something altogether delectable.

Cherry pie? I've always wanted to try cherries.

I know.

I thought you said once that you didn't like cherries.

My tastes have changed.

Share it with me?

We aren't supposed to be seen together. Your nanny is quite clever, she'll catch us. Plus, I'm often so busy during the day.

She's my governess, not my nanny. I'm now fifteen. I don't need a babysitter.

I suggest we meet at night. Midnight to be exact. We can meet on the roof, where no one will find us.

We can make it a double celebration since your birthday is coming soon.

Please. I want to see you. Like <u>really</u> see you.

Well . . . I can't say no to pie. Or the birthday boy.

CHAPTER 28
Ignacio

Twenty minutes before the Big Top show began, Ignacio was finally able to catch Jorge the tailor alone.

"I'm looking for a new costume," Ignacio said. "Something that shows off my personality better than a weasel."

The tailor tilted his head and squinted his eyes. "You'd be a magnificent albatross."

Ignacio raised his brows. "A bird?"

"What about a schnauzer, then? It's a breed of dog. Very regal. Rather smelly if left ungroomed."

Ignacio chanced a sniff at his underarm when the tailor turned away to dig into his trunk of costumes. Not smelly. He could stand to have a haircut, though. But that wasn't really important. Not when he'd seen this man holding a letter from his father. Ignacio had to know what it said or at least where the tailor had taken it.

"Do you have anything more unique?" Ignacio asked. "Perhaps something in the back?"

The tailor perked up. He grinned. "Trying to impress our Paloma Blanca, huh?"

"Of course not."

"Keep telling yourself that."

Ignacio rubbed the ring on his finger in circles, suddenly feeling uncomfortable.

"She sure is a shining star, that one," the tailor said.

She was. But not for the reasons the tailor and that ringmaster might have thought. Esmeralda's soul, her presence, her fragile but brilliant heart—that was where her magic lay. But getting to see her truly was like chipping away at granite.

The tailor snapped his fingers. "I have just the costume for you." He beckoned Ignacio to follow, which was exactly what he hoped for.

Trailing the tailor into a small office at the back of his tent, Ignacio asked, "How long have you been part of the carnival?"

"Six months," the tailor answered. He started perusing the racks of garments.

Ignacio had changed his life six months ago as well. "What made you join?" he asked.

"I had gotten myself into a pinch in my hometown. Since King Amadeo decreed all prisoners under eighty be sent to war, I figured I should make myself scarce."

"That first night I came, how did you know about my officer's badge?"

"It was easy to spot. All you law keepers have the same sort of air about you." He tapped his face. "It's in the nose. Your type always has their noses stuck high in the sky." He continued with his costume search.

"Do you see many officers enter the carnival?"

The tailor snorted. "Only the incompetent ones. No offense."

"There was an officer here last night," Ignacio said, keeping his tone light. "I believe she—"

"Ah!" The tailor snatched a garment bag from the rack. "This will do perfectly." He spun around and shoved it into Ignacio's chest. "This is exactly what you need."

Whatever was inside was hidden behind the brownish tint of the bag.

"That will be twenty silvers," the tailor said. He held out his palm.

"Costumes aren't included for carnival staff?" Ignacio asked.

The tailor whooped an obnoxious laugh. "Nothing's free here. Everything costs somebody something."

"I . . . I don't have any money." Ignacio stepped deeper into the tailor's back room. There wasn't much to it. A large table, a mannequin, an elaborate-looking sewing contraption, a standing mirror off in the corner made from the same dark glass he'd seen in the Big Top. He thought of that face within the mirror. Of the accident. The blood staining his hands as he rushed Pilar to the healer's tent.

He tore his gaze away and said, "About the officer that visited last night."

"If you don't pay, then I don't have nothing to say," the tailor declared in a singsong fashion. He snatched the garment bag out of Ignacio's grasp. "I definitely don't have anything to say about a certain tall and rather bossy creature who entered my fine tent last evening."

"I told you that I don't have any money." Ignacio's gaze flicked to the dark mirror. He swore he saw a shadow lurking within.

"Then how about that ring?" the tailor suggested. "I've been eyeing it since you arrived. Are those little gemstones inside it obsidian, by chance?"

Ignacio clutched his hand protectively. It was all he had left of his mother. The ring meant everything to him. So much so, that he only dared give it to one other person as an offering of his deepest love.

But what did that matter if he could barter it and learn something that might help the Defiant's cause? And then there were the mirrors, the ink, the accidents happening with the carnival too. He needed to find his information and get away before something else terrible happened. His mother had been an esteemed commander. She loved her country. She would have done whatever it took to end this farce of a war.

It was decided, then. The tailor was his only lead. Ignacio started to tug the ring free.

"Whatever's in that garment bag shouldn't be more than five silvers and you know it, Jorge."

Ignacio's head snapped toward the entrance. Esmeralda stood before him in the costume she'd worn last night. It was a form-fitting one-piece with silver and purple tufts of feathers on her shoulders and hips. The entirety of her legs was showing. Her mass of thick black hair hung in gentle waves down her back.

"What are you trying to sell him?" she asked, sauntering deeper into the tent to join them.

Jorge stepped forward excitedly. "Only the most perfect costume for your new beau. It's going to match yours splendidly."

She didn't argue about the title Jorge had given him like Ignacio expected. Instead, she dug her fingers into her hair and pulled out a small pouch.

He almost laughed. She still kept her coins tucked away inside her curls.

"I'll pay you five silvers for it," she said, her expression uncharacteristically neutral.

"Fifteen," Jorge countered.

"Six. You're a genius designer and seamster. You can make these costumes in your sleep. And that bag has been hanging there since before you even got here."

The tailor whispered to Ignacio, "Hell of a haggler, this one." Jorge thrust his hand out. "Deal."

Regret crossed her face as she placed the silvers into the tailor's palm.

"Whatever is inside, it had better be good," she said.

"Have I disappointed you yet, doll?" Jorge asked.

"Everyone does eventually." She grabbed the garment bag and thrust it toward Ignacio before taking his wrist. Her bare skin against his made his insides flip. She tried to tug him toward the exit, but he wasn't finished with Jorge yet.

"Wait." He turned to face the tailor. But Jorge was gone. "What? How?"

"You're in Carnival Fantástico, remember? People are always disappearing and reappearing, even if you don't ask them to. Besides, Jorge is the biggest swindler of us all. He probably wasn't going to tell you anything anyway. The man's wanted up and down the coast, and not for nothing."

Ignacio cursed.

"Anyway, I desperately need your help."

"Again?"

"Don't get cocky now."

"Why should I help you when you didn't even meet your end of the bargain after I helped you with the ostrich cage?"

"I told you me, Gabriel, and Ángel are innocent. Surely, that counts for something."

His eyes narrowed. "The jury is still out on that."

Irritation flashed over her features, but then she schooled them. She batted her lashes prettily and offered a beaming grin.

"What are you up to, Dovie?"

"You mean what are *we* up to."

She pulled Ignacio through Clown Alley and into the Backyard—the backstage dressing area that butted up against the Big Top.

Music was thumping through the tent. The march of showstoppers was already starting.

Dozens of performers were lined up inside the cramped space that smelled of sweat and overly sweet perfume. Some performers jogged in place and stretched, readying to join in on the procession. A few people greased themselves down with oils that made their skin glisten. Some helped each other dress while gossiping about whatever had transpired that day.

A few stayed back. Paco the Fire Breather sat on the ground with his legs crossed. His eyes were closed, and he was chanting something under his breath. There were others lounging on settees. Ignacio recognized them as the other acts still competing in the Running.

They passed by performers sitting before lit-up mirrors applying ample amounts of makeup. These mirrors were nothing like the ones that winked down at him when he entered the Big Top or the ones that lined the interior walls of it. These appeared to simply be mirrors, thankfully.

"I need to tell you something, and you're going to think it's strange," he said as he and Esmeralda entered a dressing room.

"Don't be angry when I judge you for it," she replied.

Ignacio licked his lips, suddenly nervous. "Have you ever seen a face inside the mirrors in the Big Top?"

"That's sort of the point of them." She stopped him and took the garment bag. "Take off your clothes," she ordered. "And do it quickly. It took me ages to find you. The march of showstoppers only lasts ten minutes, so hurry."

"Pardon?"

She shook the bag. "I'm putting you in this."

"But I don't want to wear it."

"Why were you planning on buying a costume if you weren't going to wear it?"

"I was trying to get intel from the tailor."

"A pity that didn't work." She unzipped the bag. "Now take off your shirt and pants."

He started to because he was so used to taking people's orders, but he stopped himself after he had already unfastened half his buttons. "Wait. What are you up to?"

"*We* are about to perform in the most important show of my life."

Ignacio balked. "That is the absolute last thing I'm doing."

"Don't be so uptight."

"I'm not." He peered over his shoulder at the doorway. The line of performers waiting to enter the Big Top had cleared, but still, he didn't want to say this for anyone else to hear. He edged closer to Esmeralda and watched with curious fascination as her breathing quickened. As her pupils grew wide. If he didn't know better, he might have let himself believe she was hungry for his presence.

Warmth spread through his insides as she tilted her head up to him. He loved that he towered over her. That from this angle, he could see every part of her so clearly. His knuckles ached to brush against the soft curvature of her jawbone.

This isn't what you're here for.

He cleared his throat. "There is something terribly off about this place. The ink—"

Her shoulders slumped. "Not the ink again."

"But there's some sort of property inside it. I saw it when Anella—"

"Was that before or after she kissed you?"

"Does that matter?" *Did it? Did she care about the kiss? No. That wasn't important right now.* "I saw it again right before the Sánchezes' accident. That same glinting material was in their cuffs."

Horns blared from within the Big Top. The guests roared with thunderous applause.

“Can we talk about this later?” she asked.

“But I *saw* something before the sisters’ accident. A . . . a face within the mirror. It looked evil.”

“Perhaps I hit you in the head with that golden egg a bit too hard.”

“You know me, Dovie. I’m not the type to come up with fanciful tales. That was always your thing.”

And he had loved her for it. He adored the stories she would weave into the night sky. Had he a better imagination, he might have pictured her tales come to life within the stars. But his brain did not work that way. His mother’s had, but Ignacio’s mind worked in facts, and rules, and kept all the information stored in their proper places.

“I know what I saw,” he said. “There is something inside the mirrors.”

“Then being out in front of them is the perfect place to be. Think of it. How else will you get a better view but from center stage?”

“It isn’t the vantage point that concerns me. It’s you.”

Her lips parted in surprise.

Elephants blared their trunks. Explosions went off, the beams holding the tent up rattling from the repercussions. He stepped even closer, close enough that only the garment bag lay between them, so she could hear him clearly.

“I have a terrible feeling about this place,” he said. “I know it sounds outrageous, but that thing in the mirror smiled just before Camila’s wrist snapped.”

“Come on, Ignacio. Scary stories have never deterred me.

Your little tale isn't going to work. Especially not when my own reality is far scarier." The music quickened within the Big Top. The drums grew faster. Greedier. She chewed on her lip. "Time's up. What do you say?"

"I won't go."

She huffed. "Of course not. Wouldn't be the first time you failed to come through for me."

Her words slammed into his chest. He had failed her. She just admitted it. She thought he'd failed her before. That must have been why she left him. But what had he done?

Had it been the last night they spent together a year ago? Was he terrible? It had been his first time having sex, hers too, but he'd been so nervous, he fumbled his way through. Or was it the day after? When he learned he'd been enlisted into the Blackbirds. She begged him to run away with her instead. He'd hesitated. Who wouldn't have? She asked him to turn his back on everything he'd ever known.

She started to storm away, but he threw his hand out and snatched her arm. "Wait."

"I can't. Not anymore. I have to go on."

"Why is the Running so important to you? Why do you insist on performing when you know it's dangerous? Your friend is having surgery on her ruptured spleen as we speak."

"It's this or death," she snapped. "Because I won't go back to a cold cell."

He flinched. "When were you in a cell?"

Esmeralda gaped. "You don't know?"

"Know what?"

She glared at the wall. "I was caught fleeing the city by your father's officers just after you left for the Blackbirds. I spent two months in the dark trying to claw my way out of prison like a fool."

The world spun in on him. His father had thrown her in jail and left her there alone. To rot.

Commotion sounded outside the room. Performers were already starting to funnel backstage from the march of show-stoppers. Esmeralda gnawed on her bottom lip so hard, he worried she might start to bleed. Before he could stop himself, he brushed his thumb over her lip to stop her nervous nibbling. She inhaled sharply, and a sun flare burst in his stomach.

She stepped away. "Staying on with the carnival is my only hope of being free. You know your father won't let me get away again. Especially not after I turned my nose up at General Keara's offer. And I won't be able to earn enough to purchase passage out of the country in the two months I have left."

It all made sense now. Why she would be so desperate to stay here. It wasn't because she was terrified of what Father might do. It was because she had already faced him and come out scarred.

Another awful thought came to his mind. "You won't have two months if you don't win," he said.

She frowned, confused.

"I was there when Anella was eliminated," he explained. "The ringmaster told her she had to leave that day. He said he couldn't let someone he found unworthy continue on at the carnival."

"Ángel mentioned he cut the Sánchezes, but he didn't say anything about them having to leave right away." Her tone gave the impression she didn't believe Ignacio.

"What about the previous Runnings?" he asked. "What happened to the eliminated performers?"

"I don't know. Melanie was already the lead act when I got here." Her jaw dropped. "But, now that I think of it, no one spoke of competing against her."

"Because those people were most likely kicked out. The termination letter from Ángel was coldhearted. I wouldn't put it past him to send your friends packing as soon as Pilar is out of surgery."

"So, if I fail tonight, I might be asked to leave?" She gnawed on her lip again.

The thought of Father or Keara catching her drew the very worst sort of picture in his mind. And there wouldn't be anything he could do to help her. She had to keep performing. But what about that thing in the mirror? He couldn't let her face it alone.

"I'll help you," he said.

She sighed with relief. And then, she did the very worst thing he could imagine. She threw her arms around him, the garment bag crunching between them as she squeezed him with all her strength.

Ignacio's entire body went taut.

"Thank you," she whispered into his neck.

He clamped his eyes shut.

She felt so good against him. She felt like his childhood. Like home. Like all his wildest dreams and desires trapped within the softness of her skin.

Life was so cruel, he knew that he couldn't spend most of his moments like this. He'd never be able to simply hold her and love her and be loved by her in return.

She released him and stepped back, a warm grin brightening her beautiful face.

"Now," she said. "Take off your clothes."

CHAPTER 29
Esmeralda

Her heart thundered like the drums rumbling inside the Big Top. She'd never performed in front of so many people, and she had never actually executed the act she planned to show off. Sure, she was a great climber, and the aerialists had shown her a thing or two in her time with the carnival, but messing around and performing in front of thousands were completely different things.

And then there was the young man standing to her right. She peeked at him through her lashes. Let her eyes roam over his tall form, every beautiful angle of his face illuminated by the Big Top lights bleeding through the backstage curtains. He'd always been the most handsome boy in every room. These days? He was too striking for words, currently sporting a perfectly cut suit in colors that complemented her dove costume, wearing a mask made of pearly-white feathers that popped against his coppery-brown skin. His shorn hair had grown out ever so slightly, only making him more appealing to her.

"What's your plan?" he whispered. They stood behind the other competitors in the Running.

She knew he'd hate her plan, so she said, "I will do everything. All you need to do is hold on."

"To what?"

The drums quieted to a hum. Audience members joined in, patting their hands against their laps.

The ringmaster's voice blared through a loud-hailer. "And now, friends, fans, and fiends, it is my honor to announce the final six acts in the Running to become my next lead!"

Cheers rang out.

"We have Paco the Fire Breather!" he bellowed.

The audience applauded as Paco ran out, waving his glistening arms to the crowd.

"The Flying Córdovas—the only family to perform triple somersaults on a single tightrope."

The trapeze artists ran out. Two of the siblings still limped from their run-in with Estefan.

Ángel listed the three other performers—Benicio the Bear Trainer, David the Knife Thrower, and Nicola the Escape Artist—but Esmeralda hardly paid them any attention. Everything in her body had gone numb and fuzzy. Her pulse pounded in her ears. Her fingers tingled with anticipation.

You can't do this, a sour voice in her mind said. *You will fail. You aren't good enough. You aren't worthy enough to move to the final challenge. And then you'll be thrown out and left to the wolves.*

"Hey," Ignacio said calmly. Her head shot up. "I've got you. *You* got you too."

"Allow me to introduce to the Big Top for the very first time, La Paloma Blanca and her starry-eyed companion, Paloma Amor!"

The crowd went wild. That was her cue, but her knees wouldn't move. She thought she might be sick. Ignacio took her hand in his and squeezed it tight. The act nearly brought her to tears. He'd done that sometimes when they sat on his rooftop. Whenever her thoughts would roam to her family and the scars they'd left on her heart.

He sneered. "The ringmaster just called me your love dove."

Esmeralda snorted, and her tension eased a bit.

"Come on." He tugged her out of the backstage area. "I believe in you, Dovie."

"You do?"

He seemed startled by her question. "There's no one I believe in more."

She balked, caught completely off guard.

The spotlight swiveled toward them and burned into her already flush skin. The heat of thousands of eyes seared into her soul.

"Paloma! Paloma! Paloma!"

All these people were rooting for her. They wanted to see her.

She beamed and waved the hand that wasn't still holding on to Ignacio. The audience roared. The sound rushed through every empty and broken part of her. She once thought Ignacio's presence was all she needed to feel whole. But she'd been wrong. *This.* This noise. The screams. The people calling her name. This was what she needed to fill the void. To quiet all the wretched thoughts and memories swirling inside her mind.

She waved harder as they walked toward the center ring. The hanging hoop she planned to use was slowly rotating beyond Paco's podium. She led Ignacio to the hoop and released him. With a flick of her wrist, she brushed her feather bustle out of the way and took a seat.

"What do you want me to do?" Ignacio asked.

"I'll let you know when the time comes."

"And what about right now?"

She chewed on her lip. "I was told earlier today that I should use whatever we have—or had—to excite the audience. I need you to play the part of longing lover. Gaze at me as if I am the only girl in the world."

He scoffed. "That's ridiculous."

"Please."

After a moment, he sighed. He gripped the ring on either side of her and frowned down at her. "How's this?" he asked.

"You look like I poured salt in your tea. Try harder," she ordered.

Ignacio pressed closer to her. His eyes roamed over her face like soft kisses. "Better?"

Her pulse quickened. "Not quite."

He brushed a knuckle down her cheek.

"Will this do?" he asked.

Her insides turned to mush.

"Yes. You . . . um . . . you play the part well."

He huffed bitterly. "When have you ever known me to be an actor?"

"What are you trying to say?" she asked.

"I could never fake how I look at you. I'm not like you in that way."

Her lips parted with surprise. "What does that mean?"

"I saw your reaction in the wagon when Keara mentioned my love for you. You looked . . . repulsed."

That wasn't what she had been reacting to. General Keara had almost made it sound as if she had known Esmeralda was within the carnival all along. The thought had rattled her to her very core. It made her feel as if she hadn't actually escaped. Like the comandante was toying with her, just waiting for her term to end so he could strike.

"Had it always been a lie, Dovie? Did you ever want me? Or were you . . . were you using me to . . . I don't know . . . to help pass the time? Before you went on to bigger and better?"

"How could you say such a thing? Besides, I wasn't even the one to start our friendship. You did."

"You're right. It was always me. Always me pursuing you. Fighting for you. Coming to you. But it was never enough. *I* wasn't—" He clamped his lips shut. But she'd already understood what he was going to say.

He thought he wasn't enough for her.

She barked a laugh, and his face fell. She hadn't meant to. But of all the absurd things for him to say, *that* had not been on her list. He was Ignacio Olivera! The kindest, smartest, most genuine boy she'd ever known.

"You're laughing at me," he said quietly. "Why are you always so cruel?"

She recoiled. "I'm not. Maybe you need to toughen up."

"Maybe you should learn to have a heart." He gripped the hoop tighter. "What did I do to you to make you so—"

The ringmaster's voice cut through their exchange. "The performers have two minutes to wow you, dear audience. And I need to hear your screams. I need to know which act you want to see more of!"

"Get behind me," she snapped.

"I'm so tired of being interrupted by everyone and everything." Ignacio grumbled but shoved off the hoop and stomped around to the back of her. He grasped the ring on either side, just above her own hands. "Now what?"

She sucked in a breath. "I nearly forgot the biggest part of my plan."

She released her hold on the hoop and dug into her bodice, pulling out the gloves she'd been gifted. Soft fabric slid over her skin as she put them on. That buzzing sensation she'd felt when she first wore the gloves fizzled up her arms.

"Take those off," Ignacio hissed, his lips next to her ear. Chills pricked over her skin like raindrops.

"Fat chance." She held her arms before her with a flourish, knowing the audience might be watching. The stitching of doves in flight glinted like magic. "These are my only hope of getting to the final challenge."

"Camila wore cuffs with that very same stitching the night of the accident," he said.

"Don't talk about accidents right now. That's bad luck."

"You have to take those off," he urged. "That thing I saw in the mirror. It smiled and then Camila's cuffs started to sparkle."

"Because they're made from glistening thread, genius."

"Dovie, *please*. Trust me."

"Like you trusted me when I told you your father was a fiend a year ago?"

The music began. She only had two minutes to impress Ángel.

"Quickly, stand on the hoop," she ordered. "Put your feet on either side of me, but don't step on my costume. I couldn't bear it if it got dirty."

Cursing, Ignacio did as he was asked, the hoop shifting under his weight.

Esmeralda's nerves dipped to her knees as the ring started to rise from the ground. Once the tips of her toes left the floor, they began to spin in slow rotations.

"What did you get me into?" he growled.

"Just smile," she said through her teeth. "Always smile."

When they were halfway between the ground and the peak of the Big Top, she said, "I want you to slowly lower yourself to a seated position."

"How? Your tail feathers are taking up all the room."

Shakily, she slid one of her arms up so she could clutch the top of the ring. She held on tight and released the other hand so she could take hold of the feathers draped from the back of her costume and place them over the front of her thighs.

"Better?" she asked.

He made a noncommittal sound. "Where do you want me to sit?"

The aerialists had made this look so much easier than what it really was.

"Put your legs on either side of me. I'll lift myself up and then sit on your lap."

"That isn't a good idea." His tone was stiff. Perhaps the heights were rattling his nerves. But they had both climbed up trees when they were young. The rooftop they'd always sit on was not as high as they were now, but it was close.

"Just do it, please. I only have two minutes to perform."

She raised her other arm and gripped the top of the hoop. She pulled herself up as much as her muscles would allow as he lowered himself down. When he was seated, she eased her bottom onto his lap.

She fit so perfectly against him. As if the curves of her body had been built to mold into his like a puzzle.

"What now?" he asked, his voice strained.

She tilted her head back and met his gaze. The air grew thick between them. And for a second, the world faded away as they spun in slow circles. Her gaze flicked to his lips. Would they be as soft as she remembered? Would they make her insides melt like before?

"Dovie."

His voice snapped her back into reality.

"Hold perfectly still," she ordered. "And keep your toes pointed up. I'm going to attempt to do something rather risky."

"I hate the sound of that."

His warm breath brushed across her neck. The sensation made the hairs on her arms stand on end. Good thing they were hidden away by the gloves.

"Keep steady and I won't fall to my death."

"What?!"

With all the flare she could muster, she scooted off his lap.

The audience gasped, but she did not fall. She had slid her body down the length of Ignacio's long legs and caught herself from plummeting to her doom by wrapping her underarms around his ankles.

She dangled in midair.

People stood on their feet and applauded. But not all. Many were still watching the other acts perform. She had to do better.

She flicked her fingers like she'd seen the ringmaster do countless times. The cards she'd tucked inside her gloves fanned out like a bouquet of flowers. She closed her eyes and overdramatically shouted, "Spirits, guide me." When she opened her eyes, she tucked in her legs so the hoop wove in circles. She made a great show of searching through the audience. She gasped like she'd been touched by her spirits and pointed at a tall woman dressed as a giraffe.

"You have been chosen!" Esmeralda bellowed.

She released one of her cards. It folded itself as it fluttered in the air, taking the shape of a paper dove.

"The spirits wish to show you what great fortunes lie ahead!" Esmeralda yelled.

The dove darted downward, flapping its little wings toward

the woman. The audience pointed and exclaimed their excitement as the paper bird swooped low and then fluttered around the woman's head.

"Grab it!" someone in the crowd hollered.

The woman did so, and the dove flattened into a single card. The woman's mouth dropped into the shape of an O. "It's a drawing of a storefront with my name on the sign," she cried. "This is what I've always wanted!"

Esmeralda kicked her legs once more and spun herself and Ignacio about. She repeated the act again. This time to a man sporting a lollipop mask. More people in the crowd took notice. They watched with anticipation as the dove flew into the man's awaiting palm.

He waved the flattened card in the air. "It's a depiction of twins!" He turned and kissed the man in a matching lollipop mask.

"I want my fortune told!" someone yelled.

"Me too!"

"No. Me!"

"Give us more!"

One by one, she released the cards in her hand.

"Paloma! Paloma! Paloma!"

Esmeralda's heart swelled. They loved her.

She flicked her wrists, producing more cards. The enchanted gloves warmed against her skin. Almost *too* warm.

Smiling through her discomfort, she sent more paper doves flying.

The crowd jumped and climbed onto each other's shoulders

like a ravenous horde. But they were laughing and whistling and calling her name. Everyone in the audience was looking at her now. She was doing it. She was going to pass this challenge.

But the gloves were starting to burn into her skin. And her underarms were throbbing. Surely, Ignacio's ankles were too.

Yet around and around they spun. The hoop began to whirl faster than she wanted. She couldn't stop it. The audience below blurred. Dizziness tugged at her consciousness.

She forced her gaze upward to focus on the tent roof, but that was when she saw it. A horrifying face peered through the dark mirrors that hung from the rafters. It looked like an old clay mask. Fractures and cracks littered its strange skin. The thing had a ruddy nose, a sneering grin, and glowing eyes that whirled like a spinning top.

"Pigeon," she cried out. "Look toward the rafters."

"Shit," Ignacio exclaimed.

Her gloves sizzled viciously into her skin, and she sucked in air through her teeth.

"What's wrong?" he asked.

"I have to get these gloves off." Desperate, she bit into the fingertip of her glove and tried to tug it free. Her jerky motions nearly sent her sliding off Ignacio's ankles.

"Hold still, Dovie. I'm going to lift you back up," Ignacio said calmly.

"I can't!" She squirmed. "Everything burns!"

"You can do it. You're so strong. Stronger than you realize."

The pain was searing. She gritted her teeth and groaned.

"Just focus on my voice, okay? Listen to what I'm saying. I'm going to lift my legs up. All you need to do is try and reach up and grab hold of the hoop. Can you do that?"

Could she? Could she do anything but drown in nausea and blazing heat?

"I'm going to lift you now."

He grunted. The laces of his boots dug into her armpits. It was a welcome distraction.

"Raise your arms, Dovie."

She did. His legs squeezed her, holding her in place so she wouldn't slip. But she couldn't find the hoop. Oh gods, she was going to faint. Or retch.

"Tilt your arms back," he commanded. "You can do this."

She did as she was told. Her knuckles grazed the ring. But she couldn't quite grasp on to it. Ignacio grunted again. He lifted her a tiny bit higher. Her fingers wrapped around the ring. A shock of pure agony tore through her veins.

A strong arm cinched around her waist and jerked her back. They wobbled for a second. The crowd gasped in terror.

This is it, she thought. *I've killed us both.*

But Ignacio held her tight to his body. His other hand was clenched above their heads, right next to her own hands.

They both panted as they spun. She wanted to cry from the dizziness, and her arms felt as if they were boiling from the inside out.

"Smile," Ignacio whispered into her ear. "You must continue performing or the ringmaster will disqualify you."

Despite her anguish, she did what he said.

"Keep your act going," he added.

She let more cards fly. With each flick of her wrist, the gloves burned hotter. Her only comfort was the feel of her back against his solid chest. His strong arm holding her in place.

"Thirty more seconds!" The ringmaster's voice boomed throughout the tent. "Shout out your favorite act!"

The audience exploded with praise for the doves.

Someone shrieked. Then a flash of orange light exploded upward. And the spot where Paco once stood was now completely engulfed in flames.

CHAPTER 30
Ignacio

The fire brigade stormed the tent and doused the inferno.

Esmeralda whimpered.

He held her tighter to him. "We're almost done, but don't stop smiling. Just picture yourself far away from here."

She turned her head away from the sputtering flames.

"Where has your mind taken you to?" he asked.

"To a sleepy meadow."

"And what's in the meadow?"

"Fragrant flowers and fat-bottomed bumblebees."

"Try saying that five times in a row," he whispered.

He felt her chuckle against him, and he couldn't help but smile.

"Time is up!" the ringmaster announced, as if nothing terrible was happening.

The hoop suddenly stopped spinning, and Esmeralda let out a relieved sigh.

As they slowly made their descent back to solid ground,

Ignacio watched the carnival hands cart what was left of Paco the Fire Breather away.

"Thank you for helping me keep my mind in check," she said softly. "How did you learn that trick?"

"I had a hard time sleeping while I was with the Blackbirds. I used to close my eyes and picture better times. Before long I'd drift off *with* a smile on my face."

"What times did you picture?"

He sighed and rested his cheek on her hair. "Every time I was with you."

She went silent.

He was terrified she would only offer some snarky retort, but he realized he couldn't let the fear of how she'd react stop him anymore. He needed to tell her how he felt. How she made him feel. Even if what she said in the aftermath hurt like hell.

Yet, he couldn't force his lips to work.

She was the one to break the silence. "What was that thing in the mirror?" She whispered the words as if the creature might hear her.

"I have no clue," he replied.

There was something nibbling at Ignacio's thoughts. A phantom memory he couldn't grab hold of. It had been like that since the ringmaster told him about the Valerio brothers. He'd heard their tale before. Someone else had told him about a portal to the gods. But he couldn't for the life of him remember who had mentioned such things in his past.

His eyes scanned the mirrors that surrounded the tent. But the monster was gone.

The spotlights moved away from the fire brigade and beamed onto Veracruz, who stood on top a circular platform. He raised his arm and yelled into the loud-hailer, "Do you see the dangers my performers face?! It is all for you, folks! For our glorious, most astounding, most wonderous fans of Carnival Fantástico!"

The audience roared with a ferocity Ignacio had never seen. The backstage flaps opened, and rodeo riders galloped in, performing tricks on top their horses' backs.

The ringmaster was not exaggerating when he proclaimed the show must always continue. One of his acts had just perished, and yet he so mercilessly moved on to the next. His performers were willing to do it too. They were willing to risk everything for the safety he offered. What a horrible sort of power he held over their heads.

The hoop was finally low enough to the ground that they could safely dismount, but Ignacio couldn't let Esmeralda go. This could be the last time they were so close, and he couldn't stand it. He wanted to bury his nose into her hair. To breathe in so deep, the scent of jasmine would cling to his lungs forever. Then, at least, she would always be a part of him.

But sinister happenings were afoot.

Regretting it already, he loosened his hold so she could step out of his embrace.

She faced him and tore off the gloves. She shook her head as she examined her arms. "From the pain I experienced, I thought my skin would be gone."

He swiped his thumb over her wrist and found those damn iridescent flecks that made up the enchanted ink. He wiped his hand on his pants and inspected her more thoroughly but found no burns or injuries.

"Are you okay, though?" he asked.

"Normally, I'd lie and say yes, but my nerves are too frazzled for that. And, worst of all, I fear I must admit that you were right."

Despite everything, he felt himself smiling again. "I don't think I heard you correctly. What did you say?"

"Don't push it, Pigeon."

"I told you that you could trust me," he said.

"Yeah, the jury is still out on that." Her warm fingers slipped into his hand.

His insides clenched. "What are you doing?"

"I'm taking you to the one place where we might find our answers."

The ringmaster's wagon was far outside the carnival hub and not intended for customers *or* uninvited performers trying to sneak in. Three guards lounged in front of the strawberry-red wagon, smoking cigarillos and speaking about what had happened to Paco. They made light of the fire breather's misfortune. They laughed and chattered on about who would get his prized game boards now that he was gone.

From their hidden place behind barrels of sugar, Ignacio's hands balled into fists.

Esmeralda's brow quirked. "Thinking about getting into a fight?" she whispered.

"I'd sure like to."

"Hold that thought, hero. The ratas aren't the sort to mess with. I've seen them get into scuffles a time or two with ill-mannered guests, and it never ended well for the other guys. Besides, you'll cause a commotion, and we don't want that if we're trying to sneak into the ringmaster's office." She jerked her chin to the right. "This way."

They slithered around bins of extra prizes, clusters of oddly shaped balloons bumping into each other in the breeze, and roller-coaster buggies in need of repair. "It's like a circus graveyard," he said as they hid behind a marionette booth.

"Ángel doesn't like to leave things behind, unlike some people."

"If that's meant to be a slight, I feel like you're being rather hypocritical. Seeing as you left the ring I gave you behind when you ran away. Why didn't you take it? I gave it to you," he asked. "You could have pawned it off for a good profit." The question had been burning on his tongue since the day she left him and he found the ring placed inside the box that he had kept his savings in.

"Now isn't the time to dig up things dead and buried," she snapped.

"But they aren't dead or buried. Not for me."

"Do you really think I'd want anything of yours once I heard what you said?" She turned to him so quickly that he nearly ran her over.

Ignacio reeled back, and his foot crushed down on something soft and foamy. A jubilant squeak trumpeted from under his boot. It was a clown's red nose. He winced. He wasn't so clumsy normally, but Esmeralda did this to him. She unnerved him.

"Did you hear that?" one of the guards standing in front of the ringmaster's wagon said.

Esmeralda grabbed Ignacio's hand. They dashed forward toward the rear of the wagon, but the guards were already running through the discarded bins with their flashlights aimed ahead.

"We have nowhere to hide," she whispered.

"Over there!" a rata called.

Ignacio had to do something quickly. He pushed Esmeralda against a pile of crates. He pressed his body close and lowered his face, so they were nose to nose.

"What are you doing?" she hissed. "You're going to get us caught."

"We already *are* caught. They're only yards away. Now, put your arms around me as if we're lovers."

"You can't be serious!"

A stream of golden light hovered above their heads from the guards' flashlights.

Ignacio grabbed one of her hands and flung it around his torso. The light found them. Their shadows danced onto the crates like reveling ghosts.

"Hey!" someone shouted.

Ignacio ignored it. If he were truly Esmeralda's lover, he most certainly would. He scooted closer, shielding her with his body. He moved his head from side to side, mimicking a kiss.

She rolled her eyes. "You're going to have to be more convincing than that."

Her free hand grasped his collar, and she yanked him down. Their lips crashed together. Teeth scraped against soft skin.

But the pain was numbed by the explosion blazing within his soul.

The world fizzled away. He heard nothing. Hell, he couldn't even tell if his feet were still on the ground. There was only the taste of Esmeralda. Only the familiar fullness of her lips. And the hungry ache in his chest.

His fingers splayed out on the crate on either side of her head. His nails dug into the wood, holding him steady. Esmeralda's hand slid up his back. The sensation of her touch sent a sunburst flaring inside his stomach and he groaned into her mouth.

She sighed, her breath mingling with his.

Their movements became ravenous as if they'd both been starved for far too long.

Despite his best efforts at self-control, his fingers slid into her hair, and he pulled her to him. Something metallic fell to the ground and her curls fluttered over her shoulders. He breathed her in.

"Stars, you smell good," he whispered. His lips found her neck, the sensitive skin just under her ear, her jawbone. She moaned. And he thought his knees might give out from the sound.

"Hey!"

A voice from behind him slammed Ignacio into reality.

"You two can't be out here. This area is for carnival staff only," the rata said.

He and Esmeralda tore apart then. They stood there, staring at each other in the dark, panting uncontrollably.

A flashlight beamed in Ignacio's face, and the guard gawked. "It's the palomas," he said in wonder.

The Palomas. As if they were one.

A smile tugged at the rata's lips. "Looks like you finally made up." He rubbed the back of his neck. "Perhaps you love birds should take this elsewhere, though?"

"Sure," Esmeralda said breathily. "Yes. Of course."

She looked troubled. Ignacio's gut dropped. Did she not enjoy the kiss? Did she not want it like he had? Had she been playing a part the whole time? The way she desperately gripped him certainly felt real.

Her fingers slid into Ignacio's. "We'll be on our way. Sorry to be a pest."

The rata chuckled. "Nah. It's no bother." He jerked his chin toward the main hub of the carnival. "Go on now." As he turned to head back to his post, Ignacio jolted. The man's ear! A bit of the cartilage had been sliced off like a V. He was a Blackbird. Only true officers of his father's army had their ears nicked in this manner.

Ignacio fought the urge to cover his face, but most people outside of his father's direct circle had no clue what the son of Comandante Olivera looked like. Besides their size and jawline, Ignacio looked nothing like his father. Father was pale-skinned, with light brown hair and blue eyes. Ignacio was not. On top of that, photographs of him had been wiped from all news sources and military ledgers. Insiders told the Defiant his father had done it. He was so embarrassed of Ignacio's desertion that he tried to make it as if Ignacio had never existed.

Esmeralda tugged him away from the ringmaster's wagon. After a moment, she whispered, "Is the guard looking?"

He peeked over his shoulder. "No. I don't see him. He must be back at his position in the front of the wagon."

"Good. Let's run for it."

On silent feet, they swept toward the back door of the wagon and slid inside. They stood there in the dark. The lights of the carnival filtered in, illuminating her beautiful face. Her lips were swollen from his kisses.

What would she do if I tried to kiss her again? he wondered.

"What should we be looking for?" she whispered.

Right. They weren't there for kisses.

"Anything to help us understand what is happening inside the carnival. Confirmed correspondence between the ringmaster and my father would be nice too," he said.

Esmeralda moved to one side of the ringmaster's messy desk. He to the other. He couldn't risk touching her. Not when they had to be stealthy. Not when they were alone, and every nerve in his body was screaming for him to take her in his arms and kiss her until the world ended.

He had to calm down. To remember what he was doing and why he was there.

He rifled through crunched-up papers and sticky receipts, through vendor earnings, production costs, and supply demands. The desk had no order whatsoever, and it drove Ignacio mad.

Esmeralda frowned as she shuffled through dozens of small cards.

"You were right again," she whispered. "People are betting

on who will be the main act. And . . ." She pointed at a list with a string of tally marks. "This one has an option for people to guess which performer will suffer an accident next. They're betting on our demise." She shook her head. "The ringmaster is certainly savvy. He knows how to draw in a crowd."

"*That* is your reaction to this? You give the man praise even though the gloves he gave you nearly ended you. Are you that obsessed with him?"

"At least *he* sees potential in me."

"Are you trying to say that I never did?"

"Oh please, Ignacio. All you ever cared about was being perfect. Look how far that got you. You're as much a criminal as me now."

"I'm trying to make things right. I don't run away like some selfish . . ." His brain couldn't come up with anything. He had no barbs to fling at her. How could he when his lips still tingled with the taste of hers. "You're selfish. That is all."

"You knew that about me from the first day we met."

"I never thought of you that way. You were a kid trying to survive. There's nothing selfish about that."

Her lips flattened. "You just said I was selfish."

"Well . . . yes . . . you've changed."

"Being thrown in a jail cell will do that to a person."

"And so will going to war," he snapped back.

"That settles things, doesn't it? We've both changed for the worse."

Fuming, Ignacio yanked open a drawer, then stopped. Even in the dimly lit room, he recognized his father's telltale penmanship. Every letter was capitalized and sharp.

Esmeralda must have recognized his father's handwriting too. She snatched up the note. Her expression darkened.

"I have been lenient with your antics long enough," she read. *"Release my son to me unharmed or suffer the consequences."* Her brows pinched together. "Your father clearly knows you are here. But what does he think the ringmaster will do to you?"

"I have no clue. But this proves nothing of my father's guilt. We must keep looking for something more damnable."

The note only made his father seem caring, which was the furthest thing from the truth. He scooted around her to look at another stack of paper. His torso brushed against her back, and he swore he heard her draw in a sharp breath. He bumped into a small table he didn't see in the dark because being within Dovie's orbit made him clumsy. Something clanked onto the floorboards.

Voices sounded from outside.

He and Esmeralda froze as ink bled out from the jar that had fallen. Sparkles of light winked up at him as if a thousand diamonds were trapped inside.

He knelt beside it. Dipped his fingers into the iridescent liquid. His entire hand tingled with a strange burning sensation.

"This is what I've been searching for," he whispered. "It's been with the ringmaster all along. Maybe my father is closer to Veracruz than I thought." He found Esmeralda in the shadows. "You used ink like this last year to write that letter. Did you find it in my father's office?"

"What are you talking about? When did I ever use—"

"I definitely heard something," someone grumbled from right outside the wagon's front door.

Ignacio grabbed the jar. Only a few drops were left inside it. He slipped it into his pocket.

The front door handle started to turn.

Esmeralda clutched Ignacio by the shirt. "Get up, you stubborn mule. We've got to go before we're caught again. Swoony kisses won't save us this time."

CHAPTER 31

Esmeralda

Ignacio left her the second they were out of sight of the ringmaster's wagon, claiming he needed to send correspondence to the Defiant. That was fine. She had things to do herself. Like wallow. Like pontificate. Like replay their kiss in her mind on repeat because it had left her lips raw and hungry for more. Her body had come to life under his touch as if it remembered every place where he had once kissed her, as if it remembered how good he'd made her feel the night he turned eighteen.

She should have known better than to get lost in his embrace. He had betrayed her in the worst sort of way. He had used her and left her after she'd offered him the most intimate parts of herself.

She paused.

That had been almost exactly one year to the day.

"Stars above," she whispered.

"Talking to yourself like usual, I see."

Esmeralda spun around. "Camila?"

"In the flesh." Camila limped out of the shadows. She had bandages wrapped around half her limbs, and her long black hair, which was normally braided and pinned up, fell in a tangled mess down her back. "I'm surprised to see you out here. I figured you'd still be in the Big Top enjoying your debut in the spotlight."

Esmeralda winced.

"I'm not mad at you for wanting to continue in the Running. I know how important all of this"—Camila gestured toward the carnival—"is to you. But why did you stay away? What kind of person doesn't even come to check in on a friend after a ton of marble columns crashed on them?"

Esmeralda's shoulders slumped. "I don't think I know how to be a friend," she admitted. "You don't deserve that, Camila. I don't deserve you. Maybe it's better if I let you have your space."

Camila snorted. "What sort of shitty answer is that? That's not what you should do. Not at all." With a grunt, she lowered herself onto a candy cane–colored bench. "I know you didn't have siblings like I do, or very many relationships for that matter, but let me explain how this works. If you care for someone, and you've done something that hurts them, you don't run away. You do the opposite. You wade through all the discomfort and awkward feelings and face that person head-on and admit you messed up."

Esmeralda toed the dirt. "That sounds absolutely horrible."

"It is." Camila smiled. "But love is horrible." When Esmeralda balked, Camila chuckled. "The people we love can be annoying, and irritating, and sometimes you want to grab them by the ears and scream at their pretty faces."

Esmeralda's nose scrunched.

"*But* I'd take all the aggravations in exchange for having my loved ones with me. Especially after what happened to my sister. We need each other. We gotta stick together because we are a family now." She pointed at Esmeralda. "Whether you like it or not."

Esmeralda didn't warrant this sort of friendship. She'd never done anything to be worthy of Camila. Or Gabriel. Or Pilar. Or Ignacio. She was snappy and rude. She was pushy and sarcastic. She had never been as good to them as they were to her. And that realization made her want to dig herself into a hole.

"We're leaving," Camila said.

Esmeralda's eyes shot to her friend. "So Ángel kicked you out too."

Camila nodded. "He said we could stay on until Pilar is healed, but I refuse to be here for a moment longer than I have to."

They were leaving her. She understood why, but that didn't ease the hurt gathering between her ribs.

"Come with us," Camila said.

Esmeralda blinked. "Me?"

"There are already so many mouths to feed in my grandparents' house. What's one more?"

"But . . . the carnival rules . . . I can't leave before my year is up. And I couldn't anyway because Comandante Olivera knows I'm still in the country."

"Better to face him than what's inside the carnival," Camila grumbled.

"Why do you say that?"

Camila surveyed the area, but there was only the two of them. "Something happened the night of the accident. Remember the cuffs Ángel gave me and Pilar? They . . . This is going to sound nuts, but—"

"They burned."

Camila's light brown skin paled. "How did you know?"

"It happened to me tonight. And maybe to Paco too. He . . . He's . . . he's gone."

A startled gasp came from Camila. She stood, limped forward, and grasped Esmeralda's shoulder with her uninjured hand. "We've got to get out of here before something else happens. Come with us. Please. Your officer can come too for all I care."

"He's not an officer, actually. Turns out Ignacio is also a runaway."

"Then he's one of us."

One of us. *Us.* Esmeralda was part of an *us.*

Even after she'd been nothing but a wretched friend, Camila still wanted her around. Esmeralda's heart squeezed tight in her chest.

Living in a home sounded absolutely lovely. But it was too good to be true. So long as she was wanted by the law, she would never be at peace. She would bring only trouble to the Sánchezes. Ignacio would as well.

"I can't come," she admitted.

"You're in danger, Esmeralda. I think we all are. I was so lost in the magic and enchantments. In the glitter and chaos. But I see through it now. There's darkness here."

Esmeralda thought about that thing watching them from within the black mirrors. Something truly was wrong with this place. But even so, she couldn't put her friends at risk.

"The moment I exit these gates, I'm doomed. And I'll bring you down with me."

But if Ignacio found the evidence he needed to expose the comandante's war crimes, if he took away the power Comandante Olivera had over the country, she might have a shot at a life outside Carnival Fantástico's shimmering enchantments.

"When are you planning on leaving?" she asked.

"As soon as possible. Gabriel is rigging up a motorized chair for Pilar as we speak."

Knowing how clever Gabriel was, she was sure he'd have it ready soon.

"He's coming with us too," Camila said. "Gabriel promised to help me get Pilar home and then he plans to meet up with Javier. He senses something off with this place too."

And it was somehow connected to Comandante Olivera. The ink, that thing in the mirror, the Running, Ángel, General Keara. They were all linked somehow.

"Didn't Gabriel once tell us Javi has connections within the palace?" Esmeralda asked.

"I think so."

"If you see him before I do, have him send word to Javi. Tell Gabriel to ask him to dig around and see if he can find anything fishy about the carnival." Esmeralda spun on her heel and made to leave.

"Wait!" Camila said. She held out her hand. "You're the bee's knees."

Esmeralda grinned. She licked her thumb and pressed it into Camila's palm. "And you're the cat's meow."

Camila's face turned serious. "Promise me you'll come with us. We can face whatever comes together."

"I won't bring my problems to you and your family." Camila started to argue but Esmeralda cut her off. "Which means I have very little time to figure out how to ruin the comandante before it's time for us to go."

Camila's face lit up with surprised relief.

Before she could talk herself out of it, Esmeralda slid her arms around Camila's waist and hugged her as fiercely as she could without adding insult to her already bruised body.

"What's this for?" Camila asked, squeezing Esmeralda tight with her uninjured arm.

"For you not being a shitty friend. For teaching me how not to be shitty too."

Camila's laughter rumbled through her chest. "You don't make it easy. But you're worth it."

Hot emotion gathered in Esmeralda's throat. Before Camila could make her any more of a sap, Esmeralda took off.

As fireworks exploded in the night sky, she sprinted toward Ignacio's shared boxcar. Surely, he would be there by now. Sparks fell through the air. Even from this far outside the main hub of the carnival, she could hear the delighted cheers of onlookers.

She slid the boxcar door open and called out his name. The communal space was for the carnival hands and general performers with no assigned act. It smelled of sweat and cigars and was an absolute mess. Ignacio must hate it.

Her eyes grazed over the dozen or so bunks, stacked in threes. The beds were empty, however. Their bedding was thrown back haphazardly as if everyone had woken up in a rush. She stopped when she came upon a cot with sheets so crisply folded over the corners it could only belong to one person.

Obviously, Ignacio wasn't there.

Her fingers twitched.

"Don't do it," she told herself. "Don't be petty."

But who was she kidding? She clutched his blankets and pulled them loose. "That's for breaking my heart." She chopped a hand into the center of his pillow. "That's for being so handsome." She wiggled the sheets from their home tucked beneath the mattress. "That's for kissing me into oblivion when you don't love me anymore."

Something slipped from between the slats of the cot. Esmeralda knelt and plucked up the folded piece of parchment. She opened it. Her eyes narrowed.

"What's this?" She couldn't understand what she was seeing on the page.

Tears filled her eyes as she read the words scrawled angrily on the parchment. She shook her head in silent protest.

"What the hell, Ignacio."

22nd of March, 1921

Pigeon.

When you first told me your father enlisted you into the Blackbirds, I could hardly believe it. I thought maybe you were playing some sort of terrible prank.

You weren't, of course. You were never the joking type.

I suppose that was more my thing.

But I was not joking when I told you that your father is a terrible man. And you didn't want to believe me. Me! The person who has never lied to you.

I know I asked you to run away with me, but I take it back. You won't disobey him.

You are your father's son. I saw it when we argued just now.

We aren't compatible, and I think you've always known that. There was never going to be an US. Never. You know that. I have always been meant for more. And you bore everyone around you.

I doubt you will even find this letter. I doubt you ever planned on meeting me by the dove tree or running away because you're so straitlaced. But if you did come here and you do find this letter, please forget me.

Because I will have already forgotten you by the time this ink dries.

Dovie

CHAPTER 32
Ignacio

After he sent word to the Defiant via coded telegram, telling them he'd discovered communication between his father and the ringmaster, Ignacio found himself bone-tired.

Far too much had happened in one day. He'd performed in the Big Top, snuck into the ringmaster's wagon, and kissed the only girl he'd ever loved. He deserved a break.

But when he stepped into his boxcar, he heard a familiar voice whispering.

"Dovie?" he called out.

Esmeralda whirled around, tears in her eyes. She held a letter in her hand. Not just any letter. The letter she had left for him the night they were supposed to run away together.

She shook the parchment angrily. "What in the devil is this?"

Ignacio blinked with confusion. "What do you mean?"

She shook it harder. "Who wrote this?"

Hurt stirred to life inside him. "Are you mocking me?"

"Do I look like I am?!"

She didn't. In fact, he wasn't sure if he'd ever seen Esmeralda so baffled before. But her confusion made no sense. She had been the one to write every dreadful sentence.

"Look good and hard at the letter, Dovie. That is your handwriting. Those are your words. Or maybe you truly did forget. Maybe I was another fool you swindled. Maybe you never cared a lick about me."

She sucked in a tormented breath.

But why should she feel tortured when *she* had left *him*?

"Where did you get this?" she asked, scowling down at the page.

"In the hollow of the dove tree where you left it."

The day after he turned eighteen, he had woken up feeling happier than he'd ever felt before. He and Dovie had spent the early hours of the morning together, kissing and exploring their bodies, and talking about their future. He'd given her his mother's ring as a promise. As a token of the love that he had for her that felt as vast as the universes above. But when he strolled past Father's office around sunrise, his father had beckoned him in.

Father held out a silver envelope.

At first, Ignacio thought it was a birthday gift, but the moment he saw the Blackbird seal, he knew what lay inside.

"I've been enlisted? But Blackbirds don't begin training camp until they're nineteen," he said.

"Those vipers in Dos Palos are getting stronger by the minute. We need more soldiers. And you need to pay your dues so you can take my place one day."

That wasn't what he wanted. Not anymore. He wanted a life with Esmeralda. "But . . ."

“But nothing.” Father grabbed his suitcase and brushed past Ignacio. “I’ll be back in an hour and then we will talk more about your training. Say your goodbyes, but don’t even think about doing anything absurd or there will be hell to pay. You will not tarnish my name or your mother’s legacy.”

The second Father left, Ignacio found Dovie scrubbing boots in the courtyard. She saw him approaching and scanned the empty area as if them being caught together was the biggest problem they faced. He showed her the enlistment card and watched as understanding seeped into her marrow. Her hands began to shake.

“You cannot go,” she whispered.

“I don’t want to.”

Relief softened her features, and he hated that he had to harden them again.

“But I have no choice,” he said. “I must obey my father.”

“Your father is a terrible man!” Her eyes shot around the courtyard again. She stepped nearer to him. “The comandante . . . He has done . . .” She shook her head. “He *is* doing terrible things. They are making these canisters filled with gas. When set off, they singe the skin and collapse the lungs. They’re sending those into the front lines. There’s more . . . worse things . . . like—”

Ignacio cut her off, thinking of his father’s parting words: *Don’t even think about doing anything absurd or there will be hell to pay.* “I have no choice in the matter. I cannot disobey him. I can’t disappoint him.” He took her hand, rubbed his thumb over the ring he gave her. “Will you wait for me?”

“You don’t understand how terrible this war is. Every missive I’ve been able to decode while carrying messages to and from his generals has painted a picture far different from anything we've been told in the papers. The people of Dos Palos aren't some wicked force hell-bent on destroying our kingdom. It's *us*, Pigeon. *We* are the bad guys here. And your father is leading the charge."

"Nonsense. You know my father. He's calculated. He wouldn't send us into battle for no good reason."

"Is there ever a good reason when it comes to war? To send thousands to their deaths?" She stepped closer to him. "You cannot go."

His brows furrowed. "I've been preparing for this since as far back as I can remember. My mother was a soldier, my father. I can be one too."

"You don't have to be." She grabbed his sleeves. "Run away with me. We could go south. Or take a ship east. I can't lose you."

He cupped her cheeks. "You won't. Not ever."

"You can't promise that. You'll change. You'll forget me."

"I'd never."

She started to cry. "You'll become him. I just know it. He doesn't see people like me as human. He sees us as pieces to move on a board."

"I would never do that."

"But you will do whatever he commands. If he tells you to kill, you will. And I can't stand by and watch you or your soul die. I won't stay here if you go. I refuse to sit back and wait for a corpse to return to me."

"So, you'll leave? You'll move on without me?"

She clutched him harder. "Come with me. Choose me. Choose us. Not some war that should never have been started."

"I can't turn my back on my father or my mother's legacy."

Her face paled. "Yet you can turn your back on me."

"No. That isn't true. I love you. I will always love you."

"Why do I feel like there is a *but* coming?"

"Because there is. Dovie, I am an Olivera. I must—"

She held up a hand to silence him. "I'll give you until midnight to decide. I'll meet you by the dove tree. Check your father's hidden office. See if you can't find the proof yourself. If I don't see you, I'll know you've made your choice."

He did make his choice. He would always choose her. Just before midnight, he went to retrieve his savings from the box hidden beneath his floorboards. His heart plummeted. There was nothing inside but his mother's ring. He raced out of his room and ran to the dove tree. But she wasn't there. Only that letter was.

He'd been broken over it for a year and here she was, acting as if she didn't even remember it.

She shook her head slowly. "I never wrote this."

"You can't lie your way out of this. And why would you even try? You don't care."

"I care!" she screamed. She clamped her free hand over her mouth as if her own words had startled her.

"You care about what?" he said, edging closer to her.

She stepped back, panicked.

Maybe he had been too easy on her before. Maybe he'd babied her too much. But he'd coddled her because he was so afraid she'd close herself off to him forever. Well, they were far past that. He'd already lost her. And he'd lived what felt like a lifetime with that pain. He had learned something in their year apart; it was better to learn the truth than suffer in the unknown. Now, he'd push. He'd get the answers he needed from her. She wasn't some broken bird anymore. If anything, *she'd* broken *him.*

He crossed his arms. "Neither one of us is leaving this space until we let it all out, and I'll be damned if I let one more distraction get between us. Tell me. Now. What do you care about?"

"You! You fool! I care about you!"

"Bullshit," he spat. "I'm not one of your customers willing to accept your lies. Tell me the truth."

Her eyes narrowed in annoyance. "Do you know how many nights I cried myself to sleep after you left? I thought the universe must truly hate me to give me you and then take you away."

His arms went slack at his sides. "I never left you. And I would never have stopped searching for you if not for the letter you wrote—"

"I didn't write this!" She waved the letter in the air. "I would never because I love you."

Her words pummeled into his chest.

Love. She had said *I love you.* Not *I loved you.* Not *I used to love you.* She said *I love you.*

Something hot burned at the base of his throat. If he spoke, she'd hear the tears building there.

He didn't care.

"Then why did you leave without me?" His voice cracked.

Tears slipped down his cheeks. "I was ready to run away with you. I would have followed you straight into hell if you asked."

Esmeralda looked startled. "But you *did* leave me. Your father said . . ." Her eyes went wide as if realization had dawned on her.

His heart sank. "My father said what?"

CHAPTER 33

Esmeralda

"The moment I left you in the courtyard with that ultimatum, I ran to my room and packed my things," she said. She remembered how pitiful she felt. That everything she owned in life could fit in a single satchel. But if she had Ignacio, it didn't matter. And if he chose to go to the Blackbirds like his father asked? Then she'd make do. She was not going to stay under the comandante's roof if Ignacio wasn't there—indenture sentence be damned.

"I wanted to leave the second you told me about your enlistment," she said. "But I knew I had to give you time to make that choice yourself. I didn't want you to resent me for forcing you to turn your back on your duty. Your family. I knew you idolized the comandante. Even though the man treated you more like a soldier than son, you loved him."

"I did" was all Ignacio said.

"After I finished packing my bag, I snuck into the kitchen to gather supplies. While in the pantry, I overheard the serving staff whispering about how they were going to miss you. They said you had already marched through the gate carrying a duffle filled to the brim."

Her stomach hurt even thinking of the betrayal she felt back then.

"I must have lost my mind for a moment because I dropped everything and ran after you. I figured you'd be at the train station. Or the comandante's headquarters in the center of the city." Ignacio blinked with confusion, but she went on. "Just as I exited the gates to the manor, I saw that awful motorcar your father loved puffing up the main road. I froze, knowing I'd been spotted."

The car had slowed to a rumbling halt. She remembered thinking the engine purred like a well-fed cat. The rear window had squeaked open, and the comandante eyed her from the shadows within the vehicle.

"Your father asked if my being outside the gates had anything to do with you," she said. "I had been too shocked to reply. And that was when he told me he had just been with you on the way to the station. He said you told him everything about our relationship and that I asked you to run away."

Ignacio shook his head. "That isn't true. I mean . . . I *was* with him, but he never took me to the station. And I *did* tell him about us . . . but I—"

A sob escaped her. The comandante hadn't been lying.

Ignacio took her by the arms. Tears stained his own cheeks. "I told him that I loved you. That I've loved you since we were kids."

She sucked in a breath. "You did?"

"Yes, Dovie." His thumbs brushed up her arms and chills

rolled down her spine. "But I didn't tell him everything. The moment you asked me to run away with you, I knew I would, but you left in such a hurry, and I was still so numb with shock that I just stood there in the courtyard like a damn statue."

She laughed bitterly at the thought.

"When I regained my senses, I knew the savings I kept under my bed wouldn't be enough. I ran to my room and filled my duffle bag with anything I could find of mine that was of worth. I left to try and pawn it off."

Esmeralda's knees went weak. "That was why the staff saw you leaving?"

"Yes."

He eased them onto his bunk and his hands slid to find hers. He squeezed her fingers tight. That was so like him. Always knowing exactly what she needed at the exactly right time.

"My father spotted me walking through town and told me to get inside his motorcar. When I sat on the car bench, the duffle fell on its side and the dove statue we won at the boardwalk tumbled out. He questioned me about it. That's when I told him I loved you. But everything else I told him after that was a lie. I made up some story about how I wanted to give you a gift to remember me by when I left for the Blackbirds. That seemed to be enough for him because he had his driver bring me to a pawnshop across town. He told me to leave the statue in his care, that it wasn't worth anything monetarily anyway. Then Father left me at the shop and told me to be back by supper because he was hosting a goodbye party for me."

"That was why he had our love dove statue," she whispered. Her chin fell to her chest. "I'm such a fool."

"Don't say that."

"But it's true. When your father caught me trying to chase after you, he told me there was no use in running to the station because you were already gone. I stood there shaking my head in disbelief, but then he showed me the figurine."

It was a sculpture of two doves in flight. Their wings formed into a heart. Ignacio had won it for her in a shooting game. She had teased him that one of the doves looked like a pigeon.

"Your father gave me the statue and said you no longer wanted it or anything to do with me. He said you'd only ever been my friend because you pitied me. That you bedded me the night before as a goodbye."

Ignacio's eyes flashed with fury. "He. Said. What?"

"I was so devastated. To know that I trusted you with my body and then you shared those intimate details with your father, who sat there staring at me as if I were nothing."

The anger twisting his features crumpled. "Dovie, I would never disrespect you like that," Ignacio whispered.

"I know that now. I should have known better then. But you were gone, and he had the statue, and I . . . I've been left before," she sobbed.

He grabbed her and pulled her into his arms. His warmth snapped the last strands of her composure. Her tears broke loose, and her shoulders shook with a year's worth of shame.

"I didn't want to believe you'd do that to me," she said through her cries. "But then I ran to your room and saw that most of your favorite things were gone. Your prized trophy from the athletic trials at school. The gilded frame that showcased your mother's photograph. Half of your clothes. I tore off the ring you'd given me the night before. I couldn't stand the thought of you making promises that you had no intention to keep."

The hurt was still there, writhing under her skin.

"I found the loose floorboard where you kept your savings, then went to my room and grabbed my satchel. I smashed the doves and ran away. But soon after, your father's men caught me and threw me in a cell."

Ignacio's arms squeezed her tight. His pulse pounded in her ear. "I am so sorry, Dovie."

She clamped her eyes shut. "Me too."

Silence bled between them like an open vein. She didn't know what to think. What to say. Where did they even go from here? All she knew for certain was that neither one of them had wanted to leave the other behind.

And yet, they had.

Of course *she* had. She had hardly thought herself worthy of Ignacio in the first place. He was so good. So strong and handsome. He was the son of one of the most powerful men in the country. She had believed he had turned his back on her and joined the Blackbirds. That he betrayed her to his father. He joined the Blackbirds, but could she blame him? He thought she had betrayed him first.

Her hurts slowly morphed into anger when she thought of what they'd both been through. She eased from his embrace.

"I still don't understand how you got this letter," she said. "It has our nicknames. It talks about our argument. Did your father—"

Ignacio shook his head. "He couldn't have faked something

like this. There would have been a mistake. Some sort of tell. I know your handwriting through and through. I know the bit of humor woven through the fabric of each sentence you write. There's no mimicking that."

"Unless he used enchanted ink," she offered. "Like my cards."

They both stared at each other as that possibility sank in.

"So, you didn't write those words," he whispered.

"No."

He sighed and rested his forehead on hers. "I thought you finally realized you were too good for me."

"How could you think such a thing?" she asked.

"Look at you, Dovie. You're so . . . you're . . . You shine. You light up every room you walk into. Your laughter is contagious. You aren't afraid of causing a ruckus. I always worried you'd grow bored of me. That I would disappoint you somehow."

"Never," she whispered.

His chin quivered. "An entire year of missing you. Of yearning and aching and thinking my bones might break from the weight of your absence. It could have been prevented. If I was better . . . if I didn't fail you—"

"You didn't." Tenderly, she cupped his face with her hands. His honey-colored eyes pierced into hers. Yet, he said nothing.

He didn't have to. She could see every emotion in his gaze. The pain, the regret, the love. She hoped he saw hers too.

"We both made mistakes," she admitted. "We were so naïve. How could we possibly know your father would do something like that, even if he is the world's largest prick?"

Ignacio snorted. "You've always had a way with words."

"I know. It's why you love me."

His face grew serious. "I do." His fingers slid over her own. "You must know that I've always loved you. I never stopped. Not for one second. Even when I tried to quit you, my heart must have known the truth. That our love is real. It's not some enchanted *thing*."

He had changed so much during their time apart, and so had she, but the depth of their feelings had remained. It wasn't just the physical—though, that was there too—it was more. It was the true knowing of each other. The history they shared and the future they once spoke of. The laughter and tears and comfort they gave.

Their lips found each other's, and every part of her bloomed to life.

He tasted like a warm summer night. He tasted like home. Her home. And she never wanted to be apart from him again.

The door to the boxcar screeched open, and Esmeralda and Ignacio broke away. One of the ringmaster's ratas peered in. *Does the ringmaster know we snuck inside his office?* Ignacio put his body in front of hers, shielding her from what was to come.

"We're packing up for the next stop," the rata said.

Packing up? Was it daybreak already? She didn't even get to open her fortune teller wagon once. Granted, she had been busy performing. And sneaking into the ringmaster's office. And unraveling all the secrets of her past.

"I need to pack my wagon," Esmeralda said.

"I'll come with you," he replied.

"No, you won't. All strong bodies are assigned to tent

teardown," the rata said to Ignacio. "Hurry up, we don't have all morning." The rata spun on his heels and marched off into the sunrise.

She and Ignacio sighed with relief. "Looks like the ring-master doesn't know we were in his office," she said.

Ignacio's eyes darkened. "If there's one thing I've learned in the past year, it's to never trust what I don't know for certain."

They stood. She blushed at how silly she'd been for messing up his bedding when she had first found his bunk.

She bent down to fix his sheets, but he stopped her with a shake of his head.

"Leave it," he said. "Turns out I like messy things."

She barked a laugh. "Are you talking about me?"

He wiped a lingering tear from under her eye, then kissed her forehead. "I'm talking about us."

CHAPTER 34

Ignacio

She didn't write the letter.

She didn't want to leave me behind.

He rubbed his eyes as he lay on the cot, listening to the other carnival hands softly snore as the train wheels bumped over the tracks toward their next destination. They had been chugging along for hours now but all he could do was think of her. That was nothing new, of course, but this time, for the first time in far too long, he felt a cautious sort of hope.

He had tried to find her before the train took off, but he'd missed her. He figured some sleep might do them both good, and yet, here he was, wide awake with a phantom Esmeralda plucking at his thoughts.

He turned onto his side. He should try to get some rest. But then he imagined what it would be like if she were lying beside him. If her hair were fanned out onto the pillow and she smiled at him sleepily before leaning in for a kiss.

Grumbling, he sat up. He needed to clear his mind.

Ignacio stuffed his hand under his pillow and pulled out the inkwell they'd snagged from the ringmaster.

Tiptoeing on bare feet, he quietly crossed the shared boxcar. He fumbled in the dark until he found a chair, then sat at the small desk. He looked over his shoulder at the people sleeping in cots as he lit a kerosine lantern. No one woke.

After a bit of scrounging through the desk drawer, he found a fountain pen and dipped the nib into what was left inside the jar. He lifted the inky tip to the lantern and watched as with each twist of his wrist, various sparks of color appeared in the warm yellow light.

The paintings on the posters hanging around the carnival could morph into something entirely new. Esmeralda said the sketches on her cards shifted to reveal a person's deepest desires. And then there was the note left for him within the hollow of the dove tree. Written exactly in her hand, but clearly not.

He carefully penned four words onto a blank sheet of paper.

I am Ignacio Olivera.

Nothing strange happened.

Esmeralda had said the cards shifted when her customers touched them. He pressed the pad of his pointer finger onto the ink. That same buzzing sensation fizzled through his skin.

Shift this writing into something else, he thought.

Tiny sparks bubbled up from the ink like soda pop. He jerked back his hand and watched in awe as the letters fanned out and in, transforming into words that were an identical match to his own handwriting.

No. You are not.

His brows furrowed. He dipped the nib in the ink again and penned a response.

Who am I, then?

Tell me the truth, he commanded as he pressed his finger onto the ink.

The words reshaped once more.

You will learn soon enough.

Ridiculous. This ink was nothing more than another one of the ringmaster's silly tricks.

He grabbed the parchment and started to tear it, but the ink shifted.

Dovie. I am a coward. I let innocent people die. I couldn't even protect you from my own father. I'm a failure.

Ignacio dropped the parchment and jumped to his feet. His chest heaved as more of his deepest insecurities were laid on the page.

I am a bore. I am too uptight and too serious and could never make you laugh like Gabriel. Of course you'd never love me. Look at me. I'm a disappointment. I broke the promises I made to you. I let you go.

Disgust churned inside his stomach at seeing his twisted thoughts on display. He had half a mind to flip the desk. But he knew this was but a portion of who he truly was. He was more than these thoughts. More than the negative voices inside his mind.

He snatched up the paper and folded it shut. This wasn't simply enchanted ink. This was a weapon. It toyed with the mind. And it was such a deep and convincing fake that anyone could be tricked. He had been.

This must be why his father and the ringmaster were in

correspondence. Father coveted whatever terrible magic lay inside the ink. He could use it to pretend to be anyone he wished. He could pretend to be the king himself.

A whistle sounded. The train was nearing the next stop.

Ignacio cleaned off the desk. The second he had a chance he would send his findings to the Defiant.

He stuffed the inkwell under his bed and sat heavily. His knees bounced as his anticipation grew. His father and the ringmaster were working in tandem. But then why would Father ask Ángel to send Ignacio back unharmed? What sort of power did the ringmaster hold over Father? That was simple to answer. The ringmaster knew Father was using enchanted ink to prevail in the war.

But there was more to it. There had to be. He thought back to the Sánchezes' accident, and the fire breather's, and Anella's. Every time the same glinting properties were there.

The glue that sealed Anella in the glass box was incredibly strong. The stitches woven through the Sánchezes' cuffs and Esmeralda's gloves burned hot. Surely, whatever happened with Paco came from this enchantment.

Had he seen anything like it during his training with the Blackbirds?

Esmeralda had spoken about canisters of gas used on the front lines that sucked the air out of a person's lungs. Could they be made from the same enchantment?

The locomotive was beginning to slow. Even from within the thick walls of the boxcar, the cheers of excited admirers of the carnival could be heard.

That beastly creature in the mirror played in his mind. There was a connection. He just couldn't figure out how or why.

Ignacio stood. Normally he would fix his sheets to ease the growing tension. But he left them as they were. They reminded him of her. And they reminded him that it was okay to not be so rigid all the time.

He put on his boots and marched toward the door. With a grunt, he pulled the heavy metal ajar.

"There he is!" someone yelled.

A dense crowd had formed in the valley that rested just beyond the city of Milagro. People held up signs and cheered as they waited for the train to stop.

"It's Paloma's noviecito! Paloma Amor!"

Of all the stage names to be given, Paloma Amor had to be the worst. *Love Dove.* That should have been a crime. Wincing, Ignacio raised his hand and waved, causing a group of young women to scream and swoon.

The second the train came to a complete stop, he jumped down and landed on golden grass with a crunch. He needed to find Esmeralda right away. But the crowd swarmed him like flies to honey.

"Are you and Paloma truly in love?" a woman holding a teacup-sized dog asked.

"Will you perform again tonight?" queried a man with a single spectacle resting on one eye.

"Will you be taking your shirt off for our parade, or was that a one-time thing?"

Ignacio's head snapped to the young man who had asked that last question. The young man winked.

"I'm sorry," Ignacio said. "I really need to go."

He tried to weasel himself free from the horde without being rude, but they wouldn't let him escape. His eyes flicked upward, searching for help. He spotted Gabriel, and a tiny monkey of all things, sitting on top one of the boxcars sharing a caramel apple. Gabriel laughed and shook his head before disappearing.

Thirty minutes later, Ignacio was exhausted from the impromptu meet-and-greet and had somehow lost two buttons on his shirt. He rubbed the back of his neck as he walked toward where Esmeralda's wagon should have been in the train procession, but it had already been detached and moved.

It truly was a wonder how quickly the carnival formed.

He started toward the center of the carnival, but just as he rounded the parade floats, he heard voices he recognized. He stilled.

"Pilar is well enough to move. I plan to take her home," Camila said.

"Are you sure you wish to leave so soon?" the ringmaster asked gently. "I told you that you could stay on until Pilar was in the clear."

Ignacio edged closer. He peeked around Isadora the tigress's float.

Camila nudged the dirt with her toe. "Yes. I . . . I'd like to thank you for all your generosity, but I think Pilar would fare better elsewhere. She should be with family. We aren't so far from El Sueco. That's where we're from."

After a long moment, Ángel grasped her shoulder. "I'm sorry to see you two leave us. I hate that this is how we must part."

"Not more than me," she mumbled.

A flash of anger pooled in the ringmaster's eyes, but he quickly tamed it. "I'd like to offer you and Pilar your severance pays. Your time here was cut short during a challenge I gave you. I hold myself responsible in every way."

Relief flooded Camila's features as if she'd been afraid of what he might do.

A worker called after the ringmaster, asking him about where he'd like the menagerie to be raised up. Ángel held up a finger, a signal for the man to wait. He turned his attention back to Camila.

"I better go," he said with a kind smile. "Please find the treasurer. He's called Tezcán. I believe he's in the Fun House. Tell him I said that you deserve the works."

Tezcán? Ignacio had heard that name before. *But where? When?*

Camila gulped. "Th-thank you, señor."

"It is the least I can do. I shall miss you both." He hugged Camila and patted her hard on the back. She winced, still sore from the accident. "Safe travels," he said.

Right before the ringmaster walked by, Ignacio dove beneath Isadora's float. A large man with a bald head and overalls fell in line beside Ángel. The ringmaster leaned close to the man and said something into his ear. The man's brows furrowed, and he nodded. His gaze flicked toward the spot where Camila had just been. He let out a sharp whistle. Two guards slipped from behind a nearby candy cart and slithered after her as she limped away. They had the nicked ears of the Blackbirds. Ignacio's eyes snapped back to the larger man. He had the marking too.

Why were the Blackbirds here? Why were they working for the ringmaster when the army was so busy snagging people from prison cells and thrusting them into the front lines?

Camila moved through the gaping mouth that served as the entrance to the Fun House.

Not five seconds after Camila faded into the darkness of the tent, the ratas slunk inside. Cursing, Ignacio came out of his hiding spot and dashed after them.

The Fun House was a labyrinth of peculiar mirrors. They were dark and oddly shaped. Some appeared to be invisible and had him walking forward until he ran straight into them. With each step through the maze, his reflection changed from tall to short, thin to curved, blurred to distorted. In some, he swore he saw a figure in his peripheral. But as he walked deeper into the Fun House, his reflection started to change.

He halted. One of the reflections wasn't a reflection at all. An image played from within the glass as if he were watching a picture show in a theatre. He recognized the scene. Because he had lived it. He had watched it with his own eyes. He saw golden wheat underfoot, saw the train speeding away.

This was his memory from when he first met the ringmaster.

He spun to the next mirror. He viewed a girl wearing a dove mask briskly walking through the carnival. She bumped into him and offered her apologies.

It was Esmeralda the night he'd found her.

Ignacio ran to the next mirror. Within the dark glass, he observed himself dressed in his Blackbird cadet uniform, vomiting behind a building as screams rang out. He twisted to face another mirror and watched as he and Esmeralda argued about running away together. In the next, he was younger, folding his very first paper dove.

"Hello?" Camila called out.

Ignacio jerked his attention toward the direction of her voice.

"Tezcán? The ringmaster sent me to find you. Hello?"

"In here, child."

The hair on the back of Ignacio's neck stood on end. Tezcán's voice sounded like it had been scraped from the bottom of a cavernous pit.

"To your right, my dear."

The red bulbs overhead shuddered as he spoke, and the tenor reverberated in Ignacio's bones.

Every instinct in his body told him something was terribly wrong.

He bolted through the rows of mirrors, hunting for Camila. But it was hard to track her with so many twists and turns.

Finally, Ignacio spotted her within the reflections. But where were the ratas?

As Camila spun in a slow circle, eyes searching the maze for Tezcán, a face appeared in the towering mirror behind her. Ignacio's pulse pounded. The face was slender and human, but not. His skin looked like clay. The eyebrows were too high on his too long face. And his grin was spread too wide. Where eyes should have been sat glowing orbs.

"Turn around," the man in the mirror said.

Camila whirled and gasped.

"What is this?" she asked, her voice raised to a horrified

pitch. “Is this some sort of jest? Some trick the ringmaster plays on people who leave before their term is over?”

The man in the mirror gave a rumbling laugh. “There is no trick. I am the treasurer. I ensure each performer pays their fair dues.”

“Har. Har.” She turned away from the mirror. “You all can come out now! Enough with the razzing.”

“There is no one here to laugh with,” the thing called Tezcán said.

“This isn’t funny!” she yelled.

“I disagree.”

She faced the mirror. “Go to hell.”

“I’m already here. Care to join me?”

She stumbled back, ready to run, but the ratas jumped out from seemingly nowhere, clamping their hands around her arms.

Ignacio rushed forward but skidded to a stop when a billowing fog emanated from within the mirror itself.

Camila’s skin blanched of its color.

And then she screamed.

CHAPTER 35
Esmeralda

Sitting cross-legged on the floor in her wagon, Esmeralda flipped open the tin box she had taken from Ignacio and pulled out one of the rolled-up papers. Her cheeks warmed as she read the tiny note.

> 13th of April, 1919. D+P: Age 16
> Dovie. What's one thing you don't like about me?

Esmeralda had always loved that he wrote her nickname with a period at the end of it. As if that one word was big and important enough to be an entire sentence. As if it encapsulated everything that she was and everything that he thought of her within five little letters.

She remembered thinking long and hard about the answer to this question.

> *Your ugly feet.*

Truth was, there wasn't anything she didn't like about him back then. Because she understood him. Ignacio could be uptight and sometimes standoffish, he could be a bit huffy when plans changed or things weren't in order, because that was how he was raised. That was who he had been taught to be. But in the very depths of his soul existed the kindest human alive. He was a walking cavity-maker—he was so sweet.

She chewed on her bottom lip and sighed heavily. She still didn't *not* like anything about Ignacio Olivera. He was still very much that boy. But he was more now. He wasn't the sheltered son of the comandante. He'd been out into the world. He'd seen all sorts of things.

And yet he still loved her.

Three quick knocks sounded on the door. She stuffed the tin box into the bodice of her costume before the door squeaked open. Gabriel's head popped in. Inky oil marked one cheek. He wore his signature cap but sweat coated the curls on his neck.

"Hey," she said gently. They hadn't spoken since the Sánchezes' accident.

"Hey yourself." Gabriel's gaze roamed her small space. He slumped. "I was hoping Camila was in here. I've been searching for her for an hour."

"She isn't."

"Yes," he said. "I can see that." He narrowed his eyes. "New costume?"

When she woke up that morning, she'd found a wrapped box on her doorstep with the most beautiful costume she'd ever seen inside it. It was an opal-white one-piece with feather tufts on the rear and shoulders. Shimmering diamonds had been sewn into the lacy gauze at the hips. But it was the massive wings that had her awestruck. They were angelic, and intricate, and so large they flowed down her back and swept the ground near her heels.

The notecard had given her instructions to put it on or risk being disqualified from the Running. With everything going on, the challenge for lead act was the last thing on her mind. But she did as she was told because what else could she do?

She fidgeted with one of the feathers and decided to do what Camila suggested—wade through her discomfort and be a real friend. "I know you're angry that I continued in the Running after the accident. You have every right to hate me for being so selfish."

Gabriel snorted. "Hate is a strong word, amiga. Disappointed? Sure. But Camila told me you two hashed things out last night."

"And she told me you were going to leave with them."

He nodded.

"But what about the rules? We aren't supposed to depart before our year term. There are consequences."

"What can the ringmaster possibly do to me that hasn't already been done? Will he take all the money I've saved like he did to you? Fine. Let him." He swiped at the oil on his cheek. "Rosco and I have been building a motorized chair for Pilar."

"Rosco the monkey? The pickpocket?"

Gabriel grinned. "He's great, right? I paid him in sweets to steal some of the machine parts I needed. We just finished, actually. We can leave right away."

"So soon." Esmeralda couldn't help but feel suddenly cold.

She and Ignacio couldn't possibly leave now. They hadn't found anything that would truly incriminate the comandante yet.

Gabriel swept forward and knelt beside her, taking her hand in his. He had the biggest brown eyes, the kind that seemed to always be full of mischief. Sometimes she forgot how young he was. How young they both were. But the two of them had learned how to scrape by in a world that was not kind. And that aged a person. It did things to their bodies only people like them could understand.

"I sent a telegraph to Javi like you asked. I told him to see if anyone he knows might have something interesting to tell us about the carnival."

"Did he find anything?" she asked.

"One of the snuff dealers for the king's court made it sound like the rich are all in on the game. And I mean *the rich.* Lawmakers, corporation owners, the gentry, hell, probably King Amadeo himself. They are perfectly aware that people go missing all the time within the carnival. Did you know that no one from the outside world has seen any of the acts that competed in the Running again? And the previous lead acts? Nothing. How could someone whose face is plastered on billboards across Costa Mayor just vanish? They say they *retire* but to where?"

"Why hasn't anyone tried to stop this?" she asked.

"Because we're nobodies."

Anger bubbled inside her. Gabriel wasn't a nobody. He was clever and handy and a good friend. The Sánchezes weren't nobodies. They were funny and kind and did everything for their family. Every performer and hand she'd met within the carnival was a somebody. No matter their station in life. She was so sick and tired of those with power looking down on anyone who wasn't deemed worthy in their eyes.

"Whatever is going on, we are getting out of this place before anything worse happens," Gabriel said. "As soon as I find Camila, we are—"

"Did you say you were looking for Camila?"

Esmeralda's spine stiffened. It was the ringmaster's voice. She and Gabriel both whirled toward the door.

Gabriel jumped to his feet. He took off his cap and bowed his head. "Yes, Señor Veracruz."

"I just saw her walking into the Fun House. I'm sure you can catch her there."

"Um . . . thank you, señor."

The ringmaster scooted to the side of the doorway so Gabriel could depart. But Gabriel didn't move. He peeked over his shoulder at Esmeralda, unsure if he should leave her alone.

"Is something the matter?" Ángel queried.

"Not at all," Esmeralda chimed in. She stood up. "Gabriel and I were talking about what I'm planning to do for the final challenge. He's simply nervous."

"I see. Well, that will have to wait. It is time to start the parade into town." His eyes flicked to Gabriel. "Are you coming, kid? Or did you need to find Camila first?"

"Go on," Esmeralda urged. They didn't want to raise any suspicions. "We'll meet up after."

Gabriel nodded before disappearing into the hubbub of the carnival.

The ringmaster offered his arm. "Shall we?"

Esmeralda blinked. "Did you come to my wagon to escort me to my float?"

A laugh bubbled from his lips. "Not entirely."

He gestured toward his elbow. Begrudgingly, she took it. Perhaps it was cowardly, but what else could she do? If Ángel was consorting with the elites, or whatever was in that mirror, or worse, Comandante Olivera, she had to play her cards right. She had to make sure he remained on her side. At least until she could figure out what to do next.

"Your costume fits you well," Ángel said as they walked toward the parade. "Jorge is a tailor virtuoso indeed."

"Yes. Thank you for this."

"But where are your gloves?" he asked.

She'd stuffed them into her cabinet with zero intention of ever wearing them again. "I left them with the washing crew. They got a bit smudged after the show last night."

"Ah, wouldn't want you to perform with any stains tarnishing your beauty. Speaking of beauty." He dug into his coat pocket. His brows furrowed. "Hmm. It isn't in here." He snapped. "Sí! That's right." He twirled his fingers in the air and a gilded hairpin winked into existence.

Her gilded hairpin.

He wiggled the golden piece, bits of sunlight glinting in her eye. "Looking for this by any chance?"

She'd lost it last night when she and Ignacio kissed before they entered the ringmaster's wagon. She'd felt it tumble out of her hair and land on the grass but paid it no mind. How could she when his lips were on hers?

Her pulse began to pound. Did Ángel know about what she

and Ignacio had done? She plastered on a nonchalant smile and plucked the pin from his fingertips. "That damn monkey keeps snagging my things."

The ringmaster grinned and the lines fanning out at the corners of his eyes deepened. "What a naughty little pest."

He helped her into Estefan the ostrich's birdcage. It had been repainted, and strings of pearls and diamonds now curtained the upper rim. Ángel patted her arm and started to shut the door.

"Silly me, I nearly forgot. My mind is so filled with distractions." A black envelope winked into existence. His fingers shook ever so slightly as he handed it to her. "With Paco tragically gone and Benicio sadly disqualified after one of his bears attacked the Flying Córdovas, I've been rather distraught. I have a good feeling about tonight, though. The show is going to be one we won't soon forget. But first, we shall entertain the masses with our magnificent pageant."

He shut the door and swept away, joining the bandwagon at the front of the parade.

Esmeralda looked down at the envelope.

There was that same blasted iridescent ink.

Rage boiled inside her. She itched to tear the thing into shreds.

Yet, she tore it open instead.

My magnificent Paloma, congratulations, you are now just one of three.

You showed versatility, vivacity, and now it's time to share your vibrancy.

Tonight is your final test.

Prove you shine brighter than the rest.

I am searching for my equal. My perfect match.

So now is the time for your clever plans to be hatched.

I need someone brilliant and talented and willing to sparkle against all the odds.

I will only choose the showstopper who is worthy of the gods.

**The final three performers will have five minutes to present their acts in the center ring. Make this a night my special guests will never forget, and you will be my next lead act.*

"To hell with that," she said.

She never wanted to experience what she went through in that Big Top again. And she surely wasn't going to be used as some pawn for the rich to toy with. She'd had enough of that in her life, and it had gotten her nothing but heartache.

But she also knew Ignacio wouldn't leave until he found something significant to send to the Defiant.

The parade began to move. The swing inside the cage bumped against her back, beckoning her to sit. She chewed on her cheek and searched for the boy she loved through the cage's bars. He should be here. She tried to push down the unease stirring inside her stomach.

Hopefully, he was out there getting the answers they needed so they could flee before the show began tonight.

CHAPTER 36

Ignacio

The ground rumbled under his feet as Camila's screams tore through the Fun House tent.

"No!" she bellowed. "Help!"

Ignacio tried to find his way to her through the maze of mirrors. With each step closer, he noticed something strange happening to Camila. Her appearance was shifting. Her black hair was graying. Her muscles shrinking. Her skin sagging.

"Somebody help them!" she wailed. Her body went limp in the ratas' arms, but she continued to scream for someone to help *them* as the guards holding her up brought her nearer to the mirror.

Ignacio ran hard into an invisible wall. He cursed. Tried to go right. It was blocked. He went left. Red lanterns throbbed overhead like a beating heart. Shadowy fog billowed around his feet.

He found a straight passageway and caught what Camila was seeing in the mirror. It was a living scene, like the one he'd witnessed of him boarding the train. Pilar was in this dreamscape. So were Esmeralda and Gabriel and—surprisingly—Ignacio too. They were running down a small hill. Bolting toward a quaint home in the middle of a meadow that was completely engulfed in flames.

Pilar stopped running and then turned toward the mirror, looking directly at Camila. "Don't just stand there, Camila! Our family is stuck inside!" She thrust out her hand. "Help me! Take my hand—we can save them!"

But this version of Pilar was off. Wrong. Her eyes weren't her own. They were black and gold and spun in hypnotizing circles like the eyes of the monster in the mirror.

"Take my hand, sister! Hurry. We can save them!"

The ratas dragged the aging Camila forward. Sobbing, she reached for her sister inside the mirror. Pilar's face morphed into that of the monster he had seen before.

"No!" Ignacio yelled. "Don't!"

He cut right again and this time he found the opening to where Camila stood. He rushed forward and slammed his fist into the face of one of the ratas holding her. The man stumbled back. The second rata released her and barreled right into Ignacio. Camila fell to her knees, but didn't move to escape. Tears streamed down her face, and she grew older in appearance as she inched nearer to the mirror, her hands extended toward the glass.

"Camila!" Ignacio yelled.

She paid him no mind. Her fingertips hovered an inch away from the glass.

Air rushed out of Ignacio's lungs when the second rata pounded his shoulder into Ignacio's sternum. He shoved his heels into the ground and twisted his body with a fierce cut to the right. The guard's hold broke, and he crashed into one of the mirrors. Glass shattered and clattered to the floor as he crumpled.

"Stop him!" that gravelly voice from within the reflection roared. "Do not let another mirror break!"

The first rata Ignacio had punched picked up a shard of glass. Grinning, he flipped it around until the sharpest point was facing Ignacio. The shard looked different now. It was no longer reflective but shiny black with waves of iridescent colors coursing through.

Blackbird obsidian—the same gemstone used within the soldiers' daggers and to garnish their badges. The same stones set in his mother's ring. Something clicked inside his mind. He'd heard of a type of obsidian that could be smoothed into a reflective surface before. His mother had shown it to him in an old fable she used to read to him. The very book he'd seen in his father's private office.

The rata swiped the makeshift blade. Ignacio dodged right before the sharp edge found its mark. He dodged again. But he miscalculated the third time, and pain sliced through his bicep. He clasped a hand over his burning skin.

"Do not kill him!" the voice commanded. "We aren't finished with him yet."

Sizzling heat lanced through his veins where the stone had cut. He eyed the wound. Those familiar sparkles littered his skin.

Had this been what Esmeralda felt when her gloves scorched her last night?

"Who are you?!" Ignacio yelled.

The voice laughed. "You should be asking *what* am I."

Camila's fingertips pressed into the mirror and the last of her black hair went bone white.

Her head knocked back and she howled in agony.

Holding his injured arm, Ignacio lunged forward. The rata dove after him but Ignacio dipped to the left, sidestepping him. He shoved Camila back and slammed his boot into the towering mirror.

The glass shattered.

The ground shook.

The bulbs dimmed and flickered overhead.

"No!" the monster roared. "Guard! Bring me the girl now. I am not done feasting. I need all of her!"

The rata barreled into Ignacio, and they went sprawling to the ground. Obsidian shards nicked his flesh and burned with biting heat. The rata's grip around Ignacio went suddenly limp and the sound of something gurgling snagged his attention. Slowly, Ignacio turned his head. His insides recoiled. The guard had landed face-first on an upturned piece of obsidian.

Panting, Ignacio carefully crawled toward Camila, who was slumped over. He called her name, but she didn't reply.

"Hey," he said gently. He put his hand on her boney shoulder. "Let's get you out of . . ." She faced him. And all the blood in his body drained to the floor.

She had aged by fifty or sixty years.

A soft cry escaped her lips. "Why?" was all she managed to say.

Fury boiled inside his chest. Ángel had sent her here.

"Ignacio," a haunting voice cooed. That monstrous face formed in all the mirrors that surrounded them. Camila flinched, and he wrapped his uninjured arm around her, shielding her as best he could.

"What are you?!" he shouted. "What have you done to her?"

"Come now, you already know. Your mother used to tell my story before you laid down your little head and drifted off to sleep."

One of the mirrors blurred and Ignacio saw himself as a boy. He was in his favorite pajamas. He'd loved them because his mother had brought them all the way from the palace just for him. The child version of himself looked up at the mirror, gazing at it with hope and wonder in his eyes.

"Read it to me again," he said.

He saw his mother's reflection within his pupils. She had the prettiest smile. The kind that made a person feel instantly at ease. But there was a steeliness to her too, intense enough to command the king's army.

"One more time," she said warmly, and he watched himself nuzzle deeper into her lap.

Ignacio's jaw went slack. He was witnessing the scene unfold through his mother's eyes.

"This story isn't too frightening?" she asked. "I wouldn't want you having nightmares about it."

Young Ignacio's face grew serious. "I'm brave like you, Mommy."

"That you are. But if you do get frightened, know that a man with a silly mustache was selling them on the side of the road.

He said it would be perfect for spectaculous boys like you." Young Ignacio giggled at the made-up word. "This story is a good lesson for us all, I think. There is evil in this world. Usually, we can spot it right away. But sometimes, when we least expect it, evil comes to us in disguise. Through gentle words, and alluring smiles, and, perhaps worst of all, the promise of magic. That sort of evil can sway even the kindest of men."

She turned the pages of the book in his lap back to the beginning and read the story once more.

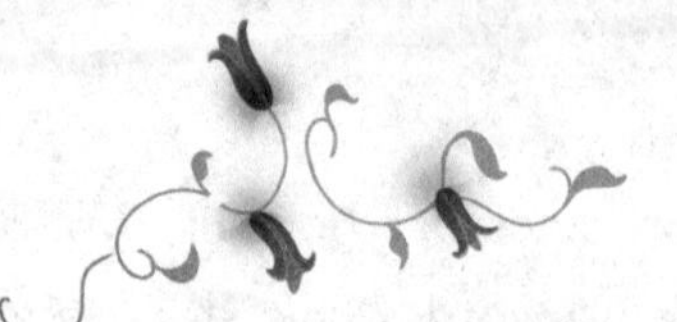

The Bell-Flower Brothers

There was once a traveling carnival that brought joy wherever it went. Fluffy white clouds puffed from the whistling train's smokestack, beckoning people from nearby towns to join in on the merriment. The Valerio brothers, orphaned when they were just eight and six but now strapping young men at twenty and eighteen, were always first to depart the rusted caboose.

It was their job to ready the fields and map out where each tent should go. The work was grueling, and no one paid them any mind or offered them respect, but the carnival was all they knew.

One day, the carnival stopped in a foreign land. With their duties completed for the day, the brothers went exploring and spotted a field of deep magenta flowers. The shape of the petals reminded the brothers of the noisy bell the carnival used during its welcome parade.

"I've heard whispers of such flowers," the younger brother said. "And of what rests within the waters." He smacked his elder brother on the shoulder and hooted. "We've found the mirror to the gods."

Yipping with excitement, the brothers ran through the blossoms until they came upon a steaming spring. The elder brother, who'd become his younger brother's guardian after their parents had perished in a trapeze accident, bent over the bubbling waters. The shallow spring was glistening in shades of black, purple, blue, and yellow. He caught his reflection in the waters. His brows rose in surprise.

Gone was his smooth skin and cheeks still rounded with youth. In the reflection, his jawline was sharp enough to cut steel. He had scruff on his chin, scars that spoke of great battles won, and wrinkles spreading from his eyes like whiskers. He was a *man*, a man no one would be foolish enough to disobey. One who could always take care of his younger brother.

A mysterious whisper came from within the hot spring. "This life could be yours for a simple exchange," it said.

"Who are you?" he asked the spring.

"The question shouldn't be *who* are you, but *what* are you," the spring replied.

The elder brother raised a brow. After years in the carnival, he found those who spoke in riddles most insufferable, but he humored the talking spring. "*What* are you, then?"

"I am a god," the quiet voice replied.

The brothers gaped at one another.

The god chuckled. "I am called Tezcán. Ruler of night and enchantment."

"We really found a god!" the younger brother exclaimed. "Do you truly grant wishes? Or are all the tales the priests tell lies?"

"I do. To prove it, I can grant you one wish right now, if you like."

The elder brother, ever astute and careful, had read enough scriptures to know that not all gods were good. He asked, "What would you want in exchange?"

"A simple trade to feed my hungry soul," Tezcán said. "I will grant you whatever you desire: wealth, true love, peace amongst humanity, anything. All you must do in return is give me someone of equal value."

"*Someone?*" the elder brother asked.

"Anyone. A perfect stranger will do," the god replied. "If it is wealth you covet, feed me the soul of someone who has great riches, and theirs shall be yours."

The elder brother shook his head. "We cannot do that. That's . . . evil."

But the younger brother rushed forward. He fell to his knees beside the hot spring. He had heard the rumors about the mirror to the gods. He knew the stones materialized and vanished at random. This opportunity may never come to them again, and he didn't want to ruin whatever chance he had to make a wish.

He gazed at his reflection within the spring. His face had become even handsomer than it already was. Beautiful women danced behind him and kissed his cheeks. People in expensive suits called out his name. He could feel their admiration. Could sense their envy.

His heart began to race. *This.* This was exactly what he wanted. He was tired of grinding away as a grunt carnival hand. As some nobody. He wanted to have women dangling from his arms, and rich men green with jealousy whenever he passed by, to be forever handsome and adored.

And he would have that no matter the cost.

"I will do it," he said to Tezcán. "I will make the trade. But we are so far from anyone. How could we possibly offer an exchange out here?"

"The answer is simple. You may take me with you," Tezcán said. "Reach into the waters and retrieve a stone. It is a looking glass. A portal between your realm and mine."

The younger brother rubbed his hands greedily. He reached forward, but his brother snatched his wrist.

"That water will burn your flesh."

"A small price to pay," the god said.

The younger brother jerked his arm free. "This is our only chance. We must do this, or we'll remain the nobodies we've always been. Don't you want more? Don't you want to be a somebody?"

The elder brother felt his cheeks burn. He had thought they were somebodies regardless of their lowly station in life. But he had to admit he was greedy to be the man he saw in the reflection. He longed to have power, to be respected and feared.

"We do this together," he said.

At the same time, the brothers shoved their arms into the scalding waters. The eldest could have sworn he felt fingers wrap around his wrist, trying to pull him in.

The ground rumbled viciously. They fell back, panting, each clutching a black stone with an iridescent sheen.

"Go," Tezcán commanded. "Summon me when you have found your trade."

The horns blared from the carnival. The brothers

needed to return before the ringmaster who owned the carnival reprimanded them.

Tezcán eventually gave the Valerio brothers what they asked for: One shone with charisma and one gained dominance. However, the brothers only grew hungrier for fame and power. The god grew hungrier too. They continued down this path, sacrificing and receiving, sacrificing and receiving, sacrificing and receiving, for many years . . .

Until one brother fell in love and realized he no longer wanted the life they led. But by then, it was too late, and sacrifices would forever have to be made.

CHAPTER 37

Esmeralda

The moment the parade was complete Esmeralda started her search for Ignacio. She hadn't seen him since they parted last night, and they needed to come up with some sort of plan because Ángel expected her to perform in the evening. And that was the last thing she was going to do.

Dread wormed through her as she checked his bunk, the Big Top, the meal tent—anywhere she thought he might be. There wasn't a single sign of him. Or Camila. Or Gabriel.

"There you are!" The tailor scurried toward her at a harried pace. The sunset cast the sky ablaze behind him. "You must hurry!"

"Hurry where?" she asked.

"Have you not heard?" Jorge gave an exasperated sigh. "Ángel is starting the show early tonight because a very important guest has arrived. The second the moon comes out the Big Top drums will sound." He took her by the arm and started to tug her forward. "Get a move on it, doll. I've been told to make sure you dazzle."

She dug her heels into the dirt. "I can't . . . I . . . I haven't found Ignacio. He's my partner."

"He's already there, silly. I'll bring you to him."

She thought about how Ignacio had suspicions of the tailor virtuoso. That he'd spotted Jorge with General Keara.

"When did you see Ignacio? Why didn't *he* come find me?"

"Can he make you dazzle like me? I'd bet my toes the answer is a big fat no. Now, come along." He tugged her forward, his grip on her wrist exceptionally strong.

But he did not lead her into Clown Alley. Instead, he ushered her to the right, moving her toward the entrance to Carnival Fantástico.

"Where are we going?" she asked.

"A quick stop to my tent. I forgot the mask I made special for tonight."

The wings she wore had to have been fifty pounds. The straps dug into her skin painfully, nearly matching the discomfort she felt inside her gut.

"Wait," she said. She tried to slow Jorge's quick steps, but he ignored her. "I said wait."

"No time for waiting," Jorge sang.

She tried to wiggle free from his grip, but he held strong. Alarm bells began to ring inside her mind. She'd made so many mistakes in her life, but what she realized at that moment was that the biggest mistake she'd ever made was not trusting her gut.

A balloon vendor walked by, wrestling with the strings of her flower-shaped inflatables. Esmeralda dug her fingers into her curls and pulled out the hairpin Ángel had returned to her. She shoved the sharp end of the pin upward. Balloons popped overhead like firecrackers. Glistening bubbles exploded out of them and filled the air. They doubled and tripled until they enveloped Esmeralda and Jorge altogether. Jorge gasped and accidentally sucked a bubble into his mouth. As he leaned forward in a fit of coughs, Esmeralda stomped on his shoe and slipped out of his grasp.

She ran through the soapy mess but shuddered to a halt when she spotted a tall and angular figure lurking behind the siren tank.

General Keara.

"Shit."

Esmeralda spun in the opposite direction and raced through the carnival, trying to put as much distance between herself and General Keara as possible. The gates must have just opened because rambunctious guests poured through the walkways and scrambled toward the Big Top.

She cut into Clown Alley to avoid the chaos.

Did the general's presence have anything to do with why Ignacio was missing?

She forced herself to peer over her shoulder. Her stomach clenched.

General Keara was marching after her, slicing a direct line through the revelers and carnival hands. But the rata stationed at the entrance held up his hand and stalled her.

"For once you've done your job right," Esmeralda grumbled under her breath.

Still, knowing how determined General Keara was to get her way, that would only last so long. Esmeralda had to find Ignacio. The Big Top drums began to thump. She quickened her speed as best she could with the ridiculous wings on her back. She bolted through the tent flap that led into the dressing area of the Big Top. She didn't trust Jorge, but he said Ignacio was here and this was her only lead.

The room was filled with performers and animals getting ready for the march of showstoppers. But no Ignacio. With Paco gone, Benicio and Anella disqualified, and the Córdovas and Sánchezes injured, the two other remaining acts in the Running, Nicola the Escape Artist and David the Knife Thrower, stood at opposite ends of the bustling space, glaring each other down as they stretched and prepared for the final challenge.

She thrust into the throng and called for Ignacio.

"I saw your beau heading toward the ringmaster's private dressing room just now," Jade informed her. "He was searching for you as well."

Esmeralda had never been inside Ángel's dressing room. But she flung herself through the open flaps that led to it.

Panting, she took in the small space. It was filled with top hats, jackets, and tall mirrors, and there was a single changing screen in the corner. A ladder hung from behind it, leading into the canvas roof.

Again, there was no sign of Ignacio.

She chewed on her lip. She had to do something. It would only be a matter of minutes before Keara found her. And then what? Esmeralda might be dragged back into a cell. She had lost her power once. She couldn't lose it again.

Movement pulled her attention to the ladder. The ringmaster's shiny boots and signature striped slacks clambered down the rungs.

Ángel's blue eyes met hers from within the shadows of his top hat. An easy grin replaced the stern look on his face. "Ready to put on the performance of a lifetime?"

"Have you seen Ignacio?" She couldn't keep the panic out of her voice.

"What's eating you, birdie?"

"General Keara is on carnival grounds," she spat out. "She's trying to enter Clown Alley as we speak."

"I see," he said.

Far too calmly.

Slowly, he finished his descent and faced her. He rested his hands on his slender hips. His coat was off, and his shirtsleeves were rolled to his elbows. One of his arms was laced with old scars she never knew existed. He took off his hat and wiped away the sweat from his brow. "I was just up there checking the rigging on the catwalk before the show begins."

"Are you going to do anything about the general?" she snapped.

"General Keara is the least of my concerns. We have bigger fish swimming inside my shimmering pond."

Her pulse began to thump hard in her chest. "What do you mean?"

"Come." He grabbed one of the sequined jackets and shrugged it on before exiting the dressing room.

"But . . . Ignacio . . ."

"Is perfectly fine. Trust me, I'd know otherwise."

She followed him. Her gaze darted toward the backstage entrance, but there was no sign of Keara. They wove through the march of showstoppers entering the Big Top. He stopped before the curtains that separated the backstage area from the arena and carefully pulled one back. He motioned for her to come nearer.

When she did, he leaned in. "Look at the center box."

Her eyes scanned over the expectant audience. Their gazes were glued to the gilded floats on full display.

She spotted who the ringmaster was pointing to.

"No" was all she could manage to say.

CHAPTER 38
Ignacio

The music playing on repeat within the carnival wasn't some made-up ballad. It was about the men who had found Tezcán. The Valerio brothers from the song were the same brothers from his mother's book. The obsidian they had found was the same stone the god was watching Ignacio from. The enchantments were coming from him. But what did his mother have to do with this?

Tezcán offered a sharp-toothed grin. "You are so like her, you know? Your mother was a beauty, both in spirit and in appearance. She was strong and mighty in heart and physicality. But, unfortunately, she was also foolish."

Ignacio shot to his feet. "Don't you dare speak of her like that!"

Tezcán's smile grew wider. "I apologize if I offended you, but it is true. Your mother loved your father fiercely. She thought her love would save him. She even got the rulers of Dos Palos to close their borders to keep us apart. She thought that would free your father from my grip. Instead, she found her demise." His face grew larger as if he were moving closer to the mirror. "Do you want to know a secret? Your mother didn't die at the hands of Dos Palos spies. She was brought to me. I devoured every morsel of her delicious soul."

"Shut up!" Ignacio roared.

"I'm afraid I do not listen to the commands of man. I do, however, happily grant wishes. I can show you what happened to her, for a simple exchange."

Weak fingers wrapped around Ignacio's wrist. He met Camila's teary gaze.

"Don't trust this bastard," she said.

White-hot fury lanced through him.

"Why did you do this to Camila?"

"She was a payment owed. Youth, I am due. I work in bargains, as you well know. I am fed the young, the fearless, the hopeful. In exchange, I bestow my enchantments."

"On the ringmaster?"

"I'll never tell," Tezcán said in a singsong way. "Unless you pay the right price. I'll make it easy for you. Give me Camila. And then bring him to me." The god's glowing eyes flicked behind Ignacio.

Ignacio's head turned toward the passageway behind him. Gabriel stood within the labyrinth. He stared blankly at one of the mirrors. He blinked hard. "Javier?"

Gabriel shook his head in confusion and stumbled closer to the mirror.

"Javi, how could you? You said you loved me."

He reached for the smokey glass.

"Get away from there!" Ignacio shouted. "Gabriel, don't look in the mirror!"

Tezcán's laugh rumbled through the entire Fun House.

Gabriel's eyes went wide, and he stumbled back. "What the hell?!"

The god popped into view in a small mirror to Ignacio's right. "What will it be?" he asked. "The girl and that clever boy in exchange for knowledge about your mother. I know you hardly remember the sound of her voice. Certainly, you'd like to see her again. To remember her—"

Camila smashed a shard of obsidian into the reflection. "I've heard enough."

The bulbs overhead shook as if angered.

"Same." Ignacio scooped her up and they wove their way through the maze to get to Gabriel.

"What is happening?" Gabriel said, confusion playing on his features. "I've never seen anything like that, and I built half of the attractions here. Why was Javi in the reflection? Why was he kissing some other fella?"

"He's a figment of your own imagination. Your worst fears," Camila replied.

Gabriel's brows pinched together. "Who are you?"

Camila glared at him.

His face paled. "Oh my. Camila?!"

An explosion sounded from the center of the carnival.

"Was that from the Big Top?" Ignacio asked.

Tezcán's gravelly laugh reverberated through the Fun House, then faded as if he were walking away.

"The show must have already started," Camila said.

"But it was barely the afternoon when we entered the Fun House."

"And I had the body of an eighteen-year-old then. I think we're past logical understandings."

"What is happening?" Gabriel's voice cracked. "Why do you look like my grandmother?"

Applause echoed faintly from the Big Top, then screams of joy.

Ignacio searched the reflections. "Where did Tezcán go?"

As if on cue, the Big Top drums began to rumble.

Pretty doves fluttered about within the mirrors. Their movement became erratic, and they began to smash into the glass. Snapping their own necks.

Ignacio gasped. "Dovie."

Gabriel took Camila in his arms and shouted, "Go!"

Without a second thought, Ignacio bolted toward the Fun House exit. He dodged and weaved around walls of mirrors that suddenly formed to block his path. When he kicked out and broke one of the mirrors, the others shuddered and let him through as if they were afraid they'd be next.

Cool air hit his skin. The smells and sounds of Carnival Fantástico enveloped him. He raced through the dense and meandering throng all shuffling toward one place: the Big Top.

CHAPTER 39
Esmeralda

"No," Esmeralda whispered as she looked out at the arena. Sitting in the prized box as if he was perfectly at home was Comandante Olivera.

"So, you *are* working with him, then?" She glared at the ringmaster.

Ángel had the nerve to appear confused. "I beg your finest pardon."

General Keara entered the box. She knelt beside the comandante and said something into his ear. Comandante Olivera's brows deeply furrowed. His lips moved, but Esmeralda had no clue what he might have said. General Keara nodded, stood, then disappeared into the crowd.

Esmeralda had to find Ignacio. She had to warn him.

With wobbling knees, she stumbled back, bumping against the ringmaster's chest. He caught her and held her in place, his warmth bleeding into her shoulders and arms.

"Easy now, birdie, don't be hasty," he said. "You must perform or risk forfeiting your only hope of being my lead act."

She whirled around. "To hell with the Running! The boy I love is in danger."

Ángel's eyes glinted with pleasure. "The lovebirds have finally found their way back to each other, I see."

"Yes. And I need to find him before his father does." She tried to move around Ángel, but he stepped into her path.

"What happens once you find him? You two leave my carnival behind and run from Comandante Olivera for the rest of your days?" His fingers took hold of her chin and tugged it up until she met his gaze. "You're a star, Esmeralda. You aren't meant to hide your light from the world."

"I don't care about being a star. Not anymore." She had been so starved to feel loved, to feel admired. She thought the roar of the crowd would drown out feelings of loneliness. But it didn't. The cracks in her broken heart could never be filled by empty admirations.

"And here I thought you were so much like me. I thought I could mold you into my glistening muse. I believed in you." He released her and stepped back. "I remember the very first moment I saw you. My guards had caught you and Gabriel trying to sneak into the carnival. They threatened to throw you on your asses outside the gates, but you said you'd rather chew off your own arm than go to the front lines. You mentioned Comandante Olivera by name. You said you'd do anything to put that man in his place. To never feel small again."

She hardly recalled that desperate day, but the reminder left a pit in her stomach, nonetheless.

"Where is that fierce firecracker now? You are willing to

turn your back on your own greatness, on becoming someone people aspire to be, all because you are afraid. You're willing to let the comandante make you cower even though I, the most magnanimous person in all of Costa Mayor, want you to be my muse. Do you not know how much that offends me? No. I am offended *for* you. You deserve more. I too have felt insignificant, you know? Like a nobody with no options in life. But look at me now. I have everything I ever wanted. And once you are my lead act, you will have it too. You're my special star. My equal."

She shook her head. "No. You . . . you're lying. You don't care about my potential. About any of us."

His mouth fell open. "How can you say that?"

"Where are the previous main acts? Where did they retire to? What about the people who competed in the Running? Why are they missing?"

"My darling, I don't know what you're talking about. They aren't missing. They've simply changed their names. They live in secret luxury, love. You can hardly expect them to flaunt their riches when we are at war."

That was a convenient explanation. Plus, there was that thing in the mirror to think of. And the gloves. All the accidents in this year's competition.

The march of showstoppers was coming to an end. The circus song faded out and the drums rumbled in full.

"That's my cue," Ángel said. "If you insist on throwing your potential away, then all I can say is good luck with your escape." He stepped toward the curtain, then halted. Over his shoulder he said, "I took you for the kind of person who would hold your head high and raise your finger to the man who had you so viciously thrown in a cell. Remember the wretched things he said to you the day Ignacio found out he'd been enlisted into the Blackbirds. Remember how he taunted your love."

Esmeralda sucked in a breath. "How do you know about that?"

The corner of Ángel's mouth twitched. "I am the ringmaster, birdie. I know *everything*. Or at least, I used to. Because I thought you wanted to show him and everyone like him that you are better than them all."

"I wanted him to rot in hell, but—"

The ringmaster spun to face her. "I can make your wish come true." He cupped her cheeks with both hands. "I can make sure you get everything you've ever desired. Safety, respect, riches beyond your wildest dreams."

Something inside her soured. She didn't want anyone to give her those things. She wanted to earn them herself. And she wanted to do that with Ignacio and her friends by her side.

An explosion went off as a single miniature firework crackled in the air. The audience roared, knowing Ángel would soon appear.

"What do you say? Shall we make a deal here and now?" he asked.

She steadied herself and said, "No."

His smile faded. "I have to admit, I had hoped you'd change your mind and make this easy. Oh well." He shrugged a shoulder and then swiped his thumb over her lips.

Heat sizzled into her skin, sealing her mouth shut. She scrambled back but strong hands gripped her shoulders. Jade. She tried to scream and jerk herself free, but she couldn't. "Hold her steady," the ringmaster ordered. He fluttered his fingers, and Esmeralda's gloves appeared. He forced them on. Sizzling pain lanced through her arms, and she shrieked into her sealed lips.

"You are a wonder, Esmeralda. And now the world gets to see it. Whether you like it or not."

She thrashed and kicked out but Ángel's smile didn't waver. "Better not make too much of a fuss, love, or I might just let Keara snatch you up. Or worse, let the monster in the mirror make your friends disappear." Her eyes widened. "Ah. You didn't think I knew that you've seen him too." He clicked his tongue. "Do you know what the creature in the mirror can do?"

She shook her head.

"He's a devourer of souls. Sucks the life right out of poor wretches like me and you. Well, not me. But you. And *definitely* Camila and Gabriel, if you don't do everything I say."

Her fighting stalled.

Ángel grinned. "That's my girl." He placed a deck of freshly painted cards in her palms.

He rolled back his shoulders and beamed. "Time to put on a show."

Ángel swept into the Big Top and a spotlight found him instantly. The crowd went wild for him. They screamed his name. He bowed and then faced her, held up by Jade in the wings. He extended his hand toward Esmeralda; then Jade thrust her into the Big Top.

The audience roared.

"Paloma! Paloma! Paloma!" they shouted.

"They love you, kid!" the ringmaster yelled.

Her pulse raced as his hand squeezed around hers.

"Paloma! Paloma! Paloma!"

The screams were so loud. The lights were so bright.

Run, she told herself. *Turn around and run.*

But what about her friends? What about Keara and the comandante and Ignacio?

How could she get out of this? There had to be a way.

"Paloma! Paloma! Paloma!"

Somehow, she and Ángel had made it to the very center of the ring, joining the other two performers left in the Running. She tried to meet their eyes, or scream a mumbled warning, but neither looked at her. They were too busy waving at the expectant crowd.

Ángel twirled her in a dizzying circle before seating her on the hoop she'd used during the second challenge. The moment her bottom was on the ring, the hoop soared upward.

She frantically clasped onto the ring with both hands. Her muscles flexed at once. The weight of her wings too great a burden.

The ringmaster's voice echoed over the eager crowd. "Get ready, friends, fans, and fiends, it is time to watch the great Paloma Blanca spread her wings!"

CHAPTER 40

Ignacio

Ignacio raced through the mirrored archway that led into the Big Top. His reflections chased after him from above. In the mirrors, his lips pulled into a smile so high, it reached his temples. His eyes glowed like Tezcán's.

The god's voice rumbled through the air, "It's a shame I cannot be everywhere all at once, or I would have gladly devoured your friends' souls *and* enjoyed the show. But this is better, I think. I do so love watching shining stars light up the night sky before I swallow them whole."

1st of November, 1919. D+P: Age 16

Dovie. I saw you when you came back to the manor this afternoon. You looked . . . I don't particularly know. Haunted? Do you want to talk about it?

I was on an assignment from your father.
You know I will not speak to you about such things.
So please drop it.

You can speak to me about anything. You can trust me with your secrets.

It is best to keep us and what I do for your father separate, don't you think?

Sure. I like that you called us US. Does that mean we are an US?

I'd be offended if we were anything less.

Good.
Because I love you.

I more than love you.

CHAPTER 41
Esmeralda

With every spin of the hoop, she watched the monster within the mirrors above. Its ravenous gaze flicked from her to the other two performers in the Running. Nicola had her arms cuffed behind her back and was stepping into a coffin filled with water. David flung daggers at a spinning bullseye with his assistants hugging each other in its center. Neither act had a clue about the danger they were in.

Esmeralda was terribly aware. She had to get off this hoop somehow. She needed to find Ignacio and her friends.

An idea came to her. She would just have to play Ángel's foul game. He wanted a showstopper. She'd give him one.

Grunting from the weight of the wings, she clambered to her feet as the hoop turned in circles. Lifting one arm, she flicked her wrists. Cards fanned out between her fingers, and people screamed with excitement far below.

Show them what my sad fate could be.

She sent the paper doves soaring into the crowd, who writhed and stretched, hungry for their fortunes to be told.

Gasps of horror exploded throughout the Big Top. Screams rang out. Audience members begged the ringmaster to bring her down.

Slowly, Ángel knelt and plucked up a card. He smirked.

"It appears our Paloma is playing some naughty tricks," he bellowed into the loud-hailer. "Need I remind her where bad children go?"

The audience's horrified faces quickly lightened. They began to cheer as if they believed this was just part of the act.

She shook her head. She tried to plead with anyone watching, but she couldn't open her mouth.

"Let me ask one of our spectators what they think," he said.

He jumped from the podium he stood on and marched toward the audience, leading to an ecstatic frenzy. The ringmaster ran up the bleacher steps and cut left into—Esmeralda nearly lost her grip on the hoop. He went to the comandante's box seats.

Comandante Olivera stood out so clearly from the crowd. He wore no mask or costume. No rouge on his cheeks. He was in his standard black-and-silver uniform. His decorated cap placed snugly on his head.

"What do you think, señor?" Ángel asked Comandante Olivera. "Should Paloma Blanca be punished for frightening my friends with her magic cards?"

The comandante said nothing. He simply glared at the ringmaster.

Ángel chuckled. "Tough crowd."

His words brought on a roar of laughter from the audience.

"What of you, friends, fans, and fiends? Should our darling dove be punished?!"

"No!" the audience screamed.

"Do you want to see more?!"

"Yes!"

"Do you want to see our Paloma fly?!"

"Yes!"

Esmeralda's hoop suddenly dipped as if the rope holding it had given out. When it stopped falling, the motion combined with the weight of her wings caused her to lose her grip. Her arms flailed wildly as she tried to catch the hoop. Her elbow hooked around the bottom tip of the ring before she fell to her death.

The crowd gasped.

One of her slippers fell off as her legs swung in the air. Grunting, she lifted her other hand up and took hold of the ring.

The hoop dipped again.

Her gloves began to sear her flesh. She screamed into her sealed lips but held on tight.

"The rope is going to snap!" a woman yelled.

Esmeralda's eyes widened with horror. The rope holding her a hundred feet above the sawdust floor had begun to fray.

The world slowed. She watched the strands of cord snap like bowstrings, one by one.

Her wings grew even heavier as if invisible hands had risen from the Land of the Dead and were trying to pull her down. This was it. She would die here, splattered onto the dirt for all to see. And she'd never get to say goodbye to the boy she loved.

CHAPTER 42
Ignacio

Ignacio hopped over the ring curb and dashed straight for the ladder leading up to the trapeze platform.

Beyond the stunned crowd, beyond the spotlights flashing and the ringmaster dancing toward the center ring, he only saw her. He only saw her holding on for dear life.

How terrified she must be. How utterly petrified. Still, his Dovie was fighting. Sweat glistened on her skin as she gripped the hoop with all her might.

Ignacio didn't spare an ounce of his energy calling out to her. His entire focus remained on climbing faster and faster.

He made it to the trapeze platform and grabbed the first swinging bar he could find. He yanked it from the hooks and gave it a tug to make certain it was secure. His gaze flicked up to the mirrors. He glared at the shadow lurking behind the cold stone before turning his focus onto the girl he loved.

"Dovie!"

Her eyes snapped to meet his. She let out a muffled sob. His heart nearly broke when he saw the sparkling flakes swiped over her lips.

"I'm coming!" he roared.

He jumped into the air. But his rope swung much lower than he imagined. He couldn't grab hold of her.

Dammit.

He swung to the platform on the other side.

"You're going to have to let go of the hoop when I tell you to!" he yelled.

She shook her head vehemently.

"I'll catch you. I promise, Dovie. I will always be here to catch you. Trust me."

The gloves she wore sparkled like the sea caught in moonlight. She groaned in agony. Her hold slipped, and she dangled by one arm.

He jumped, and right before he was beneath her, he shouted, "Now!"

She closed her eyes and let go.

His body slammed into hers. The weight of her surprised him. Those miserable wings must have been fifty pounds. *Gods*, she truly was a fighter.

Esmeralda's arms and legs wrapped tight against his torso as they swung high above the crowd. She clung to him like a frightened child.

His anger tripled in its ferocity. The ringmaster wanted this to happen.

The second both of his feet landed safely on the trapeze

perch, he squeezed her tight. He didn't care if his strength was too much. He wanted her to feel him.

"You're safe," he said into her wild tangle of curls.

Her entire body quivered.

"I've got you. I always will." He didn't move. He wouldn't do a thing until she was ready.

Slowly, she pulled back. Tears ran down her cheeks. He longed to wipe them away but didn't have the courage to let her go.

He had almost lost her.

He shuddered at the mere thought. Dovie was so special. So beautiful. So full of interesting thoughts and a magic of her own. She was his best friend. His person.

Cries from the audience below tore their attention away from each other.

The ringmaster had collapsed to one knee. His signature top hat fell to the dirt. His hair was no longer light brown, but salt-and-pepper gray with splotches of pure white. He clenched his abdomen as if he was in pain. Some of his men knelt beside him. They tried to help him rise. He shook his head vehemently and pointed upward. Right where Esmeralda and Ignacio still stood.

The ratas turned and bolted toward the ladder to the trapeze platform.

"We have to get out of here," Ignacio said. "Right now."

CHAPTER 43
Esmeralda

While Ángel regained his composure, the spotlight went to the escape artist, who was still trapped inside her watery coffin. An oversized alarm clock screamed beside Nicola's podium. She'd been under the water far too long, but no one was helping her. The ratas were too focused on Esmeralda and Ignacio, too busy climbing the trapeze ladder to capture them.

"We're trapped," Ignacio said.

Esmeralda gestured upward and tried to tell him about the catwalk overhead.

Ignacio cursed. "I can't stand to see your lips sealed like this. We've got to pry them open."

She tried to motion to him that there wasn't time, but his fingers were already brushing against her skin.

"This is going to hurt like the devil," he said.

She braced herself and nodded. As gently as he could, he tore at the glue holding her mouth shut. Tears blurred her vision. Blood seeped onto her tongue. Her lips came apart, and she gasped with pure relief.

"You were right," she panted. "That did hurt like the devil."

Ignacio's mouth found hers. He kissed her hard and hungrily, making her forget all her pain.

Just as quickly, he pulled back. "Better?" he asked. Some of the shimmering flakes covered his lips. She snorted and brushed them away. "Better," she said.

"Let's get a move on," he implored.

"We can try climbing to the catwalk. I saw Ángel using a ladder in his dressing room earlier that was connected to it. If we're fast enough, we can beat the guards to it."

She shuffled around the trapeze platform. They would have to cross a thin plank before they started their climb.

"Wait," Ignacio said.

His strong hands released her, and she thought she might scream from missing his touch so viciously. But then he took hold of the wings on her shoulders and tore them free, chucking them at the guards making their ascent. The wings smacked into the topmost guard, sending him flying back, pummeling the others as well.

"Not bad," she said, nodding in appreciation.

"Take off the gloves too," he commanded.

She was so frazzled that she'd forgotten about the heat sizzling into her skin. She tugged them free and flung them into the air.

"Okay," he said. "Time to go."

CHAPTER 44

Ignacio

They made it across the plank and up to a different perch, passing Tezcán's mirrors as they hurried on. Voices emanated from the obsidian glass. His father's. Camila's. Gabriel's. He heard a scream from within.

"Help me, son!"

Ignacio's stomach clenched. *Mother.*

"Please! Help me! I'm trapped. I need you!"

It wasn't her. Tezcán was making a desperate move.

Bastard.

Esmeralda disappeared as she clambered up the ladder that led to the catwalk and crawled onto the metal platform. He was right behind her but expected her to be halfway across the walkway by the time he made it onto the landing. Instead, he found her frozen in place.

When he stood behind her, he realized why.

General Keara was there, blocking the path to their only chance of escape. He moved around Esmeralda and put his body before hers. He knew Keara had always intimidated Esmeralda the most. And rightly so. The general was a viper.

"Let us pass, Keara," he ordered.

Keara flicked out her wrist and a baton with electrified prongs sizzled near her hip. "I am willing to do whatever I must to see you back in your father's custody."

"Like hell you will," Esmeralda growled.

She leaned around Ignacio's back and flung her slipper at the general's face. The flimsy shoe bounced off Keara's forehead with a comical thud.

Keara blinked.

Ignacio peered down at Esmeralda. Her face was splotchy, her lips cut and bleeding, but she shrugged with a humorous sort of glint. "I thought that would have a better effect. Worked with you the first time we saw each other again."

He raised a brow. "That's because you had a golden egg."

Esmeralda sucked in a breath. "Watch out!"

Ignacio pushed Esmeralda further back on the catwalk before ducking to the right, just barely evading the general's baton as she swiped her electrified weapon. Keara snarled. She swung again. Ignacio bent low, picking up Esmeralda's shoe. He spun upward and used the slipper to smack the weapon out of Keara's hand. The general growled in fury and punched Ignacio hard across the cheek. She punched him again with a left hook.

"Don't let her bully you like that!" Esmeralda shouted.

"Easier said than done!" he snapped.

He lunged forward but the general feinted right. She held out her foot, and Ignacio tripped, landing hard against the metal rungs. Keara was on top of him in an instant. He used his weight to spin onto his back, pulling himself out of her hold.

He stilled when Keara took out her pistol and pointed it at his skull.

"You will comply," she spat.

Something buzzed in the air like a thousand angry hornets. Keara's mouth gaped open as metal prongs stuck into her neck. Her skin radiated as if she had been lit from within like a candle. Her eye sockets glowed. Her teeth too.

Ignacio felt the dull ache of electricity sizzling from her skin to his.

Then, the buzzing stopped.

Keara sucked in a breath before roaring with rage. She whirled around and faced Esmeralda, who still held the baton. She jumped back before Keara could snag her.

Esmeralda smacked the baton on her palm, trying to get the electrical currents to work again. "Come on. Come on. Light back up, you fiend!"

Shakily, Keara rose to her feet. "I'm going to kill you, you little . . ."

Esmeralda swung her arm out and cracked the general across the chin.

General Keara wavered for a second. Her ankle wobbled when she stepped on Esmeralda's slipper, and she lost her balance. A yelp escaped her before she tumbled over the catwalk railing.

Someone in the audience screamed.

Esmeralda stood there, her eyes wild with shock.

More screams rang out from below.

Esmeralda flung the baton out of her grasp as if it were on fire.

"Holy shit," she panted. "I . . . I killed General Keara."

Ignacio scrambled to his feet. He eased toward Esmeralda like she was a wounded animal. "It's okay," he said in a soothing tone. "It wasn't your fault."

Her brows rose, and she blinked. "Oh, I don't feel bad, if that's what you think."

Ignacio balked. "You don't?"

"Well, sure, I do in a killing-is-immoral kind of way. I *am* human, but . . . General Keara was a witch. And not the good kind." She patted Ignacio on the shoulder. "Come on, we have to keep going while the audience is thoroughly horrified and distracted."

Ignacio could do nothing but snort. That was his girl. She was the fiercest person he'd ever known.

Together, they raced across the catwalk and clambered down the raggedy rungs of an attached ladder. The second both pairs of feet were on the ground inside a small dressing room, they ran toward the exit.

He grabbed Esmeralda and yanked her behind a clown buggy seconds before three of the ringmaster's ratas ran into the room they had just left.

More of the ringmaster's guards came.

Their hiding spot wouldn't work for long.

His eyes roamed the backstage area. There were no other exits. He needed to come up with something quick. He spotted a costume lying in two pieces on the ground not far from where they were hidden.

"I'm going to grab those," he mouthed.

He crouched low. Slowly, he poked his head out from behind the buggy. When the guards had their backs to them, Ignacio stretched forward and snatched one of the pieces. He handed it to Esmeralda before peeking at the guards again. One of the ratas turned. Ignacio snapped back, held his breath, and waited.

A small group of dancers walked in, the sequined chains on their hips swishing. In hushed and horrified tones, they spoke about the general's death, about the ringmaster suddenly falling ill. The ratas standing guard had the decency to look away as one of the performers stripped out of her garment. Ignacio used the distraction to snatch the second piece of the costume.

"Good riddance," one of the ladies said. "That woman was a witch."

Esmeralda gave him a look as if to say *See.*

"She was the comandante's hound," the dancer continued. "They have already run through all our soldiers in the war, so now they have to go after anyone they can. They took my little brother to the front lines as a punishment for stealing boots."

The performers grumbled and spoke of other stories they'd heard.

"All I know is that I'm sorry Paloma didn't take a tumble too because I'd sure like a shot with that beau of hers," a young woman with curly red hair said.

"You're terrible," the dancer next to her replied.

"What? He's so fun to look at. I bet he's fun to play with too."

Ignacio snatched Esmeralda's arm before she stomped out of their hiding spot. Judging from the fire in her eyes, she was getting ready to bop the lady right in the nose.

“Come on,” one of the women said. “Let’s go get skunked in Ángel’s caboose before Comandante Olivera recognizes any of us.”

Ignacio motioned for Esmeralda to put on the rest of her costume. For once in her life, she obeyed without complaint.

But now, it was Ignacio’s turn to complain. For he had snatched a costume meant to look like a burro. And he was the ass end of it.

3rd of January, 1920. D+P: Age 16

Dovie. What makes you jealous?

Hmm. I suppose I might get a teeny, tiny, tidbit jealous when I think of you at school. You must be the cutest boy in your class.

You know I go to an all-boys school, right?

What does that matter? The girls' school is right across the street. I hear them chatter about you as they pass by the manor. I may or may not have thrown fish guts from the compost buckets over the fence a time or two.

What makes you jealous?

Everything! It's an odd sensation. I'm jealous of time because it took so long to bring you to me. I'm jealous of air because it touches every part of your skin. I'm jealous of strangers because they get to see you for the very first time. I'm jealous of myself because I get to love you.

I like your answer better than mine.

CHAPTER 45
Esmeralda

Dressed as a donkey, Esmeralda and Ignacio filed in behind the dancers as they started for the backstage exit. A guard nearest to the exit narrowed his eyes as they passed by, but he didn't move. Esmeralda had her eyes narrowed too—but on the brat who was over there tittering about how handsome Ignacio was. When this was over, she'd give that dancer a piece of her mind.

Being the rear of the donkey, Ignacio, the handsome man in question, was bent over resting his hands on her hips to balance himself. But they weren't resting. They were squeezing. His fingers dug into her soft flesh possessively as if he were afraid she might run away and leave his half of the ass behind.

Little did he know she never intended on going anywhere without him ever again.

"Where should we go?" she whispered.

"We need to find Gabriel. I left him in the Fun House holding Camila."

"Holding her? Why? What happened to Camila?" she whispered through the papier-mâché snout.

"Um . . ."

She wove around cast members loitering in Clown Alley, gossiping and speculating about Paloma Blanca and her beau, General Keara, and the way Ángel suddenly looked so old.

A loud voice shouted from the backstage exit. "Stop that ass!"

Esmeralda jerked her donkey head in the direction the voice came from. She gasped when the person was pointing directly at them.

"Time to run," she said. "Hold on tight to me."

Ignacio's fingers dug deeper into her hips. She bolted forward through Clown Alley and cut right into the heart of the carnival. Big mistake. Most of the Big Top audience was spilling out from the main entrance. She pushed through the throng impolitely. She stomped on people's feet and shoved them aside with her snout.

Her breath caught in her throat when she saw the comandante exit.

"They went this way!" someone yelled.

"We've got to hide," she called to Ignacio.

"No," he replied. "We need to find Gabriel and the Sánchezes and leave. Where would he have taken Camila?"

She didn't even need to guess. "To her sister."

Her eyes landed on Sophia the Juggler and her rascal of a monkey Rosco. He sat perched on her shoulder, his greedy little hands—or paws or whatever the hell devils like him had—were rubbing together as he watched the wealthy crowds.

"I have an idea." She dragged Ignacio into a tight cove and tugged off her donkey head. He released her hips and stood, stretching the kinks out of his back.

Right as Sophia the Juggler passed by to entertain the growing throng, Esmeralda shoved the donkey head over Rosco's hairy body. The small demon screeched in anger, but Sophia paid him no mind—she was too busy singing a tune about swindlers and their prizes. A tune Esmeralda knew well.

As the crowd filled in around Sophia and the monkey hidden beneath the donkey head, all that could be seen was Sophia and what appeared to be a donkey walking beside her.

Two ratas ran past, shouting for the onlookers to part.

Esmeralda took Ignacio's hand and tugged him in the opposite direction. They wove through booths and tents and games.

When they made it to the healer's boxcar, stationed beyond the third ring with the carnival staff's bunks, they waited in the shadows until they were certain no one had followed them.

"The coast is clear," she whispered, finally being the one to let go.

She took a step, but Ignacio caught her by the wrist.

"Before we go in there, I feel like I should tell you . . . It's about Camila . . . she's . . ."

"Spit it out, Pigeon."

A whisper of a smile flitted over his face. "I love it when you call me that." He shook his head and flattened the grin away. "She went to the ringmaster earlier to tell him she was leaving. He said he would offer her severance pay for her pain and suffering. He sent her to the Fun House. But there wasn't anyone inside. Not anyone human, at least."

"The monster in the mirror?"

He nodded. "The god. His name is Tezcán."

Esmeralda's brows pinched. "Where have I heard that name before?"

"Perhaps from me. I might have told it to you when we were younger because my mother told it to me first. The fable was given to her by a peddler . . ." He blinked. "A peddler with a curled mustache."

"What does your mother have to do with this?"

"Tezcán said he devoured her soul. Obviously, this has to do with my father. And the ringmaster too. I think . . . I believe they feed the god in exchange for enchantments. And now . . . Camila . . ."

Her fingers clenched his shirt. "What has happened to her?"

"She's . . . changed. Just . . . prepare yourself."

Esmeralda bolted toward the boxcar. When she slid the door open, she found Gabriel holding up a crowbar like a baseball bat. He sighed heavily when he realized who it was and slumped.

"Thank the gods," he breathed. "Or maybe not. Maybe I should be saying curse the gods instead."

Esmeralda stepped through the threshold and Ignacio eased the doors shut in her wake. He took the crowbar from Gabriel and slipped it through the handles.

She ran to Pilar, who was sitting in a motorized chair on wheels.

"You're awake? Are you well?" she asked, tears in her eyes.

"It isn't me you should be worried about," Pilar said in a husky, tired voice.

"It's me."

Esmeralda whirled around. An old woman sat on a small cot. She was tiny and feeble. Her tan skin lay wrinkled across her frail bones. But those eyes. Those caring, beautiful, big brown eyes.

It couldn't be.

The woman held out her palm. "You're the bee's knees," she rasped.

Esmeralda balked. That was what she and Camila said to each other whenever they parted.

"Camila?" Esmeralda whispered.

"Don't just leave my hand out here to dry."

Esmeralda licked her thumb and sizzled it into Camila's palm. "You're the cat's meow. But . . ."

Camila gave a half smirk. "Not too shabby for a vieja, huh?"

Ignacio placed a gentle hand on Esmeralda's shoulder before stepping closer to Camila. "You've aged even more since I left you," he said.

Gabriel strode beside him. "Probably five years within the last half hour."

Ignacio rubbed the back of his neck. "We must find a way to stop her aging before it's . . ." The words *too late* hung in the air like tiny grenades.

"Can someone explain why Camila looks like she's in her eighties?" Esmeralda whisper-yelled.

"It was Tezcán," Ignacio said.

"And that evil ringmaster too," Camila added. "He sent me into the Fun House."

"Same. He directed me to go there after he heard me and

Esmeralda speculating about where you might be." Gabriel frowned. "Little did I know our ringmaster was trying to feed me to some creepy devil."

"But why?" Esmeralda wondered out loud.

"Tezcán mentioned Camila's youth was the payment for the enchantments," Ignacio said. "The god offered to tell me the truth about my mother. All I had to do was offer Gabriel to him. Give him Gabriel's cleverness in exchange for the knowledge I needed. He can grant us our deepest desires, but he requires a soul of equal measure to fulfill those wishes."

A thought slammed into Esmeralda. "The card I was given today for the final challenge mentioned that Ángel is looking for his perfect match. He needs a showstopper like him."

"An equal exchange," Ignacio whispered. "The rule-breakers and disqualified performers are enough to exchange for the magic that powers the carnival, but *he* needs an equal exchange too. He needs someone like him. Have you seen how much the ringmaster has aged as well? He needs a star. A young, beautiful, charismatic showstopper to sacrifice for his wish. Someone like you."

"I'll thank you for calling me those things later." She knelt beside the bed and took Camila's hand. Her skin was paper-thin and cold as ice. "But what do we do right now? How do we change Camila back?"

"I don't know. Destroy the mirrors?" Ignacio suggested.

Gabriel nodded. "That might sever the link between the god and this world."

"But will *she* come back?" Esmeralda looked to her friend. "No offense to the older you. You look wonderful. It's just . . ."

Camila laughed. "You don't have to explain. I understand and wholeheartedly agree."

"Tezcán said he wasn't finished feasting on her. Maybe he didn't have time to steal all her youth. Maybe we can reverse what he started. But we won't know if breaking the mirrors will work until we try," Ignacio said.

Esmeralda stood. "Then let's go try."

"What about the ratas?" Gabriel asked. "They're running about the carnival like it's been robbed."

Esmeralda winced. "That's my fault. I may have thrown General Keara over the catwalk."

"Why doesn't that surprise me," Gabriel deadpanned. "Either way, we have to get into that Fun House and destroy the mirrors. But it's got to be teeming with guards. We'll need a distraction."

"A distraction," Esmeralda said to herself.

She'd heard of intrusive thoughts before. Random things one thinks about doing even though one knows it is wrong or would cause harm. Esmeralda had had one such thought since the day she entered the carnival.

"You look like you have something devious in mind," Ignacio said.

A slow smile tugged her lips upward. "Always."

CHAPTER 46

Ignacio

He and Esmeralda slipped into the menagerie through a small opening under the canvas. They didn't want to risk being spotted within the mirrors that hung at the entrance. Gabriel had told him once that the mirrors were what kept the animals inside. Something within them—perhaps a soul-sucking god—sent currents in the air that the animals could sense and didn't like.

They ducked behind a stack of hay bales as a man in a turkey costume trotted by on the back of a zebra. Esmeralda's boot squished into something soft and odiferous.

She winced. "Good thing Pilar lent me her shoes."

Esmeralda peered over the bales. He joined her. A few elephants meandered about, their big ears flapping. Isadora the tigress lay sprawled out in her cage, her cubs wrestling over a colorful ball. There were wolves and alligators. Lions and antelope. And that menace of an ostrich was there too.

"Won't these animals hurt the guests once we unleash them?" Ignacio whispered.

"Only one way to find out." She grinned.

He scowled.

Her grin fell into an exasperated eye roll. "The lions are old. The tigress is rather sweet. The wolves are well trained. The only one to really watch for is Estefan, but he won't hurt anyone terribly bad. A few thwacks to the rump is all. The carnival hands will go after them to try to put them back, but there aren't enough of them, so they'll need the guards' help. That's the whole point. To get the ratas away from the Fun House so we can go in."

The man riding the zebra trotted by once more. Esmeralda and Ignacio darted behind another bale of hay. They were nose to nose. If he moved an inch closer, they would be mouth to mouth. Her beautiful eyes sparked in the low light. She had a smudge of dirt on the apple of her cheek. Without a second thought, he reached out and brushed it off with his thumb.

Her lips parted, and the expression on her face sent a jolt straight through his core.

He wanted to kiss those lips. To taste her.

He leaned in and so did she.

An explosion blasted outside the tent. Followed by another. And another.

Gabriel.

The two carnival hands in charge of watching over the menagerie ran out to investigate.

"That's our cue," Esmeralda said.

They hopped over the hay bales and ran for the entrance.

Ignacio grabbed a metal feed pail and threw it to her. She caught it just as he grabbed one for himself.

"Sorry for the intrusion, folks!" Esmeralda yelled as they ran past confused guests.

More fireworks fizzled to life outside.

Together, Ignacio and Esmeralda smashed the pails into every mirror they spotted. The entire tent rattled and rocked as if the mirrors were holding it up and not the massive beams. The animals startled and scurried into the center. The man on the zebra fell flat on his heinie. But the animals didn't make a move to escape.

"They're too frightened," Ignacio said.

Esmeralda tore out a gleaming hairpin and shook it in the air.

"Estefan," she yelled. "Come and get it, buddy!"

The ostrich's head popped up and his beady eyes went large. He gave an awful hiss before barreling toward her. She flung the hairpin out of the entrance, and Estefan bolted through. The elephants, smart as they were, must have realized they were free to leave. They blared their trunks and rushed forward.

But Esmeralda was too busy laughing at the damn ostrich to notice she was in their direct path.

"Dovie!" Ignacio reached out and yanked her toward him. Her breath came out in an *oof*, and her fingers splayed over his chest as the stampede rumbled by. The ground shook. Or maybe it was simply his pulse. She was pressed against every part of him.

Her gaze met his. Esmeralda appeared shocked at first, but then she giggled.

Gods, I love her.

Screams tore through the air from outside the tent.

He'd have to tell her again later. And get that kiss too. He took hold of her wrist, and they ran.

The two bolted through the chaos of fireworks blasting far too low for comfort and loose animals tearing into tents and food carts. They tucked their heads low as dozens of ratas stormed out of the Fun House and chased after the freed menagerie.

"Are you ready?" he asked his love.

She smiled bright. "Ready to smash a bastard god into oblivion? You better believe it."

CHAPTER 47

Esmeralda

They smashed mirror after mirror after mirror with the mallets they had stolen from the strongman game as they ran through the carnival grounds to the Fun House.

Haunting laughter rumbled through the tent. Esmeralda froze.

"Don't stop," Ignacio panted. "He cannot harm you so long as you don't look into his eyes or touch the glass."

They came to a fork in the labyrinth. Ignacio went right. She went left.

She tried her best to ignore the goose bumps sprouting over her arms. To ignore the fear whispering in her ear, telling her that none of this would do them any good. That they were doomed.

She raised her mallet but startled when the face in the mirror popped into existence right before her.

"Do you think this will fix what has already been done to your friend?" the god's voice rattled through her bones.

She gripped the mallet harder in her hands, steadying herself.

"I don't know. But it certainly feels good to try." She smacked the mallet into another mirror. Beautifully colored stone cascaded onto the floor in splintered shards.

Tezcán laughed. "You are a mischievous one, Esmeralda Montero." He dragged out each syllable of her name like he was savoring the taste as it slipped off his tongue. "No wonder the boy wants you so desperately. But what will happen in a year from now? In five? He'll grow tired of your sharp shards. He'll leave you, and this time for good."

Esmeralda didn't slow her assault. "Shut up."

"Suit yourself. But you know it is true. You are unlovable. I've seen your past, how your own parents left you. They knew you weren't worth the trouble."

Her heart clenched in her chest. She smashed another mirror. Another.

"Poor child. I can see your pain so clearly. I can help you with that, you know. I can take away all the things that broke you, that changed the fabric of your being. I can make you better. I can make you easy to love. Look into my eyes, and I will fix every crack and scar."

She peeked over her shoulder. She couldn't see Ignacio but could hear him hard at work. The red bulbs overhead dimmed ever so slightly with each break. The gilded frames holding up some of the mirrors started to chip and rust. The magic was waning. Every crack was weakening the enchantments in this place.

"Best hurry," Tezcán said. "If you want me to smooth out the sharp shards of your heart, if you want to be less chaotic and messy, I can change that. Change you. And then you'll be so lovable that no one will leave you behind ever again. But I cannot help you once the portal is severed."

She returned her gaze to the mirror before her. Images played across the shadowy stone. Her as a snarling little girl. Always snapping. Always defensive. Her as an early teen, growing cold and aloof. She thought it better to be alone and push people away than to get hurt. She saw herself at sixteen and seventeen. Wild and jealous. A tangle of curls and rebellion. She saw herself now. Still all those things. The broken child in her had never properly healed and she was inside her even now. Not crying but screaming, raging like a snared beast because of all the terrible things that had happened to her.

Maybe some of it was her fault. But so much of it had been out of her hands. How could a little girl know how to protect herself when she'd never been taught to? When the only adults in her life had been selfish and careless with her?

Ignacio had told her that he never blamed her for how she acted, that she was just a kid trying to survive. And he'd been right. She was a little girl scratching through the bad, trying to find some good. And she had found it. In her friends. In Ignacio. And, more importantly, in herself. She was a fighter. She was clever and strong, and rather funny too. If someone thought she was too much, then that was their loss, because she was fantastical in every damn way.

She tore her eyes from the mirror.

"Go find some other sucker to mess with," she sneered. "Actually, go back to hell."

She slammed the mallet into the mirror.

And waltzed away.

CHAPTER 48

Ignacio

Ignacio stood on his tiptoes and cracked a hanging mirror in two.

The Fun House trembled violently. The bulbs overhead swayed, casting ominous blood-colored shadows on the black walls.

An eruption of explosions boomed in the air outside the tent, followed by whizzing sounds and crackling pops.

"Gabriel must have set off every firework in the carnival," Dovie said as she met him back at the fork in the maze.

Something crashed into the roof of the Fun House. The canvas glowed orange before catching ablaze.

Ignacio took her hand. "We better run before the whole thing topples on our heads."

"Wait!" She wiggled out of his grasp and marched toward the final mirror. It was a small oblong piece that hung low to the floor and could have been easily missed. Esmeralda snagged one of the obsidian stones on the floor and chucked it into the glass. It webbed with a satisfying crack.

The ground shook. The bulbs overhead began to pop one by one. The largest of the poles holding the tent up snapped clean in half.

They bolted toward the exit. Even from inside the labyrinth walls, Ignacio could see the frenzied chaos outside. People were running one way, screaming as an angry herd of elephants rumbled after them. Horses whinnied and galloped by. A carnival hand ran in the opposite direction holding buckets of sloshing water.

The cold air slapped against Ignacio's sweat-slicked skin the second he and Esmeralda stepped out of the tent.

"Holy shit," Esmeralda panted.

The booth adjacent to the Fun House had completely crumbled in on itself and was fully engulfed in flames.

People were trying to extinguish the blaze with water, but the flames only grew.

"Look!" Esmeralda pointed to the small tent beside it.

Ignacio's eyes landed on the tent's sign:

Combustible Bubbles. For When Beans Just Won't Do.

There were tonics of numerous shades and colors displayed on shelves inside. Each had sketches of various sizes of explosions depicted on the labels.

The fire crawled closer to the jars.

"It's going to blow!" someone yelled.

Everyone began to scramble away. Bodies were trampled and pushed and kicked.

Someone rammed so hard into Ignacio's shoulder that his hold on Esmeralda's hand faltered. And she slipped away.

30th of May, 1920. D+P: Age 17

Dovie. Why did I see you climbing so high up the avocado tree this morning on my way to school?

Because I was searching for avocados. Obviously.

You should be careful.

Would you catch me if I fell?

I'd do whatever it took to save you.

I appreciate that sentiment but don't worry, I'm capable enough to save myself.

What if I fell? Would you catch me?

I fear you would squish me into the soil.
And then where would we both be?
How about this?
I'd come running with antiseptic
and clean all your wounds.

I'd prefer it if you kissed the pain away.

Why, Pigeon. What a scandalous thing to say!

CHAPTER 49
Esmeralda

"Ignacio!" she yelled.

They'd lost each other the second they exited the Fun House as people rushed to flee from the flames and bubbling tonics.

Esmeralda tried to stand on her tiptoes and search for the boy she loved, but there was no use. He'd disappeared.

"Ignacio!" her voice cracked. She knew she should run like everyone else. The fire would catch hold of those jars soon. But she wouldn't go anywhere without him. "Pigeon!"

Hands gripped her around the meat of her bicep and yanked her through the beastly throng. She bumped into torsos and elbows and—perhaps not so strangely—a few tentacles belonging to an octopus. With a grunt, she felt herself being flung behind an upturned cart of churros.

Arms draped over her shoulders and forced her against the cool grass just as the first vessel within the combustibles tent detonated. She smelled smoke and dirt and—strangely—bubble bath.

Another jar exploded. Another. Until all she could hear was

pop, pop, pop like popcorn in the kettle. Glass and pure heat soared overhead. Whoever held her to the ground grunted in pain.

When the blasts finally slowed, the arms shielding her let off. She raised her face, expecting her savior to be Ignacio but instead it was a frazzled Gabriel.

His shirt had holes burned into it. Soot covered half his face. And a bit of his dark curls appeared to be smoking on top his head.

"I may have gone overboard on the fireworks," he said, breathless.

"You think? You were supposed to cause a distraction while we snuck into the Fun House, not turn the entire carnival into an inferno."

Gabriel half grinned. "That's the greatest distraction I've ever seen, if I do say so."

"Where's Camila?"

"Safe inside the healer's boxcar with Pilar."

"Has she improved?"

He gulped, and her stomach soured.

"She's aged by another couple years," he said.

Esmeralda inwardly slumped. "Breaking the mirrors didn't work."

Wood groaned and snapped from the direction of the Fun House. Gabriel and Esmeralda peered around the cart. The final pole holding one side of the tent up crumpled in on itself in a tangle of beams, canvas, and sparkling magic.

They gawked at each other.

The music that played on a constant loop slowed and warped. The glimmering lanterns flickered, and the gondolas hovering over their heads slowed to a stop.

"The mirrors are certainly connected," Gabriel whispered. "The enchantments started to weaken after you two went inside. But look." He gestured toward the tip of the carousel, which could be seen from where they lay hidden. It continued spinning in circles. Beyond it, the lights of the Big Top still glowed a buttery yellow. "What are we missing here?"

"We're missing the rest of the mirrors. They're everywhere. We must destroy them all." She grabbed Gabriel by the wrist. "Let's find Ignacio and get to the Big Top. That's where most of the mirrors are."

Gabriel didn't budge. "About Ignacio . . ."

"What is it?"

"I saw him, just before I spotted you. He . . . he was walking away."

Away?

Her gut dipped.

"He wasn't alone." Gabriel suddenly appeared as if he might be sick. "He was with Comandante Olivera."

She jumped to her feet. "We've got to help him. Surely, he's being threatened."

"He was walking of his own accord."

She shook her head. "He would never. He wouldn't . . ."

Her mind began its familiar angry taunts: *You were never worthy of him. Of course he'd choose his father over you. He could never truly love you, a thief whose own family left her behind.*

Anger burned through those thoughts.

They were lies. Lies her own brain told her to try to protect her from potential pain. But the real pain came when she listened to them.

"Come on," she said. "We have to help him."

"As you wish." Gabriel clambered to his feet, his hair still smoking.

"Never mention the word *wish* ever again," she said. "I've heard enough about wishes for a lifetime. We help Ignacio, then smash every mirror in this place."

"Not so fast," a familiar voice said.

Both she and Gabriel spun around. Facing them was the tailor, pointing two pistols at their heads.

CHAPTER 50

Ignacio

The sharp tip of his father's dagger dug into the sensitive flesh above Ignacio's kidney.

"Keep walking, or she's dead," Father growled.

"If you hurt her—"

"You'll what? Kill me? Your own father."

"Yes," Ignacio growled back. And he meant it.

"My man has been instructed to remove her safely . . . unless you disobey me."

An explosion sounded. Moments later, the lanterns flickered out like dying stars. And the music, "The Tale of the Valerio Brothers," slowed its melody.

"Go right," Father commanded.

They rounded the carousel. It was empty of laughing guests, the golden saddles of wooden animals abandoned. Ignacio had ridden on a carousel only once. The night he and Esmeralda snuck out of the manor and went to the boardwalk. It had been the best night of his life. Watching her laugh, holding her hand in public, kissing her. Being free. It was perfect. And now that he and Dovie knew the truth about their love, they could have more of those nights. But he had to find a way to end his father's reign first.

"Keep walking," Father snarled. Ignacio didn't even realize his pace had slackened. "Don't dawdle, son, you know I hate that."

A thousand memories flooded in.

Father ordering him to continue with his fitness and tutoring regimen the day after Mother's funeral, even though he was only seven.

Father nitpicking his messy room even though there wasn't a speck of dust.

Father forever being cold.

Those memories Ignacio could handle. Knowing his father's deceptions had cut Esmeralda so deeply, he could not. Nor could he forgive the lives lost in war. He thought about what Tezcán had said about his mother. That she didn't die at the hands of Dos Palos spies. That he had devoured her soul. Who had given her to the god?

"What happened to my mother?" he asked.

"Shut up!"

Ignacio's instincts begged him not to pry further. Every time he had as a boy, he suffered the consequences. But he wasn't some timid child anymore. And he didn't care about pleasing his father. He was a man now, and he deserved the truth.

"She knew you had affiliations with the carnival, didn't she? Or worse yet, Tezcán."

"Don't speak that name," Father hissed.

"Why? Are you afraid of him? What did you do to her?"

"*I* can tell you." The ringmaster stepped out of the smokey shadows. His sequined jacket was covered in ash and ripped at the seams. He'd lost his famous top hat, and his greased hair, now completely white, flopped in tendrils over his forehead. His face had aged dozens of years but those calculating blue eyes remained unchanged.

"I can tell you everything you need to know about your mother and what role your dear old daddy played in her demise," he said.

"No, Ángel," Father snapped. "Leave him out of this."

Ángel? Father used the ringmaster's first name so easily.

The ringmaster batted his lashes sympathetically. "I'm afraid it's too late for that, Héctor."

These two really did know each other.

"Your boy came to me on his own, even though you tried to keep him away from me all these years. I knew he'd find me eventually. Especially after I rescued his runaway sweetheart. I had that suit he and his love dove purchased from the tailor ready for him the moment I realized who Esmeralda was." His eyes found Ignacio's. "And now you are right where you belong. Remember the book you loved so dear? *I* made sure you received that. Because *I* am not selfish. *I* want you to know your past. Now, do you *really* want to learn what happened to your mommy? You might not like it."

The dagger pointed at Ignacio's back flicked toward the ringmaster. "Knock it off, Ángel," the comandante ordered.

"No. *You* knock it off!" Ángel snapped. "You don't think I know what you've been up to this last year, Héctor? You don't think I have my little spies as well? I won't let you ruin everything we have built."

"We?" Ignacio rasped.

"*We* indeed," the ringmaster said. "Would you like to hear a little tale?"

Father's sapphire eyes filled with fear. "Ángel—"

"Once upon a time, your father and I were traipsing about in a foreign land. There, we found a field of bell-shaped flowers. Blackbird Penstemons to be exact."

Ignacio couldn't understand what the ringmaster was saying. "How do you even know my father?"

"Don't rush the story, kid. Anyway"—he flicked a bit of singed confetti from his shoulder—"within this stunning array of purple blooms, we came upon a strange hot spring that billowed with puffs of white smoke."

"Like the Valerio brothers," Ignacio thought out loud.

The man's eyes lit up. "Yes! Exactly like that."

"You and my father found the mirror to the gods. You made a deal with Tezcán."

With a laugh, the ringmaster raised his hands. "We have a winner, folks."

But there were no folks around to listen. They were alone, hidden in smoke and ash and secrets.

"Tezcán only works in equal bargains. To get what we wanted, certain sacrifices had to be made. Certain lives had to be forfeited. It was easy enough for me, but your father has always been a bit of a sap."

Ignacio shook his head. "How could you two possibly know each other?"

The ringmaster huffed a laugh. "I thought you were catching on, kid."

"Enough, Ángel. I'm taking my son out of here. You and I will discuss things later."

"Later?!" the ringmaster yelled. "Look what your son has done to my carnival. This is all your fault, Héctor. I told you to tell him, but you didn't listen. In fact, you tried to keep him away. Away! When he is the key to my future."

"What is he talking about?" Ignacio spat.

"Your daddy and I made a deal with Tezcán forty years ago."

Ignacio's heart dropped. "Forty . . ." Understanding took hold. It gripped Ignacio by the throat. " 'The Tale of the Valerio Brothers.' " He eyed his father. "The elder brother asked to be powerful beyond measure." He turned to the ringmaster. "The younger brother asked to be young and charming for the rest of his . . ."

"For the rest of his days," the ringmaster finished. "For an eternity if all goes to plan." He winked. "I suppose I should reintroduce myself." He cleared his throat and took a bow. "Ángel Valerio, your one and only uncle."

"Impossible," Ignacio snapped.

"What is impossible is how your father kept all this from you for so long. But there were signs. Olivera is an anagram for Valerio. Did you know that? That wasn't an easy clue, though, I suppose. I tried to warn him you'd turn bitter without understanding the truth. But he was afraid you'd hate him after you learned what he did."

"Ángel," his father growled, but Ángel ignored him.

"Your father wished to be powerful. The only way to gain such power was to offer someone who was powerful themself.

It started with the original ringmaster, the *real* Señor Veracruz, who employed us. He was our first bargain. The real Veracruz was everything we needed. He had the vibrancy, the vivacity, and the versatility to succeed at all things. He was also a great leader. Tezcán was pleased. The real Veracruz fed Tezcán, and Tezcán gave us youth and power in exchange. After a while, though, Tezcán demanded more. So, more was what we gave. Only someone like the commander of a great army would do to keep your daddy on his high horse. Someone like your mother."

"Why not offer up King Amadeo?" Ignacio asked. "He is the ruler of the entire country. Why did it have to be my mother?!"

Ángel chuckled. "The king wasn't an equal exchange. He's nothing but a mouthpiece for whomever he owes favors to, and Tezcán knew it. King Amadeo wasn't enough to satisfy our god. But your mommy, now she had vigor."

Father roared. He rushed forward, aiming his dagger at Ángel's heart. But Ángel simply leapt out of the way.

"He seduced her!" Ángel yelled as he dodged Father's attack. "He thought he'd bring her into his confidence so that she would gaze upon the mirror. And then, the sap fell in love! He tried to feed Tezcán with other powerful people like the general before Keara—kudos to Esmeralda, by the way, for snapping Keara's neck. She really was a dull dame. Anyway, the generals weren't enough to get the respect he was so desperate for. Your father knew what he had to do."

Father swiped his blade in the air, and Ángel lunged backward with a laugh. "You're getting sloppy, old man!"

Ignacio's knees weakened. Bile clawed up his throat. "You're saying my father . . . He . . ."

"He fed your beautiful mother's soul to Tezcán. And then, like magic, he was gifted the role of comandante."

"Bastard!" Ignacio yelled. He barreled forward and pummeled his shoulder into his father's back. The man wheezed but didn't try to fight as Ignacio slammed him into the ground. He grabbed his father by the shoulder and forced him to turn around so he could face him.

Ignacio shook him by the collar. "Why? Why did you take her from me?"

For the first time ever in his life, Ignacio saw tears blurring his father's blue eyes.

"I was weak," he whispered. "I was a fool. I did what I was told."

Ignacio's grip tightened until his knuckles were bone white. "Who would tell you to do such a vile, horrid, unforgivable thing?"

The ringmaster knelt next to the men. He offered a brilliant smile. "That would be me."

He brought his open palm to his lips and blew onto it with a quick burst of breath. Glittering dust engulfed Ignacio and tickled his nose. In the back of his mind, everything clicked into place. The glistening fragments in the ink, in the glue that sealed Dovie's lips shut, it was ground-up bits of Blackbird obsidian.

His body went limp, and he fell into oblivion.

CHAPTER 51
Esmeralda

Both Esmeralda and Gabriel raised their arms in surrender as the tailor pointed two pistols at their heads. Not just any pistols. Only one person in all of Costa Mayor had twin shooters with obsidian hilts.

"You're working for Comandante Olivera," she said, her voice as steely as she could manage.

"Guilty." Jorge bobbed up and down in a curtsy.

"Are you an officer?" Gabriel asked.

Jorge snorted. "I was wanted in four counties for armed robbery. I sewed all my disguises myself," he said smugly. "But then I had a slipup and got pinched. That's when General Keara found me and made me a deal. You see, Comandante Olivera knew you were here all along, Esmeralda. He sent me to work in the carnival to make sure his precious son didn't gallop in here like your knight in shining armor before the comandante's plan could be put in motion."

"What plan?" Esmeralda asked.

"You'll know soon enough. Now, kindly start walking before anyone comes searching for you. I have been instructed to get you far away from this place."

Gabriel stepped forward. "You'll take her over my dead body."

"Fine by me." Jorge cocked back the hammer. "I don't need you at all."

"Wait!" Esmeralda leapt in front of Gabriel. "We'll do whatever you say. Just please don't shoot."

"Promise to play nice?" Jorge asked teasingly.

"Yes."

Jorge waved the pistols, urging them on. "One wrong move, and Mr. Curls over here is done for."

They wove around bits of wood still burning. The animals were gone. Everyone had fled before the blasts. It was only them and Jorge and the comandante's twin weapons.

Esmeralda searched through the wreckage for something hard enough to knock the man out with. But there was nothing she could easily snatch.

"Did you know your boss is aligned with the ringmaster?" she asked.

"Isn't it obvious? Do you really think the railroad tycoons have any say over what happens within this country? They could never keep the Blackbirds out of Carnival Fantástico if Comandante Olivera wanted in. If anything, the Blackbirds are its main source of protection."

"Why?"

"It's all smoke and mirrors. A gilded carnival full of magic is the perfect sort of distraction to keep people's focus far from the realities of war."

"But the magic comes from the ringmaster feeding us to a vile god," Gabriel said.

"Yes. Yes. I know. But you got something wrong. The ringmaster isn't feeding you to Tezcán." He guffawed at the absurdity of it. "The god does not have the taste for flesh and blood."

"He's feeding our essence to him," Gabriel said. "I saw it for myself."

"*Oooh!* You were being metaphorical. In that case, you are mostly correct. The guests feed Tezcán a bit of their essence every time they enter the attractions and pass by the mirrors. They are the exchange made to give the carnival its gilded glow. And then there's the performers and staff who break the ringmaster's rules or fail the Running; those delicious souls are who the god takes in exchange for the glorious enchantments we see every night. The music, the slapdash roller coaster and the gondolas over our heads, the dazzling prizes, and the delectable treats, those are all from the souls taken. But *their* lives aren't enough to pay back the ringmaster's personal debts."

She and Gabriel shared a glance. If they wanted to end this, to try and help Camila, they needed to know more.

"I wonder what his debts are?" she said out loud, trying to sound as if she were thoroughly interested but not necessarily about what Jorge had to say. He loved to feel like the center of attention, and this would spur him.

"Take a good look at Ángel Veracruz," Jorge said. "The man is practically immortal. Aside from tonight, the ringmaster hasn't aged in forty years."

All this time, he'd been an old man hidden inside a younger man's body. *Gross.*

"I wonder what he would have to offer the god in exchange for eternal youth?" Gabriel said to Esmeralda, purposely ignoring the tailor.

"His lead acts, of course! He requires stars to feed Tezcán. He needs brilliant showstoppers who are as vibrant as he wants to be. Only the most magnificent performers win the Running. Only the very best. Don't you see? But it isn't only about their performance. It is about their ferocity, their willingness to do whatever it takes to reach the end of the competition, no matter the cost. Why do you think he makes you pass three challenges? To prove your tenacity." Jorge prattled on. "But I know a secret. Our dear ringmaster is late on his last payment. He's desperate to feed Tezcán. And you're his salvation, doll. But we aren't going to let that happen."

"We aren't?" she and Gabriel both said.

He shook the weapons again. "Keep walking. I've got to get you out of here."

"So . . . you're helping us?" she asked.

"The comandante wants Ángel gone. That's rather difficult when he's filled with magic. But if the ringmaster can't pay Tezcán, he will become his true age. He'll be a powerless geezer. And then . . ." He made a slicing motion over his neck. "Now move faster before any of Ángel's guards come looking for you." He shoved the pistols he held into Esmeralda's and Gabriel's backs.

But she couldn't leave without Ignacio. And she had to help Camila.

She stumbled forward and fell to her knees.

A shock of white hair caught her attention just ahead of them and to her left. Her jaw dropped. A little old woman was standing in the shadows. There was steely fury in her dark eyes, and in her hands, a broken piece of timber.

Esmeralda's foot shot to her side. Gabriel cursed as he tripped over her toes.

"Dammit, Esmeralda," Gabriel hissed. "I fell right on a nail." He tried to get up, but she clutched his arm.

"What are you doing?" Jorge snapped. "Get up. Get up right—"

Camila jumped out of the shadows and swung the wood in the air. It hit Jorge's skull with a *thwack*.

The tailor spun in a circle before falling face-first into the rubble.

CHAPTER 52

Ignacio

Ignacio woke with a start, and the full reality of what had happened slammed into him.

He tried to get up, but his arms and legs were hog-tied. To his left knelt his father in the sawdust, his pale skin deepening in a red-tinted rage. They were in the Big Top.

"Glad you two have finally returned from the land of dreams."

Ángel's knees popped as he bent down in front of them and adjusted their knots. He had aged even more since Ignacio was knocked out. That made Ignacio wonder how long he'd been asleep. The Big Top tent didn't have that golden glow of daytime. So, had it been minutes? Hours? Long enough to drag him and his father inside.

A thought struck him. Two, actually. Was Esmeralda okay? That thought was forever there. But the second thought pierced into his stomach. How was Camila faring if this could happen to the ringmaster?

"Why am I tied up?" Father asked.

"Because, big brother, I know what you've been up to. Why do you think I've been trying to reach you for so many months? To catch up on old times?"

Father said nothing. He simply glared at Ángel with an intensity that would have petrified Ignacio when he was young. Ignacio hated him. Hated everything about him. If he weren't tied up himself, he would tear into his father again.

"Did you truly think I wouldn't put two and two together?" Ángel asked the comandante.

A bit of dust fluttered onto Ángel's shoulder. Ignacio's gaze flicked upward. He thought he saw movement on the catwalk but couldn't be certain.

"You were going to ruin everything we have built," Ángel said.

"I was trying to make things right. I've let this go on for far too long. I let you destroy far too much."

"You *let* me? Brother, I let *you* join in on the fun. This"—Ángel gestured about—"I built this. This was all my idea. *I* was the one who came up with the idea to keep Tezcán's mirrors in the carnival. To feed him morsels of all the souls that passed through my gates. *I* was the one who knew no one would care enough about the nobodies who worked in my carnival to worry over what happened to them. This was all *my* plan. And it was one you went along with for ages. Yet now you are so desperate to destroy it."

Something clattered high above, but the brothers didn't seem to notice.

"Soon, there will be no more Blackbird obsidian to connect us to Tezcán anyway," Father said. "My troops have almost reached the far north. Between crushing the obsidian down to make weapons and the mirrors you use, there's hardly enough as it is. We've all but drained Dos Palos dry. And when we have, what will you do?"

"We'll widen our search. We find some other weak nation across the sea and take what is ours. The queen hails from Isla Cedros. We could force her to aid our endeavors."

"There's no guarantee the obsidian is anywhere but Dos Palos. You'd start a new war on a chance? So many lives have already been lost. For what? For what?! So that you can be an old man trapped in a young man's body? So that I can have power and prestige but not a soul to share it with?"

"This is what all your fussing is about? Your wife?! We agreed she had to go." The ringmaster stood, frustrated. "And now you have another choice to make. Which one of you dies tonight? Your son or you? I only need one of you to do my bidding outside the carnival."

Father shook his head. "This ends with you and me. We've committed terrible atrocities. I let my wife die. I couldn't look my own son in the face because of what I let happen. He won't become like me and you. It's over anyway. Look at you. You are aging as we speak. And your lead act is gone. My spy has taken Esmeralda far away from here. You won't be able to pay Tezcán your bargainer's fee."

"No," the ringmaster whispered.

The relief flooding Ignacio's veins was immeasurable. Esmeralda was gone. His father had made sure she got away.

"Then he'll have to suffice."

Ángel stepped forward and snatched Ignacio by the collar. He grabbed the hand mirror from within his coat. The very one Ignacio had gazed into the day he clambered onto the caboose. Shadows whirled inside the black glass. Then Tezcán's vile face appeared. His grin was hungry. Ravenous. Ignacio snapped his face away, but large mirrors were everywhere. Hanging near the exit. In the rafters. On some of the beams. He clamped his eyes shut.

"Ángel, stop!" Father tried to lunge forward, but his limbs were tied tight together. He fell on his side, grunting as he landed on his elbow.

A soothing calm crept over Ignacio's skin as the shadowy mist oozed out of the smooth stone. "Look deep into my eyes," the god whispered. Tezcán's voice sank into Ignacio's body. His pulse slowed.

"Enough of this insanity!" Father roared.

Ignacio gritted his teeth and tried to keep his eyes clamped closed, but his body was growing numb, his resolve melting.

"Pigeon."

Ignacio's eyes shot open.

He found Esmeralda inside the obsidian mirror, shivering in darkness.

"I'm so scared," she whispered. "I'm all alone and there's no one to save me."

That wasn't what Dovie would say or do at all. She was a fighter. She would be cutting her own path through the darkness.

"Please, Pigeon. Don't fail me now. Please find me. Come rescue me."

His stomach soured. She'd never speak like that.

"You aren't her."

He jerked his gaze away. The ringmaster grabbed him by the chin and forced him to face the mirror.

Ignacio slammed his eyes shut. "You won't have me," he growled. "And you'll never have her. Your time is up."

A scuffle sounded near the entrance to the tent.

"Unhand me, you asshat!"

Ignacio's heart plummeted.

Esmeralda's hands were tied together in front of her, and she was being shoved toward the center ring by the tailor. Jorge sported his signature goat mask and goat-hair shawl. In his hands, Father's twin pistols.

"What are you doing?!" Father yelled.

The tailor said nothing. *The rat.* He shoved Esmeralda with the mouth of the gun, and they ambled forward. Ignacio thought he might explode with fury.

The ringmaster grinned. "Looks like it is your lucky day, nephew." He released Ignacio and flung him to the ground. He raised his arms. "Jorge, what a lovely gift you have brought me."

24th of June, 1920. D+P: Age 17

Dovie. If I died, what would be the hardest thing to forget about me?

What sort of morbid question is that?

I was thinking about my mother. I can't remember much about her anymore and it makes me sick. I remember how pretty she was. I remember how warm and safe she made me feel. And I remember the sound of her voice when she told me stories. But that is all.

That sounds like plenty to me.
Here's my answer for you:
When you die, I'll always remember how handsome you were. I'll remember how warm and safe you made me feel. And I'll remember the sound of your voice when you told me about your day on nights we lay on the rooftop.

That's almost exactly what I just said about my mother.

Yes. Because it's plenty.

I see what you did there. You must think you're so clever.

That is a fact, not a thought.
But now you must promise me I'll die before you (once we're very old and very gray) because I couldn't stand to endure a world where you aren't in it.

CHAPTER 53
Esmeralda

The barrel of the pistol dug into her back.

She glared at the infamous goat mask. "Not so hard," she hissed through her teeth.

When she turned to face Ángel, she gasped.

If he hadn't still been dressed in his signature purple coat, she might have mistaken the ringmaster for Comandante Olivera. Like Camila, the ringmaster had aged. He had grown a bit thicker around the waist. His hair had gone completely white. And his eyes. Those crystal-blue eyes, wrinkled at the edges, were an identical match to the comandante's.

The youth he'd stolen from the previous lead acts, it was clearly drying up. Tezcán's magic would be gone if he didn't feed someone to Tezcán soon. Someone like her.

The ropes around her wrists felt suddenly too tight, and her mouth ran dry.

"Thank you for bringing my lovely dove back to me," he said to Jorge. Only, the real Jorge had been left tied up inside the weather-changing tent. Hidden beneath the goat mask and shawl was Camila. The timepiece Gabriel always wore clicked away frantically from her hip. They had only moments to get Ignacio out and run for their lives.

Camila moved the pistol, pointing it at the ringmaster. "Untie Ignacio," she said, her voice steely.

The ringmaster's smile dropped. "What is this?"

"This is your opportunity to let him go before we make you," Esmeralda yelled.

The ringmaster laughed heartily. "You are threatening me?"

He twirled his fingers, and a glittering jar appeared in his palm.

Many things happened at once. So fast that they felt slow.

The first thing that happened was Ignacio yelling: "Duck!"

Esmeralda dove out of the way, but Camila was not so lucky. The jar broke open when it crashed into her chest. Sparkling dust danced in the air around her. Her brown eyes went wide. Then she crumpled into a small heap on the ground. Camila's finger must have closed around the trigger of the pistol because a shot went off. Esmeralda balked. She thought they had emptied the bullets, but there must have already been one in the chamber.

The next thing that happened was the comandante breaking free from his bindings and pummeling into the ringmaster.

The ropes Esmeralda had hastily tightened around her wrists to look more convincing fell to the floor. She ran for Ignacio just as the first of the sparklers Gabriel had rigged up on the bale ring high above caught the fuse. There was a loud hiss, followed by a crackle, then a *BOOM!* The entire Big Top swayed.

"What was that?" Ignacio asked as she tried to undo his bindings.

"Gabriel fitted the tent with explosives. We've got to get out of here before the whole place crashes down on us."

Her fingers tunneled through the knots holding Ignacio at bay. Her nails dug into the rough twine, but it wouldn't give. Another fuse hissed to life. *BOOM!* The catwalk swayed as if it were drunk.

She growled in frustration. "I can't get you untied!"

The ringmaster and Comandante Olivera crashed into the spinning board used for the knife-throwing act. They punched and cursed and tore into each other with more vengeance and vitriol than she'd ever known was possible.

The ringmaster threw a wide punch but missed. Comandante Olivera took his chance. He barreled his fist right into Ángel's face. Ángel's head snapped to the left, and he fell nose-first into the sawdust.

BOOM! BOOM!

The explosives were detonating in full. The bale ring would fall in seconds, taking with it all the hanging mirrors. Then the entire tent would cave in, taking with it the mirrored entrance. As well as the last of the ringmaster's links to Tezcán. And their lives too if they didn't get out right now.

Esmeralda cursed. She wrapped her arms around Ignacio and tried to drag him outside.

"Why are you so heavy?" she grunted.

"Why didn't you bring a knife!"

"If I'd known you were tied up, maybe I would have."

"You came into a hostage situation unprepared!"

"No, we didn't! A pistol is a weapon . . . We just didn't know it was loaded."

"Do I need to remind you how absolutely reckless that sounds?!"

"So is getting tied up! Maybe you shouldn't have gotten yourself into this—"

Comandante Olivera stomped toward them like a charging bull. He gripped one of the knife-thrower's sharp daggers. But Esmeralda was not afraid of this man. She no longer cared what he thought or said or did. She'd kept herself alive and fed after she ran away from him, after he tried to send her to the front lines of a pointless war. She would survive him again.

BOOM!

She covered Ignacio with her arms as dust and debris fell upon them.

"Out of the way, Esmeralda!" the comandante barked.

She looked up at the man she'd once idolized. "All of this is your fault. You selfish, no-good coward of a man. If *anything* happens to Ignacio, so help me, I will tear you apart with my bare hands."

As the comandante's eyes bore into her, she thought she saw them soften the tiniest of bits, but he didn't respond. He knelt beside his son and silently sliced into his bindings as more fuses screamed to life.

CHAPTER 54
Ignacio

The ropes fell and Ignacio shot to his feet. He enveloped Esmeralda and squeezed her against his chest. "I love you."

She peeled away from him. "I know, but we've got to get out of here."

He nodded but noticed his father had yet to stand. His head was bowed low and his hand rested over his stomach. When he pulled back his arm, inky blood stained his palm.

"Father?"

"That damn bullet may have snapped my bindings, but now it's lodged inside my gut." The comandante met Ignacio's gaze. "Get out of here, son. Go before it's too late."

But Ignacio couldn't move. This man had committed the worst sort of atrocities, but he was still Ignacio's father.

"Get him," Esmeralda said. "I'll grab Camila and meet you outside."

Before he could argue against her plan, she bolted toward their friend, who was still lying on the ground.

The tent wobbled and rattled. Mirrors began to fall from the rafters.

Ignacio knelt, took his father's arm, and wrapped it over his shoulder. Grunting, he forced his father to rise. His eyes cut to Esmeralda, who was nearly to Camila. He'd take his father out and then run back to help her.

"Quickly," he spat. And the comandante obeyed.

They limped through the exit tunnel.

Tezcán's face appeared within the mirrored archway. At first, it was a thousand small versions of the haunting mask. But then they became one massive face.

"Stop, Héctor," Tezcán growled. His voice rumbled so low Ignacio felt it rattling within his core.

Father must have too, because he groaned in pain.

"You cannot break our bargain," Tezcán said.

"I'm through with serving two masters. I will no longer be your or my brother's lackey."

"You will lose everything," the god hissed.

"I do not care." The comandante's eyes met Ignacio's. "I won't let my son suffer for my mistakes anymore."

"Then you have chosen damnation for you *and* your boy."

The ground rocked. Father roared in anguish and his knees buckled. He clenched his belly.

Ignacio dropped beside him. "Come on, Father. We've got to keep going."

"I can't. But you must." He grabbed Ignacio's arm. "Go. Get out of here. Flee this country. Once the last of the mirrors breaks, everything we've built will be ruined. Our family will be exposed."

"There is no *we* here. *I* tried to stop your vile war."

"Whether you like it or not, you are my son. People will hurt you because of who you are to me."

"I'm no one to you," Ignacio snapped.

Father's face contorted in anguish. "That isn't true. You and your mother are—were everything to me."

"Enough!" Ignacio barked. He scooped his father up despite his protestations and kept walking through the haunting hallway.

"I *did* meet your mother with the intention of stealing her title, but then I fell in love with her. How could I not? Your uncle grew mad when I told him I wouldn't sacrifice her. I tried to keep my past from her, but I kept finding little things she'd been given while on duty. Pamphlets for the carnival. Books about Tezcán. Ángel was teasing me. Showing me how helpless I truly was to him. He was everywhere."

Another firecracker detonated. The archway swayed. Tezcán's screams pierced the air as the small mirrors lining the walls began to fall.

They needed to move faster. He had to get back to Esmeralda. She should be running out by now.

Through clenched jaws, his father said, "Your mother, clever woman that she was, figured out the clues Ángel had left her. She learned of our deal with Tezcán. She wanted to help me, free me. She wanted to sever the magic that protected Ángel. And she died for it. He is unstoppable. So, I did whatever he asked because I knew he might come for you next if I didn't obey."

They were nearing the exit. People were gathered out front. Holding each other as the tent swayed and groaned.

"Why didn't you just let me run away with Esmeralda back then?" Ignacio asked. "I would have been safe."

"He would have found you. I thought it was better if Keara could watch over you while we tried to end him. But then you defected from the Blackbirds, and I knew my time was up. I turned my soldiers away from hunting the Defiant and slowed all active troops searching for the obsidian. I paid Jorge to infiltrate the carnival. With his help, we extracted Melanie the Marionette before he could sacrifice her to Tezcán. That left my brother weakened and desperate for a new act. I knew this was my chance. But I never wanted you here. I never wanted you to be part of what my brother and I have done."

"And Esmeralda?"

His father said nothing.

"You were willing to let her be your pawn . . . again," Ignacio snarled.

They finally passed through the entrance threshold and found the carnival in chaos. Flames licked the rooftops of most of the tents and wagons. Gondolas had snapped from their wires and crashed into booths. Dawn was on the cusp of breaking. With the skies growing lighter, he could see that most of the glitter and gilded filigree that had once shimmered on each attraction had dulled.

Gabriel bolted forward holding a fuse box.

"Where are the girls?" he bellowed. "The entire place is about to blow!"

CHAPTER 55
Esmeralda

The wires that held the right side of the bale ring up snapped all at once. The catwalk, which was attached to it, plummeted at one end of the tent. Mirrors tumbled to the ground. With each explosion of glass, the tent groaned and shuddered.

But there were other things happening to the Big Top as well.

The golden railings within the bleachers began to rust. The vibrant colors painted on the clown buggies dulled and the wood splintered. Everything was aging. No. Everything was showing its *true* age. Without the ringmaster's payment to Tezcán, without the enchantments, what was left of the carnival was falling apart.

Good, Esmeralda thought. This place was built on the lives of the young. It didn't deserve to continue.

A mirror fell not ten feet away from her. She grabbed Camila by the shoulders and shook her so hard her teeth clicked like tiny tap dancers.

“Wake up!” Esmeralda yelled. “We’ve got to go!”

Slowly, Camila’s eyes peeled apart. The wrinkles that had formed around them were starting to fill in. Her hair was slowly turning black. Esmeralda barked a joyful, shocked laugh.

“What’s happening?” Camila groaned.

“You’re changing back!” Esmeralda yelled. “Oh, and the tent is collapsing!”

Camila smiled. “Gabriel’s rigging worked.”

Another blast rocked the poles. “I’d certainly say so.”

She eased Camila up. Together, they wobbled toward the exit.

Something cracked overhead. The largest of the mirrors plummeted toward them. She shoved Camila forward and leapt out of the way as a beam tumbled after it.

Esmeralda fell to her knees and shielded her face and neck from the fallen shards. When the dust settled, she whipped around to find Camila on the other side of the beam, unharmed.

Camila struggled to her feet. Her body still wasn’t as strong as it was meant to be.

“Go! Now!” Esmeralda yelled over the beam. “I will be right behind you!”

“Are you sure?”

“Yes. I’ll catch up!”

She had to hurry. A few more snaps and the bale ring would fall completely.

Just as Camila disappeared into the tunnel, an arm snaked around Esmeralda’s neck. A hand clamped over her mouth, sealing in her scream.

She tried to free herself from Ángel’s grasp, but there was no use—he was far too strong.

"Look what you did to my beautiful carnival," the ringmaster hissed into her ear.

The entire Big Top had changed. The black-and-white stripes had faded and turned a muted gray. The golden curtains that hung between the arena and backstage lay crumpled and frayed. Not a single speck of enchantment remained.

"But you're going to help me raise it up once more."

He pulled the hand sealing her mouth away and grabbed something from inside his coat. She screamed until her throat scratched. But who would hear her over the grinding metal swinging above their heads?

He raised the intricate hand mirror he always carried in front of her face.

Glistening eyes watched her from within the polished stone.

Stars above, I am so sick of seeing this fiend.

"Look into my eyes, Esmeralda," Tezcán said.

"I'll pass." She slammed her heel into the ringmaster's foot, then brought her elbow to his gut. He keeled over, and she took that moment of surprise to run.

But the ringmaster was upon her once more. He tackled her to the ground and then flung her around. He used his knees to pin her arms to the earth.

"This will not hurt, Esmeralda, darling," he said.

He lowered the mirror toward her. She shut her eyes.

Ángel's thumb and pointer finger peeled her eyelid back.

She screamed but her throat was raw, her voice muted over the world collapsing in around her.

"Yes," Tezcán's deep voice rumbled. "Yes, she will do. She is your equal. She will suffice."

A loud and terrible crack sounded from overhead.

The final wires holding up the bale ring were snapping.

"Please," she cried. "The tent's going to fall down on our heads."

"Give her to me now and I will save you, Ángel. I'll devour the boy too; then we will raise the carnival up better than ever before."

Ángel smirked. "As you wish."

CHAPTER 56
Ignacio

Ignacio whirled around to face the Big Top.

A lone form limped out of the entrance.

Camila.

His heart sunk.

“Where’s Dovie?!” he yelled.

Camila shook her head. “She . . . she said she would be right behind me.”

Ignacio started for the Big Top, but his father snatched his arm.

“Don’t. The entire arena is crumbling.”

“I’m not a coward like you,” Ignacio snarled. “I don’t let the people I love die.”

Ignacio tore out of his father’s grasp and bolted into the darkness.

“Please!” he heard Esmeralda cry.

Ignacio’s already fast pace quickened at the pure terror in her voice.

The moment he entered the tent he found her.

Ángel was holding Esmeralda down. That blasted hand mirror in his clutches.

Ignacio tucked his head in and ran. But it wasn't he who made it to the ringmaster first.

His father had somehow found the strength to run at full speed. He roared as he rammed into Ángel, and the brothers went flying back.

Esmeralda scrambled to her feet and staggered forward. Her eyes lifted, and she found Ignacio. A sob escaped her lips, and he thought his heart might shatter like the stone underfoot. He never wanted to hear her cry like that ever again.

She crashed into him. Her arms wrapped around his neck as if he were her only hope in the world.

"We've got to get out of here," Ignacio said while the two brothers fought for dominance.

"Wait." Esmeralda grunted as she bent down and plucked up the ringmaster's mirror. "You must end it," she said. "This is your family, after all."

"No," he replied. "You are."

But he shattered the piece nevertheless.

The center beam cracked. Slowly, it began to buckle.

"Go!" Father bellowed. "Now!"

Ignacio scooped up Dovie and ran.

The tent fell as soon as they exited the hallway of broken mirrors.

Gabriel hit the fuse box and the tunnel exploded in a cloud of sparkling fragments.

Screams of horror rang through the cotton candy–colored sky as a plume of shimmering smoke blotted out the early morning sun. Slowly, everything in the carnival began to age. It was as if invisible hands had taken hold of the magic and were peeling back the façade.

The costume Dovie wore shifted from pearly white to a dingy shade of cream. The billboards that posted the carnival rules began to crack and splinter. Glitter that had fallen to the grass dissolved into the early morning breeze.

He gently placed Esmeralda down and they faced the wreckage together. His father was in there. And Ignacio wasn't certain whether he should be devastated or relieved. Was it terrible to feel both at once? His father had done vile things, but he had loved Ignacio in his own sort of way. Still, that didn't mean he deserved Ignacio's love in return.

Fingers slid into his hand and squeezed. Ignacio's heart did the same.

He gazed down at the girl he'd loved for most of his life. And for once, she had nothing snappy to say, which made him chuckle.

"Are you laughing at me?" she asked, her nose scrunching.

Gods, I love when it does that.

"No. Well. Maybe."

She scoffed but pressed in closer to him. And he didn't dare complain.

After a long moment Esmeralda whispered, "Happy birthday, Pigeon."

Ignacio's eyes widened. He'd completely forgotten the date. Understandably.

Her arms wrapped around his torso. "I know what I shall give you for a gift."

"Oh?" He hugged her closer to him. "What more could I possibly need when I have you here with me?"

She tilted her head up and grinned. "I was thinking a pet ostrich would do."

Laughter burst from him. "Is that a gift or punishment?"

"Look!" someone yelled.

Something moved within the wreckage. A hand shot out from the edge. Father's head and shoulders squeezed through the bottom. He clawed his way out. He reached back into the canvas and then pulled out the body of his little brother, who was no longer young or charming.

Father collapsed beside Ángel, holding his still-bleeding stomach.

The few ratas that remained started for him, but Father shook his head. He found Ignacio amongst the growing crowd. For the first time in his life, Ignacio felt nothing when his father's attention focused in on him. He felt no fear. No regret. He didn't worry his father would call him a disappointment. Or stare him into submission with those cold eyes. Because, seeing him now, he realized that his father was nothing but a weak man.

Father winced and held his hand tighter to his stomach. "You may know me as Comandante Héctor Olivera. Today, I was shown by my son how much of a coward I truly am. This man who lies here dead was once your ringmaster. He was my brother."

Esmeralda sucked in a breath.

"I won't be a villain any longer," the comandante said. "I will confess, here and now, all of my and my brother's crimes."

Ignacio watched Esmeralda's brown eyes darken as the full

weight of Ángel's deceptions pressed against her. As his father's revelations cut into her mind.

He was tired of seeing Dovie bear the burden of other people's mistakes.

He turned to her and cupped her cheek. "Care for a stroll? I only got to hold your hand for the world to see once before on the boardwalk. I'd like to do that again."

"But . . . our friends . . ."

"Are safe."

She huffed a bewildered breath. "They are. We all are."

"Come on," he said. "Maybe I'll even win you a prize."

"I'm pretty sure all the games are destroyed," she said.

"It was never about the games, Dovie. It was about playing them with you."

"Oh yeah? And what happens when you lose?"

They turned their backs on the fallen tent and his broken father and all their past hurts, and strolled through what was left of the crumbling carnival.

"I won't lose," Ignacio said smugly. Before she could argue, he added, "Because I'll be spending time with you."

She giggled. "You're such a sap." His Dovie met his gaze. "I hope you never change."

The Defiant Press

A letter from Ignacio Valerio—Formerly Ignacio Olivera, son of Comandante Olivera

Printed: 28th of March, 1922

Today, just past the break of dawn, my father, Comandante Olivera, revealed to be Héctor Valerio, walked into the king's hall and turned himself in to the high court. He also stood as witness to the wrongdoings of his late brother, Ángel Valerio, formerly known as Ángel Veracruz, ringmaster of Carnival Fantástico.

Their wrongdoings in question:

Murder.

Theft.

Colluding with a god of ill intent.

War crimes.

With King Amadeo's permission, the commander of the Blackbirds started the conflict with Dos Palos.

Some of you may remember that up until twelve years ago, there had never been tensions between the countries before. So why did they start after my father took the position of commander from his recently departed wife? It wasn't because Dos Palos started a needless trade war.

But because my mother warned their leaders that my father and his brother were stealing a weapon of evil from their country. Landowners had accepted payment for some time until the brothers dried up their lands. The brothers were then cast out and, therefore, decided to take what never belonged to them.

The mineral held power. Enough to enchant the carnival. To give the Blackbirds incredible weaponry as well. It was also beneficial to the king, for he sold it in small quantities to the nobles and elites in the island kingdoms to the west.

Both King Amadeo and Héctor Valerio were taken into custody by the personal guards of the queen—who, unbeknownst to most, had been in direct communication with the Defiant and was funding their cause.

The war, the loss of thousands of innocent lives, it benefited only these three men. But mostly Ángel Valerio, who sacrificed the lives of his performers to continue his own charade as a young and charismatic ringmaster.

If you went to the carnival and ever felt fatigued afterward, it was because of this man. He has died with his circus.

The comandante has confessed his sins to dozens of witnesses who watched the carnival fall. It is now up to the queen and to the people whom she serves to do what is right. To make the changes necessary to mend the wrongs of three greedy men.

I, as a Valerio, will forever hold guilt in my soul for what they did as well as my own role in the war. And I will strive to ensure any injustices committed will not be hidden by smoke and mirrors. I will bring to light anyone who has played a part in the terrors they inflicted.

We cannot return what was lost. I cannot have my mother back. She too was a victim of the Valerio brothers. I don't know how one fixes so many wrongs. I may never know. But I can start by doing one right thing. And that is telling the truth.

CHAPTER 57
Esmeralda

Three months later

The kingdom was understandably enraged. The king and comandante had been tried and convicted for their crimes. Their punishment would be settled upon later.

Esmeralda watched as Ignacio held the weight of his father's offenses on his shoulders. She watched as he walked into each tribunal and told them everything he knew. At first, some thought he should be charged right along with his father and uncle—to end the family line. And Ignacio would have accepted that. But Esmeralda would be damned if anyone took her love away from her ever again.

She had written her own letters to be published by *The Defiant Press*. She had learned the power of words from Ignacio long ago when he'd used them to make her smile through her heartbreak. Esmeralda penned her own letters to let the world know what sort of man he was.

A good one.

A brave one.

Hers.

They stood on a rolling hill that overlooked the prettiest meadow. In the center was a large home that seemed to have been pieced together at various times over the centuries. Camila, Pilar, Gabriel, and his love, Javier, had made their way here to the countryside immediately after the Big Top fell. As did Estefan the ostrich, who had become quite the guardian for the family's farm.

Camila, nearly returned to her original self, save for a chunk of pure-white hair, had offered Esmeralda and Ignacio an open invitation to join the family whenever they were ready. But now, Esmeralda's heart was racing.

What if she did something wrong and Camila's family hated her?

What if Camila had changed her mind?

What if they didn't want her?

She pushed those thoughts away.

What wasn't to love? She was smart, loyal, and had become one hell of a friend.

"I have something for you," Ignacio said. "Close your eyes and hold up your palm."

Never one to turn away a gift, she complied.

Something light as a feather kissed her delicate skin.

"Okay," he said. "Open your eyes."

She did so and smiled. A tiny paper dove sat waiting for her.

"Open it," he said.

She obliged.

Dovie. Would you like to go onto the roof tonight and stare at the moon with me?

Raw emotion gathered in her throat. This had been what she always wanted. Love. A family. A place she called home, where she could climb up on the rooftop without sneaking around. Her beautiful Ignacio. And, most wonderfully of all, she had found peace within herself. She had found a sense of worth that could never be taken away.

"I don't have a pen to write my reply," she said.

"That's okay. You can tell me right here." He pointed to his mouth.

On tiptoes, she brushed her lips against his. Her entire body went warm.

"My answer is yes." She kissed him. "I'd like to see the moon with you." She kissed him again. "And the stars." She kissed him once more. "And whatever else the world has in store."

He wrapped his big strong arms around her and said, "Then that's exactly what we'll do."

"Do you promise, Pigeon?"

He rested his cheek on top of her head. "Always, Dovie."

Acknowledgments

As I was writing these acknowledgments, I sat at my desk, staring at a blank Word document for a few minutes in a state of shock. Five years ago, if someone had told me that I'd be writing a third book, I would have faked my own confidence and said, "Damn right, I will be!" before turning around and squeezing my eyes shut to beg the universe to "Please let that come true."

But here we are. I am living out my dreams.

A lot of it is luck. I will forever thank the universe for being kind.

Some of it is me. I was so stubborn when it came to becoming an author. I never let myself give up. I am the reason why I sit at my dining room table with my hair a mess, dark circles under my eyes, with my dog looking at me like, "Girl, it's time to wake up the kids and then feed me. We have a schedule to maintain."

But much of the reason my dreams have come true is because of the people who have believed enough in me to give me a chance.

There have been so many times in my life when I have felt

that I wasn't enough or that I was being too much. I kept trying to put myself into the boxes that I thought people would like me best in. The boxes that made sure no one saw how boring I could be, or weird, or cringy, or basic. But the community I surrounded myself with reminded me how dull it was to be stuck in a box that wasn't meant for me. The people who saw the real me and loved me and supported me *as I am* reminded me that I'm great just *as I am*. I'm worthy, no matter what box I do or don't fit in.

This book gave me that reminder as well.

I have to thank my agent, Larissa Melo Pienkowski, who saw enough potential in the seedling of the concept for *Carnival Fantástico* to help me turn it into something real.

To my editor, Bria Ragin, thank you for seeing my vision and always being there to keep me aligned. Thank you for seeing my vision better than me most days. To my amazing publishers at Joy Revolution, Nicola and David Yoon (who I get to brag that I know to everyone I meet), thank you for putting books into the world where people who are so often unrepresented in love stories get to find their happily-ever-afters. Hope you enjoyed being part of the carnival! Literally. Sorry I had to trap you in a watery coffin, Nicola.

To the team that helped bring *Carnival Fantástico* from a Word doc to an actual book: Makena Cioni, Wendy Loggia, Trisha Previte, and Jamie Johnson, thank you for all you do. To my publicist, Madison Furr, thank you for putting in the work! And for getting me to events on time. Thank you to the digital marketing team behind Underlined and Love, Underlined. It's so fun to work with you.

Thank you to all the organizers of book cons and festivals who have let me attend to chat about my books or books that I'm reading that are probably inappropriate to talk about at book festivals. These events are my absolute favorite things to be part of. Am I a sweaty, nervous mess the entire time? Sure. But the bookish community is like nothing else. We are all sweaty, nervous messes in our own ways, and I love that we can trauma bond over such things. To the authors and readers I've met during these events, thank you for being so kind.

To booksellers, librarians, book bloggers, and reviewers, thank you for loving my books and boosting them. You have no idea how much it means to see *Sinner's Isle*, *A Cruel Thirst*, and now *Carnival Fantástico* on your shelves.

I always have to show some love to my girl, Melanie Schubert. My favorite time of the week is getting to hop on Zoom and chat with you and our publishing friends. Thank you to all our *Of the Publishing Persuasion* podcast listeners. You're the best.

Huge thank-you to the authors who took the time to read *Carnival Fantástico* and blurbed it: Emily J. Taylor, Allison Saft, Emily Varga, I. V. Marie, and Katherine Quinn. You are my idols.

Shout-out to my early readers: Davona Mapp, Carolina Góvar, Rebekah Black, Krystal Ogston, Sahana Ramnath, Kate Martin, Alyssia Vasquez, Rachel Lesiw, Jennifer Gower, Hannah Laycraft, Monroe A. Wildrose, Ophelia Morris, Gretchen Schreiber, Dahlia De La Vega, Inés Lozano, Rylee Joss, Nix Damon, Shannon Arnold, Keara Rodriguez, Alexis Maragni, Laura Curtis, Melanie Schhhhubert, and Andrea Rinaldi-Perez.

If I missed anyone, it is most likely because your notes were so good that I died of excitement, and I am currently writing these acknowledgments from the underworld.

Speaking of the underworld. I'd love to thank my family and friends. Not because I think of hell when I picture your faces. *wink* But because you are so patient with me as I pop in and out of your lives. You offer me the space and love to be able to hide away in the cold and lonely hellscape that is drafting and revising and only come out when I'm done. Love you all.

Lastly, to my readers, you are so smart. You have the best taste in books. You are great at everything. You are wonderful. You are the bee's knees. You are the cat's meow. You are my shining stars.

XOXO,
Angela—your enchanting, astounding,
gloriously magnificent friend

About the Author

ANGELA MONTOYA has been obsessed with the magic of storytelling since she was a little girl. She hasn't seen a day without a book in her hand, a show tune in her mind, or a movie quote on her lips. She is the critically acclaimed author of *Sinner's Isle* and *A Cruel Thirst.* This is her third novel. When she isn't writing, Angela can be found hiding away on her small farm in Northern California, where she's busy bossing around her partner, their two children, and a host of animals.

angelamontoyawrites.com
@angelamontoya_author

LOVE
IS AT
STAKE.

Take a bite out of Angela Montoya's other fantasy romance!

"Compelling, vivacious, and filled with heart."
–Amélie Wen Zhao, *New York Times* bestselling author of *The Scorpion and the Night Blossom*

"[A] lush historical fantasy romance."
–Zoraida Córdova, *USA Today* bestselling author of *The Inheritance of Orquídea Divina*

"Both tender and fierce, a must-read for fans of good books. Period."
–Kamilah Cole, bestselling author of *So Let Them Burn*

CHAPTER 1

Lalo

Lalo Villalobos hated many things. Long walks, crowded streets, unkempt suits, people. But one thing he hated above all else was his word not being taken seriously. Tonight, he would prove to everyone he was no fool.

The parchment in his hand shook like the remaining leaves on the trees rustling overhead. He stepped beneath the light of a lantern and eyed the paper once more to make certain he had read his handwriting correctly. He had, of course. He knew this location to be correct, but he couldn't quite let himself believe it. All this time, his parents' killer had been lurking close by.

He walked past this very building almost every day and never had a single suspicion that the monster dwelled within. Even in the moonlight, Lalo could see that the three-story structure was clean and well-kept with wrought-iron awnings and a black tiled roof. It looked perfectly ordinary within the bustling city of Los

Campos. Lalo and his sister, Fernanda, lived less than four streets away, in a townhouse constructed in a similar style.

In that very townhouse one year ago, he stood by his bedroom window and witnessed his parents being murdered under flickering streetlamps. He watched in paralyzing horror as a woman with auburn hair, pale skin, and delicate hands tore into their throats and left nothing but corpses behind.

Lalo shuddered and stuffed the paper into his pocket. As he did, his fingers grazed against the wooden stake he'd carved from the root of a willow tree. Vampiros couldn't stand the touch of tree roots. Lalo thought that fact extremely odd when he first learned it, until he understood the origins of their kind. They were born from a selfish human willing to make a deal with one of the gods of the underworld. Any person who had gone to religious instruction as a child would know these gods are tricksters. Deals with devils always came with a price.

Tecuani was the first god one met when they entered the Land of the Dead. He was the hunter of hearts. His lone purpose was to ensure a person was truly deceased before they moved past his domain and into their next trial in the Land of the Dead. Tecuani was there to make certain a person's heartbeat no longer thumped within their chest and that their soul was no longer connected to the Land of the Living. If he found someone with a pulse, he took on the form of a jaguar and chased them down. He clamped his fangs into their flesh and drained their blood until there was none left.

Tecuani was bound to the Forest of Souls, the initial stop for the newly departed. If he tried to move past the tree roots that stood as a barrier between the realm of the living and the dead without an invitation, they'd wrap around him in a tight grip.

Nor could he step foot inside the river that separated his domain and the Valley of Remembrances, or else risk being dragged down into the water's infinite depths by lost souls. It made sense that the vampiros he helped create would be weakened by the same elements, ones as harmless as wood and blessed water.

Lalo hoped that tale was true. Otherwise, he would be woefully helpless once he marched inside the building where he believed his parents' killer resided. Entering some place in search of a predator with no true plan of what to do after was a bad idea, but he needed to see the monster with his own eyes. Lalo needed to be sure she was the one he saw so clearly in his nightmares. Only then would he know for certain he hadn't gone mad like everyone in town seemed to believe.

In Lalo's nineteen years alive, he'd only been to a handful of balls. They were awkward and stuffy and every mother with an eligible daughter kept thrusting them at him as if he were a prince. He didn't like dancing, and he wasn't particularly fond of small talk, which made for an uncomfortable time. Lalo was happy to be alone, but Fernanda was like their parents. His younger sister enjoyed fun. Unfortunately, his going around Los Campos warning people about a woman with fangs and glowing eyes had put a damper on her invitations to events in the last year.

He chewed on his bottom lip as his eyes scoured over the building again. He would get revenge for Fernanda. And selfishly, Lalo wanted to prove everyone who laughed in his face wrong.

He stepped forward, hands shaking. According to the young man he overheard in the public library, the trick to obtaining entry into the secret cantina was to knock once, pause for four seconds, then knock three times in quick succession. He grabbed the knocker and followed the instructions. His heart pounded as he waited. And waited. And waited.

Just when he thought he should try again, he heard the locks disengage. The door opened a crack. Thumping guitarróns and blaring trumpets poured out of the shadows but nothing more.

"Hello?" Lalo said, peering into the darkness. No one was there.

His brow furrowed, but he stepped through the threshold with caution. He slipped inside the doorway and jumped when the thick wood slammed shut behind him.

"Not the warmest of welcomes, I see," he whispered. Clearly, un vampiro didn't worry much over social norms like etiquette.

Slowly, he made his way down a dank corridor, following the music and laughter. He didn't dare brush against the walls because his jacket had only just come back from the cleaners and who knew what sort of messes monsters left behind. A few people littered the hallway, their arms wrapped around each other, their voices hushed as they whispered sweet nothings into their partner's ear.

He eased around them and entered a large room with wine-colored walls and an immense bar at the rear. It was a wonder he could see anything with so little candlelight and so much tobacco smoke in the air. His coat was doomed to go back to the cleaners now. The band played a riotous tune, and people writhed about. Lalo's eyes snapped back and forth. He prayed to whatever gods still listened that he didn't see anyone he knew. Though, he supposed they would have to explain their appearance in such a scandalous place too.

Lalo jolted. His breath caught in his throat. There, standing not twenty paces away from him, was the woman who terrorized his every nightmare and waking moment. Her long red hair was pulled into a chignon. A lacy gown stuck to her skin, showing off every sharp angle of her. And those eyes, her terrifying, horrible eyes were as red as before. He found himself frozen in place. He didn't even think he was breathing. *She was real.*

The woman slipped away, slithering toward a darkened corner. Lalo forced his legs to follow.

"Discúlpeme, por favor," he said as he bumped into a dancing couple.

"Excuse me," he offered as he attempted to pass a woman in a gown that had gone out of fashion long ago.

She turned to him, and Lalo had to hold in his gasp. Her pupils glowed in the low light like a cat's. But not with the golds or blues one might be accustomed to. This woman's eyes shone blood-red just like the killer he sought.

His already thundering heart tripled in speed.

Vampiro.

Lalo stumbled back, but the woman reached out and snatched him by the buttons of his shirt. She jerked his body toward hers.

"Your pulse is loud and strong, mi amor," she purred. One of her fingers slid up his neck. Lalo's innards coiled in disgust. "Are you here with someone?" she asked. "Are you claimed by one of my siblings?"

Siblings? There were more than two vampiros here?!

There hadn't been many police reports about attacks like his parents' that he could find. His research on humans who'd been murdered by people drinking their blood had brought him to findings from countries far from Abundancia and a single case from some tiny pueblo to the north two hundred years ago. Lalo had assumed his parents' killer was the only beast in the city of Los Campos. And now, here he was, learning he'd walked into some sort of nest of them.

He needed to know more. He needed to understand what he was up against.

"I am here for the woman with red hair," he said.

The vampiro clutching him sniffed. "I do not smell Maricela on you."

She had a name. The beast who shattered his life had a name. For some reason, that made things worse. It made his nightmares feel real.

"I am going to her now," he said.

The woman hissed and released him. "You'll find Mother in her private room."

Mother?

Maricela was this creature's maker then.

Leave, the intelligent part of his brain urged. *Get away from this snake pit before it's too late.* And yet, his feet carried him on.

He had no clue where Maricela's private room was, but he didn't dare ask. He stumbled through the throng and winced when he noticed several other vampiros within the cantina. The eyes were a telltale sign, but there were other things too. They had an almost feline way of carrying themselves.

Two vampiros wearing matching suits danced with the guests. Another one was sitting at the bar, pretending to drink bourbon as the humans he was with knocked back shots with liquid the color of blood. Another vampiro was nuzzled up to a person's neck.

Horror roiled through Lalo. He understood why this place was called *The Den.* It was quite literally a lair for these beasts to feed upon innocent souls.

This was a job for officials, for the police, for the militia. Not one nineteen-year-old boy with a sensitive stomach. Alas, here he was, in the rear of the cantina, guided by resentment and curiosity.

He stepped into a hallway that smelled of spilled tequila. The music was still loud but grew muffled as the corridor cut to the right. Lalo stopped just before a door that was slightly ajar. Candles flickered from sconces on the papered walls.

Am I really going to do this? he asked himself.

What other choice did he have? Lalo hadn't known a moment of peace since that dreadful night. He was constantly peering over his shoulder. He didn't dare let his sister out of his sight if they had errands to run after sundown. Killing Maricela was the only way to end his suffering. He would not let another child become orphaned like him. He wanted to take down every vampiro in this cantina. Though, that sounded rather impossible, especially considering he'd never even been in a scuffle before. But if he had proof of at least one vampiro's existence, he could go back to the authorities. They would *have* to come to the cantina and exterminate the rest of the foul beasts themselves.

He stuck his hand into the inner pocket of his coat. His fingers wrapped around the wood he had painstakingly sharpened, and he tugged it free. *Time to end this now.*

"Searching for someone?" a sultry voice queried from behind.

Lalo spun around.

His eyes widened.

Maricela stood before him. Her posture was perfect. Her demeanor was refined. No one would believe such a poised woman capable of the terrors Lalo had seen her inflict. That was the way of un vampiro, he'd discovered. They disarmed their victims with false humanity. But there was nothing human about the woman before him. She was a predator, hunting for hearts to devour like Tecuani.

"Pray tell." She gestured toward the stake in Lalo's hand. "What do you plan on doing with that toothpick in your grasp?"

Lalo raised the weapon in question. He could only pray she didn't notice how much it quivered because of his shaking hand. "Do not come near me, fiend. This is willow root, and I know how to use it."

He didn't. Not in the slightest. The only semblance of a weapon he knew how to wield were the knives he used to slice through seasoned meat at the dinner table.

"What have I done to deserve such vitriol? To be called a *fiend* in my own home," she asked, smiling as if this were an amusing game to be played.

"You took my parents from me. You ruined my life."

"I've ruined many lives. That is how I stay so beautiful." She batted her lashes. "I'll offer you a bit of comfort, señor. If your parents looked anything like you, I'm certain they tasted divine."

Her tongue slithered over her front teeth, stopping at the fangs that had elongated to dangerously sharp points. His insides quaked. Why in the stars did he think coming here was a good idea? That had perhaps been the problem. He wasn't thinking and simply acted. He wasn't typically impulsive. Gods, if he died tonight, his sister would reach into his grave and throttle him.

That could not happen. He wouldn't allow Fernanda to live in this world with no family. With no one to care for her. She was only seventeen, and her prospects had stopped calling when he'd become the boy who cried vampiro.

Lalo lunged, thrusting his weapon toward Maricela's heart. The vampiro simply swatted his hand, and the stake thumped to the floor.

Maricela glared at him, a dangerous growl emanating from her throat.

He spun, trying to flee, realizing he'd made a grave mistake, but something hit him, and his back slammed against the wall. Bits of dust and plaster smattered over his hair and fell into his mouth. He coughed, but it was cut off by Maricela's palm, pressed into his chest. Her other hand shoved his head to the side, exposing his neck.

"No," he managed. He tried his best to fight her off, but she was like a statue, hard and unshakable. Vampiros were strongest after they drank human blood. Maricela must have had a feast because her skin was like marble.

She opened her maw.

"No," Lalo whispered. "No. No. No!"

Sharp fangs pierced into his flesh. The sudden shock of pain clogged the scream bubbling up his throat. Just as quickly as it came, the ache dissolved away, and Lalo couldn't feel anything from his shoulders to his toes.

Saliva, his mind screamed. *Her saliva is dulling your senses.*

Her teeth sank deeper, and his eyes rolled back.

Images of his life flashed before him. Holding his mother's hand as a boy. Clapping when his baby sister took her first steps. The joy of finding a good book. The heartache of being left to his own devices as his parents gallivanted about the city, bouncing to whichever gala or ball or exhibit was hosted by the most popular socialite that week. He saw the night they died. Saw Maricela's jaw clamping down upon his father's throat.

Lalo watched the memories of him trying to tell the officials what he had witnessed. They laughed him off. Told him to stay away from horror novels. He saw himself in the library day and night, searching for clues about what he had seen. Then he saw himself moments ago, speaking to the woman with the out-of-fashion gown. He heard his own thoughts, contemplating how he'd slay the vampiros within the cantina.

Maricela tore away from him. Her irises blazed molten red. "You came here to kill my children. You thought you'd harm my beloveds?"

"You took my family first!" he cried. "You are draining my life force as we speak! Shouldn't *I* be the one who's angry?"

She sneered. "I will make you pay for your insolence, Eduardo Villalobos."

Lalo's eyes widened. "How do you know my name?"

"Blood reveals all." She leaned forward, her lips brushing against his ear. "Now that I have tasted you, I know everything. I have seen your innermost thoughts. I know your dreams and nightmares. I could go on, but I won't because punishment awaits you. Perhaps I should start with that pretty sister of yours."

No. He had to get away. He had to get back to Fernanda. "If you let me go," he wheezed, "I'll never return. I promise."

A rumbling laugh emanated from Maricela. "You know too much. You have seen my home. My children. There must be consequences to your actions. You are a smart boy, you understand this, no?"

"Please . . . I cannot die."

She brushed a nail down his cheek. "You *will* die, Lalo. But fear not, your death won't come tonight. I want you to suffer first. I want you to feel what I feel."

"What? No . . . please . . ."

"We can be fiends together." She gripped him by the hair and dragged his body into the darkness. He screamed for help; he begged for mercy. Instead, he found agony.

Lalo stumbled down the cobblestone walkway in the middle of the night. Half tripping, half running home. He dug his trembling hand into his pocket, fumbling through lint and who-knew-what before he wrapped his blood-soaked fingers around the key. He tried to disengage the lock but winced.

Everything was so excruciatingly loud.

The key scraping against the metal mechanisms within the deadbolt. The babe crying five doors down. The damn moth bumping against the lantern glass above his head. Every sound burrowed into his skull and grated against his brain.

A rodent scuttled across the road to his right, and Lalo nearly jumped out of his skin.

"Shit," he whispered.

He rarely cursed, but he figured he was owed this vice after everything he'd just been through.

Closing his eyes, he forced his breathing to calm, his mind to stop racing. He needed to focus on one simple task: opening the door.

When he heard a soft click, he let loose a sigh. The familiar scents of his past and present kissed his senses. The tallow polishes his father used on his boots. The citrus soaps his sister loved but only because their mother loved them first. Lalo breathed in deep. He never thought he'd see home again.

He glanced over his shoulder, eyeing the empty road, before shutting the door behind him. He rested his head on the cool wood. His sticky fingers splayed over the frame etched with his and Fernanda's height measurements from a childhood that no longer seemed real. The room was blessedly dark, concealing his sins within the shadows.

"Get out of my house!" a familiar voice screamed.

Lalo had but a second to duck before a fire poker smashed into the wooden frame where his head had just been.

"Get out of my house, thief!" his sister shrieked, readying to clobber him.

"It's me!" Lalo yelled. "Fernanda, it's me!"

"Lalo?" She lowered her arms but kept a tight hold on the fire poker.

"Yes!" he replied.

Though there wasn't a single candle lit, Lalo could see his sister clearly. Her almond-shaped eyes, green like their mother's. Her small nose and angular face, similar to their father's. She and Lalo shared the same warm brown skin and slender builds but that was where their resemblances ended. She was always laughing and talking to anyone who passed by. He was rather moody and preferred the company of the characters in books over actual friends.

Surprise flickered over Fernanda's features. Then came relief. And next rage.

"Where have you been?" she asked, seething. "I haven't heard a single word from you in three days! I searched everywhere. The library. The courthouse. The church. Father's business. Nada. Where were you?"

Three days? Was that all? It had felt like a lifetime. Like *three* lifetimes.

"I have to tell you something, Fernanda, but promise to stay calm."

"That statement alone has my heart rate rising."

She wasn't lying. He could hear her pulse thumping against her neck. Could smell her blood rushing through her veins. His mouth watered.

"Oh gods," he said, feeling the bile climb up his throat. "I can't believe this is happening," he whispered.

"What, Lalo? What is happening? Tell me now, or I will thump you with this poker." She shook the metal bar in her hand for proof.

He didn't doubt she would. She once threw a boot at him when he didn't tell her who asked about her in the market fast enough.

"We must leave," he said. "Right now."

Her features twisted with confusion. "What?"

"I need you to pack whatever you can. Take our most valuable items. I'll send a note to Father's advisors that we are going on sabbatical, and I'll figure everything else out later. But right now, we must get out of Los Campos."

"Lalo, what happened? What did you do?"

His mouth went dry. "I went to the cantina I told you about," he admitted.

Fernanda's jaw dropped. "You cannot be serious."

"I wish I wasn't." Saints, what he wouldn't do to take the last few days back.

"Why are you so insistent on torturing yourself? Whoever or whatever killed Mother and Father is gone."

"She was there," he whispered. "I saw her with my own eyes. She was exactly the beast I remember. They are real, Fernanda. Fucking vampiros are *real.* And we need to get out of the city. Now."

Even though they were draped in darkness, Lalo could see his sister's face go pale. "Can't we go to the authorities? Perhaps the militia? Surely there is someone who will help us."

"There is no one who will save us now. Do you remember how I told you they need human life to survive? I was right. But it isn't solely the blood. It's the existence within it. The memories. The joy. The pain. The life. All of it. That monster bit me. She *saw* me through my blood. Every thought I've ever had. Every book and journal I've read. She knows everything. She saw my research. Our family. This house. She drank and drank, and I could do nothing to stop her until I was no more."

"What does that even mean?" Fernanda's voice was shrill.

"I am dead!" he yelled. "I died, Fernanda. That miserable beast killed me!"

"You aren't making any sense. You are alive, Lalo. I'm speaking with you right now."

"I have been turned, Fernanda. I'm a monster."

She shook her head. "That cannot be true. You seem fine."

Fernanda snatched up a matchbox from a nearby table.

"Don't!" he shouted. He couldn't let her see him like this.

His sister raised her brow and did as she wanted, like she always did. She struck the match and lit the candlewick. A small flame flickered to life. Lalo hissed at the sudden brightness and tucked his face behind his arm.

His sister gasped, and his heart sank.

"Your hands," she whispered. "Your clothes."

Lalo turned away from her and examined his arms. The

sleeves of his coat were torn to shreds. And his palms were still stained with blood and the mysterious inky gore that spilled from vampiros' veins.

"Whose blood is that?" Fernanda asked.

Hot tears filled his eyes. "Everyone's."

CHOOSE LOVE.

JOIN THE JOY REVOLUTION!

Swoony romances written by and starring people of color

Learn more at GetUnderlined.com

1626f